Stealing Eyes

Stealing Eyes

An Historical Novel of Love,
Passion and Spoils of War

Martha Melahn

iUniverse, Inc.
New York   Bloomington

Stealing Eyes
An Historical Novel of Love, Passion and Spoils of War

This is a work of fiction. All of the characters, names, incidents,
organizations, and dialogue in this novel are either the products
of the author's imagination or are used fictitiously.

iUniverse books may be ordered through booksellers or by contacting:

iUniverse
1663 Liberty Drive
Bloomington, IN 47403
www.iuniverse.com
1-800-Authors (1-800-288-4677)

Because of the dynamic nature of the Internet, any Web addresses or
links contained in this book may have changed since publication and
may no longer be valid. The views expressed in this work are solely those
of the author and do not necessarily reflect the views of the publisher,
and the publisher hereby disclaims any responsibility for them.

ISBN: 978-1-4401-5888-9 (pbk)
ISBN: 978-1-4401-5890-2 (cloth)
ISBN: 978-1-4401-5889-6 (ebk)

Printed in the United States of America

iUniverse rev. date: 10/19/2009

For my children

AUTHOR'S NOTE

Although some references in this book are to historical figures, all characters are imaginary. Specifically, I would like to point out that the fictitious figure of Major Robert Street bears no resemblance whatsoever to the real Major Harry Anderson, the 101st Airborne Division's excellent Fine Arts and Monuments Officer, who served in Berchtesgaden in 1945, and was responsible for protecting, cataloguing, and returning hundreds of art treasures to their rightful owners. Fiction demands its villains, as well as heroes; and, like Commander Queeg in Herman Wouk's *The Caine Mutiny*, when a villain doesn't exist, he has to be invented.

All dates are coincidental.

AUTHOR'S ACKNOWLEDGMENTS AND CREDITS

Special thanks are due to Mr. and Mrs. Anthony Biancone whose German/American romance spanned the period covered in the second part of this novel. They graciously answered dozens of queries regarding daily life in Germany during the period prior to the implementation of the Marshall Plan.

I am grateful to Michael Ellis for hours of help on the manuscript, and to my sons, architect Quentin Dart Parker, who critiqued this book, and photographer Jules Graham Parker (known as 'Bo') whose original film treatment, *Stealing Eyes*, encouraged me to write this novel. I am also ever grateful to the late Griffen Hoeveler for her trenchant insights and knowledge of the art world. I must thank my kind neighbor, Dr. Ed Wagner, for his assistance toward the completion of the book. And lastly, I must thank my daughter, Bebe Coyle, for the many hours she devoted to the final editing and proofing, and for her patience in dealing with her mother throughout the process.

My appreciation extends to the Military Museum of Southern New England (www.usmilitarymuseum.org) for lending the authentic Nazi flag and trunk for the cover photography.

Cover photography by Bo Parker (www.boparkerphoto.com); graphic design by Hayden Chance Parker (www.chanceparkerart.com).

Enjoy,
MM

CONTENTS

Book 1

CHAPTER ONE

Monday, July 2, 1986, New York City

Bob Hermes stood under a sagging awning outside the door of his junk shop, fumbling for keys, grateful for having beaten the rain. Across the street two scurrying figures reminded him that in this neighborhood night brought danger. Drawing a quick, uneasy breath, he turned the key and released the deadbolt.

Inside, a light brush of a wall switch illuminated a room bulging with stacked furniture. Some pictures hung from awkward ceiling cradles; open drawers served as repositories for dozens of assorted small articles. Suspended particles of gray dust, not unlike fine hair, covered everything. For a moment the delicate scurrying of a mouse broke the silence, causing a ripple down Bob's spine. Then, content that the sound was nothing ominous, he dropped wearily into a sagging chair, letting his head rest against its worn cushion. A bust of Felix Mendelssohn, the nose missing, lay within reach.

"You wouldn't know it, Felix, but this place stinks," he murmured, shaking his head in quiet desperation.

Mike, his partner and best friend—as well as brother-in-law—was predictably late for their meeting. Out buying more unsaleable crap, thought Bob. Selling, not buying, was the order of the day. The weight of this message rested heavily in the pit of his stomach. Recently Bob had come to the decision that he could no longer finance their joint venture, and the time had come to tell Mike.

A few minutes later the rhythmical horn toot of Mike's old station wagon announced his arrival. As he squeezed the aging behemoth into a parking place, Bob walked to the door. Seeing Mike struggling with the tailgate, he hurried to help. Together they carried two steamer trunks into the shop.

"Taking a trip?" quipped Bob, irritably nodding toward the trunks.

"Looks like it, doesn't it?" Feeling sheepish, Mike wiped fogged glasses on his shirttail and turned on an old radio. Sensing his partner's mood, mellow music seemed called for.

"At least you're not going First Class," Bob growled.

"Lately I've had a lot of requests for old linen. I've got a bundle here—two trunks of old linen for thirty-five bucks! Not bad, huh?"

Inwardly Bob groaned. "Where are the keys?"

"I don't have them."

"You're kidding! You haven't seen the linen?" Incredulous, Bob waved a gesture of futility, his thin lips pursed in frustration.

"Look, the trunks are worth thirty-five…"

"Without keys?"

"If we've got one key, we've got a hundred." Mike handed Bob an old shoebox heavy with rusted keys. "Fish around. I didn't have time to look at the sale. The movers were there. The trunks haven't been opened in forty years."

"Did you bring beer?" Bob needed an antidote.

"You bet." Grinning, Mike headed back to the car.

Ultimately, a key was found that opened one trunk—and it did contain old European linen, full of climate stains but otherwise in perfect condition. Delicate lace and intricately embroidered patterns on the pure linen sheets came as a surprise. And they were enormous—large enough to fold back to the foot of a king-sized bed.

"We'll easily get big money for these," Mike chortled.

Bob pointed to the letters. "Even with that 'AH' monogram?"

"Sure." Mike assumed a mimicking falsetto tone to continue: "Muffy, I'm a descendent of Aldous Huxley…or Alexander Hamilton… you know."

Normally Bob would have laughed. Instead he picked through the box of keys looking for one to open the second trunk, while Mike danced around hanging the sheets to air. Soon cascading fabric curtained the room.

"Some transformation … weird, huh?"

Bob looked around. "Ghostly."

The lock on the second trunk proved more difficult. Finally, Mike produced a screwdriver. The corroded brass popped open.

Resting in the top tray was an old green passport, a few books, some letters, scattered yellow snapshots, and a pornographic sketch—quite a good one. "Nothing saleable," muttered Mike, pawing and tossing the contents. Then he lifted off the tray and exposed a Nazi flag. "Wow, Bob, look here!" Under the flag, lined up like troops clad in red velvet, were eighteen rounded bags each secured by a gold tassel.

Bob reached for one bundle and raised it, loosening the string, exposing a gold goblet; a small gleaming trumpet that could, in its own way, tattoo a fortune. "My God," he cried, jumping up.

"For Christ's sake!" Mike whispered. Stunned, he slammed down the lid and looked fearfully toward the store's plate glass windows through which passersby would have no trouble seeing into the interior. He looked at Bob whose astonished face reflected the same emotions.

"Let's get this mother to the back of the shop!" cried Mike.

Hastily, they dragged it behind a stand of used clothing.

"Did you see what I just saw?"

"Yep." Bob smiled awkwardly, his face twisted.

"Then it's true? I didn't dream it?"

"No way. You hit the jackpot." Bob slapped Mike on the back. "But first things first. Lock the door. I'll open the beers. Then open that trunk again."

Breathing heavily, they squatted before the trunk. Cautiously Bob pulled back the lid and began freeing gold goblets from their protective sacks. He uncovered eighteen, all monogrammed 'AH' in German gothic script.

"There's a fortune here," Mike muttered.

As if acting out a small ceremony, Bob grabbed a goblet and filled it with beer. With a pang of guilt he remembered the prospect of cutting off money that loomed when he entered the shop. Life had definitely changed. Yet, despite his glee, some tenacious, unwanted feeling surfaced, something human and ugly: mistrust. It wasn't that he suspected Mike would cheat him, but he never knew what Mike would do next. It was one thing to share a passel of junk, gradually accumulated with your sister's husband; another to entrust thousands of dollars, future security, or whatever, to something less than a bonded institution. Mike wasn't the most scrupulous or reliable partner you could pick. Bob's hand enveloped the heavy, exquisitely engraved metal, now sweating with condensation and brimming with a cap of creamy foam. "Who in the hell do you suppose stole 'em?" Bob asked.

Mike downed his suds with one draft and smacked his lips. Then he turned to the tray and extracted the passport. "It says here—James Albertus May, a weird name." His eyes fell to the drawing. It depicted a handsome, broad-shouldered young man, sitting slouched forward, knees apart, in throes of ecstasy in which he seemed deliriously lost. One hand steadied an erect penis extending from a garden of pubic hair.

"What a cock!" Mike exclaimed.

Still caressing the goblet, Bob murmured, "I'd say he had it all…" He turned anxiously toward their hoard. "Packed with a Nazi flag, those goblets could have belonged to only one person: Adolf Hitler." For a long moment they sat in silence, breathing heavily.

"This Kraut stuff's hot, Mike. Somebody's got to be waiting for these to surface." Frowning, Bob poured himself another beer and put up his feet, crossing his legs to prop them on a dilapidated coffee table.

Having gotten over the initial shock of their find, both were trying to come to terms with reality. Undaunted, Mike fairly danced to the small rear toilet to relieve himself, causing Bob to raise his voice, "These goblets cost one helluva lot of money."

"I can't hear you," Mike hollered, unwilling to let go of a newly found euphoria. He finished and turned to look at his own round, unshaven face fuzzily reflected in the splotched mirror propped against the dirty little lavatory. From under a mat of too much long hair, he smiled at himself and turned on the spigot. He doused his face with water, loving the refreshing coldness, and there being no towel at hand, emerged dripping, his damp shirt clinging to an extensive beer-belly.

Mike always managed to look sloppy, because faded jeans and old sneakers worn without socks formed the major part of his wardrobe. Having always lived on the edge, he appeared older than his thirty-nine years. Still, he had a friendly, happy-go-lucky air that disguised a bit of larceny crowded into an otherwise kind heart.

"We've got to move carefully, Mike. I think we should talk to a lawyer. The German government may claim these. I have no idea what the law is…"

"You're worrying already."

"You're darned tootin, I am," he cried, turning to Mike. Bob Hermes, the handsomer of the two, always seemed to be carrying the weight of the world on his shoulders, and made an ideal foil for his lackadaisical, laid-back partner. "There are people who would kill for these." He spoke, twisting a goblet in his hand, while giving the exceptionally fine engraving a closer inspection.

Bob sure could be a wet blanket, thought Mike. Still, at the mention of a lawyer and killers, his spirit took a dive. Bob's judgment was usually pretty good. He came around to things slowly, that was all. "The German government isn't going to know we've got 'em."

"Look. Let's not argue. I want us to get the best price. These are out of our league. We need some advice. Let's start with your wife."

No way, thought Mike, who began picking through snapshots in the trunk, anxious to change the subject. A small-unframed oval portrait of a beautiful young woman appeared to have been taken around the turn of the century turned up. "Somebody's mother," Mike murmured, tossing it to Bob. Another series in black and white, obviously printed abroad, showed a pretty blond girl and a boy. The boy was looking skyward. "They're probably flying kites," Mike added. "That looks like a river in the background."

Bob agreed, aware that Mike was changing the subject and wondered why.

"Here are some shots taken on a steamer. It's the same girl. It looks like she's drawing. She probably made the sketch we've got here." Mike picked up the sexually explicit sketch.

"I doubt she made that on a boat," said Bob.

"Boats have cabins," Mike explained.

"With windows?"

"Righto. I was distracted. Boats have portholes."

They were getting nowhere. Somewhere on the street a shot was fired, summoning small fears that were soon put down.

Mike separated other pictures of a different vintage, showing Alps, buildings in rubble, U.S. Army vehicles, and men in uniform—relieved that Bob seemed ready to drop the subject of his smart wife, Bob's sister. One picture of a gangly young man, appearing awkward and camera shy rang a bell. "He's the same kid in the other pictures."

"Have you got a magnifying glass?" Bob asked.

"There isn't anything that we don't have someplace around here," Mike growled, rising and disappearing to the front of the store. Soon he was back with a lens in hand.

Bob studied the faces. "You're right. Same kid, just older."

Mike produced a few snaps of a much thinner woman. "Is the girl the same?"

Bob ignored the question, and again picked up a goblet to study the engraving. "This is the finest I've ever seen…"

"You know Hitler would have had the best."

Then Mike picked up a packet of letters held together by a dried-out rubber band. These are addressed to James May in Poughkeepsie—of all places." He opened one. "They're in German. We'll have to get someone to translate."

"Funny," said Bob. "Here is a list of names." He read off: "Victoria May, Betsy Barnes, Larry Price, Frau Matcher, and Mr. Nobody, Col. Rasmussen, and so forth. It's a mixture of people." He showed Mike. "They're neatly lettered—as good as printing."

"How many names?" asked Mike.

"Seventeen," said Bob.

"And there are eighteen goblets, right?"

"Yes."

"It's a guest list for some party with one goblet for the host." Mike's eager upturned face met Bob's irritated expression.

"Hell no. You and your wild imagination!" Mike was getting on Bob's nerves.

"I guess you're right. The names don't fit, half American and half Kraut. Besides, here's a commission in the U.S. Army. By the time this list was made, Hitler was probably dead—burned to a crisp by the Russians. I read about that in one of those *Time-Life* books we had in the shop."

Bob picked up the passport. "It's all right here. James May went to Europe in 1938 and disembarked in Naples. Two weeks later he crossed to Switzerland at Balerina, stayed a few days and entered the Deutsches Reich—that means Germany. Two months after that, he came back to the U.S. via Switzerland and France. That's the whole story. You can read the stamps."

Mike, chaffing under Bob's superior tone, doubted that the whole story had been told, and would have liked to learn more about the thieving owner of the trunk. He was something of a romanticist at heart and, never having traveled farther than New Jersey, the thought of travel abroad in 1938 fascinated him. For a minute he scratched himself, putting down his irritation. "Well, what are we going to do? Shall we divvy them up?"

For a moment Bob studied his partner with more than a few misgivings. "I'm not going to carry this gold on the street in little old New York for five minutes. No way, José. We have a safe here. You have the combination?"

"Hell yes."

"Remember you didn't get working keys with the trunks." Bob had dark premonitions of eventually having to blast the safe open and blowing the goblets to smithereens.

"Look, now that we're rich, let's not fuck up. You can do what you choose. I'm leaving mine here."

Bob felt trapped. "We probably shouldn't break the set. We'll probably get more by selling them all together."

"I won't argue with you. I'll even give you a ride home," said Mike, rising victoriously and hitching up his pants, his face once more incorrigibly impish.

Carefully, they packed away the goblets, even lining the shelves with old shirts hardly destined to sell in any event. "We don't want them to get scratched," said Bob.

Mike nodded. "Even if this place burned down tonight, this safe will survive." It was the size of an armoire, almost empty and unlikely to melt.

Still, silently, Bob had misgivings.

On the sidewalk Mike locked and then double-checked the door.

The rain had stopped and the air was cooler. Together they slipped into the station wagon that obliged by starting—always a chancy thing.

"This has been some day," said Mike. "I'll never forget it, if I live to be a hundred. I've always dreamed that something like this would happen—like maybe I'd pay two bucks for a Rembrandt. I knew the hard work would pay off." He turned on the radio, again searching for mellow music.

Bob leaned back against the vinyl-covered seat, suddenly tired. Mike couldn't seem to move without music. Now that he thought about it, Mike never seemed to be working hard. Half the time the shop was closed, but he guessed that was all right.

For once Mike had hit a motherlode. He felt genuinely happy for his sister and the kid—whom he had been most interested in helping in the first place. Mike and Doris had had a stormy marriage, due primarily to fights over money or the lack of it. "This is surely going to make Doris' day," said Bob, envisioning his sister's excitement.

For a long moment Mike was silent. "Well, I don't plan to tell her just yet. She'd have it spent in a heartbeat."

"Don't tell me you two aren't getting along?" Bob groaned. Would the goblets be tied up in litigation?

"You know your sister. She has no conception of how much time this crappy business takes, always expecting me to be punctual, always thinking I'm playing around—when I'm not." Mike turned to face Bob who shot him a disgusted glance. "You know I don't play. I may look, but I don't touch."

City lights shimmered. Red and gold neon signs rippled before their eyes. Traffic slithered with them and against them, as they moved slowly through the hustle that never seemed to cease.

Christ, thought Mike. I hope Bob gets off his high horse pretty quick. He thinks he's so damned smart. I haven't heard a word of gratitude yet—not one damn word. The thoughts were distracting.

Suddenly, a big red Buick cut in front of them, forcing Mike to break, skid, and play with the wheel to avoid a crash. "Asshole," Mike yelled. "Imbecile! Mother fucker! Learn to drive!"

"Goddamn it, Mike. Learn to drive yourself," Bob lashed out, too irritated and shaken up to agree.

* ** *

The following day Bob waited impatiently for Mike. Not wanting to greet any prospective customers, he locked the front door and sat hunched on the remains of a red Moroccan hassock, staring at the monstrous safe. Acknowledging that he had been stupid, he rued the fact that he had never asked Mike for the combination.

The hand-embroidered sheets were missing. He hoped to hell that ALL eighteen gold goblets, last seen packed in the safe, were still there. At this point, Mike would have had no damned business toting them around.

Irked as he was, he didn't know what to do. He knew he belonged at work but he also knew the goblets precluded his ability to think clearly. New computers had been installed and he was rightfully terrified of forever losing reams of clients' billings simply by being distracted. Bob remembered that Mike had intimated that he and Doris had not been getting along, but he knew—as brothers know sisters—this was not solely Mike's fault. Now he wished that he had pursued the matter further. After all, he had entered the partnership thinking that one of the perks would benefit his sister, Doris, and their boy, Sean.

For a while it had seemed that providence had destined the two men to go into business together. Almost simultaneously, both had come into small inheritances—or at least what looked like small inheritances.

Two years earlier Mike had been the only heir of an old lady who, for many years, he had tried to help as a kind 'Mr. Fix-it.' The estate consisted of a rundown house in a poor neighborhood, mortgaged to the rafters. Over a few beers, Mike had said the house was loaded with antiques. The antiques turned out to be an almost worthless assortment of broken-down period furniture and plastic junk. By the time the funeral was over, the lady buried, the cats disposed of, the debts and taxes paid—and some shyster saw the will through probate—Mike had put out seventy-five dollars to collect his dubious inheritance. He had no place even to store the so-called antiques.

About this time Bob and his sister had come into a plumbing business through their father by the same means. Ah, destiny! No sooner was the old man cold that the costly tools and equipment walked out of the business, leaving an almost empty shop with a few irate customers, an old beat up truck and a stack of accounts payable.

Knowing nothing about the plumbing business, Bob had shrugged off the inheritance as an albatross around his neck, especially when his sister washed her hands of all responsibility—except to sell the truck and keep the money.

Then Mike had a bright idea, again over a few beers. They could combine their so-called assets to form the Hermesdorf Trading Company and, as partners, open an antique shop. Bob had gone along for want of any other viable option. What looked like individual liabilities could be combined into a joint opportunity. With Mike's wife, Doris, and his then-girlfriend, they worked nights and Sundays cleaning, painting and getting set up. But the disappointing location had been matched by the dilapidated inventory, and, in the end, neither had a legitimate gripe with the other's contribution.

Before long it became clear that Mike wasn't going to make a living as a junk dealer. He trusted people. Having bought for cash, he sold on credit. Mike had not kept regular open hours. Talking, he'd forget to write sales slips. Dust and cobwebs flourished while roaches died of old age. The City of New York came down hard on them for business licenses, sales taxes, property taxes, improvement taxes, *ad nauseum*. Doris also got sick of supporting her husband.

Bob picked up a photograph he had paid no attention to the previous day. It showed a group at a table in a sidewalk café. Smiling, they had beer glasses raised in a toast. In the background swastika banners hung from a building. Everyone seemed to be having a wonderful time celebrating some *Blitzkrieg*. He thought that he could identify James May with one arm around a beautiful girl who appeared in many of the photographs. Again he checked the dates stamped by border officials in May's passport, and remembered that the United States was not yet at war in 1938 during May's two month stay in Europe. Forty years later these people are probably all dead, he surmised. Then he picked up one of the frayed letters—undoubtedly a love letter read many times—postmarked a year later, and remembered a friend who taught German. He pocketed the batch.

He was about to abandon the tray's contents when he spied a small sepia photograph of one of the handsomest men he had ever seen. The subject, wearing a German officer's hat, gazed suavely out of the picture, as if he were a Tyrone Power or European matinee idol—perhaps a professional model, he was so photogenic. Yet the quality of the sepia print indicated that it was no publicity shot, but a carefully posed, personal portrait made in an expensive photo salon. This too, showed signs of wear. The officer seemed a little sad—nothing like the arrogant bastards Hitler's officers were reputed to have been.

* ** *

Meanwhile, Mike was up early, having slept only a few hours. Surprisingly keen and refreshed, he skipped breakfast and rushed to the shop. For once, there was no parking problem. With the imagined skill of a racing driver he pulled the long fat vehicle into an open spot in front of the door. Once inside he threw himself into the job of gathering up the sheets that had been left hanging the night before. The trunk repacked, he hoisted it to his shoulder, feeling the adrenaline of excitement harden his muscles, and headed for the laundromat. The trunk seemed to weight ten pounds instead of fifty.

As he hoped, he was the first customer. He set his loads humming, and then while the machines did their work, went out for a leisurely breakfast. Supremely happy, he ate as he roughly mapped out his day. Then satisfied, he paid up and boyishly slipped back to where his loads were winding down. He loaded the dryers, and sat down beside a pair of gossiping women, so blissful that not one word of their conversation entered his head.

After checking twice, he decided that the sheets were dry. The women, seeing his struggle to fold them, came to his aid, marveling over the virtual explosion of exquisite handwork.

"These sheets haven't been washed in years," he volunteered.

"You know," said the older of the two, shaking her head, "you really ought to wash your sheets more often. It's not good for clothes to lie around dirty for years on end."

"Yeah," Mike agreed sheepishly, making a quick exit.

He headed for a shop called Nostalgia, where a spinsterish Miss Rigby was opening up when Mike arrived. He had his story prepared. "I have some of the finest linen sheets you'll ever see. They're heirlooms which, sadly, I'm forced to sacrifice. They were part of my grandmother's dowry when she came here from France."

Miss Rigby eyed him suspiciously.

"They were made for a high French double bed," said Mike, "but they'll fit today's king-size beds. Let me show you."

Before she could refuse, Mike dashed off for his trunk. After his effort in hauling it, she was obliged to give him a moment. Her eyes widened, as one by one, he began unpacking the linens, revealing yard after yard of embroidered linen.

"I'm sorry they aren't ironed. My wife won't even iron my best shirt," said Mike.

"The handwork is lovely," she murmured, daintily fingering a border of lace.

"I don't think they were ever used. You see, my grandfather deceived my grandmother about living conditions she'd find here. She saved them, waiting for better days that never came."

"Oh, how sad! I'm afraid the 'AH' monogram is a problem."

"Not really. They're obviously heirloom linen." Mike then expanded his tale. "My kids with their sticky little fingers could poke holes in the lace, so at home we can't use them."

"Indeed, that would be a shame." Miss Rigby swallowed revulsion as her Rolodex brain flipped on. "How much do you want for them?"

"I can't take less than one hundred apiece," Mike replied, hitching up his pants.

"I'm afraid that's out of the question, Mr. Dorf."

"There's over fifteen yards of Irish linen in each sheet. I've measured them!"

She picked up a pencil to calculate. She also wrote down Angie Heywood, Alice Hamden, and Andy Hammerstein, three customers who came to mind. "The initials are limiting, but, as you say, they are heirlooms …"

"Make me an offer," said Mike, starting to pack up.

"Four hundred for the lot. I'll have to have them professionally laundered and ironed which will be expensive."

That some people had insisted on ironed sheets never ceased to amaze Mike. For a moment he cursed himself for not having ironed them himself. Then he realized it would have taken a week, and today there was a cash shortage. "Five hundred."

"Sorry, four hundred is the best I can do."

"Okay, my back is to the wall. You're getting a steal."

Miss Rigby's eyes widened. "I hope you're joking."

"Of course, who'd steal sheets?"

"I guess you're right." She smiled.

Back in the shop, pleased with having disposed of the sheets so profitably, Mike was sorry not to have someone to crow to. He thought of his wife, and for a moment actually felt he caught a whiff of her perfume, but then dismissed the thought as preposterous. Last week she had kicked him out of their loft, but Mike had refused to think about this. Doris had thrown him out before, and he had always found a safe haven where he could room cheaply for a few days until she softened up. With a pattern established, he had not worried. In fact, he had almost enjoyed a few days of complete independence while his wife raged, although he truly did miss their son. Today he realized that he should have told Bob about his problems with Doris. The fact that he hadn't, demonstrated a lack of confidence, which wasn't the case at all. He had thought the fight would simply blow over, and was sensitive about it.

Noting that the German letters were missing, he decided that Bob had been to the shop. Mike knew the shop well; he knew the dust, the cobwebs, the running toilet. Even if nothing had been touched, he knew with an animal-like sense that his territory had been trespassed. And if Doris were serious about wanting a divorce, he didn't want her to know about the goblets. This would mean that valuable time would be lost in disposing of them—which might not suit Bob either. It was important to talk to Bob—immediately.

When Bob could not be reached, he decided to call Doris at work. For good reason, she refused to talk to him.

＊ ＊＊ ＊

That morning, Doris—as compact and soignee a woman as her husband was loose and laid-back—had visited the shop looking for Mike. Determined to end the marriage, there were points to hammer out: she wanted full custody of Sean, the loft, and for him to remove his possessions from their home. Also, she did not want to pay him alimony.

She entered, every muscle in her body taut as finely tuned violin strings. She stood around for a moment, noting that in the months since she had been there, nothing had changed. Continuing her examination, she walked to the back of the shop to where the great green safe stood. While I'm at it, I might just as well have a look in this, she decided. Then she dug in her pouch bag for her wallet, where at some point she had had the good sense to record the safe combination and, blessedly found it.

Immediately her eyes focused sharply on the eighteen red velvet sacks. When she opened one and found a shining goblet, she thought for a moment that she had to be dreaming. The gooseflesh rising on her arms convinced her that she wasn't. Finally she breathed; Mike has hit pay dirt! She placed one goblet in her purse, closed the safe, called a taxi, and in less than three minutes was out of there.

Riding to work in the taxi, Doris nursed a good many conflicting thoughts. She immediately recognized an article of great value and rightly felt—anyway she looked at it—that the cache was something beyond Mike and Bob's expertise.

Fortuitously, since high school Doris had worked for Aaron Hirschfeld, a wealthy, elderly Jewish investment banker, whom she knew was considered a connoisseur of quite an array of fine arts. Even his office housed a collection of bronzes which occasionally he had taken the time to talk to her about. Hirschfeld could give her an idea of the goblets' worth, and then she could deal accordingly with Mike.

The fact that Aaron Hirschfeld's initials were 'AH' was not lost on Doris; however, it never occurred to her that 'AH' also limned Adolf Hitler.

With considerable trepidation Doris waited for Hirschfeld to get off the telephone so that she could show him the goblet, hot enough, she felt, to burn a hole in her purse. At last he concluded his conversation, and she knocked on his door.

"Sir, if you have a moment, I'd like to show you something," she said, handing over the red velvet sack.

Knowing that anything so neatly packaged would be of value, Hirschfeld gingerly removed, and then studied the goblet. Finally he looked up and smiled at his employee. "You have a nice chunk of gold here, Doris. The German engraving is very fine."

"Someway my husband has acquired eighteen of these. I saw your initials and thought you might be interested in buying them." Doris waved to a row of ancient bronzes on a high shelf behind his desk and added, "You have many valuable pieces right here."

"Eighteen you say…?" he murmured. "This collection points to only one man, my dear: Adolf Hitler. You see, only royalty or a government could afford eighteen, and besides, there is no coat of arms on the goblet which a princely family such as the Hohenzollerns or the von Humboldts certainly would have used in lieu of initials. However, a great many Germans would have been able to afford a few gold goblets—but hardly eighteen."

"Oh, my! I didn't think of Hitler, but of you."

"Yes, I might be interested. I'll arrange to meet a friend for lunch today who would be able to give me a factual appraisal and," he laughed, "I'll try to be fair."

"I'm sure you would be," replied Doris, her voice dropping, "but then, considering the Holocaust, you might be offended or repulsed by something that belonged to Hitler."

"That's very perceptive of you, but a work of art is a work of art, and the goblets might also be my sweet revenge—beyond that of living, that is." He smiled the smile of a man loath to reveal anything more personal than the time of day. He nodded her a goodbye.

* ** *

Bob Hermes entered a small bar that carried good German beers and ordered a Beck's. With the letters from Germany in his pocket, a German bar seemed a good choice. He had spent most of the morning waiting for Mike, of whom there had been no spoor. "What a helluva way to run a business," he ruminated. Then, like a bolt of lightning it struck him: TODAY two representatives from the computer company were to be in his office for a training session. They were being paid fifty dollars an hour, and undoubtedly could do nothing awaiting his arrival. His boss, Mr. Wright, by now would be close to catatonic over his absence.

He bolted the bar, hailed a cab, and prayed for some sort of deliverance. His conjecture over his reception was right on target. Consequently, Mr. Wright told the receptionist not to disturb Mr. Hermes with any telephone calls for the remainder of the day, but to refer all calls to him personally. Mr. Wright, on hearing Mike's voice, politely denied Bob was in the office and promised that Bob would return the call when he came in. The training session and the overtime extended until late.

* ** *

This day Aaron Hirschfeld took a three-hour lunch. He returned to his offices with three stamped *bona fide* appraisals. Doris noted the one from Christie's—vetting the goblets at $10,000 apiece. The other two appraisals had a differing range of less than five percent. "I'll buy them myself, Doris. Soon my wife and I will celebrate our fiftieth wedding anniversary—with what will be only a family celebration—but I think the goblets would be an appropriate adjunct to our table."

Doris agreed.

"Can you bring me the other goblets today? I'd like to study them. They will be safe here in the vaults." Hirschfeld was a man accustomed to moving fast.

"I think so," Doris replied with baited breath. "I'm only concerned about the neighborhood. Will your chauffeur drive me?"

"Naturally. And, by the way, I think your husband and brother would profit considerably—tax-wise—with an exchange, perhaps in stock, rather than a cash sale. I can explain that to them in detail. However, if they would prefer cash, that is also no problem. I'm simply trying to be helpful, suggesting they avoid taxes—not evade them."

As luck would have it, Mike was not in the shop when Doris, quailing at the thought of meeting her husband, and the chauffeur arrived. With her door key and the safe combination, in no time the great green box was left empty, except for a few old shirts lining the shelves and some totally nondescript artifacts Mike liked.

In the evening when Doris returned home, there was a message on her machine from Bob inviting her to dinner, even promising to pay for a baby sitter. Grateful, she called him back.

He warned her, "It won't be fancy, but I presume you've been sitting home alone for a week and would like to get out."

"How'd you guess?"

"I've had a rough day, correction, rough week, but things have picked up," said Bob.

"I know what you mean," she replied, rolling her eyes.

During dinner Bob first queried her about Mike, and then listened to her gripes, all of which he had heard before and personally was well aware of. However, this time she added infidelity and confessed that sometimes she had been frightened of him. At this point her big dark eyes filled with tears, but they were not the kind that fall.

So, she still cares, thought Bob. "Dry up, Doris. You're dead wrong. He doesn't play around, and he'll never hit you." Mike had guts and street smarts, but when they had disagreed, he had never been frightened of Mike. His braggadocio had always been couched in good humor, and Bob had passed off his amusing, although dire, threats toward others as nothing more than grandstanding. "You have to understand him. His back has been to the wall. The shop was failing, and he considered it his fault—as it was. In desperation he strikes out at you verbally because you're the only one he can strike out at. But I know him pretty well, and some of this is my fault. I, too, began hounding him, complaining, putting on the pressure..."

"That's still no reason to go after me."

"Yes, it is."

"Besides, he knows how to push all the right buttons..."

"And you explode," Bob interrupted, "which is what he wants. It shows you care. You're an attractive woman, Sis—not as attractive as you once were as you've put on weight in the beam—and you'll always attract men. But you'll never find a better father for your boy. Listen to me. A lot of women find Mike attractive. He's open, simple, and warm—and he can be very funny."

"As my brother, you should be taking my side." Her dark eyes flashed. "Whose side are you on anyway?" A napkin crumpled in her hand.

"Your kid's. Actually I'm an impartial observer."

Bob could feel her tension rising like an electrical current about to short out or light up a stick of dynamite. "Relax. Honestly, Sis, if I thought you were in the right one hundred percent, I'd back you to the hilt. If I thought that Mike would physically abuse you, I'd see that you got out of your marriage before the sun comes up. Mike's a nice guy, and they are rare. Furthermore, we have our enormous inheritance banking on him, and I think he is going to make some money on our investment. Give the guy a fighting chance."

Other diners looked harder than necessary, for those two made a strange couple, one hard to read. Bob signaled for the waiter to refresh their wineglasses, and then continued. "I have to give you what I think is my best advice. I'd be ashamed to do otherwise. You can take it or leave it. It's your life."

Good old reliable Bob, thought Doris. "I have missed Mike," she confessed. "I'll give what you say some thought." She raised her glass to him, slightly tilting her head as she spoke. "Now tell me, what do you know that I don't know?"

That bitch can smell money, thought Bob, without rancor.

"Well," he said, "apparently business has picked up. Mike's been working nights, collecting old debts, and he's made some pretty good buys."

Doris smiled her best Cheshire cat smile. "If we get together again, he can't continue working nights."

"I don't expect him to. Businesses always need time to get going. After all, he had to learn the junk business." Bob signaled for the check. "It's not the world's greatest." Figuring on a victory, he smiled.

Doris had done some quick thinking, and wanted to be really sure that she had Bob on her side. "Bob," she said calmly and controlled, "I have the gold goblets."

"You WHAT?"

"I stole them tonight. They're in Aaron Hirschfeld's vault. We're calling a meeting tomorrow morning." She gave Bob a pause to catch his breath, and then added, "Please be there. I may need you badly. He's going to buy them."

There was nothing for Bob to do but try to find Mike immediately. He had to catch him before he discovered the goblets were missing, even if he had to sit in the shop until dawn. Bob's instincts were right on target.

Thoroughly disgusted and wanting distraction, even lonely, Mike went to the movies. Rodney Dangerfield was playing in *Easy Money*, a topic close to Mike's heart. As far as Mike was concerned, the movie was a heartbreaker. He left the theater in search of food. Having forced down a pizza that would have choked a hyena, he decided to drop by and check the shop.

With the deadbolt securing the front door and the front lights dimmed, he felt quite safe in the rear; once again he was reminded of his wife, as if he could smell her scent when sadly he knew she neither could nor would have been there. Bob was the only one who could have come in looking for him, he hoped. Then he decided to open the safe, as if just looking and feeling the treasure would warm the cockles of his woebegone heart.

As the great door opened, he got the shock of his life. The goblets were missing. The partnership agreement was also gone. At first, utterly stunned, with the scaffold of his life collapsing around him, a few expletives ensued. Then he could feel his hair standing on end. No doubt about it, Bob had come to the shop, taken the goblets, determined to handle the sale himself. This amounted to a tremendous loss of trust. This explained why Bob had been unreachable all day. It was enough to make him sick. "It's enough to gag a goat," he cried, tears filling his eyes. After a few minutes shock and crushing disappointment turned to rage.

It was then that Bob was unfortunate enough to enter the shop hoping to find Mike. Mike bounded through the dim room toward him yelling, "You thief!" Before Bob could utter a sound, one good swift uppercut from Mike sent Bob flying through the air as if motorized. He landed flat on his back, looking up at a cluster of brilliant stars and meteorites cascading to earth around him.

Then he saw Mike standing, straddling him, ready to punch him again. He simply closed his eyes.

Mike would not hit a man who was down, and after a minute Bob could murmur, "Doris took them."

"WHAT?"

"They're safe in Hirschfeld's vault. There will be a meeting tomorrow in Hirschfeld's office. He has had them appraised."

After sufficient words of apology, the whole story came out. "Your marriage is on shaky ground, but I wouldn't say it's over. And I just told Doris I was never afraid of you. Well, I am now."

* ** *

One by one, a shaky quartet entered the offices of Aaron Hirschfeld. Quite naturally, Doris was the first to arrive. Her apprehension over the way Mike would act blew all her concentration—although for the sake of appearances she had tried to look busy. Hirschfeld had arrived at his massive desk punctually as usual, and not long after both Mike and Bob were announced by the receptionist. To Doris's surprise, the younger men who had been up all night, fighting, drinking and talking, looked more than contrite—almost whupped. It was a good sign.

"Please, gentlemen, be seated," said Hirschfeld with a wave of his hand toward two leather chairs facing his desk. Doris stood to the left, smiling wanly. "I have given your acquisition quite a lot of thought, and I believe I can offer you an advantageous exchange. Here are three independent appraisals, which you will see are close enough to be virtually equal and, therefore, I think quite fair and accurate." With that he handed over the papers for his guests to peruse.

"Doris, ahem, tells me that you will probably want to see some cash immediately. That's understandable." Hirschfeld then outlined an exchange for the major part of the value of the goblets in publicly traded stock. "This will reduce both of our taxes considerably. Also, if you don't mind, I would appreciate it if you would keep this business private. I have gone over all of the goblets very carefully looking for a manufacturer's stamp, and found none. I have also checked the records for stolen property both here and in Germany, and the goblets are not listed even as Hitler's personal property. In case you wondered, they are truly, solid, eighteen karat gold. Please excuse me for asking Doris to bring in all of the goblets yesterday, but I had to check them all, presuming that you did not have a provenance or title. Right?"

"True," replied Mike, now guessing correctly that Hirschfeld had no idea that Doris had taken the goblets without conferring with either him or Bob.

While Hirschfeld droned on about what his legal department could or could not do, and exactly which stocks he was offering them, Mike hoped that Bob was listening because he found himself on an entirely different train of thought. From over Hirschfeld's desk his eyes rested on his wife and all he could think of was how much he loved her. He felt his love emanating in great pulsating waves and wondered if she could feel their bombardment, because his feelings were so strong. Yes, he loved her today and he had loved her always, he decided. He loved her face, her hair, and the way she moved, and the way her hands—always such capable hands—brought him so much pleasure. He thought of their years together and of how negligent he had been, how much she had given, how hard she had worked, and how seldom she had complained. All he wanted now was to take his clever wife in his arms and hold on to her tightly and forever. Here he was supposedly listening to old man Hirschfeld carry on about a lot of silly things. The only thing that mattered was his little family, and he knew that come hell or high water, he wanted to hang on to them. Then he realized that he should not be staring at Doris, and that surely any minute Hirschfeld was likely to ask him some question and he wouldn't know diddley-squat.

Then he watched Doris busily put together the papers all of which she handed to him with a soft touch. "We can talk this over at dinner this evening," she said, effectively muzzling him while turning to her brother, "Bob, you'll join us, won't you?"

It was in the tone of her voice, gentle and caring, that he knew everything was going to be all right. He could move out of that cheap little rooming house.

Bob turned to Mike. "Are we together on this? I think this is a fair offer."

"Sure… sure," Mike replied, silently heaving a great sigh of relief. Neither he nor Bob had mustered one ounce of bargaining or bartering spirit. They rose to leave, thanking Hirschfeld. Mike used the opportunity to kiss his wife, knowing—the way men know—that he was going to make out.

Book II

CHAPTER ONE

August 1938, New York City

Apprehensive, James May stood with fellow passengers waving from the deck of the *Conte di Savoia* as the tug towed her from the New York dock. A rousing band momentarily drowned out the deep sonorous ship's horn, while confetti streamed from railings, forming festive ties to shore. For a few minutes he could make out Betsy Price's bobbing blond curls, as she jumped up and down to see over the crowd of zealous goodbye-wavers.

I've got to remember that it was swell of her to come, thought Jim. She didn't have to. Today he felt that he had wasted so much love on Betsy—just thrown it away.

Relief partially quieted the tension of the last few weeks, and the deck felt good under foot. He spent a few minutes watching the skyline, then he stepped back, giving those behind him a chance at the rail while he walked toward the less-populated bow. It would have been nice had his mother appeared, but she was being petulant. Dead set against his going abroad, her not visiting the ship was just one more way of saying so.

Under the auspices of the Otto Mannheim Foundation he was bound for Berlin via Italy for a year of graduate study abroad. Taking a ship that stopped briefly in Naples would enable him to debark for a tour of Italy and Switzerland, a jaunt otherwise not financially feasible.

Getting away had been harrowing. Because of the political

uncertainty in Europe, the foundation granting him money had almost rescinded his grant. Hitler, deploring the plight of Germans in the Sudetenland and Austria, had threatened a need to restore order, and Jim saw his hopes of studying abroad fading. Then Hitler announced that Germany had no territorial designs on the rest of Europe and only wanted friendship with the United States. The foundation board relaxed; and, in the nick of time, the check came through.

Betsy Price had been another matter. She was the sister of his best friend and college roommate and the daughter of his wealthy mentor. For years he and Betsy had indulged in an off-and-on-again affair. He was enormously fond of her, and could have married her—had she not been so relentlessly promiscuous. She was good-looking, smart, fun and rich. During times when he loved her deeply, she would haul off and screw somebody else, tell him about it, and leave him crushed. When Lawrence Dodge Price, Sr. died, Jim, in the interest of self-preservation, dumped his overworked sense of duty and gratitude into the casket and closed the lid.

Betsy had come to see him off bearing an enormous basket of goodies. Then the crazy girl had threatened to stow away. "I'm going to sail with you," she whispered, beaming.

"But you don't even have a passport or clothes," he had stammered, feeling entrapment returning. "You'd have to take the same ship back home…"

Fortunately, a steward spotted her.

By the time the *Savoia* reached the Statue of Liberty, Betsy was following aboard a New York City fireboat, still waving madly from the pilot's cabin. When she disappeared for a moment, his face froze; knowing that she was trying to get the waterspout turned on the *Savoia*.

Apparently reason, or the fireboat's captain, prevailed and the fireboat turned back. It was a wild send-off, typical of Betsy. He felt a pang for something precious—something that could not be.

Many of the details of the voyage would become lost in the shuffle of time, but because he was a Child of the Depression, the memory of that ship and her prelude to the grandeur of Europe would stay with him always. To the students the *Savoia* was a marvel, a 48,000-ton floating palace. They gawked at their brief glimpse of the First Class lounge--its inlaid marble floors, marble columns and baroque statues. The vaulted ceiling somehow managed to convey a whiff of the Sistine Chapel, despite pink-sashed cupids swinging garlands of roses. Deep inside the bow was the first stabilizing system for a passenger ship—three gyroscopes, each weighing more than a hundred tons. The captain permitted a ship's officer to explain the machinery to the interested passengers. So it was in the bowels of the ship that Jim met two other graduate architects, George Chauncy (a well-brought-up young man from Texas) and Bob Street (a not-so-well-brought-up Californian), also bound for Germany.

"I feel I'm on the threshold of a new age—not just a new continent," George said, wide-eyed, obviously awed by the machinery.

Jim concurred. The vision of harum-scarum Betsy in the fireboat, his agony over the indecisive foundation, and the cold draft of his mother's farewell, all receded as giant twisting screws and whirling wheels propelled him into another life.

"If you intend to move in the best circles, you'll need polish," Bob interjected, smugly. "You'll get it in Europe."

Jim blinked, never thinking about 'best circles.' He wanted direction in modern architecture. Looking at Bob, he recognized a pompous fool. "I'll keep that in mind. Then I'll come back and make my debut." The remark was a mistake that he would pay for…

It was a precipitate architectural period in which several important schools were simultaneously evolving: a purely American style, led by Frank Lloyd Wright, and a European counterpart with the Bauhaus in Germany and Le Corbusier in France.

On the Italian line, Tourist Class was akin to Steerage, so most students traveled Cabin. Here the ceilings were not so ornately decorated, still, the service was impressive. Jim soon floundered under mounds of pasta pressed on him by genial waiters in snowy white coats. The only antidote was the exercise room.

"A year of eating like this will ruin me," puffed chubby George, working out on an exercise bike.

"Look out for the delicious German bread," Jim warned with a smile. "I remember my grandmother's."

George pedaled harder. "I've heard about the girls," he puffed. "They're pretty free."

Feeling the shadow of Betsy, Jim skipped away, taking a circuitous route, moving through the gym with uncommon grace. Telltale signs of strain flickered on his long grave face, high cheekbones and large deep-set dark-blue eyes. He would never have admitted that he was lonely—even to himself.

Evidencing no fatigue, Jim came to a halt. His thumb flipped a lock of damp brown hair from his forehead, and a pensive smile returned. "This year is it for me, George. I've got to make a clean break with the past. Some people I had to get away from; continuing my education was a good excuse."

George nodded in agreement. Grateful for a pause, he stopped pedaling. He's got girl trouble, George thought, wondering why.

Someone opened a door to the outer deck letting in a great gust of wind, cooling their moist skin. Jim moved off again. He couldn't say more, let alone to someone who was practically a stranger.

George observed his new acquaintance from all angles. He's a natural athlete, he thought enviously. Jim seemed the acme of bachelorhood—gentlemanly, perhaps Rodinesque. "Why did you choose Germany?" George called from across the room.

"It was a natural. I speak German. In college I met the son of the German ambassador. He told me a lot about Germany's progress under National Socialism. He says that what we read in the newspapers and *Time* is simply not true—or grossly exaggerated. It made sense. After all, he wasn't trying to stir up people and sell newspapers."

* ** *

To Jim's chagrin, Bob Street, tall, dark and fashionably snobbish, moved to an empty chair at their table. "I think we architects should stick together. Besides the Swiss at that table are unbelievably dull. They're actually scared of Hitler."

Jim barely heard the remark—which he would later recall with considerable pain—seeing for the first time a sloe-eyed girl at a nearby table. Short dark hair curled becomingly about her face, and her complexion, creamy white, appeared inexpressibly soft. Most striking was her bosom, ample enough to have sufficed two women. Several times during the meal he caught her eye, and finally she smiled.

While tapping a Camel on a handsome crocodile case, as if to add credence, Bob Street was holding forth on the Bauhaus with textbook authority. "Although the best architects have immigrated to the United States, I want to study the Gropius complex at Dessau, particularly that all-glass shop block he designed in '25. There the concept that walls…"

Jim felt an animosity toward Bob that he didn't want to bother analyzing. He was headed for the prestigious Technische Hochschule in Berlin's Charlottenburg district. Here Professor Tessenow, branching off from the Bauhaus, advocated principles of simple craftsmanship, which Hitler approved and permitted to exist. But Tessenow's theories appealed to Jim anyway, and for postgraduate work the school seemed ideal.

"I can't understand why you chose Berlin," Bob taunted, distracting Jim from the girl. "Tessenow ignores changing times. We're moving toward what can be machine-made, not handmade."

What Bob was saying was true, but Jim felt his irritation rising and threw Bob a mocking look. "Sorry, I say 'Bau' to the Bauhaus. I don't find water heaters and radiators worth looking at, despite their honest purposes. Nor do I like to see a washing machine on someone's front porch—for an entirely different reason. If you want to watch three gyroscopes keep your wine steady on the table, have it your way. It's not mine."

"You're exaggerating. It's time we uncluttered."

"I'll go along with that, but less isn't always more. A lot of simple crafts are art forms that get short shrift in America."

Bob rolled his eyes in disdain. "Jim, you're being corny. I'll bet you have a birch bark canoe on your mantel and a stuffed alligator footrest." Everyone at the table laughed.

Swallowing his irritation, Jim looked the other way. But he knew that lines were being drawn, paces marked off. Humor was called for, but the Muse of Mirth had departed—so had the sloe-eyed beauty.

George was anxious to smooth things over. "We're in for a period of catch-as-catch-can. This year should show us where the world is headed. This could be advantageous."

And, indeed, it would be—but only for a few.

The atmosphere on the ship was changing as people relaxed and felt free to open conversations. Little old ladies were getting their sea legs and becoming accustomed to ship's time announced by incessant bells. Girls, doing their junior year abroad, already donned the ubiquitous walking shoes that, without resoling, could have made it over the Alps with Hannibal. Bridge players found partners who played at their own level, and others buried their faces in *Gone with the Wind*—some sensing a prophetic title. Several times, feeling that he was missing something that should be part of an ocean voyage, Jim walked the deck hoping to meet the voluptuous beauty, but she had disappeared. His private stateroom with its small bunk seemed…rather wasted.

The following day and days to follow, he watched the unforgettably magnificent skies seen only at sea. Clouds formed a veil of soft fleece, then a field of drifted snow. Opalescent light and rainbows colored the ship's spray. Still—no lady.

Breakfast and lunch were marked, not by her presence, but by Bob's poses that bordered on insults. Recognizing a man who played dirty pool, Jim bided his time. Finally he determined not to let Bob ruin his meals and found his chance…

That evening, while Bob showered, Jim wadded tinfoil from an empty cigarette package and poked it into the small lock on Bob's stateroom door to jam it. A DO NOT DISTURB sign added the final touch. Two hours passed before Bob was freed. Raging, he immediately complained to the captain.

"*Meeester Street*," the captain replied in a ringing Italian accent, "apparently someone doesn't like you."

Bob was stunned. "Suppose there had been an emergency—a lifeboat drill?" he sputtered, aghast.

"I guess you can be grateful the prankster didn't choose to take the joke that far. Indeed, an alarm would have been terrifying."

Subdued for the remainder of the voyage, Bob almost became tolerable, although it seemed to Jim that he was always lurking.

When at dinner the pretty girl still had not appeared, Jim felt the spirit of the ship was such that he could inquire. With an air of nonchalance, he stopped at her table.

"I hope the empty chair doesn't mean that your beautiful dinner partner is seasick," Jim said, addressing one of the group.

"Oh, not at all." The man smiled. "She spent the day on the bridge with the captain. She's dining with him in First Class."

So, that's how it is, thought Jim. "The captain has eyes, too," he replied, managing to laugh as a little dream evaporated.

In the evening people packed deck chairs like herring. Jim and George, joined by two nice faces, visited the bow and stern to watch the phosphorescence. Furrows of silvery foam glistened like mother-of-pearl far out over the sea's surface. The night seemed incomparably romantic. Jim had paired with a redhead, Jane Sablehouse, who was on her way to study voice in Italy. The girl with George was her pianist. Jane took Jim's arm to steady herself as they walked, but whenever Jim drew her close enough to embrace her, she pulled away.

"With all this beauty about you—you don't want to be kissed?" he whispered, disappointed.

"That's right," she replied, avoiding his eyes. Then, sensing that he was hurt, she turned to face him. "You're a nice person—a handsome man. I like you, but I don't want to go to bed with you."

Still, the voyage was not destined to be one of celibacy but of brief encounters. A touch of bad weather—or possibly other interesting and important passengers warranting attention—occupied the captain. Once again the dark-haired beauty took her assigned place in the dining salon. Jim was quick to grab an opportunity and invited her for an after-dinner drink.

The girl had practically nothing to say, which at first imparted an air of mystery. By leading her to his cabin on the pretext of needing to change his shirt and quickly taking her in his arms, his goal was accomplished.

After a lingering kiss she pulled away from him, and with almost professional efficiency, slipped out of her clothes. Mounds of soft creamy flesh readily accepted him. The slow rocking of the ship, followed by gyroscopic correction, magnified his metered plunges until, with one great blast, coincidentally announced by the ship's horn, he released his own pressurized flood. He immediately fell asleep, soon only to be awakened by her humping him. He was glad to oblige her with more. The next day he bedded her again, but she soon became one of the most boring girls he had even encountered. She moved on to more attentive men, while Jim spent many hours with a married woman, a mother of two, joining her husband in Burgundy. Together they watched the dolphins cavorting off the Azores. As a university professor's wife, she had something to talk about—and he gave her something memorable. Besides, she played good bridge.

He became curious about an elderly fellow traveler. Day after day a distinguished old German occupied the same deck chair. Once, with some hesitancy, Jim struck up a conversation, explaining that this was his first trip abroad.

The old man smiled and put down his book. "Travel gets in your blood. It's almost a disease—itching feet. I know Java, Sumatra, Borneo, the Pampas, Andes, Himalayas, the Sahara—not to mention the world's capitols. Still, I find myself traveling."

Jim felt he had already contracted the disease; the symptoms were undeniable.

A very different disease was taking over Europe. Those traveling abroad would be privileged—for one year—to see the end of a dying era, already consumptive and coughing, but not yet spitting up blood. For the students the Chianti would never again seem as good; the food—deemed marvelous—would never arrive with such flourish; and travel would never again be so easy, so comfortable, so promisingly rewarding in culture.

On the last night at sea, Jim proposed a toast. He refreshed each glass from a pitcher of red wine that invariably graced every table. George Chauncy could hardly conceal excitement over their debarkation. He can't help showing everything he feels, Jim noted, fondly. Bob Street busily sniffed the wine and deemed it adequate. Several soon-to-be-forgotten faces beamed. "To us, to the Old World that will soon be our New World—and everything not covered by *Baedeker*. Let's live the next year to the fullest."

"I'll drink to that," they echoed, laughing as glasses clinked.

"What about the girls? You didn't mention them," said Bob, looking superior with a smutty smile to puncture Jim's moment of pleasure.

"I said everything not covered by *Baedeker*," Jim growled.

Soon after, Jim left the table for a last walk on deck. There alone, looking out over the vast reaches of water and a sky rich with stars—so many never visible on land—he felt utterly insignificant. The feeling did not wear well, and he headed for the bar where George and other friends were vowing to stay in contact. Bob lost no time in horning in, perfunctorily offering uncalled for advice, until finally Jim rolled his eyes in disdain. Bob turned quickly and caught the look. Jim knew at that moment Bob had guessed correctly who had locked him in his stateroom. Fortunately, thought Jim, there isn't time for him to retaliate.

That turned out to be true only for the time being.

The following day, walking down the gangplank under the comforting umbrella of familiar smiling faces on the deck above, dodging baggage cranes, lorries, and screaming porters, it seemed to Jim that heaven was near. He was certain when an elderly American couple from First Class invited him to share a taxi north to Rome.

Traveling at breakneck speed with the driver's hand almost continuously on the horn—when not waving obscene gestures out of the window—they arrived at the Eternal City, certain that they had narrowly escaped three serious accidents. The indignant American refused to pay what he considered an exorbitant overcharge, bringing them all perilously close to jail before the old gentleman reconsidered. Eventually Jim staggered into a cheap *pensione*—seemingly the noisiest in the city.

Closeted, loosening his tie, he thought wistfully of his shipmates and regretted not being able to compare notes. Even Bob's reaction to the rundown quarters, easy to predict and fun to snicker over, would have been acceptable. Bob had no money problems, he remembered, tossing his bulging wallet on the dresser. The thousands of colorful lira seemed like Monopoly money—prettier and larger. Like Betsy, the ridiculous money wouldn't last long either. Funny that I should think of her now, he mused, when she's out of my life forever.

Her threw himself down on the bed only to discover that he still carried the motion of the ship with him. The bed rocked as the ship never had. Hungry, tired and reeling, unable to speak the language, he felt … shipwrecked.

In later years James Albertus May would look back on that voyage and realize that it marked the time when his life got properly started. Until then, everything would fade from memory as if he had spent twenty-some years in the womb. It was not that afterward his life would never be the same—because that was certainly true—but as though he had never even lived, so great was the contrast. The good times would be so good that he could cry remembering them, and the bad times would be so bad that he would remember nothing of them.

But, for the moment in Berlin, he felt sure everything was going to be just ... swell.

CHAPTER TWO

Jim arrived in Berlin early in the morning and spent a few hours walking around, map and newspaper in hand, looking for a room to rent within walking distance of the school. The city burst upon him with all its strength, breadth, and vitality, constantly distracting and amazing him; yet, he felt he was standing on firm ground. Speaking German was like slipping into the security of his childhood, when his happiest moments had been with German-speaking grandparents.

He would soon discover that he would be known as 'Herr May' or simply 'May' pronounced 'My,' come hell or high water. Despite his pleas, no one would accept the familiar first name. It was just as well, he decided, anxious to be on with his new self that included a new name.

The posters condemning the Jews came as a rude shock—although he knew they shouldn't have. He had heard about them, but their viciousness far exceeded his expectations. His reaction came so early on emotionally that it had to be dismissed. He blocked it out.

A number of rooms for rent were listed in the *Tageblatt*, but in walking around, looking for the most promising area between the Centrum and Charlottenburg, he spotted a sign: *Möbiliertes Zimmer zu vermieten*. The walled masonry house was convenient and looked prosperous. A middle-aged aproned woman answered his ring and led him into a large airy room on the second floor with two windows facing the street.

"The price is twenty marks a week with breakfast. You'll have to share the bath with another gentleman. He's been here for many years," she told him.

May felt the bed, which seemed comfortable, noted a desk and a good light for study. The parquet floor was so magnificently polished; he almost slipped on the small Oriental rug. A great ticking radiator, armoire, dresser and two straight chairs lined up in styleless Pullman-fashion, reminded him of the stiff furniture arrangement in his grandmother's house.

"I'll take it," he said, obviously pleased.

"Will you put down a deposit of five marks?" she asked, now scrutinizing him.

"I'd like to move in immediately. I'll give you the full month's rent. Now please, tell me, what's my new address? I'd like to have my baggage delivered."

May gave her a fountain pen and his card. Her eyes brightened.

"I'm Frau Kruger, the housekeeper. Breakfast is coffee, a roll, butter and marmalade, and on Sunday an egg. Shall I serve it in your room or would you prefer the breakfast room?"

May smiled inwardly. "I'd like it downstairs, if you don't mind." He was not accustomed to being waited on.

With these formalities settled, he found life for the next year coming into focus. A striking air of tidiness, formality and regimentation would characterize his homelife, which suited him perfectly. He would live in the home of Frau Matcher, a spinster too old to be addressed as 'Fraulein,' and her brother, who for no obvious reason, rented two rooms. Frau Kruger presented him his keys on a large brass ring. There were keys to the front door and his room, two smaller ones for his armoire, three for his dresser drawers, and one for the storage room.

Standing beside the polished walnut balustrade in the foyer, Frau Kruger also told him he was free to put his overcoat in a closet under the stairs—for which he would not need a key. (He said a silent prayer of thanks for this.) He could also use the umbrella stand in the foyer. Here, two stained glass panels framed a massive front door and transmitted enough light so that two perfectly matched aspidistras on ornamental stands survived. Two closed curtained French doors on both sides of the deep foyer afforded privacy to all the other rooms on the street floor.

Had it not been for his grandparents, who had been so kind and adoring of him, May might have been intimidated by Frau Kruger's business-like manner. Her explicit instructions made it clear that everything else was *verboten* or unacceptable.

Congratulating himself that he had a sound roof over he head, he walked to the admissions office of the Technische Hochschule to present his admittance papers. Returning to his new home, inspired, he stopped at a corner flower stand and purchased a small bouquet for Frau Kruger, only to learn that they were a slight embarrassment. She blushed from the bun on top of her head to her bunioned toes, but although he did not know it at the time, he would find two large cookies on a plate every evening.

The key ring and its keys, of course, were impossibly heavy and cumbersome. Rather than carry them around, he discovered a small glassed-in Madonna in the front yard where he could hide them.

"He's a nice young man," Frau Kruger assured owner Frau Matcher as she dusted the parlor.

"I'm sure he is," replied Frau Matcher, standing beside the sheer curtains that veiled a view of the garden. "I've noticed that whenever he comes and goes, he pauses before Our Lady for a brief prayer."

* ** *

The first days in Berlin were strenuous. The lectures exposed May to a new vocabulary, which he thought he had prepared for, but still, his comprehension was strained. In a large workroom he was assigned a drafting table and given a project, which would be criticized weekly by a team of professors. He soon learned that much was expected and that deficiencies would be embarrassing. But, for the first week the faculty understood that buying supplies and settling down took time.

Berlin demanded exploration. An elevated train system—perhaps the best in the world—ringed the bustling city. It seemed to May as if he had found a pulsating center of the universe.

Everything was tidy, tended and organized. The streets were clean, the houses painted, the gardens manicured and the parks flourished. Money spent for public buildings and armaments had alleviated unemployment, and an unparalleled building boom surged. The architectural features resembled fortifications, especially the new Templehof airport, but May kept these thoughts to himself.

He walked for hours, drinking in the city. He browsed the lively shops and cafes on the Kurfürstendamm, climbing the great gates to the city and treading the cobblestones of the *Altstadt.* A soft blue light, sometimes eerie, bathed the buildings and trees as if they were paintings. People were well dressed, although often uniformed; they ran the gamut from women daily sweeping the sidewalks to chic and elegant ladies, swathed by Schiaparelli, stepping into a chauffeur-driven Mercedes.

May felt incredibly alive. The blood coursing through his body had taken on some new, exciting, life-giving element. The infusion of the mysterious quickening substance made him light-headed and joyous. Street sounds, night sounds, small clatter which he never before had noticed, now were picked up and magnified into sonatas, or at least arias with their melting tessitura. The sudden awareness was surprising and thrilling, leaving the familiar past colorless in comparison. The air seemed fresher; the food tasted better; sleep was deeper. Never had he been so stimulated.

He marveled over this, sensing that the boost came from within himself, saying that it was only the strangeness, foreignness, that made his blood tingle. Yet his excitement in the newness was constant. From the moment he opened his eyes in the morning until he fell into bed at night, everything he had taken for-granted as background suddenly had moved to the foreground. In this excitement, he fought for objectivity. It wasn't easy, if only because life had become so interesting. In its insignificant way, even brushing his teeth in the morning with a new odd-shaped toothbrush and antiseptic powder became an experience. Still, he tried to weigh, digest and reserve judgment.

Yet, behind it all—the patina of antiquity and the vigorousness of the present—May noted the lack of freedom invariably intruded. Surprisingly, the Germans seemed unaware of this, accepting regimentation as a fact of life, a price they paid for creature comforts without a deeper harder look. The axis of the world turned on National Socialism.

Also it surprised May that every communal building included a memorial chapel for victims—not Jews, but those who died in war or for the movement. Finally he brought up the point with a colleague, who, perched on a stool, was also willing to put down his pencil and take a break.

It had been a twelve-hour day, and the few still in the drafting room were finding little creative impetus, "Without doubt," said May, "Hitler's so-called 'timeless' art and architecture provide something to think about, but it strikes me that the cultural linking of the masses with architecture includes an awful lot of ceremonies honoring the dead. I don't understand this concern. Bronzes and parks make pleasant spots to meet pretty girls and eat French fries, but why the chapels when there are plenty of churches—rather empty, too?"

A new friend, Norbert Buth, whom May found the friendliest of his colleagues, explained, "The party captured the young people in schools and youth programs. All that reference to the dead—remember four million died in the Great War—grabs the old people. There's something for everyone in the program."

"The dead would never get that mileage in the States," replied May, "because, of course, they can't vote."

That quip brought a good bit of laughter.

"The vitality of the regime is impressive," May continued, thinking of the Jews who had left, "but you've lost many inventive thinkers. One day you may feel that loss."

Buth stretched his neck, looking for words. "Everything has its price. You can't make an omelet without breaking eggs. We now have a collective thrust instead of an individual one. We hope to get back to the old traditional high standards. Change is always painful."

"Just make sure that in getting back to the old, you're not going to the obsolete," May continued.

The room grew silent and May dropped the subject, suddenly aware of a truly embroiling nationalism. He had made a mistake, and hoped that he had not pushed Buth too far. Like May, Buth was young and eager, working hard at seeming sophisticated in a rapidly changing world.

May did his best to dismiss recurring qualms. Architecture was an ideal escape, a monstrous devourer of time and creative energy. Even though nothing he had designed had been built, his spatial vision was such that he could take pleasure and pride in his paper creations. These he struggled over. When things got tough, he picked up a pencil and let work take over.

* ** *

Not far from the main boulevard, Unter den Linden, May found an inviting sidewalk café and decided that he was bushed. Flags were out everywhere, and he needed a beer to keep pace with the hustle and bustle around him. Then he noticed what was happening.

Storm Troopers were parading down the street to the rousing strands of *Die Fahne hoch.* They stopped and stood immobile in flawless formations beneath long lines of swastika banners. A wild infectious exuberance buoyed those on the sidewalk. Observing from the café, he sat mesmerized, feeling himself a part of the action. All the world loves a parade, he thought, and one thing was certain, the Nazis knew how to put on a good show. An Indian summer smiled on the city with benevolent warmth and brightness. The action moved on, yet for blocks the *oom-pa-pa* of kettle drums resounded. Finally a trickle of cars returned to the street. People, erasing proud smiles, settled down to business. For a few minutes May felt himself taken in, even a trifle bamboozled. I'm too gullible, thought May.

A tall blond looked into the café and turned to the terrace to take a table in the sunshine. It seemed to May as if the parade had returned with all its pomp and glory. Then he knew he was hearing a different beat. It came from within himself, brought on by the magic of her fleeting smile.

"*Herr Ober, bitte,*" he whispered to the nearest waiter. "Do you know the young lady who just took a table on the terrace?"

"She's Fräulein von Haas, an art student."

"How can I meet her?"

The waiter shrugged. "I'll deliver a note. It's all I can do."

May extracted a card and wrote: "*Dear Fräulein von Haas, I am a student from the U.S. sharing your interest in art. Will you share a table?*" He signed it, "*James A. May, Architect.*"

At such times he was very proud of his professional status.

Seeming not half so self-assured, the girl picked up her purse and sketches to join him. It was not improper, May knew. The Germans were always quick to be friendly to foreigners. He stood to offer her a chair. They smiled self-consciously.

"Right now there's only one thing worrying me," said May. "How in the world can I afford to tip the waiter sufficiently for this pleasure?"

She threw back her head and laughed, dazzling him.

Inge von Haas had a rare combination of blond hair and brown eyes. In the clear white sunlight of the terrace her irises appeared flecked with pyramids of shattered topaz. The dominance of these strong intelligent eyes eliminated the washed-out look characteristic of so many blondes. Her body seemed boneless to May, so lyrical and flowing were the lines under her soft dress.

May explained the 'hows' and 'whys' of his visit and his interest in getting to know her country. "Frankly, Germany hasn't had a good press in the U.S., but I don't know anyone who can teach me more of what I want to know than Professor Tessenow. That's it in a nutshell."

"Don't talk about politics."

"I'll try to remember that," he replied. "It seems to have a way of intruding."

Again he fastened his eyes on her. She was trying to be helpful, not snide, he knew. "You're in art school?" he asked, wishing to change the subject. He didn't want to offend. She stared at him for a moment, and in that brief second both of them knew that something inevitable had passed between them. "I'm studying art—a lifetime occupation."

"One of the best that I can think of. Are you good? Actually, the word I mean is serious."

"I try hard."

"May I see?" he asked, nodding toward her sketchbook.

"I don't mind. You'll like my work or you won't. Anyway, it won't grow on you like a... fungus..." She laughed.

May leafed through a few pages. "You are good." Her sketches were fine line with nothing superfluous. "Your work is clean. I think you have talent and style." He folded the book. "What more can I say?"

For a moment she was silent. "That it doesn't make any difference."

Her remark surprised him. "That's true."

Looking at her, May was incapable of connected thought. On one beer he felt intoxicated. A sudden flash of giddy drunkenness forced him to sit back, gathering poise. He would have liked to abandon himself within the aura of her personality, and yet he sat there feeling awkward, aware of his own face and form, and wanting desperately to be acceptable—liked.

She switched to a less personal topic. "You'll like Berlin. You'll love Berlin," she corrected, jubilantly. "There are other beautiful German cities with finer cathedrals and squares, but compared to Berlin, they are only overgrown small towns. At least Berliners are sophisticated, and they have vitality, not just sentimentality, which I suspect the Germans invented."

"Or, the Italians. I've just come from two weeks in Italy. I saw an awful lot of Renaissance art. At first I was bowled over, struck dumb—perhaps I overdid. I ended up bored with the art, but not with the food and the people."

"Hum," she mused. "You really surprise me." Candid eyes met his. "I've never heard such an idea put forward."

"Perhaps I shouldn't have been so frank. You'll think I'm stupid or blind, as I was also taught differently. But something about you demands honesty. And I'm sure I'll love Berlin."

"Like London, Berlin has an architectural solidarity which says a lot about us—though art and architecture have never been our forte. Being practical people, one might expect this—and not the music. Germans set the world to music."

In that moment May could not have agreed with her more. He knew that she was speaking of a combined Germany and Austria and the old Great German Empire that had stretched like a giant paw over Europe. But he was hearing something else—light, lyrical and incomparably sweet.

"I'd like to meet some of your friends. The people I've met at the university take themselves pretty seriously. I can see it in the way they dress. I'd feel naked around them without a vest."

"The academic system is pretty rigid. However, you'll soon see another side." She laughed. "When your friends relax and get into the foam and Schnapps, you'll see they're like giant cream puffs. There's a party tonight. Would you like to come?"

"I'd love to."

"There'll be mostly artists there," she warned.

"Good. I'll look forward toward seeing the Bohemian side of Berlin."

They had been speaking German, but suddenly Inge switched to English. "Are you pulling my foot?"

May laughed. "You mean your leg. No, I'm happily contemplating seeing you again. Nothing more."

"I'd like to practice my English with you—if you don't mind."

"I wouldn't mind at all."

Inge wrote down a name and address. May wanted to ask her to include her own, but thought better of it. He didn't want to push his luck, and there would be time. Despite her banter, he was afraid that she was very young.

She glanced at her watch and rose quickly. "I must be going. Thank you for the beer."

May rose, feeling awkward, almost tripping over his chair as he looked down at her extended hand. He shook it warmly, wishing that he had mustered the continental art of bowing slightly and kissing a lady's hand. Then he remembered the gesture was only appropriate for married women. She vanished, and he walked home on air.

He knew, the way some men know, that he could love this girl with all his heart, and that he would want her to be his wife. He could not know the unmitigated grief this desire would cost him.

The evening was not without its panic; he could not find the little piece of paper with the address, which he had slipped into his pocket. Disbelieving, cursing his carelessness, over and over again he went through a dozen pockets. Sick with disappointment, he finally discovered a hole in the jacket lining where his damp hand had slipped.

Two other oversights added to his consternation. He had forgotten to ask the time. He did not want to be the first to arrive, and he did not want to miss anything. Finally he decided eight-thirty would be appropriate. His *Helpful Hints for the Traveler* emphasized that a bottle of wine and flowers for the hostess were expected. This was written in stone. It was late and the shops were closed. Frau Kruger, the housekeeper, came to his rescue, producing both. Through the backdoor of a nearby florist she obtained a modest bouquet. The wine, easily replaceable, came from Frau Matcher's cellar.

The party was in a working-class part of town. A small, unsteady, birdcage-like elevator took him to the sixth floor. From the hall he could hear voices and laughter over the music. In a haze of blue smoke the hostess finally appeared and accepted his gifts.

"Thank you. I'm Gretchen Baumgarten, and I'm delighted Inge included you. I'll put your flowers in water and introduce you around."

Unsure, his eyes sought Inge.

She stepped into the brighter light of the foyer to greet him. "I'll do the honors," she told Gretchen, smiling at May and leading him into the throng. "Gretchen has troubles with names," she whispered.

Open double doors expanded the living area to include the dining room, a small balcony, and what was obviously a sleeping alcove marked by a fold-up bed now draped with fabric. At least twenty guests overflowed the main room, spilling into adjoining conversational groups. May shook hands with everyone and did his best to remember names. Although most guests were young, several were middle-aged and one, a Russian countess, appeared ancient. Wrinkled as a Shar-pei puppy, she was dressed in a high-collared, long black velvet dress with rhinestone buttons running down the front, making a trail of little lights that stretched from her long neck to the floor.

"Are you enjoying your visit to this country, Herr May?" the countess asked, a smile further wrinkling downy skin.

May drew a deep breath. "Very much, although I would have loved to have known Europe earlier, when narrow streets were not crowded with autos, and people wore native costumes. Then you could tell nationalities apart. Germany, especially, is becoming modern—mechanized." He hoped he hadn't said too much.

"Let me tell you something beside the fact that you speak German beautifully. When I was a young girl growing up in Russia, people told me that the English constantly discussed the weather; the Italians were always in hysterics; the French thought only of getting you into bed; the Swiss were boring beyond redemption; the Hungarians would steal you blind; and the Germans were always crying in their beer. And, my young friend, it's all still true." She paused for a prophetic moment. "I think you'll find that you've come just in time…"

"I don't know how I can reply to that," May stammered. "But, I promise you, I'll never forget it."

He would not. Sunken beady Georgian eyes met his. Worry was unmistakably reflected in them.

Later Inge would confide that the countess's dress had been made from curtains, and that for years she had been living on the proceeds from the sale of her jewels, but her china painting was exquisite.

There were others present whose careers May would follow, lesser artists who would produce highly saleable pop art for the Nazis, and one or two who would have to wait many years for recognition. A tabletop victrola ground out jazz. Someone rolled up a rug, and he danced with Inge—a very good dancer.

"I hope you're having a nice time," she whispered, intrigued with her new, tall, handsome, outspoken friend.

"I am."

"There's some food if you're hungry."

He had seen the table where little open-faced sandwiches, cookies and tidbits were laid out. Each platter was beautifully garnished. "I made the deviled eggs," she told him.

"Then I shall certainly try one of them."

The music stopped and she moved to talk to another young man, yet May could not take his eyes from her. He had not remembered that she had such a lovely neck or that her breasts spilled so fully into her dress. Tonight a soft blue fabric better revealed her figure. He found himself keeping his ears alert for the sound of her laughter, wondering what she was saying, wanting desperately to talk to her alone.

He danced with another exotic looking girl, a schoolmate of Inge's. "Inge always finds the most attractive and interesting men," she murmured poisonously. "Tell me, where did she find you?"

"I can't say she found me. I think I found her."

"By the way, in case you've forgotten, my name is Hildegard. I'm an actress. I'm playing *Salome*. You must come see me."

"I would like to," he lied, forcing a smile.

"Come backstage afterward."

"Thank you. My favorite Aubrey Beardsley's drawings illustrated Oscar Wilde's play. It is interesting, I think, that he found inspiration for his finest work in a play he never liked and by a writer he cordially disliked."

"It shows how silly artists can be," she replied with a wink, obviously putting down Inge, a futile effort.

May did not notice. Inge was departing with another man and wished him goodnight. He had not reckoned on this, and to ask for her address and telephone number now was unthinkable. "Thanks for a lovely evening," he managed, feeling helplessly trapped.

He stayed quite late wanting to throw off his disappointment over Inge's leaving.

The evening mellowed as others departed and wine loosened tongues. A short, rotund, balding man, wearing an ascot, approached May.

"Interested as you are in modern art, Herr May, it's a shame you could not have come here before 1936, when the modern section of the Berlin National Gallery was open. Did you know that we once had Europe's finest collection of modern art? The director, Ludwig Justi, a very dear friend of mine, made a major breakthrough in recognizing the various schools—Impressionistic, Cubist, Expressionist, *und so weiter.* The modern section was, of course, the first museum that German fascism marked for total destruction. *Schade!*"

"Believe me, I would have liked to. What happened to the modern works?"

"Some of the best will be auctioned off this coming March in Lucerne—snapped up for peanuts by people who know what they are doing. Works by Manet, Rousseau, Monet, Cézanne, Renoir, van Gogh, Picasso, Braque and Gris have been spared destruction, on the whole, mind you, only because they have international market value." He paused to wipe a hand across his brow. "But many fine modern works, particularly by German artists, have been burned. Most of us can understand how painters of social protest, such as George Grosz, Otto Dix and Käthe Kollwitz would have fallen to purges. They stuck their necks out. But so much destruction has been senseless. Book burning is only a symbolic gesture; after all, there is always another copy somewhere. But paintings are another matter."

By the time the speaker had finished, he was talking in a whisper.

"I've seen the waste in the departure of many Bauhaus artists," replied May. "I don't adhere to their thinking particularly, but I can appreciate what the founders sought and I'm glad the school developed. It has been stimulating."

"Good modern art flourished for thirty years in *Deutschland.* Then the people became so totally disheartened by the Weimar Republic that they were ready to throw over everything associated with that period."

"Are you saying that they threw out the baby with the bath water?" May interjected.

"Exactly. The young girl, Inge, who introduced you, has real talent, but it will never be brought out. She can never develop here. She will only be able to paint another *Judgment of Paris*—of which there are already dozens—or *Reclining Nudes* in the School of Pubic Hair."

May had to laugh. "I don't remember your name, but please don't give it to me now. I appreciate you speaking so frankly and openly."

"That's kind of you. I'm sure I've talked too much to a stranger. Blame the wine. I'm Mr. Nobody. I'm not a good artist, but I recognize those who are. I'm a skilled craftsman who under National Socialism will make an adequate living, turning out banal crap—over bright landscapes and battle scenes. I'd give my right arm for real talent, and then I would get out!"

Mr. Nobody walked away, which May also took as a signal to leave.

May had always loved art, but at one point he realized that he did not have the imagination for prominence in this field and he was ambitious. His discrimination and appreciation were such that he could never find satisfaction in painting. He was too critical, especially of himself—of his own talent. Still, he had a wonderful, innate, intimate understanding of beauty others tried to convey to the world. These insights moved him profoundly.

The walk home gave him a chance to think about what he had heard from Mr. Nobody on the destruction of the modern art in museums in Germany—surely exaggerated. The work of the Impressionists, Expressionists, Cubists, Pointillists, Fauves, and other cliques flashed before his mind in a procession of stills. Apparently, with the exception of a few pieces of modern art held privately and secretly, the state had snapped up all it could get its hands on and then destroyed it. Much had been eliminated through channels, in other words, burned!

Still emotionally keyed up by Inge and his conversations with the odd assortment of personalities—even including Hildegard—he walked toward the Centrum hoping to work off some of what he was feeling. He passed a state museum, staunch with Victorian grandeur, expressive of governmental power in block and stone. The night was crisp and clear, almost devoid of traffic. Then he noticed a faint whiff of smoke, and when he passed the entrance to an arched courtyard, he could see silhouetted, black uniformed figures, warming their hands before a low fire. What he saw boggled his mind.

The men, now bent forward, stood out against the bonfire's multicolored hues—colors spawned by the pigments in some modern artist's palette. Gold and silver picture frames, now empty windows packed in the shadows, were stacked high as the men could reach, their contents in ashes. For a minute or two he stood transfixed—aghast— steadying himself with a hand on a column.

Earlier in the courtyard over three hundred modern paintings had been burned. Hitler called them 'unfinished.'

As the full impact hit him, May felt himself stiffen and gasp. His breath came coarse and heavy. Disbelieving until this moment, he stood, fixing the courtyard scene in his mind, letting it score his heart. It was one thing to hear of such an atrocity secondhand, another to witness it. Then, fearing that he might explode in anger, and knowing that he dare not, he raced home where his rage dissolved in despair.

I came here, thought May, for direction in architecture. Maybe I'm destined to get more than I bargained for.

No doubt he had said too much in the school. Occasionally he had caught colleagues exchanging knowing glances, as if they thought he might be guilty of seditious behavior. I must be more careful or I could end up in some Nazi prison. Under this regime anything is possible. Such thinking was right on course. One thing had saved him: the curriculum was so tough, the days so short, the workload so heavy that so far nobody had had the time to report him.

CHAPTER THREE

With no modern art to look at even in books (which had been pulled off library shelves), Inge could hardly pass judgment on modern art. Once at the dinner table, with the candor of youth, she had lapsed, expressing reluctance to accept, hook line and sinker, her teacher's opinions. "I should be able to look and make up my own mind," she had lamented.

Her father had become furious, crushing his napkin in his fist. "You have no choice but to accept what your professors are saying. Do you understand me, young lady?"

Her father, a banker, had adopted the Nazi Party's policies, averring that Germany's financial problems had been brought about by the Jews, even though he did not approve of their treatment. "My joining the party has been necessary, if not expedient, to rebuild our family fortune. I thought that I had made it clear that, under this roof, criticism of the system would not be tolerated." Herr von Haas was not an evil man, but he was also no fool. His admonishment had come with such severity that Inge never forgot it. Blanching, she had swallowed the scolding with her soup. Not to obey his command would have been unthinkable disobedience.

For a couple of days May's thoughts lingered on what he had seen in the courtyard, causing him to retreat into a silence that his colleagues attributed to homesickness. Meanwhile, he rationalized that the periods of turmoil and social unrest during the Depression that produced Hitler, at the same time produced great artistic strides. It was hunger and abuse that prompted artists to speak out, exploring new avenues. Prosperity could consolidate those gains, he reckoned, but did not have the force to produce them. That settled in his mind, he wanted to talk to Inge, but without her address and telephone number, he could only dog the café where they had met.

The old waiter considered May his personal customer. "She usually drops in often, but honestly, I haven't seen her."

May groaned at his rotten luck. Since the night of the party his work had suffered from distraction. That morning when the examining professors made their rounds, he had also been severely chastised. On one drawing he had forgotten that he was dealing with meters and centimeters, not feet and inches. He was deeply embarrassed.

"Don't be upset," consoled Norbert Buth. "Your work is exceptional. They see it. They enjoy shaking you up. Remember, you're an American. We Germans envy you—you and your cowboys and open spaces…"

May carried his disgruntlement to the café and resumed his vigil. His iron table on the terrace offered views of the street in both directions so that little could escape his scrutiny. It was mid-afternoon and traffic was light and only the comfortably employed sauntered by. Lacking business, waiters chatted, occasionally breaking out of huddles to brush a crumb from a chair or refill a sugar bowl. The bored waiters knew why he was there, and their bemused sympathetic glances said that young love is painful.

Suddenly he noticed a *Schutzstaffel* van come to a halt across the street. Four SS men exited quickly and vanished in a doorway. The waiter's voices dropped to whispers and their expressions froze. Has there been a robbery? May wondered. The only other customer on the terrace buried his head in a newspaper. May turned to question a waiter, but the waiters had vanished.

Soon the SS men reappeared. A small family was quickly hustled into the van. The door slammed, and the van took off. May was puzzled over what he had seen, obviously an arrest, but why the whole damn family? For some minutes he kept reliving the scene, hearing the sound of the van's doors and the curious vibration of the Mercedes diesel motor, convinced that he had witnessed something terrible. Then an unusual busyness followed as people, who obviously knew one another well, appeared, conversed, and separated. Bodies were tense, moving with quick, ant-like fervor and unmistakable anxiety. May turned to the man reading the newspaper. "Excuse me, sir, but what has been going on?"

"*Gar nichts.* I didn't see a thing," he replied, folding his paper. Not waiting for a waiter, he went inside the café apparently to pay his check and departed.

Eventually May's waiter appeared to inquire whether or not he wanted another beer. He would, but the little drama still absorbed him. "*Herr Ober,* let me ask you a question. What was going on with the people who live over the camera shop? Were they arrested?"

"I don't know. It's a big city," he stammered, retreating for the beer.

Slowly but surely, May was beginning to see National Socialism in a different light.

The finality of the waiter's answer foreclosed further questioning. May was not going to be rude. Dourly, he downed his beer, paid his check and abandoned for another day his wait for Inge. Walking back to the school he passed the offending doorway. The name on the door was Kaplan.

The incident slipped May's mind for a while only because of the more absorbing distress of not finding Inge, coupled with the need to redo much of one project. His old anodyne, work, saw him through the next few days, yet a pall hung over him. On Monday mornings a *charrette*, or large cart, carrying bells, rolled down the halls picking up the students' work due that week. The faculty would not grade what was not put on the cart. Sometimes the cart moved along with one or two students hanging on, still madly drawing, as, of course, some plans were not finished and never would be. May always laughed about the late ones, and, having laughed, he wanted to avoid their predicament. The pressure of making a good showing, a sort of the-honor-of-my-country-is-at-stake attitude, had forced him to work long hours. Now love beckoned while *charrette-ing* loomed.

Worn, unshaven and haggard, having worked most of the night, he was nursing an afternoon's beer when finally Inge appeared. She looked gay and lovely, like something blooming.

Brimming with relief, he moved toward her and confessed his consternation. "I've become this establishment's most devoted customer waiting for you. You have no idea how I've looked for you…"

Her voice seemed to sing despite her explanation. "Mother has been ill. Everything that she usually does, fell to me."

"I hope it isn't serious?" He did not want to face more waiting.

"It was. She was dreadfully ill with the flu. She even had a nurse. My little brother needed tutoring. What do you say—the sky dropped?"

"Fell. But, will you have dinner with me tonight?"

"Herr May, I'm so behind…" That was true. Then, hating to disappoint him, she remembered that her father was out of town and she knew she could handle her mother. May's presence in some way destroyed all other intentions.

May pushed. "I'd like to take you to the Hotel Adlon. I won't be able to take you there often. It's expensive. But I'll come for you in a carriage drawn by six horses if necessary." He laughed.

"Like Prince Charming?"

"Like James May."

"You make it impossible to turn you down."

Elated, May excused himself to telephone for a reservation. "It's all set," he said on returning.

So began an unforgettable evening. Inge wore a long, satin, Grecian-cut gown and her mother's ermine jacket. He wore his white dinner jacket and discovered it made him look like a waiter. When he voiced his chagrin, she admonished: "Don't be concerned. You're an American, which is chic. Germans love everything American."

He hoped that would remain true.

After a superb dinner, which included champagne and chateaubriand, they danced. The orchestra played *Poor Butterfly,* and the vision of Inge in his arms, reflected in a mirrored column, the folds of her white dress falling from her shoulders to her waist revealing her satiny back, would stay with him always.

She twirled, causing her skirt to wrap around her legs. This made her look to May like the legendary German Lorelei, a beautiful nymph, clothed in white with a wreath of stars in her golden hair, who threw a string of pearls into the Rhine, calling it to rise and save her from capture.

"I've never danced with a better dancer," he said, brimming with sincerity. Since the night of the party he knew that she followed easily, but the cramped quarters had not allowed much movement. Now he could show off his partner with a sort of oh-to-be-young-again nostalgia, as they portrayed a storybook pair few could turn their eyes from.

They talked quietly about their disparate backgrounds. She decided she had to be honest. "Herr May, you can't expect to see me often. This is the first time I've been allowed to go out alone with a man outside of our family. My father guards me as if I were money in his bank."

This bit of news was at first startling, but from his perch on cloud nine, he only marveled at his luck. Her escort at the party must have been kin, and he felt sure he could handle her parents. There was a niceness about May that mothers fell for.

Late, they left the Adlon to stroll under the chestnuts and elms that gave the beautiful boulevard its name. Even as they walked down the wide sidewalk lit by bronze streetlights, they could hardly keep from moving as one. They chose the long, moonlit walk, anything to prolong the evening, stopping to dance whenever a strain of music, like a little night-light, drifted from a shuttered window. Even without music, he would sweep her into his arms for a few steps before proceeding further. As Orion wheeled over their heads, they laughed over absurdities, and a lost barfing drunk; she forgot entirely that she hoped to practice her English.

At her gate May looked down at his feet and saw a cigar band from a Corona Corona, Havana's best. The embossed paper, flattened but entire, glittered like a gold, ruby and sapphire ring. Laughing, he picked it up and slipped it on her finger; with her hand thrust high, it seemed to command a falling star.

He should have made a wish, yet it was enough that he stood at her door, drawing her into his arms to kiss her goodnight.

She looked concerned. "Don't think me fast, my prince," she whispered, trying to quiet her rampant heart.

May had to confess and blurted out, "I think of you constantly. Is that fast?"

"We have a language problem," She smiled, turning to leave him.

May pressed. "How many men are in love with you?"

Inge slipped her key into the lock and replied, "There's only room for one cuckoo in the clock."

Inge's mother, Gertrude von Haas, considered her husband's stringent and over-protective attitude, old-fashioned, and sympathized with her daughter. During her illness Inge had demonstrated a maturity she was ready to reward. Both recognized a first date would represent a point of no return that Herr von Haas, when he returned from Dresden, would not be happy about.

Inge, not her brother, Otto, was Herr von Haas's favorite child, and her father had very fixed ideas, if not aspirations, as to who might make a suitable husband for his beautiful daughter.

"For heaven's sake," cried Gertrude, the following morning when the storm broke. "You've paid for three years of ballroom dancing lessons. What for? To dance with Uncle Fritz?"

Without ever having laid eyes on James May, Herr von Haas thoroughly disliked him.

"That's the wrong tactic," Gertrude would insist—many times.

Frau Matcher's household revealed itself slowly to May. It took a couple of weeks to learn why two rooms were let: Frau Matcher wanted the security of a young man in the house, and yet she had a horror of throwing out a student whom she knew. So she waited for a report from her devoted cook and housekeeper, Frau Kruger, as to whether or not Herr May was a satisfactory boarder before she stepped into the entrance hall to greet him.

The second boarder was an old family friend who came for a few days and stayed forty years. He occupied the other bedroom on the second floor. A family courtesy thing or so May was told…

Frail and unsteady, Frau Matcher had not been upstairs in years. Her social life centered on the telephone, which she used incessantly, far louder than necessary—like most people for whom this invention came late in life. Her conversations, overheard by May, trumpeted his favorable acceptance. He also learned from Frau Kruger that Matcher, the *Herr im Haus*, was seldom home, apparently an inveterate traveler. He had met such on the *Conte di Savoia*. The memory of that brief conversation stuck with May as he tried to envision Herr Matcher.

"He'll show up before the year's end," Frau Kruger explained, "if only because of his sister. It's lonely for *die gnädige Frau*. The footsteps on the stairs of someone young and lively help."

* ** *

The news was not good. Germany took the Sudetenland. Then, as quickly as the crisis came, it passed. There would not be a war, but 'peace in our time,' words that May would always remember.

Letters from his mother and George Chauncy arrived. May opened George's first, noticing that the letter had been opened and resealed. This struck May as strange because George was within the country. George wrote in German. But May realized his friend believed they were being watched. George began with a reference to their *many, dear, mutual friends* who, of course, did not exist. Although the letter went on to describe projects and rigorous studies, scattered double meanings dotted the pages. A German proverb, *Eine Hand wäscht die andere,* in German meaning 'one good turn deserves another,' translated literally meant 'one hand washes the other.' The fact that George had written in the roundabout fashion indicated that he was alarmed. May thought of the posters, propaganda, and the arrest he had seen. Possibly George had seen a lot more. He, May, had been letting everyone's kindness and good manners obscure something very sinister. He read George's letter several times, hating its implications.

Victoria May's letter, which apparently escaped the censor's ink, didn't help and was predictable to a point. She was hurt when he did not cable his safe arrival. Must she always feel hurt? thought May. She quoted ugly newspaper editorials referring to the Nazis, as well as a brief quote from Winston Churchill's October 5, 1938 speech to the House of Commons, which had not been printed in German newspapers. *'All is over. Silent, mournful, abandoned, Czechoslovakia receded into darkness.'*

May saw clearly he was totally cut off from world opinion. One thing was certain; his mother would have to be careful of what she wrote him. He didn't want to be jailed as a spy.

* ** *

Frau Matcher was small, utterly feminine, and like most European aristocrats, never grew heavy. Under a benignant mien, her skin seemed to May as transparent as a rain puddle, glowing with pearl-like pinkness underneath. He had no idea what to expect when she invited him to tea.

He suggested a day when he knew Inge had classes and could not meet him; he arrived downstairs for tea, bearing flowers.

Her parlor was light and spacious yet everything about the room seemed so fragile. May sat down on a Biedermeier chair with great care. Sheer curtains, which ended with a band of lace a foot deep, screened window banks where jade plants and sculptured bonsai flourished in Dresden jardinières below baskets of ivy. Pale Aubussons carpeted the parquet floor. For a minute May anticipated a party. Clearly, Frau Kruger had worked for hours preparing the little cress sandwiches garnished with carrot curls, rings of cucumber, and radishes cut like roses. Tiny teacakes, strawberry tarts, candied ginger, assorted cookies, and a nut confection waited on silver trays. But there were only two cups and plates, therefore no one else was expected. Eyeing the spread, May congratulated himself on having thought of the flowers. Frau Matcher's eyes twinkled proudly.

"Frau Kruger has gone to a lot of trouble," he murmured, unable to take his eyes from the delicacies resting on her Zwiebelmuster Meissen. He didn't want to sound a paean, but he was truly impressed.

Frau Matcher, seated beside him, poured tea. "We were all hungry once. Having property made no difference." Then gesturing with a spoon, lending emphasis to her words, she met his eyes as she spoke about how bad things were after the Great War, what he knew of as World War I. Yet no matter what they had seen, her eyes were never bitter and her mouth showed no signs of defeat as she described the indignities of combating starvation.

"Herr May, I have eaten scrambled rats and poodle-dog meat, and been grateful for them. Sometimes there were not enough rats. Then I vowed that if I lived through it, I would eat well. I've kept that vow."

"*Mein Gott,*" said May, feeling it hard to imagine the bright little lady in circumstances any different from the present.

"When people are especially hungry, they play with their palates. Nicodemus smacked his lips when his chef presented him with a dish of anchovies, which in reality were turnips cleverly disguised with oil and spices."

May helped himself to a cake. "When I come home, and the air is filled with the heavenly aroma of Frau Kruger's baking, I think of my German grandmother's cooking."

"You enjoyed Italian cooking?"

"Very much."

"And Swiss?"

"Flavorless French."

Frau Matcher clapped her hands like a child. "Oh, Herr May!

We agree. Wait until I tell my brother. Dull people cannot produce interesting food. Their food is attractive but tasteless; like their Alps, beautiful but barren."

"They don't want to spend money on spices, I guess," he said.

Frau Matcher refilled their cups. May talked about his work, mentioning the difference between German and American approaches, and, of course, his concern over the political situation. "Frau Matcher, I could be called home or kicked out at the drop of a hat."

"My brother says that we Germans prepare for war like precocious giants, and for peace like retarded pygmies. And, Herr May, I am afraid that we will repeat the terrible pattern. We have become fatalists during this regime. We sit back and say, 'What will be, will be' regardless of the course our leaders take. I'm frightened for the young men like you, but enough of this talk. You must try one of these tarts. Don't be ashamed. Young men and boys are always hungry."

May laughed, helping himself to several. "I've met a lovely girl I'd like you to meet." Inge was never very far from his mind.

"I'd be honored. Bring her the next time we have tea. I have a feeling you are quite smitten." Frau Matcher regarded him for a moment, her drooping eyelids crinkled at the sides. Then she busied herself pouring more tea, passing the milk and sugar as if to distract from the confidentiality of her words. "I believe people recognize immediately those they could love. Love can come very quickly."

The words rang in his ears. "I can almost say that it was love at first sight except that I don't believe in that." He smiled at himself. It was unlike him to confess his innermost feelings so readily, but Frau Matcher had opened his heart, and hence his mouth.

"I was once engaged to a fine man of whom I was very fond, although we had never spent five minutes alone together. Then a young cousin of my fiancé came to town. For us it was love at first sight. Unfortunately, I was caught in this man's arms. To make a long story short, my fiancé challenged his cousin to a duel."

May looked up in surprise. The soul of composure she continued. "I was fifteen. The choice of weapons was pistols. The duel was held at dawn on the *Grüne* where the Spee meets the Havel See. The man I loved was not a good shot, even though he was an army officer, but there was a haze and he had better eyesight. He won the duel."

"I was afraid of a different ending," said May.

"As fate would have it, during a training exercise, the younger brother of the loser shot my love in the back. I doubt that his guilt could have been proved, but he confessed. He was court-martialed and died before a firing squad. That was 1871, a long time ago."

"I am shocked."

"I have told you this because you discounted love at first sight when I have known three men to die over it. You would do well, Herr May, to cherish the good times when you can."

"Seneca said, 'When shall I live if not now?'"

Frau Matcher suddenly looked tired. Stirred by her advice, the thought of talking to Inge was now uppermost in his mind. Thanking Frau Matcher for an absorbing afternoon, he told her goodbye.

Although he had a mountain of work to complete for Monday's evaluation, he wanted to take the day off. He phoned and found Inge at home. "Winter is coming soon. Let's go out on the water while we can. The break may inspire us both."

"We could take a steamer on the Wannsee down to Potsdam and back. I'll show you Sans Souci."

"Bring your sketchbook."

They left from the village of Wannsee, south of Charlottenburg, steaming into the Grosser Wannsee. The sun was brilliant, making the grass and trees shimmer like velvet cloth spread over the landscape. Before terraces where people stood, boathouses flaunted dozens of colorful flags, waiting for small regattas to begin. Like a fresh wash, the little flags flapped in the cool air, whipped by a brisk breeze that anticipated the coming of winter and tidied the silky sky. The late season had reduced the crowds, but the inveterate sailors had formed boating parties, heading out to sail around the Pflauinsel. May brought his Leica, and when he could bring himself to step from her side, he photographed her.

During the simple lunch, washed down by a Mosel, *Bernkasteler Doktor,* May told her about the tea with Fraulein Matcher. "Next time I promised to bring you. Of course she's full of advice."

Inge took a deep breath. "My grandmother used to say that advice only helps the one who gives it. I think in the end that people do what fate and breeding dictate." Her eyes met his. "Some people don't have a choice."

May looked up surprised. "Darling, you speak like a fatalist. Many people do as they want. Someday I'll have to drum it into your head that you can and should determine your own life."

"I love your word 'darling,' but in Germany what you say is very hard to do." She had to warn him.

"We'll see," he replied.

"We probably will." She was sure of that.

It dawned on him that Inge was too resigned, too subjugated to the will of others for her own good. This seemed to be a malaise which women were prone to in the 'Old World.' There was only one thing to do: wrap his arms about her, draw her head to his shoulder, and stabilize them both.

They walked to San Souci, the beautiful and relatively small palace of Frederick the Great. Inge knew her national heritage like a tour director.

"See the way the falling ground around it is terraced, so that the building and the glazing make the palace appear to stand above a waterfall."

"It should be higher. Seen from below, it seems cut in half."

She turned to face him, delighted by his perceptive eye. "You're right, but this is Frederick's fault, not his architect's. Emperors get their own way."

"As do dictators." He felt he knew her well enough to refer to Hitler, however skirtingly.

"Yes, I'm afraid so."

There were ugly posters about condemning the Jews, which had to be ignored as if they were 'No Parking' signs. She stopped before one with water in her eyes. "These are awful. I am ashamed, but there is absolutely nothing that I can do about them."

Instantly he caught her pain as if she had touched him with a fevered hand during a highly infectious lethal illness. "I know it." He grabbed her arm, propelling her into motion, trying to dispel politics. In a blinding moment he knew that loving this girl would not be easy, yet love her he did.

Someway or another, like the infectious fever, she knew that she loved him too, and that it was an impossible love.

Now and then a modicum of privacy prevailed, when he could draw her into his arms for kisses that made it clear, he did not hold her accountable for the sins of her nation. As they walked back to the steamer they knew their relationship had reached another stage. Communication was slivers of thought, bound by touch, ending in mounting desire. Their minds had met but their bodies demanded more.

A buffet was laid out on the steamer. "Did you like my deviled eggs?" she asked him, holding out an egg for him to bite. Eggs had reminded her of Gretchen's party.

"I didn't try them," he confessed. "I was so upset by seeing you leave with another man. I didn't think I could eat for a week."

"It was one of those unavoidable things, set up long in advance. Tell me, what could I have done?"

"Poisoned one egg."

She laughed. "The man was my first cousin, Karl Heinz, my favorite cousin. Didn't you see how fast he dumped me?"

He hadn't, but it was his turn to laugh. "I must work tomorrow, but next week let's have a picnic."

"I'll bring everything but the ants." She hoped it would be possible, but a vision of her father loomed. He had no idea that for several afternoons, she and May had been meeting at the café. There was no choice but to banish the thought of her severe parent as if putting on another record.

They returned and a block from her home, May paused to kiss her good-bye since in daylight he could not kiss her in her own doorway. He leaned with his back against a tree, pulling her close, pressing his lips to hers. He could feel her knees trembling against his own. His fingers pressed her back, and moved to cup her quivering buttocks. He wanted her as he had never wanted anyone before. Walking away, never had his penis ached so badly. The only saving grace was that, undeniably, he knew that she wanted him, too.

CHAPTER FOUR

October 1938, Berlin, Germany

A professor, honoring the foreign students, held a compulsory breakfast. Originally, the annual affair introduced the students to each other and German home life. Now there was little consideration given to the fact that the event took place a few weeks too late for either purpose.

The young men stood around making polite conversation, while trying to restrain appetites in view of the rather sparse but well-garnished food (which was all they were interested in). May did a lot of smiling of a kind he did not like, and he did a lot of handshaking, also of a kind he did not like. As soon as it was socially acceptable, he escaped. He then began a long walk through the prosperous but unfamiliar neighborhood, eventually coming to a tram station.

Waiting on the tram platform, still hungry, he asked for a *Bratwurst* from an old woman pushing a two-wheeled cart. While he was being served, a young man, thinking the old crone distracted, stole a sausage and ran away with it. Out of the corner of her eye she caught the act and shrieked, "Thief! Stop the thief!"

Unfortunately for the poor wretch, two policemen appeared from nowhere and took off after him. May watched the chase on the long platform and, much to his horror, saw that the thief, now caught, was being brutally beaten. It seemed too much for only a few *Pfennige*. May threw sufficient money into the woman's hands to pay for the man's sausage and rushed to the aid of the youth, hollering, "Stop! Stop!" to the police.

Such an interruption in the administration of justice was unheard of. Aghast, the police turned on May, their anger and indignation further rising like thunderclouds.

"*Meine Herren Polizisten, bitte, bitte,* the *Wurst* is paid for. It's all been a mistake," May stammered. Then suddenly seeing their expressions, he realized the enormity of his indiscretion.

"You! How dare you interfere! You are aiding and abetting a criminal. You too are under arrest."

"Excuse me, sirs, it's all a mistake. The woman will tell you," May cried, turning to where the cart had been, only to see that the cart and the woman had vanished. An ogling crowd now formed around them. With May's impudence, the police had lost face. Aware of his error and the precariousness of his position, May felt his heart sink. Their violence would now fall on him. He had to steady himself; at his back, handcuffs were snapped on his wrists. Then, already embarrassed enough, he looked up, horrified, to see Inge approaching.

A brief prayer that the earth would swallow him went unanswered.

Having seen May arrested, Inge gathered courage and strode into the fracas. By sheer luck, she had recognized one of the policemen who used to moonlight by guarding at her father's bank, and quickly enough, she thought of a story that might keep May from going to jail. Catching the desperation on his face, she summoned strength and nodded graciously to the police.

"*Guten Tag,* Herr Zimmermann. Is something wrong? This is my fiancé, an architect from America. Surely he hasn't committed a crime." May could hardly believe his ears. The two policemen telegraphed waves of surprise.

"I'm sure Herr May will be able to explain and, certainly, if there should ever be a theft at the bank, I hope you would be on duty."

The charm and clout had an immediate impact. "Luckily, you appeared just in time, Fräulein von Haas," Zimmermann explained. "You should explain to your young man how we do things in Germany."

Inge forced a sweet winsome smile. "Oh, I'll do that, rest assured."

The officer now turned to the crowd, ordering everyone to get moving. An approaching tram made the order unnecessary. Inconspicuously

May and the thief were released. Mortified but grateful, May followed Inge who was now boarding the trolley with her classmates.

"Those bullying thugs," she whispered, just as the folding doors snapped between them, guillotining further talk.

The bloodied and beaten young man had also disappeared. Anxious to be free of the whole episode, May fled back to the street rather than wait for a tram going in his direction.

The now middle-class neighborhood was free of pedestrians, since most businesses had closed for the noon meal. Small ochre buildings stood close together, and the smell of cabbage cooking permeated the air. May walked rapidly, trying to digest the police episode, when suddenly the young man whom he had spared reappeared in an alleyway, gesturing for May to join him in a small secluded park.

"Please, for your own good, sit down at the other end of the bench," he pleaded. May did and, at the man's insistence, looked the other way as they talked. The battered, hallow-eyed man explained that he was a Jew. "I can't begin to thank you, but I've got to try. I'm not a thief. I haven't eaten in three days, and ignoring dietary laws, I grabbed the first food I could get my hands on."

"My name is May. I'm an American graduate student. I'm glad I could help you, although, frankly, for a minute I had my doubts that I could. The inside of a jail is not a tourist attraction I ever want to see. I don't mean to be flippant, but I can't remember being more uncomfortable about my own actions as I was today."

"What you witnessed, Herr May, is no isolated incident. Germany has become a brutal police state." He then talked at length about the indignities people of his religion had suffered and the way most of them, after being arrested, simply disappeared. His voice cracked. "Thousands are missing; the jails couldn't begin to hold them."

May turned abruptly. "Where can they be?"

"Where do the dead go?"

"Lord, I don't know. Why are we different? Why am I here and you there?" May asked.

"Nothing makes any sense, and yet it is happening. Believe me, a terror is raging that is hard, almost impossible, to grasp."

They talked on for some time and May was profoundly moved. He asked simple questions for which, beyond attributing everything to the ravings of a madman and his cohorts, there seemed to be no answers. Occasionally, he turned to look at the man who had become a deep voice coming out of the shadows, touching him as if he were a brother, a fellow traveler on some uncharted course, wondering how to proceed. Around them the slanting afternoon light illuminated patches of earth, as if cutting through windows in a cathedral of great old trees. Such little parks were scattered all over Berlin.

Clearly, the man knew what he was talking about. Everything sinister about Germany that May had sensed, seemed to crystallize, filling him with a great wave of compassion. He knew that if he left this man without helping him, he could never live comfortably with himself again. But what? How? As a student, and on a grant at that, what could he do? He had no power. He could not involve any Germans he knew. Then an idea took hold. Again he turned to take a good look at the man, comparing their physical similarities. They were about the same height. Their coloring would appear the same in a black and white photograph. At the end of their conversation, he again acted imprudently with a daring gesture. He gave the man his passport and all the money he had on him, saying, "Friend, get out of Germany. Tonight! You can't wait. After dark, come to my house. I'll give you some American clothing that will help you get over the border to Switzerland. You can bluff your way through it. Don't knock at my door. It might disturb some good people I can't involve. Throw a stone at my window, upstairs on the right. Within a minute I'll appear. Above all, you must not tell anyone—not even your family or what is left of them. You must simply vanish. From Switzerland, go to France where you should be able to get work on a ship going someplace—anyplace. Once you're safe, please mail me back my passport." May laughed feebly. "I may also need it."

The Germans had issued May a student identification card, which sufficed for most purposes. Eventually he might have to report his passport missing, undoubtedly stolen, but a new passport would come from American officials—the embassy. In the meantime, the man would have time to escape. He could not do more, but he could not do less.

He could not even tell Inge what he had done.

The Jew's sincerity and utter desperation were enough to make concern for himself pale in comparison, although that night, pacing the floor in his room, in some moments weighty misgivings crossed his mind. It was too late to turn back, and May finally sat down on his bed, waiting for the light ping of a pebble on the window. A complete change of clothing, including shoes, and a little food were bunched together at his feet. "I only hope the Gestapo doesn't murder him," he told himself, bolstering resolve.

The sound came and May jumped to his feet. Then, warily, he slipped downstairs into the dark walled garden where he handed the package over to the ghost-pale youth. The Jew's eyes glistened with tears of gratitude. Words failed them both. They shook hands, embraced, and the man left, disappearing into the night.

On the off chance that someone, perhaps walking a dog, had observed him leaving the house, May stood beside the spruce tree for a minute, his heart hammering, hands in his pockets, looking up at the sky as if he had stepped outside for a casual breath of fresh air.

Dog-tired he returned to his room feeling as if, in twenty hours, he had aged twenty years.

The next morning as he walked to class, he stopped dead in his tracks when he noticed a neighbor's gardener picking through some crumpled, vaguely familiar clothing that had been left under a hedge. The sight brought back the previous day's events with an unexpected jolt, jarring him with a sudden sense of alarm. Probably he had made a terrible mistake, one he could pay for for years. He picked up his feet and walked rapidly on. The exertion helped. By the time he reached his classroom, he acknowledged that he had taken part in a weird experience that could impinge on his life in so many ways, that he simply would not let himself think about it.

During the morning the need to talk to Inge kept intruding on his work, and finally he put away his pencil, T-square, and triangle to telephone.

* ** *

Inge was also shaken over the previous day's incident with the police. Were her father to learn of her role in the affair, bandying about his influence, it would have been hard to imagine the consequences. Just the thought summoned a horrible dark sickness. Hardly allowing herself a decent breath, gnawing at her lower lip and playing sick from school, she waited for May to call.

With the call a commitment was born, one not necessarily to May, but against the Nazis. A milestone had been reached and a course set for years to come, regardless of whether or not May remained in her life. "We must not talk about this," she whispered. The receiver weighed heavily in her palm.

"Of course not," he replied, "but thank you again."

To her classmates she had passed off the incident as an amusing lark without a word of truth in it. After a few days she saw that the little drama, although foolhardy, had tested her mettle and proved strangely satisfying. With her courage bolstered she told her parents that Sunday she would be making a picnic for the American. Following Gertrude's advice, her father did not make a scene, although his disapproval was clear.

*   ** *

Sunday, with no idea what would be in store for him, May called for Inge. Thinking of little except that he wanted to take their daughter to bed, he was decidedly uncomfortable meeting her parents.

Herr von Haas had imparted his height to Inge. There, his input apparently stopped. Piercing eyes and considerable muscular action with his nose—prompted by a chronic sniffle—did little to put May at ease. Possibly to offset her husband's manner, Frau von Haas, short and plump as a capon, effused charm. Clearly, beneath her padding lay a bone structure like Inge's. The gangly little brother Otto was on good behavior—bound to be of short duration, mischievous eyes promised.

"Otto has tormented me for ten years," Inge confessed, announcing his age.

May did not believe her.

The von Haas's living room was impressively large, representing old wealth, yet lacking in the airy delicacy of Frau Matcher's parlor. The room was dark, the furniture massive. Persian rugs overlaid more Persian rugs that, in turn, overlaid carpeting. Ancestral portraits gazed sternly beside a rural image by Franz Marc, which struck May as an indication of artistic appreciation somewhere in Inge's lineage, perhaps from a grandmother. Unread leather-bound classics in sets stood behind beveled-glass doors. May stuck as close as possible to the imposing foyer where a great oak-paneled door offered escape.

Herr von Haas, not unlike the style of Franklin Delano Roosevelt, twisted a cigarette into a long ivory holder. May quickly produced a lighter.

"Where do you intend to go on the picnic?" Herr von Haas inquired, looking up at May, but in effect looking down. "Why not consider our own garden? The flowers are lovely right now."

"So I noticed, " May replied, "but that is entirely up to Fräulein von Haas."

Little Otto grinned. Inwardly, May squirmed.

"There are many lovely spots," Inge's mother chimed in, turning to her daughter, as if some unseen SOS between mother and daughter had been broadcast and received. Then, smiling, she suggested several sites guaranteed to be public.

Inge, ready to spring free of them, nodded acquiescence.

"Will you be home for dinner?" Herr von Haas asked.

"We've been asked to join friends," May interjected and turned to Inge. "Providing this is acceptable to Fräulein von Haas…"

"Whatever you'd like," she replied, relieved.

Again Otto grinned, enabling May to turn to him. "I hear you fly kites. I used to build them. Perhaps one day we can fly some." He knew he sounded patronizing, yet he was unsettled by the grin, a definite put-on.

Dutifully kissing her parents, Inge hastened their departure. As May reached for his gloves, a large toad jumped out, startling in its unexpectedness.

Eyes blazing and embarrassed to the point of exasperation, Inge shrieked. "*Mutti, bitte,* must he always behave like this?"

"Think nothing of it," May enjoined, now having to smile. "Once I might have done the same—if I'd had a sister." Then picking up the basket, he ushered Inge out, heading for the tram, leaving the household to settle its problems.

"I should have warned you. That toad could have popped out of your pocket. Otto is a menace—a scourge." Her topaz eyes met his. "Are all little boys so poisonous?"

"I thought it was funny," he lied. "Lordy, Inge, he has a sense of humor. Don't try to squelch him."

She sighed good-naturedly. "You handled Father well. I'm surprised he didn't ask you if you were a doctor. That's one of his favorite put-downs. Of course he thought you might have been, which would have been self-defeating."

Inge seemed to May breathtakingly lovely, and once again he felt his reason departing. "The friendly bankers are the same the world over. I'm glad I don't need to borrow any money."

Walking leisurely, they laughed. He longed to hold her in his arms and was ready to devour her with kisses, yet he still found casual words. "By the way, where are we going?"

"To the Tiergarten. It's a separate world."

"While I think of it, because I'm really thinking of something else, open that picnic basket carefully when we get there," he said.

Berlin's magnificent Tiergarten, a huge park, encompassed not only a zoo, where they got off the tram, but miles of winding paths among trees, lakes and streams. Deep in the park, even on Sunday, they could find privacy. Like forest animals that learn camouflage, they made themselves disappear. With Inge leading them deeper and deeper into the wood, May's heart beat faster and faster. Without words, he was certain that she was telling him that she wanted him. Finally she found a spot she liked, and May spread his raincoat. They sat down beside a small stream. Only later would he see its beauty.

"I must talk to you seriously," he blurted. "I love you. Frankly, it worries me, because it has happened so fast. You've become vital to me—my whole existence." Gently he pushed her back to recline in his arms. He kissed her lightly, anxious to know how she would react to his outpouring.

Sealing his lips with a finger, her eyes met his. "Don't say things to me that you do not mean, even to make love to me, because I will believe you," she whispered.

"But I do mean it!" He was emphatic, almost angry that she could doubt him. "I want to marry you."

She sat upright, startled. Then covering her surprise, she reached for a blade of grass. "*Liebling,* I have my studies. For at least two more years ..."

He pulled her back down to him, his hand cupping her breast. "I'm speaking too soon. I might not have a whole year in Germany. These are tumultuous times. My God, I almost went to jail!"

She could not know his desperation or how much she was loved. Nor could he tell her about the Jew he had helped or the world opinion of her country. He felt as if he were either tongue-tied or foaming at the mouth. He swallowed his saliva, giving her a desperate, hopeless little laugh laced with chagrin.

"I never knew love could be so painful," she told him. "I'm baffled too. And you, you frighten me. You're a desirable man, and knowing you has made me feel alive. You make an ugly world beautiful."

Her voice was like music. She reached up to wrap her arms about him. He could feel his heart beating outrageously and his blood churning as passion within built in an aching explosive tension. Then the music changed when she said, "I'm only afraid of losing you, because we may have an impossible love."

"Don't think that way!" he cried, unbuttoning his trousers so that he could make love to her. Finding her lips, he struggled to control himself, knowing that she lifted an impossible weight, but her words imposed another. "You must learn courage and to trust me," he whispered running his hand under her skirt up her thigh to stroke her. There he found a damp spot to massage. Then he said, "I'll never again buy a stolen *Bratwurst*!" They laughed as a fleeting remembrance of the awful situation crowded past their passion.

"You will take care of me?" she asked, again serious as he felt her. "You're doing something very nice to me right now."

"Always. I'm a responsible man."

"I want you to take me. That's why I brought you here."

Her words catapulted him into a pool of immeasurable joy. His lips closed on hers, ceasing all talk.

He, too, had planned to make love to her this day, but wanting something perfect, he did not want to seduce her. He wanted her to come to him freely without his having to plead. Despite his screaming need to explode within her, he brought her to a climax and protected her with a condom before he came. Puffs of wind in the treetops made flickering shafts of sunlight, animating the afternoon's perfection. Finally, the most beautiful girl in the world lay in his arms, having become his. Lovely topaz eyes, reflecting prisms of amber light, had stolen his heart for all time.

The picnic basket was not booby-trapped. They ate and when the day began to die, they made love again. In days to come, they would perfect their lovemaking, better synchronizing, rising to greater heights, dying more deaths; but the first time marked a commitment of crushing intensity. Utterly sweet surrender, fresh and unspoiled, brought them to the point of perishing in newly found ecstasy.

Arm in arm they walked back to the Zoo Station for the tram. At May's house she freshened up, and instead of joining friends they went dancing. Moving close to her, May thought he would die of happiness. Here was the love he had always wanted, the great love that Betsy, who had dominated his love life during his college years, would have kept him from. It was the first time in weeks that he had thought of Betsy, he noted with satisfaction, but it was Betsy who had taught him how to make love—really well, in fact.

At five in the morning when he let himself into the drafting room, he knew there was a price to pay for everything. For the moment he paid it gladly. He had six hours before he would hear the bells of the *charrette.*

* ** *

The next week passed in relative quietness marked by a mountain of work. Professors had no sympathy for love affairs, even those they knew about. Inge invited him to dinner.

"I'm sure you'd rather eat someplace else, but my parents want a better look at you. Awful, isn't it?" This wasn't quite the truth; it was the only way her father would let her see him.

"I'll take anything short of a poleaxing to be with you," he told her.

"*Liebling*, there's no guarantee…"

Otto, who used his spending money to purchase trick gadgets, gave May a few embarrassing moments. The most distressing was a whoopee cushion that emitted a noise loud enough to shatter anyone's equanimity. Previously, every member of the family had been exposed to this hoax, but the offending article had been forgotten. Herr von Haas was polite but hardly cordial, yet the conversation flowed more easily than Inge had expected. Otto wore a jacket, which permitted a fake rubber flower to peak out of a buttonhole on his lapel. In his pocket, connected by a small rubber hose, was a squeezable bladder containing water. Fortunately, the spurt of water missed May, and Otto was spared a good cuff.

The following Saturday, hoping to put an end to his tomfoolery, May and Inge took Otto to fly kites on the *Grüne* by the Spee River near where Frau Matcher's lover and fiancé had dueled. There they talked about Inge's field, art.

"Believe me, Inge, there's been significant work done since Cranach, Boucher, Goya, and the old masters, Rembrandt and Leonardo."

She eyed him suspiciously. "No one will ever achieve the greatness of Rembrandt and Leonardo, or so I've been told."

"Not unless they are Hitler's favorites like Makart, von Amerling, Defregger and Grützner."

"What do you mean?" she asked, his sarcasm having gotten through to her.

"Your professors, like mine, don't want to lose their jobs, so they've cut off the moderns who have made some of the world's finest art. You need to study outside of Germany." To no avail he tugged sharply on his string, trying to get his kite in an updraft. It crashed to the ground.

"You come here to study and then have the nerve to tell me I should leave!" Her eyes flashed angrily. She looked so attractive, even irritated; May took his camera from its case and shot several pictures of both her and Otto.

"I've had different schooling. I can sift. In class sometimes I can even read between the lines and understand what Tessenow is saying, which is always guarded. I don't think your countrymen can de-code it."

"The art program has been the one redeeming feature of this regime, and now you're telling me that it is no good." Her kite was falling. "I feel as if you are pulling my teeth." She looked up at him defiantly, momentarily forgetting her kite. The lapse in attention was fatal; her kite crashed, too.

"I didn't say it was no good. I said it stopped. I'd like to help you, that's all." There would be time to open her eyes. It would be a mistake to throw everything at her too fast. Besides, she was awfully angry about her kite.

Later May would remember those early discussions, ruing the days that he had been so hard on her, knowing that he should have gone more slowly before she left him....

* ** *

November 9, 1938, May awakened to find Inge sitting at the foot of his bed, let in by Frau Kruger, upset but reluctant to disturb him. For a few minutes before consciousness he had been aware of someone present, and, as if in dream, remembered an incident. He had been asleep on an old iron bed with sagging springs in his grandmother's house. Inexplicably his mother had been there when he awakened.

"Son," she said to him, "something happened during the night. A man named Lindbergh has flown across the ocean. Imagine that! This feat will mean much in your life, I'm sure." Her eyes brimmed with excitement and enthusiasm. Young and beautiful in 1927, her life was still full of promise.

Victoria's face soon receded, and Inge's came into focus. "Something terrible has happened!"

"What?" queried May, sitting up, shaking free of his dream.

"Listen. Hear the noise across town. There'll be no classes today. The Nazis are on a rampage against the Jews. Stores have been ruined. Synagogues burned. Those poor people! It's on the radio. They are calling it *Kristallnacht.*"

"The night of broken glass…"

"I'm so upset."

"Come here," said May, moving to make room for her and patting a place on the bed by his pillow.

She settled down close to him, taut and on the brink of tears. He hardly knew where to begin. He relived the arrest of the Kaplan family that had somehow become submerged in his consciousness. The apartment over the camera store had not been reopened. Then the young Jew who took his passport flashed before him. The Jew had told him that hundreds, perhaps thousands, had been carted off, never to be heard from again. But Inge had been brought up under National Socialism. She was a victim of years of propaganda. Now, apparently, formerly covert Nazi brutality was being exposed to all Germans.

He sighed, not knowing what to say. "Inge, I'm frightened for you and your people. The Nazis will stop at nothing to hold their power. Germany is headed toward no good end. And I don't think there is anything we can do about it." He turned to face her squarely, trying to put down his own personal fears.

She began to cry, "I was always so proud of being German. Hitler promised so much, but the price is terrible. I'm ashamed."

"Inge, for heaven's sake, be quiet about what you feel. It's nothing you've done." He patted her.

"You don't understand. It's MY country."

"I do understand."

"I feel betrayed."

"Well, you have been."

"I'm completely disillusioned."

May's arms closed about her, and he rocked her back and forth. "Darling, we all have to learn to face disillusionment. There's no inoculation against it. Governments—politicians—are all mad.

He shared her woe, but he was more frightened than he dared let on. Their world could crumble overnight. He wheeled to the edge of the bed, thinking. This action on the part of the Nazis would not sit well with the governments of the free world. The most immediate threat was that all Americans would be ordered home. Worse, of course, was the possibility of war. Suddenly his heart felt heavier than he had ever remembered. He would have to get Inge out of Germany.

As soon as Inge left, somewhat quieted—he tackled the onerous task of writing his mother asking for her engagement ring. Many times she had promised it to him. Even before he sealed the letter, he knew the cold response his request would bring.

Sadly, he remembered Victoria's misguided intentions had always been 'for-his-own-good.' At such times her face would freeze, and then her lips would tremble for she hated to oppose him. He shuddered. Banishing unkind recollections, he thought of Inge.

Her family would want a proper engagement and a big wedding, he naively decided.

Then he remembered: *He had no passport.* Without that little green book he stood deprived of the protection of the United States government. Perhaps now without it, he couldn't even marry Inge. For the first time in his life he had no resources to fall back on. He had been a fool. Horrified, he banged his head against the wall.

As if disarmed before battle, he was afraid, presciently afraid for Inge and himself.

CHAPTER FIVE

After the *Kristallnacht* May and others knew that by decree, Jews had been deprived of their work and property, and that they were stalked like animals in a nationwide pogrom. Good people felt a national shame that after a few weeks was blacked out, because there was little to remind them. Inge, Frau Matcher and Frau Kruger met the crisis with sadness and horror. Former shipmates scattered about Germany telephoned to compare notes.

"What in the hell is going on?" George Chauncy asked.

"I don't know any more than you do—just what I read in the papers—and the posters, of course."

"I'd feel safer in the Belgian Congo with cannibals."

"I know. It's barbaric. Have you trimmed down since the *Savoia?*"

"No. Like you said, it's the bread."

"George, they may just eat you."

George had to be jockeyed a little, thought May, momentarily relieving his own anxiety by teasing. "I'll bet you're as round as a Viennese cream puff."

George had to laugh. "I never did travel light."

Bob Street also called, wrecking the vestige of amusement George had afforded. "I haven't had the chance to see Berlin, and I was hoping you'd set me up with some hot chick. I'm afraid the climate is becoming unhealthy."

"I agree, but you'll have to find your own girls. I'm not running a dating bureau."

Later May was sorry he hadn't been more cordial, but he still couldn't stomach Bob Street.

While studying at home, May occasionally looked away from his books, gazing for a moment out of his window to rest his eyes on the apple and cherry trees that framed the front walk leading to an iron gate. A blue spruce obscured the corner of a low wall topped with wrought iron. There was seldom anything to see but the garden itself or a neighbor walking a dog, but the view was satisfying. Then late one afternoon, May looked down at the irregular stone walk and saw an elderly, heavy-set gentleman with a handlebar moustache. He was wearing a black fur-collared overcoat, a bowler and carried a furled umbrella. For a long curious moment the gentleman's eyes met his own. Then two men, carrying a trunk, broke the spell.

May knew Herr Matcher had returned. The following morning when he came down to breakfast, Herr Matcher was just finishing his. May introduced himself as Matcher rose, extending a hand. "My dear sister tells me that you have been a welcome adjunct to our little household."

"The pleasure has been mine," May replied, immediately noting the effortless elegance in the older man.

"When you can find a few minutes to join me, perhaps only for a nightcap, please do."

"That's very kind of you, sir."

It was not long before the occasion arose. One night May came home to hear the final notes of a piano étude coming from the floor above. Feeling he would enjoy a drink, he continued up the stairs and knocked. He was ushered into another world.

"I'm not disturbing?" May asked, seeing that Matcher was wearing a soft velvet smoking jacket and house slippers.

"Not at all. I was becoming bored with my own playing. I don't do Chopin justice and I'm afraid I never will."

May had often wondered about the third floor. Stair carpeting and paintings promised no ordinary attic. Now looking about he saw a Bösendorfer concert grand under the highest point of the mansard roof. It was surrounded by an interesting assemblage of *objets d'art* collected over many years of traveling. Tiger and zebra skins overlaid carpet. A 'degenerate' Gauguin stood on an easel for want of wall space. The bed was concealed behind a Hasagawa Tohaku folding screen, worthy of a museum. Bronze sculpture from Greece and woodcarvings from

Bali mingled with cloisonné vases. Portraits of beautiful women and sportive men, endearingly signed, recalled another decade.

"What a comfortable spacious apartment," May exclaimed, admiring and missing nothing in the eclectic assemblage.

"Everything I have carries memories, and has stood the test of time." He urged May to sit down and poured two brandies. "At this hour nothing serves the stomach like fine cognac; it keeps impeccably, and is always so nice to come home to. By the way, I have just returned from your country, having moved my financial interests to America." Matcher leaned back, swirling the crystal snifter, viewing the liquid in the light with a squinted eye.

"Where have you most enjoyed traveling?" May asked.

"Oh, there are right moments, perfect moments to have been almost anywhere. One wants to enjoy a flowering of a culture when you can be on top of it."

"I think I know what you mean, but please explain," said May, sitting back, feeling the warmth of the brandy, smoother than any he could remember tasting.

"There are times when you would prefer to be anyplace else. Years ago I was young and on the *Nellie Bligh*. She found me in Java. I was there, picked up in Sourabaya. She was in the coolie trade to the China islands then. Have you heard of the trade?"

"Vaguely."

"Captains were paid for what they delivered. The ship was packed and, of course, some died. The *Nellie* was not a ship to choose if you knew better. I didn't. We had a Dago captain from Chile, and we got to China, all right. There were some close calls—such as weather and British warships. We had three hundred coolies on the *Nellie*. One of them looked at me as he came aboard, and I'll never forget that look. After that, I checked the hatch gratings. I wanted to be sure they were sound."

Matcher swirled his brandy. Somewhere outside dogs were barking. "The *Nellie* was making such good time, I wasn't sorry to have left Java the way I did, but I'd forgotten the Chinamen. Then we heard a ferocious howl from below, like a man being knifed. I looked down. The coolies were swarming to the deck, clinging to the ladder like bees. Most were armed with boards they'd chipped off from below, maybe with their teeth or fingernails. The leader was scrambling over the coaming toward us. I lifted him up by his pigtail and dropped him on the others. I was a big strong man then." Matcher shook his head.

"Somehow we were able to make those hatch gratings fast, but the coolies were howling at us. Wolves would have looked prettier. Then that fool captain came up with a pistol. He was trembling and half-crying when he fired into their faces. Those coolies began to leap and scream."

May sat speechless as Matcher continued, "One shot had set a shirt on fire. I almost thought it was funny the way a man tore his shirt off, but it wasn't funny when someone blew on the rag to keep it burning. The captain thought he was done with the mutiny, but I knew better. Smoke began to pour from the hatch. Of course the Chinese were reasonable, intelligent people. The captain wouldn't let them roast, would he?"

"Not if he wanted the fire put out," said May.

"He had the puzzle of his life before him. The coolies were clamoring to be let out, pointing to the fire. They thought they had the captain this time, and he was about to let those maniacs loose to save his ship, but they didn't reckon with a burly sailor with another gun. "Let them roast," the sailor ordered, making another mutiny.

"To make a long story short, by the time we had the lifeboats provisioned and away, all was quiet again, except for the flames. My boat made the Pelew Islands. I never heard what became of the other two. But I never went back to China without seeing those faces—from jinrickshaws or in cars or among smiling waiters. Man's inhumanity to man astounds me."

"Mein Gott," May exclaimed. "What a nightmare."

"I've come back with considerable trepidation, May."

"Recent events have left us all stunned. Berlin is not the Pelews or China. Let's hope it is over!" He had to tell himself that.

A look on Matcher's face said he felt differently. "We may be seeing only the tip of the iceberg. I made a little tour to Genoa. The factories in Milan go day and night producing armaments."

His drink finished, May took Matcher's story to bed as fixed in his memory as a dream of his own.

* ** *

With an eye toward increasing the birthrate, the Nazis encouraged free love. In Inge's social class, however, this license was slow in arriving. "I want to announce our engagement," said May, smiling expectantly.

"Liebling, my school hasn't finished, and my parents wouldn't hear of it."

Her words cut him. "Is that because I'm a foreigner and might take you away?"

"That's part of it."

Until now it had never dawned on May that her family might find him unacceptable. His pride was smarting. "Inge, it's your life."

"Already they've been making little noises over the fact that I see you exclusively. They expect everything to move much more slowly. Usually couples and their families have known each other for years."

May knew what Inge was saying was true, but she could not tell May that her father did not like him and that her friends disapproved of the affair. "If we said anything now my parents would do their best to stop me from seeing you. I'd have to lie about where I was. Getting friends to lie would not be easy."

She pressed his hand to her cheek. Her nearness almost comforted him.

As much as he hated this state of affairs, he felt obliged to bow to her instincts. Work mounted and May was anxious to spend all the time he could with Inge. Desire for her clenched itself around him. Winter had set in, and they could no longer make love in the Tiergarten. Before long Norbert Buth came to his rescue.

May was the better architect. Stationed at the next drafting table, he had often been able to help Buth with constructive criticism before the evaluating team chopped Buth's designs to pieces. Suggestions that arose from May's less rigid schooling had spared Buth considerable grief.

Finally May confided to him about Inge and his frustration in finding privacy.

"I'll give you a key to my place," said Buth. "Why didn't you speak up earlier? The apartment isn't in the greatest neighborhood. And it's never tidy but it's warm and private, and I go home on weekends."

"Maybe someday I can repay you."

"You already have."

In Buth's apartment, 'untidy' was a gross understatement, but May and Inge could make love unhampered. Afterward, conversations in the dark charted the small maneuvers and upheavals that colored their love. Understandably, there were times when Inge was fearful over discovery…or even a pregnancy. Accidents did happen.

"Why not? It would settle things for good," said May.

Neither doubted that they were inextricably bound together. "You know we can't afford to get married right now."

May ran his fingers through his hair in desperation. "You must understand the way I think. I hate sham and pretense. We survived *Kristallnacht* without my being dragged back to the States. There may be other crises. If we were married, we wouldn't be separated. We have to make our own luck." He knew he was being churlish. It wasn't her fault she was young and unsure. Feeling sorry, he reached out and touched her face, ivory gold under the lamplight. It had a promise of maturation he had never seen before. "I will not wish your life away. You'll be handsome in middle-age and better yet in old age." He cupped her chin in his hand. "The right bone structure is there."

Gravely, she returned his gaze. "I'd give up five years of my youth to have you."

She did not know it, but it would have been no sacrifice.

* ** *

The secrecy that May despaired over continued to impart a spice, poignancy and animation that kept them vibrant. An inherent high voltage ran through them both, which found grounding in their trysts. They loved and talked. Inge was enormously curious about life in the United States. Most of her impressions had come from the movies. Hollywood versions of rags to riches, cowboys and indians, and cops and robbers produced some rather strange ideas May had to straighten out. There were things to laugh about and serious moments when the current between them shorted out. When May tried to undo what Inge's teachers taught, she fought back.

"I can't expose you to what has been eradicated here, but I have to tell you what I believe or I won't be giving you the best of me." He talked about the staggering variety of painting done in the twentieth century. "To urge artists to make concessions for the sake of communicating with a bunch of farmers or factory workers is stupid. Serving only a government dilutes the artist's individuality."

"You're decrying patronage under which art has always flowered."

"The artist must be free to paint what he wants the way he wants. Why paint like the Renaissance? We're not in it—at least not the old one."

She frowned. "When I look at modern art I see less than I want to."

"My dear, you haven't really seen any modern art. The only modern art you've seen are grotesque remnants the Nazis preserved to illustrate their point."

"I'm confused. I don't know freedom as you know it, but I've always felt secure and safe. Granted, my security is a cocoon. Then I met you, and slowly and surely you are pulling away the silk web."

"And out will come a beautiful butterfly," he replied.

"To be gobbled up before she can fly." Inge shuddered. "You must think of that."

"I do, and don't think I'm not alarmed."

Calmer, she was now sitting cross-legged. Her hair, pulled loose and high, shimmered in the soft light. Her arms squeezed her shoulders. "Having met you, I'm a one-eyed woman in a country of the blind," she acknowledged bitterly.

"That makes you a queen." He picked up her sketchbook. "You have tremendous potential."

"Potential talent is a terrible burden," she murmured, and began sketching him nude on the bed. Because of his erection the drawing might have been pornographic had it not been for her talent. She pressed one of his hands between her thighs and cautioned him not to distract her. "Don't you dare move." Instinct would not let him obey.

"You're cruel."

Finally, after sketching and teasing him for about an hour, she let him make love to her.

"This sketch I'll always keep," he promised admiringly.

"You can't. It's too intimate, too revealing."

"I've no intention of showing it to anyone."

"But it shows you terribly vulnerable," she replied, unwilling to let go of it.

"I am, and I want to pose again."

She laughed. "I'd like to paint this room, but I wouldn't dare. It's been the home of so many delightful hours that deserve recording or they might become lost. I suppose I might have to paint wings on the bed, and take the cracks out of the mirror, but the hardest part would be to convey the quality of the time spent in this room."

She turned to look at him but he was asleep.

* ** *

Feeling Tessenow's influence, May extolled his as he and Inge lunched. "He's not rashly modern, but in one sense he's more modern than the other professors."

"And so you like him?"

"He's inspiring. He's enormously bright, and if you look closely, his buildings express what I can only call a profound experience. Like many great teachers, he is a catalyst. Now he feels we are in a period of decay, but this is a subject he must dance around, flinging all seven veils over our eyes and ears."

The thought of May's group of fifty students dancing with veils was ludicrous. "I must paint that," she said, almost collapsing with laughter. "You will dance naked, of course, like a centaur or Pan. And I'll toot the panpipe."

Her laughter and the picture she described made May feel like a fool. "You're not being funny. Besides, you can't toot and paint at the same time."

Seeing his irritation, she quieted. "I'm sorry. Go on."

"He compares our civilization to the last days of Rome, citing the decline of morals, inflation, *etc.*; not being too explicit, he ends his tirades with hope for the future. However, first he says we must come to something like a rain of brimstone."

Inge's eyes widened incredulously. "How does he dare come out with that?" The man was in danger.

"Oh, yes. Hope for the future will appear when the handicrafts in the small towns can once again flourish."

"And hope for the future gets him off the political hook?"

"*Jawohl.*"

May explained, "He doesn't speak from a podium. Maybe that's why I felt his influence slowly. He says style comes from the people, and that it's only natural to love one's native land; true culture cannot be international because it comes from the maternal womb of a nation."

"That's the sort of thing Hitler would love to hear." She broke apart a roll.

"I disagreed with him."

"You WHAT?" She was shocked.

"I told him that it was easy for me to see and understand that theory in Germany and France; both are sort of closed corporations. But I can visualize art evolving in the United States, in time, almost international in scope, because the country is so diversified. If so there, this could become worldwide. It could become a very important movement, more important than *Der Stil.*"

"What did he say?"

"Well, he looked surprised. Then he said he would give my point further consideration." May appeared pensive, and then added, "I hope I didn't offend him. I wouldn't want him to notify my foundation that I was a troublemaker or a heretic."

Inge swallowed hard, unrelieved. Now her man was in danger. May had to be careful about expressing his outlandish opinions. The 'International Style' was un-German. However, not wanting to harp, she resumed a resigned tone. "Apparently you like Tessenow-on-architecture better than Tessenow-on-art."

"That's right."

"*Liebling,* art is the expression of human emotion, however subtle. It gains or loses, depending on its power to move the viewer, nothing more. I don't think it has anything to do with national boundaries." Deadly serious, she shook her fork at him, dropping her voice almost to a whisper. "Don't show off your brilliance. You could get in terrible trouble!"

He smiled. "I always knew you were a work of art."

Later he decided he had been foolish to express a contrary opinion. He doubted that Tessenow would hold it against him, particularly if he never did it again. Through frequent reports, Tessenow would surely try to maintain a close connection with the foundation's board of governors. The thought made him antsy. But there were also others in the class listening. The others could be like a younger Herr von Haas, and this thought made him decidedly uncomfortable.

* ** *

As a gangling, yet pretty child, Inge hung back among her family, seldom revealing her inquisitive mind. Despite her parents' efforts to hide their gloom over the dwindling family fortune during the worldwide Depression, she grew up feeling its stifling effect. Accustomed to being rich and unable to cope with less and less, Gertrude and her husband struggled with pride. Inge was baffled. In public money was a dirty word. In private it was the only topic. Inge found refuge in the world of her imagination. With pencil and paper her fantasies took shape.

By joining the party, Herr von Haas had been able to stem the tide of financial ruin. He began wearing the Nazi insignia on his lapel, as did his friends in similar circumstances. Soon Inge could not mention politics within the family without her father coldly raising his eyebrows. She quickly learned discretion.

Driving with her parents for a Sunday dinner with her uncle Fritz at his hunting lodge, Inge's rebellion crystallized when her father made a few unkind words about her cousin, Karl Heinz. The relative silence in the backseat (Otto remained home with a cold) had loosened her father's tongue.

"I have to dismiss Epstein and Abronovitz."

Gertrude was shocked. "How can you do that? They're also stockholders, not to mention, old friends. They've always been with you at the bank."

The sudden shift in Gertrude's voice alerted Inge and she began to listen intently.

"They happen to be Jews, my dear wife. That being the case, their high position doesn't mean a damn. Even big fish are coming under the hammer."

"Surely, you can do something."

"I've tried—stalled. I can't any longer. There are laws. I can't break them."

Inge remained still, so still that the deep green trees of the *Grünewald*, pruned clean and straight as if they were already electrical poles, seemed to be whipping by the car. Behind the first row of trees, the view almost immediately gave way to utter darkness, to which she would have loved to escape.

"What about their stock?" Gertrude spoke, playing with the clasp on her purse until it snapped with a brittle crack, lending unexpected emphasis to her question.

"The sale will be handled by outsiders, officials from another city. That's the way things work. Local hands must be kept clean."

"But…but…you're the one who has to fire them."

Epstein and Abronovitz, prosperous widowers related by marriage, had lived together by choice in a large home in a wealthy neighborhood. A daughter, Sadie, had been a classmate of Inge's until she was forced to drop out of school. One Epstein son attended school in England; the other was gaining banking experience in the United States.

Herr von Haas's eyes remained fixed on the newly completed *Autobahn*. "I know. More than once their money pulled us through. I don't like this anymore than you do, but I have to hang on to what we have. I know the way to do it, the only way: play ball!" He sniffed, cleared his throat, and continued. "Heading a bank entails a lot of unpleasant tasks. That's what I'm paid for." His tone was unconvincing until he glanced in the rearview mirror and caught Inge's shocked expression. "Inge, you're not to speak of this. You know I'll do what I can."

His feeble attempt to mollify her only summoned more disgust. She knew he would do nothing.

*   **   *

Shortly after *Kristallnacht* Sadie Epstein called Inge, quiet desperation in her voice. "Please see me. I know the dismissal of Father and Uncle Max was not your father's fault. Still, I have to talk to you." A new hum on the line alerted them both.

"Let's meet in the Tiergarten where we used to play. I'm leaving for England tonight."

Clearly timing was important. Inge agreed.

Later Inge was shocked at the sight of her friend, stepping from behind a large tree near a small clearing. Now thin as a wraith, her hair hung limply around her face.

Inge reached for her friend's trembling hands. "It's good you're getting away, Sadie."

"Father and Uncle Max are in terrible trouble. They can't come home. They're living on the street, sleeping in parks. Inge, once your father came to us virtually begging, and my family's money saved your father's bank. Now I have to beg a favor of you. Will you hide them in your attic? Perhaps only for a few days…it won't be for long. Believe me, without your help they will die."

Inge was aghast, shocked speechless over the enormity of her request. "Sadie, I can't help you. Things at home are not as you remember them during the Depression. Now there are servants living in the attic—a maid, a gardener and a cook. As much as I would love to help you, I can't jeopardize my family."

"Inge, I beg you."

That Sadie would make such an impossible demand, even out of desperation, angered her. Fallen leaves cracked under her feet, now carrying the dead weight of her body. Like a stone figure in a garden enclosing a heart that was alive, she held her ground, unyielding.

"I am so sorry."

Sadie's plea would ring in Inge's ear for the rest of her life. She hardly heard her friend's words of disappointment, so wretched was she over the cruelty of the request in light of her own obligation to refuse.

CHAPTER SIX

Inge's affair with May deepened into perilous frenetic love. He became her salvation. Only with him, enjoying the wild pleasure he afforded, could she forget Sadie and her family.

Herr von Haas noticed a letter from Sadie postmarked London on the console in the foyer. The cheap envelope was almost transparent, and he picked it up and was holding it to the light when Inge entered the room. Embarrassed, he surrendered the letter to her open hand, catching an icy stare. Later he asked casually, "Did Sadie mention her father and uncle?"

That he was honestly hoping that they had escaped the country went unnoticed by Inge. "They're all fine," she replied, tight-lipped. She had not opened the letter. Knowing that Sadie would be asking for HER forgiveness, guilt overwhelmed her. Aware that her father had done nothing to get his directors out of Germany, she was unforgiving. He's such a fool, thought Inge, disgust crimping her eyelids. Then she realized, looking at him—his face bent over his plate as if watching his dinner cool— that he was worse than a fool.

That fall the longer her father waited, the cheaper the Epstein and Abronovitz shares in the bank had become for him to buy, and buy them he did, in a legal and tidy transaction through an intermediary.

The purchase was marked by an unheralded bottle of *Dom Perignon.* Once Inge learned the reason for the expensive wine, not bothering to plead illness, she fled the room for fear of gagging. The thought of her father's action was so painfully shameful, she had to temper it. Had her father urged them to leave (as he might have), they probably wouldn't have listened, she told herself. Like so many other Jews, the damned fools wouldn't have acted, sold out, or left!

* ** *

May looked forward with boyish enthusiasm toward Christmas. He bought Frau Kruger a silk scarf, Matcher a brandy, and some excellent tobacco for the other roomer he almost never saw, Herr Rosenberg. He commissioned Inge to sketch the house for Frau Matcher. He called on his mother in the States for a magic set for Otto. *"Any sort would be perfect. Little flags that come out of a sleeve or even trick cards would do. No chemistry sets like I used to have, or he'd blow the roof off the house,"* he wrote. He sent his mother an adjustable bread slicer, telling Inge when she disapproved, "She loves gadgets."

For weeks he watched the mail, expecting his mother's ring for Inge, but it did not arrive. When a box finally came with the magic set, bitter and resentful he picked through the packing several times to be sure. He also received a tie from the States with his passport. The young man who used it, obviously successfully, had waited for the rush of Christmas mail to avoid detection. This made May feel a little better.

For Inge's parents he found an angel dressed in beige velvet with a wax head and gilded wings. It was only a decoration and therefore appropriate. Inge's gift presented a great problem. Finally he commissioned a red leather desk portfolio. On the front cover edged in silver were her initials in elaborate copperplate calligraphy. It was lined with soft gray-green moiré, and contained a supply of monogrammed writing paper. It was exquisite, not too personal but personal enough.

Christmas began with the four Advents. Not until Christmas Eve were the trees lit with dozens of little candles. Then the exchange of gifts followed an elegant supper. May told Inge they would have to divide their time between the two houses. "Frau Kruger has been baking for days. In that elderly household, think of what we represent—hope for the future."

Herr von Haas threw a monkey wrench into the plans. This arrangement would have been a statement of sorts, signifying an alliance that he vehemently objected to.

"You're going to spoil the day for your daughter," Gertrude warned. She had recognized the symptoms of young love: the dreamy silences, the dancing movements to incessant English popular music, and the obvious neglect of old friends.

"I don't like whatever she's up to. I'm going to put a detective on her," said Herr von Haas. His wife stared in icy disapproval.

"*Mutti, bitte,* it's an elderly household. They're not social. They have no children," pleaded Inge.

In the end a compromise was reached. May could come to their home, but afterward it would be inappropriate for her to go to his. "I'm sorry, my dear, but your father will go no further."

Later, in a restaurant, Inge told May her parents' decision, disappointing him to the point of anger. "Obviously their wishes come before mine. That hurts."

"I live under their roof. Please, don't make things worse."

Inge picked at her food and drank too much wine. Her cheeks were flushed when she went to the restroom. May shoved his plate away and looked at his watch. Twenty minutes elapsed before she returned. "You were gone a helluva long time," he growled.

"I'm sorry."

"So am I," he lied. He wanted his way, and her non-conformity bruised his ego.

"I was sick."

May paid the check and without another word saw Inge home. Christmas would be clouded by their first quarrel. That evening he told Frau Matcher that Inge would be unable to attend her dinner. She gave him a little twisted smile and a nod, accepting her refusal with such understanding that Inge's family was somewhat vindicated.

Christmas Eve, shortly after dark, he arrived with his gifts and a bouquet of red roses. Inge was obviously strained. The hit of the evening was the magic set that transported Otto into a world of Harry Houdini. It was as if he had received instructions and means for a disappearing act. By eight o'clock May felt free to depart with his presents: a duplicate drawing of the one Inge had done for Frau Matcher, a scarf from her parents, and a wooden toad Otto had carved. Inge saw May to the door. There she laid her head on his shoulder so that he could feel her breast against his arm. "I was afraid I would never see you again."

He could only say her name.

Dinner at Matcher's without the dominating presence of a child was a sophisticated affair. May changed to evening clothes.

Frau Kruger loved to cook the way some love to gossip or pray or sing and dance. Tonight, in a starched apron and cap, she lit the candles on the tree and shared a glass of champagne with her employers. She would serve the meal and then eat in the kitchen with her elderly cousin. The exchange of gifts was a minor aspect of the evening, although clearly Frau Matcher was delighted with Inge's drawing. "*Gut,* Herr May, your Inge has talent." She beamed in appreciation, and May's heart swelled with pride.

He received two leather-bound books from the Matchers, obviously selected by Herr Rosenberg, and a tin of cookies from Frau Kruger. For the first time May noted Herr Rosenberg found his tongue. "Twenty-eight hundred years before Jesus broke bread for his children, a wise emperor in China compiled a great cookbook, the *Hon Zu.* In forty-seven centuries we have not learned much more about food than it tells us. However, a few French chefs and our own Frau Kruger always manage to earn my gratitude."

Everyone agreed, and at that moment Frau Kruger appeared bearing a lovingly garnished carp on a large Meissen platter.

"One must always come to the table hungry and never angry," said Frau Matcher, giving May a twinge. That evening he had disobeyed both principles. Still, the insatiable appetite of the young covered his sins.

As always, Herr Matcher dominated the conversation with chuffy candor. "Nothing is quite so alienating for a Christian as Christmas in a non-Christian country or, for that matter, a Muslim or Islamic here during our little ritual. Virtually everything outside the home closes down for the unwary traveler. I'll never forget one Christmas, steaming toward Alexandria, feeling incredibly lonely. It was my first Christmas away from home. The day had not been marked by even a cinnamon bun. We were still three hours away from sighting land when suddenly sailors began shouting and pointing at the horizon.

There before us, inverted in the sky, was a full-scale mirage of the city, luminous and trembling, as if painted on satin. I could make out the Ras El Tin palace, the Nebi Daniel Mosque, the Arab quarter, and the Goharri Mosque. The mirage hung there in the sky with breathtaking splendor for perhaps half an hour before it melted into the horizon. Ahead of us, the sea was brighter than the sky, a smooth expanse as if made of some luminous element. While I was seeing this so plainly, an officer in uniform handed me a yellow telegram." Matcher paused for a moment. "It was from home, wishing me a Merry Christmas. The message had been picked out of the sky." Reaching toward the ceiling and a glittering chandelier, he chuckled and shook his head. "I glanced behind the telegraph messenger and wondered if he had left his bicycle around the corner. An hour later the real city appeared."

May sat spellbound, remembering the *Savoia* and the changing seas. With what struck May as wizardry, Herr Matcher could pull tales from his head and act them out, and had Inge been there, the evening would have been perfect. Later, over liqueurs Matcher said as much.

"I'm sorry your friend could not join us. Lovely ladies add immeasurably to the table. Tallyrand said two things are essential in life: to give good dinners and to keep on fair terms with women. And from what we read about the ancient Greeks, they barred wives from all banqueting, and only invited the *hetaerae* to come in with the final wines for, ahem, philosophic dalliance. This bit of information indicates that we have made some progress."

"The loss is hers," said May honestly.

The year 1939 began slowly as if Old Father Time had trouble getting the hang of the bells. On New Year's Eve Inge and May joined her parents at the Adlon. The bank now provided Herr von Haas with a car and driver. Obsequious waiters catered to him and the coterie of other Nazi bigwigs in the now raucous, garland-festooned ballroom. May danced with Gertrude and maneuvered her like a little hen so adroitly through a series of numbers, like *I'll Follow You*, that she could not stop raving about his dancing. Her appreciation was such that May felt obligated to repeat the invitation, and then regretted it when the orchestra moved into *Poor Butterfly*. Wearing an expression that telegraphed gloom, he caught Inge's eye. She was making the best of a similar situation with an autocratic nobleman, while obnoxious Nazi officers and their partners pushed and shoved their drunken ways around the floor.

Later, watching exploding fireworks through the high ballroom windows that for the occasion were marked by swastika banners as well as drapes, May said, "I'm out of step."

"Coming here has been a terrible mistake. I hated dragging you to this, but I'd have been miserable without you," Inge murmured. May agreed.

Cronies of Herr von Haas, who may have felt duty-bound to dance with his wife, were happy to meet this obligation by choosing the daughter instead. Finally Inge refused all requests, pleading fatigue.

Taking a stroll for air, she and May found a corridor where, despite the green carpet, they could hear the music and dance, "It wouldn't be so bad if I could forget the first time we came here," said Inge, hoping to make him feel better.

When they returned to the ballroom, her father clearly was displeased. "Where have you been for so long," he demanded, greeting them.

"Father, we've been dancing in the hall. If you could dance with Herr May—and see for yourself what a good dancer he is—you would understand why I prefer to dance with him instead of those old, fat, puffing clodhoppers." A napkin crumpled in her hand.

In a silly red paper hat Herr von Haas stared at his daughter aghast. Gertrude picked up the cudgel. "I understand how she feels. We do want her to have a good time, don't we?"

He was hardly mollified. "Herr May is our guest, Father," said Inge, shaming him into saying no more that evening.

Chimney sweeps with blackened faces carried little pink pigs, squealing as they were kissed for good luck. May felt he needed it. They saved a paper bucket of noisemakers and foolscaps for Otto—to May and Inge, seemingly significant trophies for the outrageously expensive and disappointing evening.

1939 was not destined to be a good year.

* ** *

May did not know it, but at this point Inge's disrespect, even hatred, for her father had reached the point where she almost went to May, begging him to marry her. They would have to elope. Then she would have to tell May that her father hated him. May would read her sudden acquiescence for what it was: a need to escape her home—not a good reason to marry. Inge knew that as much as he wanted to marry her, he always wanted to do things right. He wanted his mother's ring for her—a large, but not particularly flawless diamond. It hadn't come and never would. So the moment in time, when their lives might have been inexorably altered, did not happen.

During March war came perilously close. German troops stormed Prague and the prematurely senile Czech President Emil Hacha signed documents of surrender in the Adlon Hotel. Inge, May, Norbert Buth, and other students were photographed under Nazi banners. May saved the photograph. Not to have joined the celebration would have been undiplomatic. War had been averted, but for how long?

Letters from the foundation advised him to be prepared to leave on a moment's notice. Friends from the *Savoia* called.

"What do you make of things, Jim?" asked George Chauncy.

"I'm not ready to pull up stakes until I absolutely have to."

"I guess the foundations feel morally responsible for us. One thing is certain: if we go home now, we won't get back anytime soon."

"That's the way I see it," May replied.

But it wasn't the way he felt. He was growing sick with apprehension, hanging on to each day by his fingernails, grateful for a chair every time he had a long distance call.

Bob Street also called, which surprised May, considering their last conversation when May had been downright rude. "Do you think the party's over, Jim? It's been lovely, but I don't want to get caught in the crossfire."

"We've had these scares before."

"Then you're sticking?"

"As long as I can."

"How long do you think it'll be before some Jew steals your passport?"

"Bob, I've had enough problems already. Do me a favor and talk to somebody else." With that he slammed down the receiver. It was incredible that way that man could always come up with exactly the wrong thing to say. May shook his head in wonderment.

* ** *

Germany was alive with new prosperity, and without the joblessness that plagued England and France. Herr von Haas felt Germany finally had Europe by the tail. He believed what he read in the papers, and felt that soon Inge could have her pick of any man in Europe. His long-smoldering dream of having a title in the family could be realized. At dinner he reminisced. "Remember when you were a little girl, Inge, I promised you a prince?" Then he smiled a loving but paternal smile. "Don't give up that dream."

"Father, that was your dream," retorted Inge, shuddering and fleeing the table. There was no way that she could explain her father's aspirations to her lover.

May came down with a terrible cold. Between wheezes and sneezes he watched the operation of the household, not previously witnessed. A hairdresser came to wash Frau Matcher's hair, a seamstress to mend. He had seen bushels of potatoes, apples and cabbages, and cases of wine lugged into the cellar for storage. Truckloads of coal gushed down a chute, seemingly enough for three winters. The mechanics of life moved forward, dutifully oiled as if the grease job carried a trouble-free guarantee.

In many ways these people know how to live, May decided. The so-called good life was not restricted to the upper middle class. Daily, some cultural event, a band concert, concerts of the singing academy, the cathedral choir, or philharmonic, all free and well attended, took place. Afterward the beer restaurants, the Tucher-Brau, Lowenbrau and Münchner Hofbrau, beckoned. Four major art museums and many minor ones offered diverse showings, making cultural events available to all. Yet he knew something in the system had gone wrong, something likely to topple everyone, including the sweet, gentle people he loved.

As soon as May was deemed out of the infectious stage, he and Inge were invited to tea. Because it was Saturday, Herren Rosenberg and Matcher joined them.

"There seemed to be a lot going on this morning," said May.

Frau Matcher blushed, and the other men chuckled. Inge, looking beautiful in a pale blue sweater and a single strand of pearls, teacup in hand sat nearby. "It was a dreadful experience," Frau Matcher confided. "I have a little *corsetiere* who lives in one room and keeps her sewing under her bed. Bedbugs dropped into a garment that was delivered to me this morning. I tried it on and was immediately bitten. I screamed. Of course we stripped and fumigated the room."

It wasn't funny to Frau Matcher, but it was to the others, who laughed. She cried, *"Schadenfreude,"* playing an abused role to the hilt. "I'm frightened over the times." She spoke, thinking of the bedbug incident as representative of a country gone to pot. She looked to Inge and May. "Your lives are still before you. You'll have to make your own destinies, but you'll have to swim against the tide."

May hoped Inge was listening. "Which is never easy," he said.

Inge had heard. "Frau Matcher, if you were my age, what would you do?"

Frau Matcher did not hesitate, "Put myself out of the reach of dictators."

"I'm hoping she'll marry me," May interjected. The older men clapped, then a long silence followed in which something passed between Inge and Frau Matcher. Frau Matcher had immediately recognized Inge's background, and that her parents would never consider such a match. She turned to May. "You'll make a fine husband."

When they were alone, May pressed Inge. "Are we or are we not engaged? If we are, let's announce it."

"You'll have to speak to my father, but I know what he'll say. You'll only be angered and embarrassed."

He did not believe her, having not known that Herr von Haas had become more amiable only because he could foresee May's departure soon. Before long, what appeared to be an opportune moment arrived. Sunday dinner had been excellent, and Herr von Haas was in a rare loquacious mood. He sat back, cigarette in hand, enjoying a brandy. He told May: "Ours was a small family bank, conservatively run. No one could have anticipated the inflation in store for us. People who had borrowed good solid Reichmarks were able to pay off their loans with worthless paper. Much earlier we could have foreclosed many accounts, when borrowers had no hope of paying, but we did not. We were so badly burned that I dipped heavily into our family fortune. In the end, we were forced to join a chain. It saved the bank, but we lost half the company."

"I know that can happen when a government keeps printing money. I've seen photographs of money in wheelbarrows," said May.

"I've seen a woman pass a basket of money on the street, then dump the money and steal the basket," Herr von Haas added, laughing maliciously.

"How did joining the chain save you," May asked, "beyond an influx of more capital?"

"We gained inside information—learned what the government was going to do next. Moving into foreign currencies, we profited as the mark seesawed."

The apparent confidentiality seemed like an opening to May. "Herr von Haas, I'm sure this is no surprise, but I want to marry your daughter."

Herr von Haas turned red then yellow. "She's too young," he replied with unmistakable vehemence. Both men sat without moving. The father's face was full of hatred and controlled anger. The lover's planned monologue on his earning potential, love of Germany, and future aspirations were swallowed, as an iron collar closed about his throat. Inge and her mother appeared, and eventually the collar loosened. He managed to utter goodnight and feeble thanks.

The next day Inge tried to console him. With the coming of spring the Tiergarten had come ablaze with new leaves, and there was boating on the lakes. "Father is difficult. Only mother influences him, but slowly." It was only half the story.

"Inge, you'll never get permission to marry me."

"Take heart. Nothing has changed. It's been this way all along."

"A lot has changed. While we've been studying, our worlds have been on a collision course. Hitler is not to be contained. Germany has been stockpiling grain. Something will break soon. Hitler expects and wants a war."

"How do you know this?"

"Through friends and some knowledge of what to look for in the German papers, which I read very carefully," he replied, temporarily silencing her.

There was much to see and do in Berlin. Like a man running out of time, May felt a compulsion to do and see it all. Dozens of majestic monuments—Bismarck's, Victory, William I's, Frederick III's, and the Peace Column that stood over sixty feet high—dressed the city with all the finery of a grand old lady in velvet and pearls. There seemed no way to equate the city and his friends, the good people, with the low class thugs in control and hell-bent on war. May and Inge walked the streets clinging to each other until eventually they would reach Buth's apartment where they could talk.

She told him, "You do give me the ability to see in another dimension—things that I never saw before—about so many different things."

"Don't let me get you into trouble." He spoke with large feeling, more than love, in which approval and exasperation merged. He wanted to help her and spare her simply because he had no other choice. From the moment he first laid eyes on her, she had made him come alive in some inexplicable way. Besides, knowing what they were about to do, he was finding it hard to concentrate or talk. Heat built in his loins, as he watched her pouring wine from a bottle they kept cool on the windowsill.

"As to art, even Rembrandt had to face outrageous criticism because of his innovations. Why are you different?"

"Despite all you say about the moderns, I feel at home with classic art. It reflects study, not paint slapped on canvas. I can recognize things. Frames enclose loveliness."

"In 1904 Picasso, poor as a church mouse, etched *The Frugal Repast.* The man's hands, done by a thousand tiny openings in the wax on the metal plate, are great; the slightly hungry, distortion elegant. Two years later, better fed, Picasso painted a self-portrait. This time two major strokes established the arm's shape, weight and robust strength." May was now stroking her, playing with her breasts.

"Why are two strokes better than a thousand?" she asked, hardly able to follow his train of thought.

He laughed. "You know, at this point with you near, I'm not sure." He pressed a long leisurely kiss on her lips, while his hand moved up her thighs.

She pulled her lips away. "I like a thousand strokes, but go on..."

He was reaching a point where talking was difficult, but he gave it his best. "Every good modern artist must first learn to paint realistically. Then he must develop his own style and unique way of interpreting something beyond which the eye can see. We don't see it until he paints it."

Inge grew impatient. "*Liebling,* stop talking and get to the business at hand."

They moved together until both found answers. Later he wondered if she'd gotten as much out of his little lecture as he had.

* ** *

Summer came to Germany with unmatched beauty. As Matcher putted in his garden, he talked to May about appreciation for the land. "While you're here, you should see the battlefields around Verdun. It's been twenty years since the Great War, yet hundreds of hectares are still a wasteland where nothing grows, not even weeds." He snipped a rose. "Never before has land been so decimated. We've watched three years of war in Spain and have seen the way all of the people are involved and in danger, not just the fighting soldiers. Another war will change the face of Europe. It may become uninhabitable."

May expressed these fears to Inge. They always carried a small bag of crumbs for the birds that had learned to be fearless. Inge put the crumbs on her shoulder, and the birds pecked her ears for attention and food.

"I have to go home soon. We'll have to elope."

"I want to marry you, but I can't right now." She looked toward a lake, hating the thought of his leaving so much that it even made her bones ache.

"You're an impractical artist, seeing things others don't and never will, but you have blind spots."

"Where would we elope to?"

"Switzerland."

She looked at him now with mounting distress. He didn't understand. Nothing was so pat and simple. While the light lasted they sat on a bench, holding hands. Under a somber exterior, she was utterly distraught. "I'm going to have to go with my parents to the Riviera for three weeks," she finally blurted out. "The reservations were made and the tickets were bought a year ago."

"I assumed something of the sort, nothing having been said about vacations for a long time." He did not want to hear more.

He took her to dinner at a little place called the Fürstenhof. It was in the old quarter, where the cobblestone streets were winding and narrow. Two-story ocher buildings seemed to be holding one another up. Their exterior walls, decorated with folk paintings and signs in old Gothic script, spoke of another age despite bookstores, antique shops and cafes. The restaurant was crowded with laughing people whose very presence and happiness offended May. He had cashed his last check that morning.

"I have orals coming, and every waking moment I should be studying. After exams I'll have to turn in my thesis. Assigned projects and lectures will be over then."

The weight of responsibility toward the foundation made him feel badgered, and in those moments he understood sacrifice. His insights were reinforced by a late night visit with Herr Matcher. "My sister and I are taking a few weeks in Baden Baden. The waters at the spa should be good for her."

"I didn't know she was ill."

"She has a very weak heart, and may soon be a complete invalid, unless we can reverse the trend, which is doubtful."

Life in the household came into deeper focus. No wonder I've seen so little of her, thought May. She's been dying, and I've been so concerned with my own problems I haven't seen what's been going on around me.

Then he told Matcher that Inge would not elope. As always, Matcher turned the conversation, trying to take May out of himself. "None of us know where we are going in life. Let me tell you a little story. It may help you to be more flexible in your thinking."

May shrugged.

"Once, on a steamer heading for Bangkok, traveling northward through the Gulf of Siam from Singapore, I met a young girl. The captain had told me that I could go on the bridge whenever I felt like it—these fellows are usually very accommodating. For a moment I thought no one was there. The girl was like a shadow when I stood next to her. The ship was in the blackest night you could imagine—even the stars were hidden—apparently going nowhere. There was nothing in sight. Only the surging engines put us on earth. Soon I saw she was weeping. She asked me about Bangkok. I could see she was frightened, and I couldn't understand why she would be going to a country like that alone. Then the story came out. A native prince had sent her money, and she was going to marry him."

Matcher paused, placing his hands on his knees, emphasizing confidentiality. "Do you know what that means?" I asked. 'How many wives does he have in his harem?' She had taken the repulsive prince's money and spent it, frittered it away—quite a few hundred pounds. Now she had no choice. She was bound, she said. I had to leave her in Bangkok. When people are bound, there's nothing you can do about it, May."

May thought he had never heard such a pointless story, but to honor Matcher he replied: "When the king says it's midnight, underlings look at the stars. I've never been able to understand underlings, Herr Matcher."

"You will someday," he prophesied, " as there are a lot of them. Don't judge Inge too harshly."

"God loves the meek. He made so many of them," May murmured.

The departure of Inge and the Matchers allowed him to throw himself into work, but one evening Herr Rosenberg invited him to dinner. "I think you need a break," he said.

May had not often seen Herr Rosenberg, who owned a bookstore on Wilhelm-Platz. His room had its own lavatory where he peed at night. Because he used the bathtub only on Saturday nights, not even the sharing of the bathroom offered contact. To May's surprise, Rosenberg took him to an elegant restaurant, Berlin's best, Horcher's, where Rosenberg was greeted warmly by the *maitre d'*. Circulating violinists played gypsy music, while waiters hovered. Rosenberg recommended the lobster thermidor and selected a vintage wine. "The place is full of Nazis," he confided, "but the food compensates. Also, I'm not Jewish…"

Wearing a pince-nez that seemed to drop magically into his hand, Rosenberg evidenced considerable charm. "I thought you might enjoy this restaurant as it is the best Europe has to offer. Unfortunately, it's the sort of place most students never get near. Not to sample this side of European life, however, is not to see Europe."

"I've been twice to the Adlon," May confessed, "and once I paid."

Rosenberg laughed. He lived in literature and suggested books on almost every topic. Those on architecture came very close to what Tessenow had recommended. After dinner he invited May to his room for a drink. The gesture proved to be one of trust. His room was much larger and better furnished than May's. There, lining the walls, were all the 'degenerate' books, many of them leather-bound first editions, housed in walnut cases that almost reached the ceiling. Books that had been abhorred by Hitler were all there in hiding, works by Thomas Mann, H.G. Wells, Sigmund Freud…

"This year has been a great experience for me," said May. "More than I'd hoped for, but it has been rigorous." He hoped he didn't sound bitter.

"To some people much is given; from others much is expected. The latter may be the lucky ones as they'll be the stronger. I read that somewhere," said Rosenberg.

*   ** *

On August 22nd at Obersalzberg, Hitler ordered his commanders to invade Poland. Germany and Russia had signed a mutual non-aggression pact, announced on Radio Berlin. Regular programming resumed with a rendition of *Deutschland über alles.*

On September 3rd, Britain and France declared war on Germany. When the doorbell rang, May, breathless, knew it was a cable from his foundation ordering him to return immediately. The war news brought Inge and her family hurrying back. Inge had been miserable separated from May, and once again May was determined to win over Herr von Haas and called at the bank to see him.

May was ushered into a series of private rooms, secluded by double doors. Herr von Haas, assuming May had some financial problem in departing, was quite friendly. As far as he was concerned, no ocean between his daughter and May was wide enough. A cordial greeting caught May unaware. "I'm sure you know why I'm here."

"*Ja, ja!* Foreigners are all having money problems."

"Herr von Haas, it's not money. I want to marry Inge,"

The square Aryan jaw dropped. "I'm surprised you're here on such a fool's errand." As he spoke his face twitched as if he had trigeminal neuralgia. "You are a fine young man, but totally unacceptable. The U.S. is clearly sympathetic to our enemies, and it would hardly be a congenial atmosphere for Inge. The answer is *NEIN.*" May had never heard words more final or icier.

He was half-drunk when he met Inge who was grateful she had rehearsed what she had to say. "Now I must be the practical one for us both. Don't feel I don't love you enough. I can see that thought in your eyes." She sealed his lips with her fingers. "I love you more than anything in the world, but I cannot leave."

Actually, he would have had barely enough money to get them home.

Farewells at the institute were simple. The thought that he might one day be at war with these people seemed unconscionable. Then he heard the Nazis goose-stepping down the street to cheering crowds, and his heart caught a more normal beat.

The Matchers rushed back for which he was thankful. Leaving without bidding them goodbye would have been more painful. As his taxi carried him off, Matcher, his arm around his sister, stood in the doorway with Frau Kruger and Rosenberg in the background.

He and Inge met for the last time at Buth's. He devoured her with kisses, kisses that drew from her mouth until her lips were ready to bleed. Then he moved to her breasts, her navel and finally between her thighs. For a few short moments passion absolved their sorrow. Later, clinging to each other, they wept quietly. He dressed while she lay silent, inert, aware only of her heartbreak. Like Matcher's little girl on the boat to Bangkok, she was bound.

On the street he turned once more to look at the window. Seeing nothing but a flapping curtain, he no longer believed in happy endings.

Since the French-German borders were closed, he took a train to Switzerland and walked over a bridge into France. He spent three days in Paris, grateful for both his inability to speak the language and the monumental distractions the city offered. He was too obsessed to notice the food. By a stroke of luck he had found space on a freighter. Cherbourg was crowded with panicked Americans, all looking for a passage on ships, now packed with people in every possible way.

Throughout the voyage he kept to himself. He thought of the friends he had met on the *Savoia*, now probably carrying troops to Africa. On seeing the Statue of Liberty, he tried to be optimistic, but the impact of Germany would be too great. He felt as if he were going into exile.

Yet, after National Socialism, there was something satisfying that he couldn't quite put his finger on about setting foot on good old American soil.

Book III

CHAPTER ONE

1939, Poughkeepsie, N.Y.

James May returned to the U.S. feeling like a castaway. The golden year of graduate work in Berlin came to a crashing halt at his mother's house where he soon became an introverted, muted Jimbo, viewed by his baffled mother as having 'changed.' He had, of course, undergone a tremendous intellectual and emotional experience that marked a crucial era in his life. The extent of his demoralization was not readily apparent, for cultural shock took over.

After the emotional color, excitement and pulsating war fever of Nazi Germany, returning was like leaving high drama in the theater for a deserted street. People plodded about their businesses. Cars, big as buses, moved slowly, although smoothly. Drivers in cushioned comfort flipped radio dials past the news reports to find their favorite songs. Complacency was rampant.

For a few days his mother, Victoria, babied him, cooking dishes he had always liked. Unfortunately, as a cook Victoria was hopelessly out classed by every German cook whose meals he had sampled. Having lived alone for many years—and never having had a large family—she was at best inept. Recently, frozen foods, which she overcooked, had come on the market. Considering the simple directions on each package, Jim was impatient. Wanting only to be left alone, he did his best to be polite.

"Eat your chicken fricassee, Jim. It's new and expensive."

"Mother, I think you do better starting from scratch. Also, I believe I've reached an age at which you don't have to tell me to 'clean my plate,'" he replied, dutifully picking up his fork.

"Apparently that isn't the case," she huffed.

"I'm sorry, Mother. Now please don't tell me about the starving Armenians or whoever is presently starving, because I'm not interested."

A change of subject seemed wise. "Did you have a nice day?"

He had looked for work. "No, there doesn't seem to be any hiring in architecture, and I'm still too short on the required office experience to take the State Boards."

"You see, you'd be better off now if you hadn't spent the last year gallivanting all over Europe. Well, what's done is done."

"That's right, Mother. I'm afraid you'll have to carry me a little longer. If it hurts too much I can always pump gas."

"After your fine education, I wouldn't hear of such a thing."

"I'm sure Uncle Sam'll be breathing down my back any day now. I should be able to get an officer's commission because of that 'fine' education."

Silenced, Victoria resolved to say no more. The thought of her son going to war stuck in her craw as Bird's Eye chicken never had.

For the first few days Victoria had prettied herself. She could never have approached the simple elegance of Frau Matcher or the dressiness of Frau von Haas, but she had tried. Her disappointment in Jim's attitude soon stymied all her good intentions. He had not remembered his mother as dowdy as she now appeared.

Her hair, uncombed, remained in aluminum clamps until noon, but even more offensive to Jim, were stockings rolled around garters below her knees.

"Dresses are getting shortened to save cloth," she explained. "If I pull my stocking up higher, my garters cut off circulation."

Jim shuddered. "Then get a garter belt! Those tires look dreadful."

Victoria retreated into a perpetually dirty silk kimono. She had lived alone too long. Besides, dry cleaning was expensive. In the name of charity Jim swallowed his disdain with thinly veiled impudence.

As much as she loved him in her own way, his presence pinched her financially. She returned from her shift at the local telephone company office to announce that in her spare time, she planned to sell Silver Seal aluminum cookware through demonstration dinners. Over supper she explained the vitamin-saving ware. Jim was flabbergasted.

"By the time you spend fifty dollars buying the demonstration set, and learn to cook with two tablespoons of water to preserve those precious vitamins, the manufacturer will have converted to defense production."

Victoria reconsidered.

In one year she had aged perceptibly, and Jim was certain she had foregone proper food in order to send him extra money. The few nights when he was not home, she was content to open a small can of something. The little tyranny grated. But their financial position and his smoldering resentment was nothing compared to the pain of losing Inge. It had not lessened. The thought of her catapulted him into a silence hard to break out of.

"Why don't you go to a movie? Several good ones are playing." The movie section of the paper dropped to her lap as her eyes fell on her son, lying on the sofa, lost in some other world beyond their small living room.

"Mother, did you say something?"

"I suggested that you go to a movie."

"I don't feel like it."

"Can I get you an aspirin?"

An aspirin, good God! He shuddered inwardly. "No thank you, Mother."

"Then look up some of your old friends," she rose, put her hand on his hair and yanked it playfully.

Unwilling to banish her from her own living room and unable to bear her for another minute, he went out for a walk.

The night was cold and he quickened his pace, covering more ground than he had intended. Just as he decided the exercise and brisk air had done him good, and he would head back, he spotted a large building under construction. Undoubtedly the builder would be rushing it to completion before winter closed in. He had spent a good many summers working on construction jobs, and although he was over-qualified, the prospect of work loomed. He was not a skilled tradesman, but he would make a competent overseer. The next day he had a job.

"What will you be doing?" Victoria asked.

"Everything that doesn't interfere with the unions. I'll be finished early, giving me time to look for something better, because the work will end with this job."

"Your luck has turned. Oh, by the way, you have two letters from Germany."

He fairly jumped out of his skin reaching for them. The script was immediately recognizable. Inge had finally written! Apparently both letters had traveled on the same ship. The first was dated October 1, 1939. It read:

"Liebling,

"I have been looking at the bleary afternoon moon thinking you may share that too. What a little thing to share after so much. I walk to the Tiergarten, not aimlessly or lovingly as we used to, but purposely searching for paths we covered, as if miraculously you might appear. Two little birds always land on my shoulder, and blessedly, in my doldrums I have not forgotten crumbs. They, too, feel the vacancy of your space beside me.

"Father is tight-lipped. Mother constantly complains. They whisper a lot. 'Wouldn't this be nice,' or 'Wouldn't you like that?' they ask. What can I say? I have already said it all. That devil, Otto, stands around wide-eyed, cleaning the corners of his mouth with the tip of his tongue. There's no one to trick, no one to bribe, no one to help him with his kites.

"Speer is designing madly for Hitler, war or no war. The papers are filled with his grandiose building plans.

"I sketch without concentration and so, of course, nothing is good. Don't stop writing. Ich liebe dich.

"Deine, Inge."

Somehow finding composure, he opened the second letter, dated three weeks later.

"Liebling,

"Can I handle a culture that brings out new car models every year, where broken things are thrown away, not mended, where beds are not aired in windows, and clothes not boiled? I remember every word. My

wish box is no longer filled with questions, but with answers you have given me.

"Sometimes I am angry, other times I simply weep. You have not only absented yourself, but you have taken with you the continuity of my life, the habitual things that make my life secure, not to mention joyous, and all expansive thought. I know it is not your fault, but I cannot blame my parents for everything. I cannot horsewhip them every night in my dreams. Nights are too often spent reliving days with you.

"Deine, Inge."

The two brief letters at first thrilled him and then threw him into remorse. Abruptly he left the house, letters in hand. When he found a bus bench and a streetlight, he sat down to read them over and over again, becoming angry that she had not written more. Then he remembered the censorship and German mail regulations and almost understood.

For the next two months he worked as a jack-of-all-trades, expediting the construction. He made sure the men always had the tools and materials at hand for the job, and that their work was up to snuff. He also saw that an 'As-built' set of plans was kept up-to-date. Buildings in the U.S. were expected to depreciate three or four times with several renovations and face-lifts in their lifetimes—not to last three hundred years. In due time architectural work came along, although the thirty-five dollars a week was disappointing. He had been making fifty.

"That's all I can pay a draftsman, which is what you are until you become registered," said William Finch, a portly, traditional architect. "You'll actually cost me money while you learn the ropes. You'll also have to learn what's still available. Manufacturers are turning to defense contracts. Right and left, lots of materials are disappearing off the market."

Jim had already seen that. "I understand, Mr. Finch."

Finch tapped his pencil and pressed his lips. "I'll expect you to letter in my style so the drawings won't be a hodgepodge. I do the designing; you do the working drawings. Clear?"

So began pure drudgery.

Lavina Rawlings, Mr. Finch's secretary, immediately blossomed in a new wardrobe. All personal conversation was frowned upon in the office, but Jim couldn't help overhearing Finch. "That's a pretty new dress you're wearing today, Lavina." It never occurred to Jim that he had anything to do with Lavina's sudden interest in her appearance. He found her pleasant in an unspectacular way. She had soft brown hair and eyes, but a trilly telephone voice. She wore bright red lipstick and long red fingernails that made scratching noises as she typed specifications. In all respects she was a far cry from all the preppy collegians he had known. Her hips swished as she walked, and she had one of the tiniest waists, broadly and tightly belted, that he ever remembered seeing. She was almost pretty.

She had been in Mr. Finch's employ since graduating from high school and she was efficient. Soon she was making the coffee stronger, as Jim liked it, and keeping his many pencils as sharp as Mr. Finch's.

Typing specs, usually taken from *Sweet's Catalog,* she had learned quite a bit about building. She also knew what materials were becoming scarce-to-unavailable, and those too shoddy or expensive for the job, thus sparing Jim some mistakes. What friction there was in the office was only between Jim and Mr. Finch over design. Finch did not appreciate initiative, much less suggestions.

Jim had been too besotted with Inge to even think of dating, but Lavina invited him to dinner.

She lived in a two-room garage apartment behind a house built during the twenties that looked like every other house on the block. The apartment was reached by an outside stair covered by a small roof. The living room was furnished with a sofa, lamp, one end table, a straight chair and a Philco radio with legs. A card table, attractively set for dining, was candle lit. He brought wine.

From a tiny kitchen with a kerosene stove, curtained shelves, and a lavatory-size porcelain sink, she put the last touches on a simple but tasty-smelling dinner. "I hope you like Swiss steak," she remarked from the doorway.

He joined her in the kitchen. "I do very much. Mother fixes frozen food now. I find it leaves something to be desired."

"Frozen peas are good." From a windowsill, she reached outside for ice to chill the wine. He could see the dessert cooling there.

"The wine is already cool. I walked."

"Oh, that's good." She handed him a corkscrew.

"I brought German wine, not knowing what you'd planned. I find German wines go with everything." Suddenly he felt like a pompous fool. "Actually I've just returned from a year in Germany, and German wines are the only ones I know." That out, he felt a little better.

Ceremoniously, he opened the wine, carefully wiped the mouth of the bottle, and poured himself a small amount to sample. He rolled the wine around in his mouth with his tongue. The old familiar taste brought back a hundred shattering memories. For a moment he sickened, feeling his knees might fold under him. But they didn't, and he regained his poise and pronounced the wine drinkable. He filled her glass. She sipped.

"If my dinner tastes as good as this wine, we're in great shape." Her eyes sparkled.

She changed the subject. "I know you feel restricted working for Finch. He's conservative, but so are his clients. People seem to want what they're used to. Also it's difficult to get modern plans approved. City Hall is just as conservative."

"Clients have to be educated to want something more. Thomas Jefferson wouldn't build Monticello today, over and over again."

Lavina put dinner on the table and asked him to bring another chair from the bedroom. "I'm slowly furnishing this place. Next month the sofa will be paid for, and I can start saving for a new rug." She gave a little embarrassed laugh.

They talked about movies he hadn't seen, and after dinner moved to the sofa.

When the wine was finished, Lavina made two large Scotch-on-the-rocks, and sat down close to him.

"Tell me about Europe."

For a moment the sudden request silenced him, and again the rush of memories had to be dismissed. "I worked hard. The Germans are preparing for war on a major scale. I suspect we'll be drawn into it, despite what we read in the papers."

"Are you glad to be home?"

"No, it was a very good year." Dear God, he thought. What an understatement.

Blessedly he felt the liquor taking hold and breathed more freely. Lavina slipped off her shoes. A faint spill of light from the kitchen painted her hand with pale luminosity as she placed it on his thigh. She didn't move the hand but let it lie there. He knew he should kiss Lavina, but a vision of Inge loomed and vanished. To clear his mind he focused on a piece of framed embroidery, hung somewhat crookedly. She leaned across him to put down her drink on the small end table, and her breast brushed him. He put down his drink and pulled her toward him for an embrace and a long drawn out kiss. He kissed her several times, breaking only for air, trying to divorce the memory of other lips. One hand reached into the V-neck of her dress and caressed her breast. Her firm warm flesh fit nicely in his hand while her hand moved along his leg, then fumbled with his fly. Something wasn't quite right, he knew. He had not expected that.

"Why don't you put out the light?" he suggested, hoping darkness would help. It didn't much. To his embarrassment he couldn't get a hard-on, but with his hand he brought Lavina to a climax.

* ** *

"I'm going to buy a used car," he told Victoria. "The prices will only be going up."

"Gas will soon be rationed."

"I don't care. I'll be able to help you with the shopping."

Pushed a few times, Victoria came up with fifty dollars. He had saved two hundred, thinking of a ticket for Inge. The black Plymouth sedan in good shape cost five hundred. Monthly payments would run for three years, an eternity.

The car brought further invitations from Lavina. A simple loveless relationship ensued that, at first, was inexpensive and undemanding. At the same time, Victoria's demands grew. Her weak heart kicked up, resulting in a plethora of doctor's bills. These bills plus car payments threw Jim in a financial bind that from his standpoint equaled the national debt. In buying a car he had envisioned dating so-called eligible girls. He remembered Bob Street's remark that, after Europe, he could move in the best circles. Broke, he saw that he could move nowhere.

College, the great mating ground, was so far behind him that old girlfriends—excepting Betsy—were now married with children. An impending war rumbled, a tom-tom calling young people into hasty marriages. The monotony of his life stretched before him like the eternity of a poorly performed opera.

Lavina's telephone calls offered an easy escape from despondence and loneliness. Happy enough to simply go on a ride, she soon had his fly open. Once he had found release, he felt guilty. Lavina's swishy walk, roving hands, décolletage, the little games, were all-effective, because there was no alternative. At the same time she was omnipresent, marvelously adroit at seeing them thrown together. At night, wherever he went out, by some strange coincidence, she would show up. These accidental meetings always ended up in her bed. He was usually careful to carry condoms, and if not, she relieved him with fellatio. Later he cursed himself for having followed her, like a hound tagging a bitch in heat. But her bed offered the only pleasure, limited as it was, that he knew.

"You have no idea how much I love you," she told him. "I'd die for you."

"That won't be necessary. Please, Lavina, don't talk that way. I don't want to hear it. You're a nice girl, and you're very sweet to me, but that's it. I'm not in love. I'm not remotely interested in getting married, even though everybody else seems to be doing just that these days."

He knew perfectly well what she wanted, but not wanting to hurt her, he let the bondage grow, cemented by a myriad of small tyrannies. Little unwanted surprise gifts—tacky drugstore adult toys, which she thought cute—often awaited him. Romantic notes that included poems cut from the newspaper, or worse, booklets of sentimental mush popped up on his drafting table. He viewed her with a jaundiced eye, but Lavina was flattering when no one else was. Only a callous person could have ignored the labor going into the knitting of argyle socks, the homemade brownies brought to the office, or whatever…

At first he felt like a heel, but before long, he found himself in a hysterical, impassioned death grip that left him exhausted and somewhat exonerated.

At every opportunity she had his fly open and her hand in his lap. There were times when he broke with her, finding any excuse to be angry, only to be drawn back by her tears and threats of suicide. Hating his weakness, he resented her, and hated himself. Never had he been so distraught over a girl he cared nothing about.

* ** *

The affair came to a crashing end, as anyone would have expected.

Victoria wanted to can some apples, and Lavina knew of a commercial orchard that still had some remaining fruit, free for the picking. Dutifully, with Lavina, Jim drove to the country, making the excursion an opportunity for a long quiet talk leading to actual deliverance. But she was happy and sweet, and he found himself diverted, absorbed with driving. Freshly changed oil, a grease job, and a full tank of gas seemed to exhilarate the little Plymouth that responded with new smoothness to his touch. The slightest pressure to the clutch and gearshift was all that was needed to make it hum and zoom like a hornet. The power was infectious, the fun of driving like magic. The road was almost empty, and the car, whipping past farms and small towns, lifted his spirits, imparting a new tempo to the afternoon.

They finally turned off on a side road, and reaching the orchard, parked on the verge and worked their way deep into the trees. It had been a week since he had been in bed with Lavina. She was wearing brief shorts exposing a crease at her crotch. He had to hoist her up high to reach a limb, and then hold her, his hands tight around her thighs. Inevitably as he lowered her, his hands brushed under her shorts, landing in her moist pubic hair. The touch moved her into his arms. Then she dropped to her knees, and opened his trousers. His erect penis, suddenly freed, sprang forward into her lips. Abstinence and the momentum of the long ride had caused a powerful build-up of semen. Fellatio soon had him reeling. Then she stopped.

"It's not fair. I always see to your pleasure. Sometimes it has to be my turn. This little pussy has got to have you," she cried, pulling him down.

"I don't have a rubber," he whispered, now feeling the cool air on his penis, made cooler by evaporation.

"Come on, honey. Give it to me. You can pull out in time. Please…"

Within seconds she was out of her shorts, prostrate, her knees apart, making way for him. The sight of her and the thought of *coitus interruptus* stopped all rational thought. He entered her. He had to admit, it felt so, so very good.

"It's wonderful without that boot," she cried. "Jimbo, it's like fire.

You really know how to do it." Before long she made him roll over so that she was on top of him, riding waves of pleasure.

"Stop! Stop for a minute," he begged, almost losing control. Instead she kept thrusting.

"I can't quit. It's heaven, and I'm about to come," she panted, continually pounding him into her.

"You've got to quit," he pleaded.

Then she had a devilish thought, possibly knowing the consequences. "You can pee in me if you want, but I can't quit."

To stop himself, he tried the biological impossibility, but delivered sperm instead.

Driving home and during the three weeks that followed, he nursed a premonition that he had made a terrible mistake. Finally, she coyly announced that they could expect 'a little stranger.' "I guess we should get married as soon as possible," she murmured.

He felt sick. The words trumpeted in his ears. An echo remained as if nothing could put a stop to it. In one moment of shame he knew what he had to say or be doomed. The whole period became so unpleasant that, years later, he disbelieved it had ever happened.

"Lavina, I'm not going to marry you. That's final." His voice was firm and flat. He wanted out—forever. He found the courage to look at her as if he liked looking at her, turning slowly and cautiously to see her face, seeing only tears. He felt her pain like the menace of an inferno.

"You know it's your baby."

"Of course I do." He also knew he was being cruel. His eyes focused on her with distaste that she missed. "I'll find the money to take care of this, but I don't want to get married. I've told you that before—many times."

"This time it's different."

"No, it isn't. I may be responsible but I won't add calumny to calumny. Let's backtrack over a worn path. I'll take care of you while you have the child; I'll support and educate it. Or you can decide not to have it; if you do, I'll pay for that, too."

"Abortions are dangerous."

"They are performed everyday under illegal but aseptic conditions."

It took several confrontations, agonizing whispered conversations and pathetic notes, until in one hysterical scene, Lavina saw that Jim was unbending. "Lavina, you will never know how sorry I am this happened. If there were any way that I could turn back the clock and repair this wrong, believe me, I would. But because a great mistake occurred accidentally, I will not make another deliberately."

Realizing that his decision was final, in a last ditch effort to keep Jim, Lavina visited several abortionists. The best wouldn't touch her for six weeks. The interim was pure hell; Lavina withered before his eyes. Abhorring his cruelty, but knowing that there was no way that he could endure marriage to her, he stuck to his convictions. The doctor's fee was three hundred dollars, payable in advance and in cash. In the end, he had no recourse but to borrow the money.

He wrote Larry Price, his college roommate, explaining that he had knocked up a girl he wasn't about to marry, and he had to have some money to take care of her. *"I can't imagine myself in this predicament, but it happened."*

By return mail he received a letter and check, dated January 22, 1940.

"Dear Jim,

"Enclosed is my check. I believe you when you say you're having one helluva rough time. This sort of thing always happens to nice guys. I now see the small advantage of being considered a heel; girls take care of themselves.

"Of course, as a rumble seat Romeo, you always made out better than I did. Based on the law of averages, this was bound to happen sometime.

"Remember the Easter vacation you spent at our house—the whole time in my sister's pants, I might add? She told me later, 'When shy, quiet Jimbo walks in a room, girls get an itch, and he sure knows how to scratch.' Of course, we both know my darling sister is a goddamned whore. Now she's engaged to moneybags like you wouldn't believe. Her diamond is the size of a Packard. But don't think she's settled down. Not one bit.

"Don't worry about repayment. The family business just landed a fat defense contract. The day may come when, equally desperate, I'll call on you, harking back to those days at Columbia when brains were more of an asset than political pull.

"Hail Columbia,

"Best, Larry."

Although grateful to Larry, he had no one to talk to. He walked the streets at night, craving to blurt out his problems to any stranger who looked the least bit sympathetic. Until the ordeal with Lavina was over, he never drew an easy breath.

Fortunately his behavior finished him with Lavinia. He applied for a commission in the U.S. Army. Regardless of how unpleasant Army life was, it would offer blessed escape.

CHAPTER TWO

Within a few weeks of applying for a commission in the U.S. Army, Jim was scheduled for an interview. He was eager to the point of being an hour early in appearing before the recruiting officer, a captain. One of the many copies of his application was on his desk.

"How well do you feel you know the Krauts?" asked the interrogator, sitting back in his heavy swivel chair, hands locked behind his head, his arms forming wings.

"I spent the winter of 1938 - 39 in Germany studying architecture." This information was in his application.

"German heritage?"

"My grandparents on my father's side were German immigrants. I lived with them as a child."

"Then you speak fluent German?"

"Yes."

"What do you know about art?" asked the captain, leaning forward, looking into Jim's eyes.

"Something more than the next man, but I'm no expert."

The captain held up two color prints. "Can you identify these?"

Spotting the sign or logo of a flying dragon in the corner of one of them, Jim replied, "I'd say Cranach the Elder, between fourteen and fifteen hundred."

"BC?"

"AD."

"It says BC on the back…"

"Well, the back is wrong. The other print is a Pierre Bonnard, titled *Beach at St. Tropez,* 1934. The painting is well known."

The captain wrote: art expert.

"May, the Army anticipates the need for German-speaking art experts once things are over. A lot of stolen art has been bandied about Europe since Hitler's been on the march. There's no doubt that we'll be drawn into the war and, of course, we'll win. The missing art will have to be located and returned. There are plenty of art experts, but not many are young and speak German, *et cetera*. You'll be with the State Department, assigned to the Army."

"Then I'll have time to prepare for this assignment?"

"Oh, yes. You'll have until the end of the war. You'll be stationed in Washington, where you'll have access to the Library of Congress, all the museums there, and whatever sources you might need. You'll be given an indoctrination course first, which will have nothing to do with your field. You'll learn the ropes, how to handle a gun, *et cetera*. I'm going to recommend you. I trust you're not a Nazi sympathizer?"

"Captain, not at all," he replied, meeting the man's eyes squarely. "I doubt that any of the Americans who were in Germany during the same period are. We saw a lot."

Apparently, his opinion was noted. "You'll hear from the Army within the next few weeks. Channels, *et cetera*."

Jim decided the captain liked the sound of *et cetera,* and took his leave.

The few weeks stretched. The thought that he might work with George Chauncy, who could also be drawn into this project, was appealing. They had kept in touch although George left Germany before he did. He closed his eyes and thought of Inge. As a German, she would hardly be an appropriate Army wife. There was no longer the slightest possibility that she could come to the States. He did not know how he could deal with that. Clearly his government was gearing for war despite newspaper articles to the contrary. Even sustaining a correspondence with Inge was difficult, if only because the mail now took many weeks. A letter written April 10th arrived June 15th.

"Liebling,
"This letter contains more bad news than what you would have read in the newspapers reporting Germany's invasion of Norway and Denmark. Frau Matcher died yesterday. Herr Rosenberg called me. His voice trembling,

he did manage to say that she had failed markedly after you left, and refused any new students. To hope for another Herr May was seeking too much. I agreed.

"We Germans seem to have an infinite capacity for suffering. Look at our greatest legend, the Niebelunglied. It tells of people who believe that the power of good is shown, not by conquering evil, but by continuing to resist, even facing certain doom. Victory comes with death, and courage is never defeated. What a terrible heritage!

"I'm sorry about your heavy doctor bills. Mostly it pains me to tell you that another life has been extinguished.

"Deine, Inge."

Her next letter was dated June 10th, 1940.

"Liebling,

"The beautiful house where you lived is suddenly closed. A neighbor confided to me that Herren Matcher and Rosenberg have gone to Brazil.

"It seems strange to me that you will be an Army officer in only a few weeks. How can they teach you so much so quickly?

"You have been like a great painting to me, a silent voice, so vibrant, so learned, with still so much to be discovered. I hope for us. I have your letters. They are for keeping, rereading, rethinking. I will keep them forever. But the beautiful writing portfolio that you gave me is becoming tear-stained. I awaken to find myself crying.

"Deine, Inge."

Her letters always disrupted his sleep, bringing him to consciousness before he felt equipped to face the day. He could see her, writing each letter, sealing it, and posting it at the corner as he lay watching the morning light fall through his window. First, the leaves and branches of the giant elm made shadowy shapes. Then he could see the tracery of the limbs and leaves. The color was the last to come, and then it was morning. He could hear Victoria clumping down the stairs, and buried his head in his pillow. Only half awake he would reach out for Inge, and then coming up with nothing, he'd pull himself out of bed. In the bathroom he would jack off, not wanting anything to do with girls at this point.

There was no new work at the office, and he felt certain that when the working drawings on his drafting table were finished, he would be given notice. Mr. Finch was also applying for a commission, undoubtedly a higher one. Lavina no longer spoke to him unless it was absolutely necessary. Still her presence was an intolerable weight. Victoria did not make Jim's wait any easier. She kept referring to those 'warmongers.' He could do nothing but hope for a telegram from the U.S. Army. It came, and it began: 'Greetings.'

In his last few days at home he tried to explain to his mother that not all Germans were Nazis—not the people with whom he lived and certainly not Inge.

"You keep saying that, but it is all I see. You came back a different person, and I think that girl did it," said Victoria.

"You're probably right, Mother," he conceded. "Maybe if you had sent me the ring as you always promised, things would be different." That was not the case, but it felt good to lash out at someone.

"You had only known her a few weeks." Victoria twisted the ring on her finger. It seemed to him to have lost its fire.

"Mother, it was long enough."

"Perhaps I made a mistake. You've certainly made me pay for it."

He needed patience. "I'm sorry. I appreciate the sacrifices you've made for me—and kept me well aware of them. I'll be out of your hair soon."

"Jimbo, that's not what I want." She was weeping.

He refrained from adding more, and felt guilty, but not guilty enough to comfort her. There was no longer any comfort left in him. Victoria had become a sickly, menopausal, neurotic woman, and he was sure he was partially to blame. Yet he couldn't have given her a life. It was unfair for her to think so—as illogical as his thought that marrying Inge would make his life. As war approached, the possibility of marrying Inge grew more and more remote. Still, he could not think of a future without her.

He did not cope with the ensuing months particularly well. He went into the Army, and the complete change of scene helped; however, before long, he had to take an extended leave when Victoria died. He sold the house and its contents, gave her clothes to the Salvation Army, and repaid his friend, Larry Price. He wrote Larry, enclosed a check, and brought one period of his life to a close.

"Dear Larry,

"I'm sure you wrote off the loan long ago, but here it is with interest. Some special words of thanks are due for seeing me through an ordeal. I can hardly express myself on this without embarrassing us both. Somehow a debt still looms in my mind. May I leave it at that?

"Two months ago mother died. I managed to bury her, but not much of my sense of guilt that always colored my relationship with her.

"By the way, I ran into your sister Betsy a few months ago at a Washington cocktail party with no less than an admiral in tow. You will be relieved to know that she has not changed. In light of her talents, the family fortune seems secure.

"Hail Columbia,

"Best, Jim."

* ** *

Letters from Inge came slowly, prolonging the agony. She wrote:

"Liebling,

"My dear cousin Karl Heinz is dead. Uncle Fritz is devastated and will see no one but Mother. Friends sind gefallen.

"I force myself to think of better days. Paris fell, but with limited fighting so perhaps one day we may still visit her as we once dreamed. Otto has grown 20 cms. since you left. He is repairing the subway station between Wittenbergplatz and the Zoo. He's too young for this work, but he's big. It's the bombing season. I heard Father say, 'I should have spared Inge this.' Mein Gott!

"The cigar store has a window full of cigar boxes and cigarette cartons but none are for sale. They are there for morale purposes. The storeowner confessed to me that they're all empty. We have ration cards in seven different rainbow colors for different food categories. Ich liebe dich noch!

"Deine, Inge."

* ** *

While other Americans were in action, including George Chauncy, and were dying on foreign shores, Jim was safe and sound in Washington preparing for the aftermath, yet not missing out on the brisk social scene. His bachelor status, skill on the dance floor, and uncommon good looks—made even more dashing by a uniform—stood him in good stead. He even bought an apartment, having decided he liked Washington and wanted a career with the State Department.

Most waking moments were spent studying art, but not sketching and painting as he had in college. Now he was studying to recognize thousands of pieces of reported stolen art. Millions and millions of dollars worth of European art—not entirely Old Masters, but including many—had been stripped from museums, castles, and private collections, wherever the Nazis were. The U.S. government knew that this art would have been protected from bombing, and hoped that it could be discovered in good shape. It would be identified, properly handled, crated, and finally returned to rightful owners. Jim felt this was an unprecedented action on the part of the government and, consequently, determined to do a bang-up job.

CHAPTER THREE

1941, Berlin

After the *Anschluss*, or annexation of Austria, Austrian Baron Kurt Montag used the shortened form of the family name, von Montague to Montag. As an officer in the Austrian Army, Montag found himself in the German Army, bound for the Eastern Front. He was in Berlin awaiting his unit's transfer to the East and conducting some banking business when he met Inge's father. Impressed with his title, land holdings, and good looks—not to mention Austrian charm—Herr von Haas latched onto Montag as an ideal suitor for Inge.

Inge, non-communicative and refusing to see old friends, had not been herself since May departed. A year of this weighed heavily on both parents. Gertrude felt they had lost their daughter forever, and often told Herr von Haas so. "Can't you at least bring some personable young man by the house?" she demanded.

"There aren't any nice young men around," he retorted with a scowl. "There's a war on, remember?"

The Germans were in control of the continent. Activity in the Balkans had stalled. The High Command's *Operation Barbarosa,* a three-pronged attack on Russia, left Montag free for a brief leave in Berlin. He received a very different reception from Herr von Haas than James May had.

Thinking that she would be seeing Montag for one evening only, Inge came out of her shell to be nice. Not only was Montag tall, sensitive looking, and wildly handsome, but he was also devoid of the arrogance so common to German males.

After dinner the young couple was allowed a few minutes of private conversation before coffee was served. Montag was serious, self-assured and deep-voiced. "I'm not a Nazi," he said, frankly. "I'm a pawn and I expect, unless I'm terribly lucky, to be little more than cannon fodder. It's a humbling thought. The German officers get the new fast tanks, and we Austrians get the old ones, the traps. Having come to terms with that, I had business in your father's bank."

The statement was made in such good humor, Inge was surprised. "You seem to take death very lightly."

"Oh, don't think I did at first." His dark eyes met hers. "I walked around in dazed fear, sick with it. Then one day I told myself, enough of this. Why ruin what's left or what may be left? It was easier to do than I'd thought. Now I'm grateful for every day, and think no further than the next meal."

"I guess what you say could apply to civilians. They're as likely to be casualties as those on the Front." She replied, herself a victim of a depression she had done little to shake. "Unless this world becomes a better place, I don't relish growing old in it."

"You could make this world a much better place if you would see me tomorrow. I'm due in Breslau the day after."

To refuse struck Inge as selfish. Tomorrow she would tell him that she was carrying a torch for another man, but there seemed to be no point in allowing him to walk the streets alone. He was easy to talk to, and she could not talk freely with anyone else. Possibly, he could not be open with those close to him either. Inge's soul-searching came to an end.

"Where would you like to go?" she asked.

"I'll leave that up to you." To him the entire room suddenly seemed airy, and it showed on his face.

She didn't want to go anyplace she'd been with May, which made almost all of Berlin sacred territory. Finally, she suggested they meet for lunch in the old city at a restaurant she had often wanted to try.

The remainder of the evening passed easily enough. Her father crowed with good will, and her mother did her best to disguise over-eagerness, making Inge grateful. She no longer despised her parents for the pain they had caused her. Now they seemed only pitiful old fools.

Over a simple luncheon of *Bratwurst* and good Berliner beer, they found a lot to talk about. "Unfortunately, we Austrians joined Germany in the Great War, and losing, ended a prosperous Hapsburg empire that had lasted for seven centuries," Montag explained. "The victorious Allies carved us up to satisfy the national yearnings of the Czechs, Hungarians, Serbs, and Italians. So, from a nation of fifty-one million we were reduced to seven—cut off from all harbors. Then in 1938 we really became the biggest loser in modern European history as Hitler had us for lunch."

"I'm no Nazi, so I can freely sympathize," said Inge. "As a matter of fact, I've been in love with an American. Everyday it grows more hopeless, but I'm still emotionally involved. I have to tell you."

"I thought meeting you was too good to be true," he murmured.

"If you can be happy with a friend in Berlin as a *confidante*, and happy to write you, I'll be your friend. I'm sorry, I can't be more, but friendship is something."

As the sunshine spilled through the stained glass window, catching the topaz prisms in troubled eyes, it seemed to the handsome Austrian, seated across the table, that divine providence had brought them together. "You had to be attached to someone. The fact that he is American is pure luck."

"I'm not sure about that…"

"Then you believe that the United States will enter the war, and that Germany will again be defeated?" he asked.

"I am certain of it."

"You don't talk like any girl I've ever met. I'm not used to women who are open and frank. It's delightful. Austrians are trained to say what others would like to hear. It's never important where the truth lies, only that it be heavily sugarcoated. One of our simple legends illustrates Austrian charm perfectly."

"Tell me…"

"Remember, it's simple: There used to be a rivalry between Salzburg and Vienna, and once in Salzburg a magnificent black bull grazed in a pasture. 'He can't be happy black,' said the people. 'Let's wash him white.' They tried and the foaming suds ran from the Salzach to the Danube to Vienna; the Viennese saw the foam and decided the Danube had turned to milk, so they scooped up all the foam in buckets until the water ran clean. So there you see what simpletons we are—sentimental, unrealistic, hard-working and foolish."

For the first time in a year Inge found herself laughing, amused that a man could openly admit to the weaknesses of his people. How unlike the German's haughty superior stance. "You're refreshing," she remarked.

"I think it's the good beer that's refreshing you. Your choice of a restaurant is perfect."

"It was luck. I've often passed this place. The patrons always seem to be smiling, which must have been due to the food; a smile is so rare lately. We never expected to be bombed. But let's not talk about the war. Tell me about your home."

He threw back his head as if his collar were suddenly too tight. "That's a difficult subject for me, although a lesser one than bombing. I've been homesick like every other man in the Army. My home is on the Mondsee with marvelous views of the Salzkammergut region. Steep mountains that rise majestically, straight out of their depths enclose the lakes. It has to be one of the most beautiful regions of the world, and it has one of the oldest cultures. If you're interested in archaeology, relics in this region date from the eleventh century BC."

"And your home?"

"A small Gothic, which means rundown, barony in which only a few rooms out of a hundred are used because of leaky roofs and a lack of heat. Granite and timber, mountains of both, enable us to survive. Someday, when the world settles down, and people can once again enjoy resorts, the main building would make a great hotel. My father would never consider such a thing, but he's ill and won't live much longer. Mother's more practical. I think she would consider selling the family jewels for such a purpose, because she loves people. With a ski lift and a *patinoire,* in winter we could offer winter sports, and in summer boating, fishing and riding. My sister and I have dreamed of this. Father has seen our wealth dissipate, but in his gentlemanly way, and having no business sense, he sits back dreaming of the good old days, unable to cope. The sheer beauty of the place dispels anxiety. It's another world."

"You have no brothers?"

"Only one sister, Olympia." He sat back in his chair, and a warm tender light glowed in his eyes.

"Named after Olympus, the mountains of Thessaly, the abode of the gods. How apropos."

"I doubt Mother thought of that in naming her. Olympia's doing her best to hold things together, escaping when she can to Linz. With me away, that isn't often because someone has to manage the quarries."

"That's an unusual occupation for a girl."

"Commanding a tank is an unusual occupation for a man. And, for an Austrian, riding in a German tank is even odder." He spoke with no malice, but it was easy to detect his sense of entrapment.

He had given her the facts, an accurate representation of what his life had been. Surely, there was more. "You haven't mentioned a girl."

"All social life came to a crashing halt in 1938 when we lost our automobiles. There was no way to see the girls I knew in Vienna. Also there was no way to foresee how long this situation would last. It was much harder for my sister. I was not in love."

"You sound close to her."

"She's bright and pretty, but she walks with a limp from polio. For a long time she was sensitive about it. Yes, we are close."

"Is there anything you have to do today? Any errands?" she asked, knowing that in the early evening he would be leaving for camp.

"I'm glad you reminded me. I sat for a photograph, having promised Mother one. The proofs will be ready. If you don't mind, we could stop by."

"Certainly."

"Sitting was a pain, and I must have been scowling, because the poor man kept asking me to smile. So I'm not too optimistic."

It was not far to the Kurfürstendamm, and a pleasant walk, so they set out on foot.

The atelier was the most expensive in Berlin, or on the continent, for that matter. The shop owner, a master photographer, and a bevy of underlings bowed and scraped as Baron Montag entered the store. They were immediately ushered into a private salon where the proofs were presented with considerable flourish.

"You are a magnificent subject, sir, " fawned the master. Indeed, thought Inge, with such a handsome man, not making a beautiful photograph would be a crime.

One view was quite serious, shot like a matinee idol with a seductive glamour designed to stir women. The visor of his cap was pulled well down to achieve a sexy mysterious air. In the other shots he gradually worked up a smile that made him look younger and more ingenuous.

"What do you think, Inge?"

"They're all good, but I think your mother would like the one of you smiling. The eyes are right on the viewer, which is nice. Surely, she remembers you this way." Inge then eyed him critically. "Yes, your right side is your best side."

They were words she would always remember and regret.

Montag agreed. He ordered two large sepias for his mother and sister, and three smaller ones for friends. Without a word about cost or payment marring the social exchange, they were obsequiously ushered to the door.

On the street Inge braved a question. "You never mentioned money? Is that customary in such expensive establishments?"

"Oh, indeed, otherwise he would doubt my title. He knows it will be a long time before he sees his money, so he'll sock it to the next Nazi."

They laughed.

As they walked along talking, she felt new vistas opening up. It was nice to be out, going on with the living. Her mind focused on the attractive man beside her. Like James May, he was stimulating and had interesting opinions of his own.

"Class does have its privileges, even under this regime," he remarked. "You can't erase hundreds of years of ingrained attitudes overnight, thank heaven."

"Another friend often despaired of that," she murmured.

"I can't take you to dinner. There would not be enough time, but we can have coffee at some place like the Sacher."

She led him to a *Haus* known for *Schrammel-Musik,* the nostalgic sentimental songs of Austria, played on two violins, an accordion and a guitar. They drank their coffee which almost tasted like coffee, ate *Kuchen* smothered in whipped cream, and listened to Johann Strauss's *Beautiful Blue Danube.*

"I hope that when you see *Die Fledermaus, The Gypsy Baron,* or another Strauss operetta, you will think of me," he said sadly.

"I will, and I promise to write."

She accompanied him to the Lehrte Station. Lofty grime-coated girders towered over their strained faces. In the eerie light of the cold cavernous room they joined another group of parting couples, the men in uniform, clutching their girls in desperate, heart-splitting farewells. Clouds of blue steam hissed about their feet. The grief was infectious, and Montag suddenly grabbed Inge to him, holding her tightly, one hand cradling her head, pressing it to his neck so that she felt the pulse in his throat.

She had not wanted such a moment. The day's outing had been a lark, yet here she was, suddenly thrust into the drama of terrifying poignancy. How many of those men, even Montag, might never come home? She thought of Karl Heinz. The air in the Bahnhof was freezing, and the only heat seemed to come from Montag's arms around her and the softness of his breath on her ear. Suddenly, swept by the sadness of the moment, she felt incomparably grieved, as bereft as the other women. Fighting to be brave, she felt her throat swelling, pressing up tears. Pushing free of his arms, she turned and fled.

A week later she received a letter from him. In many ways, it was remarkable. The stationary was the finest snowy-white linen, obviously hand-pressed, that she had ever seen. His full title, Baron Eberhardt Alexander Kurt von Montague, and the city, Mondsee, Austria, all the address necessary, were handsomely engraved. His handwriting bordered on calligraphy. He thanked her for every moment of pleasure during his leave and apologized for his impetuous behavior in the railroad station.

"I know the embarrassment of being in love with one person, only to find yourself suddenly in the arms of another, must have troubled you. Forgive me. You have been so kind that I have been unable to put you out of my mind. I can dwell on our happy interlude when there is little but abject misery around me. The men do nothing but gripe. Heaven knows, they have reason to. A tank must be the most uncomfortable vehicle ever devised."

Inge, as she promised, was quick to reply, assuring him that he had no reason to apologize. She, too, hated the day to end. So much heartfelt emotion had erupted around them, which neither had been prepared for, and had spread like a fever.

"I left the station feeling mortally wounded," she wrote. She also told him that she was making a strenuous effort to come to terms with her parents, and for that blessing he was responsible. *"If you can say, 'why ruin whatever is left?' I certainly should be able to show more consideration for those who love me."*

She was not at all ashamed of her own writing paper, a gift from May.

Soon after, walking down the Kurfürstendamm and passing the portrait studio, she looked up to see Montag's picture in the window. Unhesitatingly, she entered the shop and asked if she could order a small print. She wanted something smaller than a postcard size, which was the smallest they made. "I want something in a leather folder that I can carry in my purse," she said. She had no intention of carrying it in her purse, but the leather folder would keep it hidden. Otto snooped. The shop owner, charging for a special order, was delighted to oblige. He remembered her and offered to put the additional print on Montag's bill.

"No," she replied, "I'll pay for it."

Swallowing his surprise, he accepted the money.

It would be easier to write him with his picture at hand, she rationalized, but it was more expensive than she had imagined. Leaving the shop, she almost regretted the extravagant impulse. Later reading the paper, she had no regrets.

On June 22nd, 1941 the entire Eastern Front erupted in a rain of fire and steel. On the first day of *Operation Barbarosa,* Montag's corps advanced over fifty miles through a wide gap in the Russian defenses. By June 26th, von Manstein's panzers captured the city of Dvinsk. Days passed before Inge heard from Montag, and she began to fear for his life.

Finally a letter came through. *"Much to my General's chagrin, we were halted. Our flanks are not vulnerable as long as we are on the move and retain mobility. By stopping we invite warfare totally unsuitable for tanks. When we finally got permission to press on, the opposition was tremendous. Now the situation seems well in hand. I feel very lucky to be alive."*

It was a long letter that described some of the men with whom he was serving and the devastated countryside they had left behind. *"Long after we stop moving, my ears still ring from the noise, and I find myself shaking with fatigue. Am I really living this? It seems like such an awful dream."*

Inge not only found herself anguishing over his predicament, but distressed over the position in which she had allowed herself to fall, by becoming interested in a man at the Front. She had thought a great deal more about Montag than she would have believed possible on such a short acquaintance. Her separation from May was painful enough, but at least it had no overtones of peril. As long as May was safe on the other side of the ocean, she had no fear. With the accelerated RAF bombing, she had been the one in danger. Also she felt a sense of duty about writing Montag that she had never felt about writing May—from whom she could only be better off by letting go. Now her concerns were shifting, too flimsy for focus, but they were there.

December 9, 1941 the United States entered the war. Facing the reality of what could only be a death struggle, Inge wrote May to say farewell. Clearly, it would be many years before they could marry, were they to live. A terrible winter's fighting in Russia marshaled sympathy for Montag that filled the void she had created in her life.

The theater and movies continued to thrive in Berlin, and to divert the Baron, she wrote about the entertainment, always closing with a few bolstering words. During the next two years, although they never met, she and Montag grew closer through their letters. Then one day he wrote that he loved her deeply.

She wrote that she loved him also.

Dire as the circumstances were in Berlin, a remarkable spirit of camaraderie pervaded the city. She wrote about that too. She was sent to work in a shoe factory, making boots for the soldiers. There she picked up many amusing anecdotes to make him laugh. One such story involved a friend with a snobbish neighbor. Having been snubbed a few times on the street, her friend had been forced to knock at the neighbor's door. "My name is Fraulein Stadler. I realize that I should have called you before coming, and I beg your pardon for intruding this way, but your house is on fire."

She wrote him about the confusion into which May had thrown

her by his contempt for Hitler's art program. *"He was not taking away without trying to put back, but there was nothing to illustrate what he was talking about. I was left very unsure of myself. When I pick up a pen or pencil, I feel as though I'm about to write a rubber check."*

Everything that she had done for months seemed unbeautiful. Only her correspondence with Montag afforded sustenance for her spirit. She wrote Montag: *"I woke up one day feeling different, having written James May to say goodbye. I felt exhausted but peaceful, as if my temperature had broken over a long fever, as if an end or a limit to some capacity had been reached. Nothing would be quite as bad again—I thought. I never dreamed that, with only one day shared between us, I would learn to feel for you as I have—that I could break out in a cold sweat fearing for your safety or life."*

In early July the German *Blitzkrieg* stormed across Russia. Montag's corps was one of the Northern Group ordered to take Leningrad. Roads, climate and terrain slowed their advance in what had been designed to be a short war. When the weather was dry, dust stirred up by boots and tanks hung in clouds as high as a house. When it rained, tanks and trucks got mired in mud. When Leningrad did not fall, the panzers were withdrawn and transported to the Central Front to attack Moscow from the north. The fall of Moscow seemed imminent.

"Our spirits are high," Montag wrote, *"only because we see an end in sight. Our drive has been slowed while engineers and work crews patch the highway. The roads and dirt tracks that pass as roads in Russia have turned into oozing quagmires. Supplies of all kinds are mired in the rear. I've been stalled a few times without fuel."*

"The Russians have a new T-34 tank with sloping armor plates that deflect our shells. Their wide tracks nimbly roll over the roughest terrain and they have a powerful 76mm gun that can cripple our panzers with a single shot. We're lucky to make eight kilometers a day. I find myself dreaming of you as we creep along. The thought warms me more than my light coat. Winter is setting in fast."

Then in another letter he confessed: *"I am warmed by the thought of you, and fired by other thoughts. I am a jealous man. I am jealous of James May for the year he had with you when I only had one day. Often I imagine him in a Russian tank, one supplied by the United States, and I fight like a demon. This is irrational I know, but so is war, and it helps. For this you must forgive me. Life is too perilous for reason and nicety. I must call on and hone every primal instinct just to survive."*

By December, against Hitler's orders, commanders were thinking in terms of defense, not offense. The attack on Moscow had run down. The Army had suffered nearly a quarter of a million casualties, but Montag was still alive. Finally he wrote her: *"If you tell me that we can be married, I will live for that. There's little chance that I will be wounded since the wounded die fast and sweetly from shock and frostbite. Many have frozen to death in stalled hospital trains. I want to live if it can be with you."*

Aided by 'General Winter,' the Russian counteroffensive began. The temperature continued to fall. The Russians planned the encirclement of Montag's group, and had this succeeded, Montag would not have survived. The Russians were not taking prisoners. But he was saved from the trap before it closed. He wrote: *"Stalin saved his capitol by bringing in hoards of men. When a man fell there was always another in a seemingly inexhaustible supply to take his place. Young, untrained, unseasoned troops, transferred from every village in this vast nation, offer an endless blood transfusion to the Russian Army."*

Sometimes his letters ignored the war to talk about his childhood. Other times he fastened onto James May with an unreal hatred that was frightening. By reducing Hitler's stupid war to something personal, he found reason to fight. *"These powerful personal emotions enable me to fight like a werewolf."*

The German Armies were first stopped outside Moscow in the winter of 1941 – '42. Then Montag was transferred to the banks of the Volga for the siege of Stalingrad during the winter of 1942 – '43. By January, on the Eastern Front, only 495 German tanks remained operable. Montag's outmoded Mark IV was still among them.

During the spring Montag received a short leave, but by this time Inge had fled Berlin, and her address was unknown. Not finding her, he returned to Austria where his father was dying. Grieving over his father and having missed Inge, he returned for the Battle of Kursk.

The Germans assembled massive forces: 570,000 men, 10,000 field guns and mortars, supported by 2,000 aircraft and tanks. More than 3,000 armored behemoths became locked in the greatest tank battle ever fought. May was assigned to a new Ferdinand tank, a hapless giant, terribly vulnerable to infantry attack since it did not carry a single machine gun, but depended on riflemen on either side. This tank proved deadlier to its own six-man crew than it was to the Russians. When the Ferdinand lost its defenders, Soviet infantrymen, 977,000 strong, could approach safely from any direction, disable the tracks, and destroy the monsters at their leisure.

To Montag's dismay, low flying Soviet aircraft dropped men around them, some with parachutes, some without. The plan relied on deep mud to break their fall and save the men, under the fiendish conception that injured men could still shoot.

When Montag's tank was disabled, rather than be locked in a deathtrap, a crewman opened the overhead hatch for their escape. Montag held back to let his men go first. A Russian was waiting with a flame-thrower. The erupting snake of fire burned all except Montag, in what would have been agonizing death, had Montag not drawn his Luger and fired killing his own men. Several of his ricocheting bullets entered his own body. Hours later he was picked up by an ambulance and worked on by surgeons. Under their knives he lost his right arm and portions of his shoulder. The right side of his face, or what was left of it, was hideously burned.

Shattered mentally and physically, and unable to bring himself to write Inge even if he had known her whereabouts, he underwent a series of reconstructive operations. In one of Inge's last letters to him she told him she was going to Berchtesgaden and would be there waiting for him until she was allowed to cross the border into Austria. *"I will wait for you,"* she promised, totally unaware of his condition.

* ** *

In June 1945, Jim was packing to return to Europe. In his baggage was the last letter from Inge, dated December 10, 1941. She had forgotten Christmas was coming. It read:

"Liebling,

"Your letters are fewer. Honestly, they come as pleasant surprises, not as eagerly awaited epistles. Neither of us is to blame, I'm sure. The time was not right even though we were.

"Please don't write me again. Don't make my life harder. It has been bad enough. Clearly, any chance for us to get together again is years away.

A day never passes that I do not think of you, but thank heaven the pain is gone, as is so much else that you would remember.

"You are thinking that I have met someone else. Perhaps. I have the feeling that I could care for this man if I could free myself of you. There should be no limit to the love a human heart can hold. Certainly, one chamber of my heart, perhaps two, operates with a blockage that chokes the free flow of emotion as not before. Life here is perilous, and much more frightening alone, but I am learning courage.

"The Leutzensee is shrouded with camouflage nets to confuse the RAF that pounds us nightly. The wail of sirens, like screeching cats, sickens me.

" A friend will take this letter to Switzerland for posting, sparing the censor's blots. I will write when I can, as a caring friend, to keep you aware of the most important changes life throws or drops my way. Thank you for the most memorable moments of my life. They will never be surpassed. Thank you, thank you,

"Love, Inge."

Jim also carried a letter from Herr Matcher in Brazil, dated October 5th, 1944.

"Dear Herr May,

"This note will be brief to let you know where Rosenberg and I are, in the modest hope not to lose track of you, because we have moved several times. Apparently, not much is left of what we remember in Germany. The house in gone. I can only be grateful my dear sister did not live to see the worst of her fears become a reality. You gave us a very warm feeling for Americans that we still carry with us. You would make a fine good-will ambassador anywhere.

"So often I think of the wonderful evenings we spent together, when you listened patiently to an old man rant and rave over those unspoiled corners of the globe from Port Said to Chochin or Macassar's beaches to Billingsgate.

"Did I ever tell you about the fish market in Celebes? Well, sometime, perhaps. The Italian jewelers of the Renaissance never approached the easy opulence, the variety, and the wild ornamentation of what I saw there. I promise to supply the cognac. We will miss Frau Kruger's Kuchen.

"Rosenberg and the finest from his library are here by me now. Between

frets over climate strains, he sends his best wishes. Little silverfish worry him. Mein Gott, I must tell him about leeches. That's the tropics for you. We have a little monkey who has adopted us. He sleeps on my handkerchief.

"This place swarms with Germans. They're all Nazis, except for the Jews. They only speak when they have to. What's new?

"Fondly, Matcher."

Jim had heard from pilots who had returned to Washington from Europe, and from the newspapers, that not much was left standing in Berlin. So Matcher's letter with word of the house did not come as a surprise.

May 30, 1945, James Albertus May reentered Berlin in a C-47. He looked down on a sea of rubble. As the plane banked he could make out the Brandenburg Gate, the charred shell of the old Reichstag and a derelict Reich Chancellery. The East-West axis, made up of several boulevards, was clearly visible, but it seemed to be swarming with sheep. As they descended, in preparation for landing at Templehof, he saw that the slowly moving mass of sheep were people. He looked away, deciding that he had grown callous.

Resolving to send Matcher a first hand report, May, now pronounced like the month, braced himself for a landing.

Suddenly he heard a voice behind him. During the flight from England the man had been sleeping. Now he was peering out the window.

"What a crock! I missed the goddamned experience of the age! For four years I've cooled my heels while my buddies gave those bastards a dose of their own medicine. Now I'm up to bat, and there's not a damn thing down there worth pissing on!"

It took May a minute to gain perspective. *The Germans got what they has coming to them.* He would have to forget the people he knew as individuals and concentrate on the great crimes against humanity which, as a nation, they had been a party to. There was no avoiding it.

Book IV

CHAPTER ONE

1945, Berlin

Lt. James May checked in at the Kaiser Wilhem Anthropological Institute, home of the American Military Government in Germany.

In a jeep with an assigned driver, he was driven around Berlin. None of the stories he had read or heard prepared him for what he saw. He knew that seventy percent of the city's twenty boroughs lay in ruins, but he never imagined what must have happened to the people. A long column of bedraggled refugees streamed endlessly through the city, always east to west. During the previous month over one million had trekked through Berlin, and people were still coming.

"They have no place to stay and after forty-eight hours they're made to move on," the driver explained.

"My God, Inge, where are you?" May muttered, scanning faces.

Though he knew the city well, in directing the driver, it was necessary to creep no faster than he could walk. Avoiding people and rubble, they moved down Wilhemstrasse, passing ruined embassies and the new Reich Chancellery, which was more intact than it had seemed from the air. Berlin was a wasteland. At the corner of Pariser Platz, May stared in disbelief at the Hotel Adlon. Its ornate façade was miraculously unscathed, having been preserved by sandbags with all its nineteenth-century elegance.

"Stop here, please," May ordered. Then he saw the broken windows.

"Do you know this hotel, sir? It's a wreck inside."

"I never spent a night here, but I know it." Feeling choked and remembering a dance, May blew his nose. His head cleared, he felt better.

"It's the dust, sir. It covers everything," the driver said kindly.

May found his voice. "It's been six years, and it sure has changed."

They turned on to the Kurfürstendamm at the Französischer Dom that now had the shape of a man without arms. The devastation took May's breath away. The elegant shops, cinemas, and cafés were charred ruins.

"Wait until you see the Tiergarten, sir. You know, the garden of tears."

"I've heard about that, but there are a couple of houses that I'd rather see. By the way, Tiergarten means garden of animals."

At first May could not fine Inge's house, then he realized that the whole goddamned block had been destroyed. He questioned half a dozen people emerging from caves—that had been cellars—before he found an elderly man who told him that both Herr von Haas and his wife were long dead. He had no idea where Inge and Otto were, or if they had survived.

"But they weren't in the house when it was hit?"

"*Nein*. Half an hour later they…"

May erased the thought of what Inge had come home to. "I knew them," was all he could say, climbing back into the jeep.

The old man called out, "You haven't got a cigarette, have you?"

May tossed him a pack of Camels. He turned sheepishly to his driver. "You have no idea how important the news is that he just gave me. Two people that I once knew may still be alive."

"I guess that was worth a pack, but they were MY cigarettes."

The Matchers' house was also gone. Most of the rubble had been removed and May knew why: the cellar had been full of food and coal. The major trees in the yard survived, and there were patches of the garden wall left standing. For about ten minutes he walked around, gathering memories like pebbles in his hand. Then he remembered the party at Gretchen Baungarten's flat. Perhaps she would have some word of Inge. If that building still stood… It meant crossing town again. Certainly it was worth a try.

It took them almost an hour to reach it, and miraculously, the building was still there, damaged like everything else. The elevator no longer functioned, so May walked up six flights. The stairs were almost impossibly dark, and they stank of urine. After repeated knocks Gretchen came to the door.

"Fräulein Baumgarten, I'm Herr May. In '38 I attended a party here."

"I'm sorry, but I don't remember you, but you're wearing an American Army uniform, so I should pretend to. American soldiers are very good to know."

"Inge von Haas invited me."

"Oh, I do remember you. Come in. The place won't look the same. I haven't had a chance to redecorate. Quite a few people live here now—I'd say about twenty. They're out scrounging for food."

"Do you know where Inge is?"

Gretchen leaned against the door to the living room. "No, I'm sorry. About a year ago she headed south, walking. It was a good thing too. She would have been fair game for the Russians. I'm afraid that's all I can tell you."

"That's a lot." Fortunately, May had taken another pack of cigarettes off his driver with a promise to repay. "I arrived in Berlin today, and tomorrow I go to Munich. Let me give you my APO number. Please send word to me if you hear of her. Hopefully, you can trade these cigarettes for something."

"You don't know what you're giving me." Gretchen reached eagerly for the pack, fearing that he might change his mind. "I'm sorry you're leaving." She swayed and stepped closer.

May shifted his weight and backed off. However subtle, the approach was there. "I'm lucky I thought of you." He wrote out his mailing address and handed her the card. *"Auf Wiedersehen. Ich danke Ihnen."*

"Das Vergnügen war meinerseits."

May fairly ran down the stairs. Her words, the pleasure was mine, rang in his ears. Even living in rubble, whoring, the Berliners were still polite.

* ** *

May returned to the BOQ, reeling under the day's impressions. Inge might still be alive. A light spring rain fell as he walked to the hastily improvised officers' club. Even with the devastation he had seen, there was something romantic about the rain.

He was sitting at the bar when Bob Street, whom he had not seen since the *Savoia* walked in. May found himself glad to be shaking Street's hand, one indication of his misery. "How've you been?"

"I'm alive, which in this day and age is something. Have you come to a donkey market to find a camel?" asked Street.

"Apparently." For a moment it occurred to May that Street might know what his job would be—locating plundered art. Then he dismissed the idea as preposterous.

"Looking at the mountains of rubble, I can't say Berlin is flattened, but it sure is shaken up," Street remarked. "Will there ever be a city here again?"

"Not next week."

It was then that May noticed Street's oak leaf. "How'd you make major so fast?"

Street smiled smugly. "Five years in the service has to be worth something." Then he boasted. "I always managed to make the select five percent eligibility rating, and being an expert…"

May knew it was lucky timing. Basically, promotions came with time and grade, but when losses were high in one rank, those next in line were promoted quickly. May covered his chagrin with a little laugh.

"How did you make out with Tessenow?"

"From an educational standpoint, the year was first-rate."

They ordered scotch-on-the-rocks. When the drinks came, Street raised his glass. "To us. To the Old World that will be our New World. Remember your toast? I think our *Baedeker's* are out of date."

May remembered. He also remembered a vague feeling of animosity toward Street that somehow time had dimmed; but with a hovering sense of distaste, he felt it coming back. His drink weighed heavily in his hand.

"I was headed for the Pacific," Street was saying. "Then someone woke up to the fact that I come from a long line of West Pointers, generals, in fact. I was moved into an area more in line with my ability." Street grinned, making light of his bragging.

May remembered that Street was from San Francisco, and the servants in his home had been Japanese. "Today I saw remnants of a house that I know contained a Hasagawa Tahaku screen along with a lot of art I would love to own."

"Say, I seem to carry the impression that you were once hooked on a Fraulein. Her house, by chance?" Street swirled his scotch, an eyebrow cocked.

"No, not hers. I lived in a house with some very fine people and many beautiful things."

"May, I swear, you were blind as a bat. Germany was one big Nazi camp. Listen, I lived among them, too, but without stars in my eyes. Oh, don't think I didn't have a ball! Never since have so many broads spread their legs for me. Sometimes I banged two a night. They weren't like American girls. No, siree. They'd do anything. They're out there right now, skinny as crows, still ready to fuck you bandy legged for a couple of cigarettes. Cigarettes are the coin of the realm. Go to the flea market at the Brandenburg Gate.

"There, American cigarettes, coffin nails, will get you anything in the city still in one piece. But you won't find a Nazi. Oh, no! You couldn't find a Nazi with binoculars."

The man is still an abomination, thought May, downing his drink. "Major, I'm bushed. Have a good tour."

"Say, I haven't offended you, have I?"

"Berlin has. Tomorrow I'm flying to Munich. I have to be at the airport early. You know, hurry up and wait, the old Army game."

The night air was almost refreshing.

* ** *

May's flight made a landing at Rhein/Main Airport that afforded an aerial view of Frankfurt am Main. The panorama, like that of Berlin, was a vision of the apocalypse, but with one noble exception. The I.G. Farben building was completely intact. Across the street not one building was standing.

"Precision bombing at its best," someone commented.

Darmstadt, which he previously thought of as George Chauncy's 'Garden City,' appeared as a small brown patch among potato fields. Manheim and Ludwigshaven, two heavily industrialized cities facing each other on the Rhine, seemed totally obliterated. The plane climbed, and they flew eastward, following the Autobahn over Stuttgart, Ulm and Augsburg to München-Reim Airport.

Munich, although heavily damaged, still retained a vestige of grandeur that had disappeared from Berlin. Only one-third of the inhabitants had lost their homes, making the city look good in comparison to the capitol.

On learning that his plane had already departed, May was forced to accept land transportation. Eventually he was assigned a jeep and a driver, and they headed toward Berchtesgaden. Observing, while someone else was having to cope with the road, May surmised the Germans would find the peace harder than the war.

As soon as they were out of town on a highway, now free of cars except for Army vehicles, the foothills of Ober Bayern and the Bayerische Alpen appeared on their right, serene and majestic. Once again, what May remembered as the real Germany—the old Germany of his grandparents—pastoral scenes and quaint villages not too badly damaged, appeared before the backdrop of the Alps.

Still there were many people, hungry people, tired people (many shoeless) trudging the highway. Some lucky ones had been given rides on Army vehicles, always going in the opposite direction.

"A lot of these people are Czechs, anxious to get into the American Zone. You heard what the Russians did in Prague?" asked the driver.

"Christ, don't talk about it." May saw suffering everywhere.

To avoid mountains the dusty road cut north around Simmsee and then south around Chiemsee, a much larger lake. These areas had not been heavily bombed due to a lack of industry, as well as farsightedness on the part of someone who knew that Germany's spas would be badly needed as rest and recreation areas for battle-weary troops, the worst of whom were paratroopers, dropped in front of advancing armor.

So long as they did not look closely at the people staggering along the highway, the scenery was spellbinding. May told the driver, "Hitler used to stop here at a village inn for coffee and pastries on the way to Obersalzberg."

"How come you know that, suh?" asked the driver, a Corporal Brown.

"I spent years researching what the Nazis were doing with stolen art, and other things came to light."

He had avoided conversation with Brown, a black man with cavernous nostrils and a trumpet of a nose that, frequently, fighting the billowing dust, he sounded into a handkerchief. It was not Brown's relative unattractiveness that stilled May, but he needed to look at the world undistracted. He felt numbed, but then pain and shock pierced his narcosis, and he found himself troubled by memories. Summoning inner resources, he found he could regain a more normal sense of curiosity. Unless he did, he had to retreat.

"This ain't the first time I've made this trip," said Brown. "Now there ain't no coffee to stop for."

"When was the last time?"

"The day Field Marshal Albert Kesselring, Commander of the German Armies on the Western Front, surrendered to Major General Maxwell Taylor. I'll never forget that!"

"I guess you won't."

"Whew! It was scary."

"Why? Tell me about it," said May, feeling friendlier.

"There wuz at least half a million German soldiers in these mountains ready to fight 'til they died. Most of them still had their guns. We'd won, but we never knowed what could happen."

"Fanatics?"

"Crazy people, suh. The day started when two jeeps--I drove one-- and a Packard limo with General Taylor left the Berchtesgadener Hof and headed down this so-called Alpine Highway. We met head-on the first lines of the beaten army on a long hill—it's coming up soon. Before we made the turn we could hear them rumblin' motors, hundreds of trucks laborin'. I ain't never seen such a bunch of heaps! There wuz standard diesels with soldiers on hoods an' draped across runnin' boards, an' three-ton Model A Fords—musta been twenty years old— radiators spoutin'. Diesel freight trucks wuz draggin' trailers, tractors an' anything with wheels, always jammed with soldiers—their mudguards nearly scraping the ground—comin' at us. One lil' truck wuz even towing five motorcycles. Suh, they looked like a line of giant drunken bugs lookin' for a place to die."

May had to chuckle. He had never thought of the German Army in those terms.

"The bridge over the Ache River had a new name on it, the 'Ernie Pyle Memorial Bridge.' German officers wuz directin' traffic with American soldiers watchin', helpless as trucks broke down and everything piled up. The German officers cussed and prodded their men. All of a sudden their army seemed like a big bad joke, passed off on the world by some clown. Seein' 'em like that made the whole war unbelievable."

"It was pretty believable for a long time," said May.

"That feelin' passed. Them trucks was dirty, rusted. Some had wooden bodies that ain't never seen paint. They sounded like riveting machines. There wuz girls in uniform, too. When we finally got to Saalfelden, it wuz really weird. We wuz in a German camp, and we wuz the only Americans in it! German soldiers wuz in the street, but there wuz dogs and civilians mixed in, and mixed up with them wuz dozens of officers in spittin'-clean uniforms, salutin' like it wuz a dress parade. Then I saw that dark-blue wagon-lits train on a sidin'. General Taylor got out of his Packard, and went inside. Somebody closed 'em fancy curtains, an' I guess the surrender conference started. Boy, that train was somethin'—it wuz polished like a showroom Cady. Even the pistons wuz spit-polished."

"Right in character for the Germans," said May.

"Goin' back to Berchtesgaden, we got into another fuckin' traffic jam. The Kraut generals behind us got out to clear up the mess in person. Kesselring wuz sittin' in our limo, gabbin' with General Taylor like he wuz at a tea party the whole time." At this point Brown maneuvered a wild curve. "Imagine meeting a Sherman tank right here! We did. The officer in my jeep stood up and hung out cussin' and wavin' at trucks to pull over."

"That had to be the most memorable ride you ever made. It would've been mine," said May, shaking his head.

"At night they had a sort of tea party with cognac and cakes. In Berchtesgaden the German hot shots got the whole hotel. Kesselring met the press with Taylor beside him. Kesselring sat there, puffin' on a cigar. That man's eyes wuz always movin', but he tried to look friendly even if his teeth wuz yellow. When he smiled he reminded me of an ole tomcat my momma used to have that curled his lip thataway when she took away his kill."

May laughed.

"It wuz like there hadn't been a war—like this sort of thing was like winnin' the Wimbledon or windin' up the World Series."

At the foot of the mountain, the Obersalzberg, May was driven through the half-timbered village of Berchtesgaden. It shimmered like a bright jewel in the early summer light. They passed the hotel where the press conference had taken place. American Army signs with arrows reading 'To Hitler's home' dotted the road. At the edge of the town they crossed a simple rustic bridge over the River Ache, and shifted into low gear for the steep climb ahead. The vistas were superb—pine forests, Alps, and green valleys and small tidy houses clustered here and there. Grazing cows, cherry and plum trees, and roadside flowers lent an ambiance of peace and contentment. *It's almost too pretty,* thought May.

The first gatehouse, a little Bavarian cottage, had an archway across the road and barbed wire fence on both sides.

The second gatehouse was more ominous. Built of wood and stone, it was saddled into the mountain. The fortress-like construction indicated the Führer might have been afraid of someone. They turned sharply to the right, crossed a steeper grade, and emerged on a road running along a granite shelf cut into the mountainside. Then, as far as the eye could see, was a vast tangle of green, bombed-out buildings, now piles of cinderblock, wooden beams, cracked plaster, pipes and wires, jumbled together haphazardly, now sprouting weeds.

"Holy Toledo," cussed May with a whistle, turning to Brown in astonishment. "Is this all that's left of the Berghof?"

"Right, sir. You'll find Colonel Rasmussen in the barracks—they're still standin'."

Obersalzberg is the mountainside area where Hitler came to live after being released from prison in 1924, having served time for his botched Munich Beer-hall *Putsch* of the previous year. In time the property expanded to over two hundred acres. It always remained his favorite retreat. Here he finished *Mein Kampf* and entertained state visitors such as Mussolini, Chamberlain, and the Duke and Duchess of Windsor. And it was here that his closest aides and cronies: Borman, Göbbels, Göring, and Speer also seized nearby property from intimidated residents and built homes. "My greatest plans were all made at Obersalzberg," Hitler said in a 1942 broadcast. However, it was also here that the Holocaust and the invasion of Poland, which brought England and France into the war, were planned.

May, as Fine Arts and Monuments Officer for the American Military Government attached to the Army, had been instructed to report for duty under Col. Saul Rasmussen.

As he jumped from the jeep, every muscle in his body suddenly ached. Around him was nothing but devastation. He turned away from it and stretched. With a handkerchief he wiped his face clean of dust, ran a pocket comb through his hair, and adjusted his cap.

"Well, Brown, here goes it. I'm in the Army now. Thanks for a memorable ride and a great tale."

"I knows it's right peculiar reportin' for duty in a place like this." Brown waved aimlessly toward the rubble. "It's windy as my grandmomma's ass here, suh."

May chuckled. He entered a ramshackle cinderblock building, traversed a long corridor, addressed a sergeant, and was ushered into the colonel's office. May saluted, and the colonel rose and returned the salute. He then extended a short stubby hand while the other dug into a pocket of his jacket to scratch a rounded belly.

"Have a seat, May. We're still just settling in."

The colonel had a friendly, open, middle-aged face. Tufts of gray hair sprouted from his nostrils and ears, which May sensed had grown only because the hectic tenor of the last few weeks had left little time for cosmetics.

May let his commanding officer do the talking. "I'm worried that you may not find much to do as an art curator. The RAF bombed the bloody hell out of the Berghof and the adjoining Nazi bigwigs' estates. Then the French took over, followed by souvenir-hunting GIs. There are tunnels under the Kehlstein, and there may be something up in the Eagle's Nest, but the engineers haven't gotten around to getting the elevator to work. The road up there is impossible."

The colonel paused to blow his nose. "This country has an awful climate. Traipse around, take a good look. Apparently a helluva lot of art is missing. If it's not in the tunnels, it's been destroyed in bombed-out warehouses or hustled off by the Russians."

"I look forward to serving under you, sir, for as long as I can be of service," May replied, considering himself politely dismissed.

"Oh, by the way, how did you come in?"

"By jeep from Munich."

"There's a perfectly good runway here—Hitler's private airport, the Ainring. You could've been flown in and saved that miserable ride. I thought you would have." The colonel bellowed for a sergeant. "Check why May didn't get the flight."

"It was a good ride. I left Germany in '39 and wasn't prepared for the change. I wanted to see it. It turned out that my driver was part of the motorcade attending Kesslring's surrender. He told me about it in detail. I don't begrudge the trip at all."

"I'd like to hear more about that sometime. Richards will assign you quarters and an office." His eyes fell to a folder on his desk, which he picked up. The cover read: JCS 1067. "Are you familiar with this?"

"No, sir."

"Then read it," the colonel ordered, handing it over.

The sergeant appeared in the doorway. "Major Street in Munich used his priority for the plane, sir."

May's eyes opened wide. "Would that be Major Robert Street, sir?"

"Yes. Officially, you'll be working under him. However, his duties are such that he won't always be on post. Do you know him?"

"We've met several times over the years," May replied, seeing steadily mounting difficulties—first, the extent of the Allied bombing, and now the obnoxious Street as his boss. He saluted and then departed, feeling the colonel's eyes on his back.

May's astonishment at what was left of the compound increased. It was a wilderness of devastation. Cataloging *objets d'art* could hardly take fifteen minutes, fourteen completing the headings on Military Government forms. That was bad news, but it could also mean that rather quickly he might be transferred out from under Street. Slightly encouraged, he turned to the business of settling in.

For years he had dreamed of getting back to Germany, never fully realizing what he would find. Seeing Inge again had been part of his goal, if only to lay a few ghosts to rest. Now, struck by the enormity of the change, he saw his dream crumbling. I might not even recognize her, he thought, picking through his suitcase in search of a packet of snapshots. They were not there. At the last minute he had transferred them to another carton coming with the major part of his baggage. Dismissing an indistinct picture of Inge that could not be clarified, he sat down to tackle the colonel's assignment.

Within minutes his attention was riveted on the pages.

While in Washington he had heard of the Morganthau Plan— vaguely. His rank, a First Lieutenant, hardly made him privy to top secrets on a policy level of this scope. Had his country lost its collective mind?

What he now read was shocking beyond belief. It struck him as so ridiculous, it would never be implemented, at least not for very long. Then, knowing the Army, he knew that was not the case. That anyone could conceive of such an asinine policy was unbelievable. And the peace treaty called for five years of occupation!

"My God, am I going to have to live with this tripe AND Street?" he cried aloud, slamming down the booklet, rolling his eyes to the ceiling, hoping it wouldn't fall on him.

CHAPTER TWO

For the first three years of the war, the von Haas household functioned on a timetable as predictable as that of Monday following Sunday. Then, in one of the biggest RAF daylight raids on Berlin, the great stone house suffered a direct hit. Herr von Haas had been unwell and was home. When the air raid warning sirens wailed, he and Gertrude had not availed themselves of public shelter, but had gone instead to their own cellar.

The bomb, like a giant sausage, crashed through the roof, screamed down the stairs and finally exploded in the foyer, sending debris upward and outward in a booming thrust. Immediate flames gathered into an inferno. RAF raids on the city brought severe destruction that day and it took several hours for pump trucks to arrive. When they did, it was too late. Within twenty minutes fire had destroyed everything the bomb may have missed.

Inge had been at work. From a block away, seeing the crowd of people in the street and the fire engines pulling away, she knew what had happened. Her neighbors, arms outstretched in sympathy, walked in a wall to meet her.

She stood in the street, stunned, looking around, not knowing where to turn. Nothing remained but crumbled stone and ashes filling the cellar. A few charred beams protruded at crude angles from the rubble, looking like dilapidated cemetery markers on the ill-kept graves of the poor. On seeing Otto a few minutes later, her forlorn expression changed briefly. For once he looked like the angel Gabriel, who would bring glad tidings. But he had been visiting friends when the bomb hit and knew nothing.

By early evening when her parents did not return, their fate was no longer in doubt.

The bomb's thrust was such that all the nearby houses were severely damaged, and for a few weeks Inge and Otto found shelter in a neighbor's windowless home. Everything they owned was on their backs. Then the State intervened, and Otto, being underage, was sent to the safety of a farm.

In a very real sense the destruction of her home wiped out the past. Inge grieved, especially for her mother, whom she felt deserved a kinder fate, if only because, like so many women of her generation, she had had no control over her life. She also recognized some sort of payment due for her own transgressions. Sadie's family, whom she had turned away, came vividly to mind. Her loss seemed retribution.

Isolated within herself, she threw herself into the war effort, never thinking of victory, only the end of the war. The effort offered companionship and oneness with the *esprit de corps* that characterized Berliners. They were not fooled by the propaganda blaring from their radios. Work meant food and survival on a day-to-day basis. Strangely, as the war droned on and on, and the Americans joined the RAF in the bombing, she could not equate the Americans with the enemy, which made the radio communications all the more ridiculous.

Only to Kurt Montag, the one important adult left in her crumbled world, could she pour out her shock and sorrow. He understood her regrets, and when her grief subsided, filled her dreams with gossamer visions that reality no longer afforded. With him, in his castle in Mondsee, there was hope for the future and a rebuilding of her world.

The Russians were another matter.

Until Montag's letters stopped, he described the Russians as an enemy to be feared—a demoniacal ruthless horde to be avoided at all costs. His opinion was confirmed by other seasoned soldiers who spoke of primitive Mongols set loose to plunder and rape. One day she picked up a newspaper to read of another 'temporary setback' on the Eastern Front. That afternoon diligent authorities informed her that Otto had run away from the farm. She waited several days for him to appear, then decided that she was in greater jeopardy than he. When the Russian offensive in the Ukraine gained momentum, she headed for Austria, thoughts of Montag acting like guiding stars to lead her south.

Naively, she misjudged the time the trip would take, time in which Otto would be looking for her. On the awful trek she was often hungry, sometimes hungry enough to eat grass. In villages she picked up newspapers, which invariably minimized the bombing damage. However, they also served a more honest purpose as bedrolls. But on clear bright days, looking from the hilltops, she could see the cities, view the ruins, and know that the end was in sight.

It was a good summer for the defeat of a nation. The benevolent weather that aided the bombing also helped her to survive.

Most farmers or their wives needed hands, even a girl's, because the men were still away in the Army, and likely to be shot if they deserted. Walking southward, she would stop, work for a few days so that she could eat and build strength, and then take off again. She developed a simple motto that stood her in good stead: stay alive. She forced herself to say it over and over again, like a mantra.

Eventually she found herself on a potato farm owned by the Hoffmanns, not far from Berchtesgaden.

* ** *

"Stay alive," Inge repeated sleepily, aloud but to herself. She didn't know whether the words applied to a plea to Kurt Montag or as an admonition to herself. The dream always involved him. Dreams were always ragged fragments, a mixture of past and present in which romance and the horrors of war combined in poignant yet painful experiences.

Then the loud call, "Inge!" woke her abruptly.

"I'm coming," she replied, jumping up, shaking out the worn blanket that had kept her off the hay. A web, with a spider curled tight at the center, hung from her shoulder. She brushed it away, and hurried down the ladder from the hayloft to the kitchen, where Herr Hoffmann and his wife were about to sit down to a morning's porridge.

Her presence grated on Frau Hoffmann, who felt hired help should be obsequious, if not cowering, to an employer. Didn't that fool girl realize how important today was?

Inge always walked straight, her head high, moving easily and effortlessly with the fluidity and natural grace of one trained at making appearances. This, Frau Hoffmann couldn't bear. No matter that her clothes were worn and shabby or that she had been allowed no time for toiletries, her breeding showed.

Frau Hoffmann scowled. It was not that Inge was not a hard and tireless worker; she was. But there was something about the girl, something about the yellow-flecked eyes that made her feel clumsy and uncomfortable, if not envious. Frau Hoffmann knew her place and station in life in a small closed community, but the quiet young girl—who did not act aloof—disquieted her as much as if she had been an alien, foreign to the ways of good Germans.

The trek had left Inge painfully thin, her skin coarsened by the sun. Still, finely chiseled features and gentle ways bespoke an upbringing and heritage in which physical strength was not the important end-all. Frau Hoffmann could not verbalize any of this, but like a canny animal, sensed these qualities, and felt not only crude and cloddish, but also powerless, which was ten times more disquieting.

"Have you forgotten that we're slaughtering a pig today?" she asked crossly, hardly looking up from her bowl.

"A seven-hundred pounder," her husband added, his voice kindlier. He shared none of his wife's antagonism. "The meat inspector, a professional butcher, and the state controller will soon be here. They cost a lot of money," he explained, "so we have to be ready for them."

For some days the trio's arrival had demanded considerable preparation and concern. A giant meat-grinder, spotlessly clean, sat firmly mounted on a workbench. The firewood was piled high by a copper kettle, normally a washtub. Outside another table had been set up for the meat cutting. Additional firewood was piled nearby to keep the outside chimney going. Smooth wooden plugs had been scrubbed and neatly stacked.

A knock on the door interrupted Frau Hoffmann before she had a chance to vent her ill humor. A jar of plums was missing, and she was about to question Inge when two women arrived on bicycles. She put down her spoon and moved to answer the bell; it had a loud ring, one strong enough to bring men from the fields.

Inge heard her say haughtily, "Yes, you can have five pounds of potatoes but you'll have to dig them yourself. When you're finished, come back here to weigh and pay." Looking self-satisfied, wiping her hands on her buttocks, she returned to the table, having forgotten about the plums.

As suppliers of food, farmers had come into their own with unbridled tyranny.

The expected officials arrived promptly and immediately went to work. One frightened squeal and a few curses announced the demise of the pig. Inge, inside doing the breakfast dishes, cringed, while Frau Hoffmann hovered outside, attempting to hold her excitement in rein. Then the preliminaries were over. A few slugs of schnapps followed the signed statement that the pig was fit to eat. The inspector and the state controller left.

Outside the butcher hacked away. Inge and Frau Hoffmann began hauling great steel platters, loaded with mountains of meat cut in stew-size pieces into the house.

Herr Hoffmann washed what looked like miles of shimmering white gut, one end of which would be attached to a small spout on the end of the grinder. Having seasoned the meat, Frau Hoffmann ordered Inge to turn the grinder, making the machine groan and clank, while spewing out a steady stream of ground pork and spices to fill the casings. With a flip and a twist Frau Hoffmann marked off individual sausages that, still joined in long meter strips, would hang to dry.

"The first batch is ready to be smoked," Frau Hoffmann announced to her husband.

The butcher paused for a moment. "Who is the pretty girl?"

"A *Wandervogel*," Hoffmann replied with a shrug. Wandering girls, called birds, a somewhat disreputable title, came and went. There were hundreds of them scattered along the highways.

"She has no shoes?" the butcher asked, having noticed Inge's bare feet.

"She's saving them."

When the butchering was finished, he hung around like a stray dog wanting a bone. Eventually he was invited to join them in the kitchen for a bowl of soup. Throughout the brief meal, Inge was silent, ignoring the butcher's stare. Finally he asked bluntly, "Don't you like me?"

In the pause that followed Inge looked down at her hands, clutched in the lap of her bloodstained apron. "Why should I?" she asked. Then she got up, cleared the table and washed the dishes. Rightly guessing his cause was hopeless, the butcher left. She knew he could have guessed that she was sleeping in the barn and she decided to pull up the ladder that night. Their work continued.

The smell of blood, meat and sausage was all pervading. Night fell. Fire still cracked under the great copper vat. The first batch of dark red *Blutwurst* was ready. Frau Hoffmann ladled out bowls of the blood sausage to be eaten with chunks of gray bread. They ate silently, then work resumed at a frantic pace. "Seven hundred pounds of meat is a lot of meat," said Inge.

Finally, the pig had become bacon, ham, lard, pork roasts and sausage. The skin would be tanned into leather. They were exhausted. "Tomorrow I'll cook the bones," announced Frau Hoffmann.

Once the bones had given up their gelatin, they would be dried, and it would be Inge's job to grind them into meal for the chickens. But now she scrubbed the kitchen. "We've used everything but the Oink," she said wearily, leaning against the tiled oven for welcome support. For the first time the Hoffmanns laughed. Blood spattered aprons were put to soak, and Inge crawled into her loft, remembering to draw up the ladder after her.

Dawn came quickly. This day Inge rose without needing to be called. She found the Hoffmanns sitting dourly at the kitchen table. Without a greeting, their eyes rose simultaneously to meet hers.

"The war is over," Herr Hoffmann announced, standing up like a man with a lighted match among explosives. "Imagine, we surrendered. I just heard it on the radio." Then he hitched up his pants and went downstairs to the cellar to check his rabbit hides, stretched on boards.

Frau Hoffmann lifted her head, jutting her chin forward, and addressed Inge. For once her voice was mechanical and atonic. "Our son will be home soon, and then we won't be able to use you anymore."

Inge panicked. She was being thrown out. "I speak English. Maybe I can get a job with the Americans." The horrendous prospect of again needing food loomed, obliterating the importance of Herr Hoffmann's news.

Frau Hoffmann shrugged. "You can sleep in the loft until you do. I'll expect a few chores."

Suddenly the real impact of Hoffmann's message hit like a sledgehammer. His solemn words reverberated with an echo that would not stop. Long thin fingers combed through her hair in steady unconscious sweeps as if she were mindlessly separating flax. She looked transfixed, oblivious to everything around her.

Frau Hoffmann studied her, thinking that the girl looked as if she were going to cry any minute. But then, she often looked that way, thought Frau Hoffmann, scraping the last of her husband's uneaten breakfast into a bowl for the pigs. When she looked down at Inge, tears were flowing from the girl's face.

Her tears were tears of joy, but Frau Hoffmann did not know that.

Then Frau Hoffmann dropped her wooden spoon and the bowl on the table, and eased her large frame into her husband's chair. She covered her face with her hands and began to sob.

Inge looked at her aghast. Blessed defeat had come. Her son was safe, but this fool woman didn't have the sense to rejoice.

The scene would stay with her always, indelibly etched upon her memory. On the kitchen wall a carved wooden cuckoo popped out of his clock to chirp his sharp toots that seemed to trumpet a great new beginning of the world. Ravishing sunlight streamed through a small window and bounced about on the white tiles. The broken figure of a woman slumped over the disorderly table made a shocking scene. It was memorable as if etched in stone. One day she would have to paint it all—except there would be no way to portray such stupidity and misbegotten grief.

Art should not need explanatory titles, thought Inge, looking down at her hands and noting that it had been years since they had held a pencil or a paintbrush. She felt thoroughly incompetent. Then she thought of how long it had taken her brain to react to Herr Hoffmann's news. The awful war was over, and she had only thought of her own stomach. *Mein Gott,* if I'm not brain dead, what kind of animal have I become? she asked herself.

In any event, it was important to hide her feelings from the Hoffmanns. There was no point in unnecessarily antagonizing them. As soon as possible she would have to walk to Berchtesgaden to try to get work translating, but no longer would she be in danger of getting strafed on the highway.

She would have to wash her hair, and she hoped that she could still get her feet into her shoes. She was still a woman. Then it occurred to her that never again would she have to say, "Stay alive" and felt a little better.

CHAPTER THREE

For months May had been familiarizing himself with the details of Hitler's home and the Berghof compound. Martin Bormann had spent years buying up farms, chapels and small buildings that together made up two and one-half square miles behind barbed wire. Inside this fence were a dormitory and barracks, a hotel for prominent guests and a smaller hotel for lesser Nazis, a complex for employees, a vast garage, and palatial residences for himself, Herman Göring, Joseph Göbbels, Robert Ley, and finally, Hitler's own public residence. All the homes were joined by tunnels. Hitler's home also was known as the Berghof. May knew the two publicized sitting rooms contained a Bardone nude, a Titian nude, Anselm Feuerbach's *Nana*, an early Spitzweg and a Steinle; all bought by Hitler himself.

Now, as if in a dream, he was there.

Although Hitler's poor taste in art was laughed at abroad, May felt certain the private rooms, tunnels, and possibly the Eagle's Nest atop the Kehlstein contained much more. Hitler hardly would have flaunted stolen art before the eyes of Neville Chamberlain, King Boris of Bulgaria, the Duke and Duchess of Windsor, Charles Lindbergh, Benito Mussolini and other leaders who visited the Berghof. The plundering of museums was well established, but there was no record of where the art ended up. Gobelins were known to have hidden motion picture screens, deep Persian rugs had covered floors, and spectacular Austrian chandeliers had been described. All led credence to May's suspicions that there was more art around than Albert Speer ever saw. Was anything left, and if so, where was it?

The complex looked like a moon landscape. The roads, once

macadam, were pitted rocks and dirt. Huge perilous craters were filled with green water. Shattered brown tree trunks leaned in every direction. Wreckage and ragged green metal sheets used for camouflage were strewn everywhere. Comically the remains of basement garages, now holes in the ground, often still bore 'No Smoking' signs.

The three-story lesser hotel, the Platterhof, was in usable shape. Here, in low-ceilinged, cell-like rooms, the 101st Airborne was now housed. However the French had destroyed many of the furnishings, smashing windows, and making off with china, silver, glassware and all the wall decorations. It combined to make a picture May would never forget, seemingly a perfect storybook ending for a regime noted for destruction.

Bombs had spared only one building, the Eagle's Nest, topping the Kehlstein pinnacle, now towering above May. It was probably too hard to hit, he mused, gazing skyward. He moved on to what was left of Hitler's house. Here a gum-chewing GI was reading a comic book while guarding Hitler's rubbish-filled entry. To keep warm he had a small fire burning briskly on the marble floor. Seeing an officer, he jumped to his feet and saluted. May explained his business.

"Hitler's main living room is there," he said pointing. "When you go upstairs, don't fall on the steps. They're about to collapse."

The salon was a monstrous, dismal, fire-blackened cavern, also marble-floored. One end, where Hitler's famous 30 X 12 foot plate glass window had stood, was carpeted by a mass of splintered and melted glass. He noted that the fireplace still held a few decorative tiles depicting Storm Troopers carrying a banner, but most of the tiles had been chipped out by souvenir hunters. An adjoining room might have been a billiard room, he decided, finding a few scraps of green felt. Not a smidgen of art remained.

"Some mess," May said to the GI, conscious of looking bug-eyed.

"You get used to it, sir."

The soldier showed him how to ascend the loosened marble steps leading to Hitler's sleeping quarters above the living room. "Move fast, sir. They could give way."

Having managed the leap safely, he moved from the spacious hall to Hitler's bedroom. There was nothing left of the furnishings. They had burned and congealed with dust and more melted glass. A great hole in the wall afforded a view of Austria. Hitler's modern bath, tiled in emerald green, was relatively intact.

Eva Braun's adjoining suite still carried a few vestiges of furniture— an overturned rosewood desk and matching chair now splintered. Neither piece had been valuable, being baroque reproductions with too-shiny varnish and a smattering of inlay. A crystal chandelier, missing most of its prisms, hung precariously from one wire. A cold draft fluttered scraps of paper in one corner. With every step broken glass crunched under his feet. It seemed to May as if he had stepped into some surrealist film sequence. From a blown out window he could see the mauve and pewter sky above leaden shadows that was Austria. Shivering, he moved on.

In the next room Eva Braun's bed was still there, the mattress sprouting springs. Her bath was tiled the same as Hitler's, but included a bidet. Of her personal belongings none remained except boxes and boxes of Germany's best brand of sanitary napkins.

Having seen enough, May went back downstairs.

"The Germans' eyes popped out when they saw what was hoarded here," the guard volunteered. "Dozens of cases of food, candy, wines, liquors and linens, all have been hauled off to the Berchtesgadener Hof—it's the officer's mess now. But there are still plenty of unexplored tunnels."

"I'll pretend I'm a old mine hand."

"I don't envy you, sir."

"Thanks for your help." May had seen enough for one day.

A figure loomed. "Here's my relief."

May returned his salute.

*   **   *

"You must have seen the mess," said the colonel, bellied up to the bar. "You look as if you're ready to turn around and go home."

May shook his head resignedly. "It's discouraging. It looks as if I wasted a lot of time preparing for a job that doesn't exist anymore. But the alternative, concentrated party-going in Washington, probably would have been a bigger waste."

"Don't give up. There are the tunnels—said to be miles of them, but they may be booby-trapped." The colonel frowned. "Be careful."

"Yes, sir," he replied emphatically.

The colonel introduced arriving officers. "Bridges heads Military Police, Richards is Quartermaster, Cohen is Military Intelligence, an oxymoron if I ever heard one, and Walkowsky heads the Motor Corps. Kempe and Hass, here, work with the local government. I'm ready to eat. Why don't you join me?"

"Delighted, sir." Having politely acknowledged the introductions, he followed Rasmussen to a table.

"We found things pretty much as we expected. You'll soon adjust."

"At least we officers can eat like civilized people," said May, looking around at the charming hotel.

"Have you had a chance to read the directive, Morganthau's Plan for Germany, JCS 1067, that I handed you?"

"I did and I'm not excited about it, if I can be frank."

The colonel raised a kindly eyebrow. "I don't mind telling you, I feel bitter about the Germans-—and most of my reasons are dead American soldiers—and what these people have cost the world. I also see an awesome job for the next five years."

May chuckled. "I doubt that I'll be here that long."

Rasmussen ignored May's remark. "As you read, the plan is designed to shut down German industry—an impossible scheme economically. We're in farm country now, and the Germans here will eat. There are millions in cities who won't. Even if we get farm production up, there won't be a work payroll to buy food. We're shipping their machinery to the Russians. The Germans will starve or the American taxpayers are going to have to feed them. In the chaos Germany could go communist. I don't want to win the war and lose the peace."

Now assured that the colonel's opinion coincided with his own, May felt his spirits rising. Still, this was only one small part of Germany, one command in many. Rasmussen and May ordered their dinners and the wait afforded time for May to air what he knew. "In Washington I dated the daughter of a general. Of course I can't mention his name. She confided some scuttlebutt she'd picked up from her father,"

"Huh?" burped the colonel. "Go on."

"Well, as you know, Roosevelt had an unprecedented number of Jewish brains in his immediate circle: Henry Monganthau, Jr., Felix Frankfurter, Bernard Baruch, Benjamin Cohen, Samuel Roseman, *etc.*

Naturally, the Jews began doing everything they could to get their people out of Europe. Unfortunately, our State Department acted just about as anti-Semitic as it could." May paused, grimacing. "No doubt, through delays and simple red tape, Assistant Secretary Breckinridge Long's mean-spirited obstructionist policies spelled a death sentence for thousands of Jews. But the fact of the matter was—and it bothered a lot of Army people, not just Jewish Americans—that there wasn't much that anybody could do, because the great majority of European Jews were inaccessible, trapped behind Hitler's lines. Morganthau must have raged. Understandably, his hatred of the Germans knows no bounds. But until today, I never read his plan."

"The plan also reflects the current mood of the American people—fed up with war," replied May, "but in '39 they couldn't stop it."

Soon their dinners arrived and May attacked his pork chop, while the colonel continued to air his opinions. "Our allies are no damn help. The Brits are out for Germany's markets, and after their bombardment, their covetousness is understandable. They're lucky fools. Even Julius Caesar got a headache thinking about them." The colonel dropped his fork in a gesture of despair. "The Russians are thoroughly untrustworthy. All the same, May, our personal feelings have to be put aside. As Occupational Forces, we have to obey Washington's directives, dreamed up by a bunch of politicians whose bread and butter comes from a bitterly bereaved public, wanting further revenge. Not one of those bozos in Congress has to live here. JCS 1067 is vengeful, petty and mean-spirited."

May glanced at the officers behind the colonel, whose expressions, almost jocular, indicated that they had heard the same lecture, and although they may have been in accord, they didn't much care. May felt that minor parts of the plan, such as forbidding the passing of potato peelings or used coffee grounds to the Germans were downright ridiculous.

"Colonel, I spent the best year of my life here. My big loss was that I couldn't marry a German girl—I hope she's wandering someplace now because that would mean that she's alive. And seeing the destruction everywhere, I'm about ready to say that everybody has suffered enough—excepting, of course, the Nazi sadists whom we'll prosecute. I simply don't believe in vengeance. The death of six million Jews can never be balanced. It's that simple. Justice for all is a crock, except in a limited legal sense. Let's hang the leaders and try to build a democratic Europe."

"I'm glad you're with me, regardless of the reasons. I spent a great year here myself. It came out a little differently; I married the girl."

They laughed in sudden camaraderie.

"They had so much and blew it," said May, wistfully. Dozens of small memories crowded in on him, including the great stabbing pain that losing Inge inflicted. He thought he had outgrown the loss, but being back in Germany had brought her back so clearly that, once again, he could feel the forgotten heartache. Loneliness almost swamped him.

Later that evening Major Robert Street strode into the club, gloating over his position of authority over May, pretending to take an exaggerated amusing stance. The opportunity had been a long time coming, he thought. Finally he could settle a score dating back to the *Savoia*. He was now certain that May had been the one who had locked him in his stateroom. Since then, May had continued to snub him. Now, sitting in the catbird seat, he was in a position to enjoy sweet revenge.

"Good evening, sir," said May. Bolstered by several scotches and his easy rapport with the colonel, he was unwilling to hide his chagrin. "You might have told me in Berlin that I'd be dancing to your tune."

Street smiled smugly. "I want to squeeze as much satisfaction as possible out of life's small pleasures."

"That figures."

Street's face took on a sudden hard cast. "Also I'd like to put something straight. Just because we're old friends, don't think that's going to cut any ice. I'll expect you to follow orders in line with Army regulations. Is that clear, Lieutenant?"

May groped for a response that would conceal the slow burn Street always managed to light, but finding none settled on, "Perfectly, Major," offered with an infuriatingly broad grin. The thought of knuckling under to Street's command foretold an intolerable professional relationship. The pleasant relationship with the colonel was unlikely to help, the chain of command being what it was.

"By the way," said Street, "there's a non-fraternization rule in effect."

"I've read JCS 1067. But if we're going to starve six million Germans plus dismantle their factories, maybe it's just as well we can't talk to them. I'd be at a loss for words."

"There's a sixty-five dollar fine for speaking to a German except in the line of duty. As an officer you could be subject to general court-martial. GIs simply get a reprimand, and the fine, of course. I won't have much sympathy for those under me in this respect."

"Major," breathed May, "the Germans will look on non-fraternization with inexpressible relief, but we are going to get sick of playing with ourselves."

"God, how true!" piped up someone from the laughing group who had heard May and Street's conversation. It marked a round May had won.

May put down his glass. "If you'll excuse me, I'm going to hit the sack." It was after hours, and he was unwilling to endure Street's presence a minute more than he had to.

May could sense when to depart or when to hang up the telephone that often put others on the defensive. He had learned this in Washington from a tipsy commanding officer. "Always be the one to hang up," he had told him. At the time it seemed an odd tip, but he soon saw that it worked. People seemed to respect an ability to walk away from a sticky wicket.

Later, after reading for an hour and then brushing his teeth in the BOQ, he heard from Walkowsky that Street had sulked until he retired. "Tell me," May queried, "how do you go about meeting German girls and avoiding the no-speaking rule?"

"It's simple. Write a note," Walkowsky replied, rolling his eyes. "But don't think I know anything about cupid's ways. I'm a total innocent."

They laughed.

There were complications. A curfew for Germans was in effect, which kept them in their homes after sundown. Still, soon after May arrived in Berchtesgaden, illegal kitchens were already being set up. German women were willing to prepare food secured from mess kitchens (and tote some home). May quickly saw that when people are hungry, it did not take long before the exigencies of the times took precedence over directives from Washington. The GIs, being friendly men, chaffed under the unnatural restrictions.

May was billeted with three other officers in a four-bedroom house, which the owners had been given twenty-four hours to vacate. There it was: losing a war is costly. May remembered high school history courses in which the painful results had been hidden under a blanket of phrases about reparations-paid-to-victors in millions of dollars and cents with no explanation of the real meaning. Maybe if politicians knew that the reparations would also mean losing their own homes, they'd think twice before starting a war, he decided.

The best houses, invariably owned by the biggest Nazis, were the first taken. The dispossessed moved out into whatever they could find—barns, empty garages, attics, and cave-like bombed out structures. *Raus dem Haus*, or get out of the house, was all the incorrect German any soldier needed. They had had enough of sleeping in trucks, shaving in helmets and bathing in cold streams.

In moments May felt numbed by the harshness, but he had only to imagine himself in the range of a Krupp cannon, having fought his way across France, to understand the way the Fighting Army felt. Now a greatly-reduced-in-size Occupation Army was taking over, chiefly made up of reenlisted fighting forces.

During the war, sometimes May had dreamed about Norbert Buth, and in a recurrent nightmare he had had to fight him. When the dreams stopped, he knew that Buth was dead.

* ** *

The first tunnel May entered was off Hitler's pantry. It went down five flights of stairs. At the bottom to the left was a room filled with machine guns, what GIs called 'burp-guns,' rifles and pistols. Boxes of ammunition reached the ceiling. In the corridors in darkness only a slow drip of water from the ceiling could be heard over his footsteps. Fearing that he might become lost, he turned back. To survive the war only to meet one's end in one of Hitler's dungeons seemed the height of folly.

Still the paranoia of the moles that had so boisterously ruled Germany in 1938 flabbergasted him. All the time Hitler was buffaloing the world with his bravado, his slaves had been digging. To think of this was to remember Inge. She had been the gauge by which he had measured women ever since, and none had stood up as well in comparison. Now that he was back in her territory, hearing German on the street and looking at buildings bathed in the natural, bluish, eerie light so characteristic of the land, he felt haunted by her. He might have missed her had it not been for a tattered red sweater that caught his eye.

Inge was crossing the street below the Rathaus when May went for mail and happened to look out a window, down to the side walk, half full of people. Spotting a girl he thought was her, he raced from the room and down the stairs taking two steps at a time. In the street in a moment of panic, he lost her. She had disappeared from view when she ducked into a doorway. Then like a miracle, he saw her again. For a few minutes he held back, still fearful she might be someone who closely resembled Inge. He drew closer, strangely relishing the moment, completely forgetting that speaking to her was against regulations. When sure, he stalked her like a hunter, knowing the assurance of happiness that he had not felt in years.

He stepped around people, bumped into people, ignoring people in a frenzy of excitement, bound only by her trail. He overtook her as she turned from the main street, climbing a small cobblestone street, a slip of paper in hand.

"Inge, Inge," he cried, his voice too high, shocking him by its strangeness. She turned and recognized him. A startled, reticent smile crossed her face.

"Herr May," she whispered, drawing on the formal address to summon courage. Then she bit her lip, constraining her very mixed emotions.

"Thank God, I've found you. Are you all right?" That sounded weird, he knew, but he didn't know what else to say. His hand reached for her arm, and then lost force as her formal address and pained expression sank in. He had not remembered that her eyes were so large, nor had he ever seen her so thin. She had always been so... elegant.

"Almost. A little war-torn, but aren't we all." Feeling awkward, she gestured like a tour guide toward the people in the street around them. Having May find her so impoverished, so at the end of her rope was unnerving. Then she also remembered that she was deeply in love with Kurt Montag, and another great wave of confusion swamped her.

On his part May had never envisioned a public reunion marked by the confusion that also smote him. That she had survived someway he had felt quite sure of, but he had never anticipated this initial distancing.

He felt awkwardly stymied. Swiftly, as a blow from a hammer, he realized that they were now two vastly different people. She was a waif, bringing home to him the disaster of a continent.

"I looked for you in Berlin. Gretchen Baumgarten was my last resort," he murmured, still too overcome to have found poise. "Where are you living now?"

"In a hay loft."

"Where?"

"On a farm on the road to Köngssee, only a couple of kilometers from here."

"Are you looking for work?"

"Yes, indeed."

"Let me see what I can do. Here's my address. Come tomorrow. I'll have arranged something. Someway…"

An MP slipped between them. "Sir, you are subject to a sixty-five dollar fine for speaking to a German."

As if growing horns, May drew himself up and turned on the soldier. "This is a person I would give six-hundred dollars to speak to. She's no Nazi, and I intend to see her hired by the American Army. Write this incident up if you must, but I promise you that I'll see you eat the ticket. This conversation is in the line of duty!" He spoke with such unexpected anger, and seemed so sure of his convictions, the MP backed down.

"I'm sorry, sir. I didn't understand your business."

"Then walk the other way," May growled.

Being new to such a situation, and unwilling to take on an adversary with State Department rank so sure of what he was doing, the MP did. Apparently this was not the usual pickup as he had assumed.

"I believe you have forgotten to salute," said May, curtly.

The MP obliged, and May returned his salute. As soon as the MP walked away, he turned back to Inge with an embarrassed laugh. "This may not always work so well, but find me or I'll find you. That's a promise."

She blushed. She had never seen May behave in such a way. He had changed, but so had she. He saw that she was close to being in rags. Her hair hung limply around her face. Her topaz eyes were lifeless, her skin coarsened. Long bony fingers reached for her throat as if to hold down a deep swallow. He dug for his wallet, pulling out every piece of paper.

"Here. Take this. Get yourself food, whatever. I know there's not much to buy."

Pride rose. "I can't take this…"

"*Mein Gott,* Inge, don't try to explain or make excuses." He didn't know what else to say and settled on, "The war is over," which didn't make much sense. Suddenly, looking at her, he knew he had to flee. She could not be the one to leave. Going first was his only chance. He fled, and it seemed to him that he had left something precious on the *Bürgersteig.*

* ** *

Luckily, Major Street was not on post. Rejoicing, May sought Colonel Rasmussen.

"I've found an old friend that we must hire. She speaks beautiful English. She's intelligent." He tried to appear calm but inwardly he was agonizing.

"Not a Nazi?"

"Certainly not in 1939." He remembered that she had changed.

"You know, we group these people as to when they joined, because they're all Nazis."

May's heart sank.

"We lump them in five categories: The first are officials of the Nazi government. Next come the pre-1933 Party members, likely to be fanatics. The third group joined between 1933 and 1936, when many believed that the Nazi government would moderate in time. Those who joined between 1936 and 1939 did so knowing the government was planning a war of aggression. And, lastly, we have those who joined because Party membership was forced on them. Job promotions were limited to Party members. It spared people embarrassing on-the-street confrontations."

May swallowed hard, having just come from one.

Rasmussen flipped a pencil, meeting May's eyes. "I would advise your friend not to lie, because there are records. Where these are incomplete, there are other Germans quick to tattle. It's a dog-eat-dog world."

May listened impatiently, suffering over the possibility that

Rasmussen would turn him down, but at the same time, being aware of the limb that he was climbing out on. Six years had passed. What had Inge become in six years? Was she married? Helping her could be complicated. Helping her illicitly could be next to impossible. "I feel that I must do something to help the girl. She's decent. Now she's a wraith."

Rasmussen was painfully long in replying. It was easy to surmise what he was thinking. An old girlfriend could spell a pack of trouble for his new officer, and Major Street was away. Hiring should be done on the basis of ability and political leanings, not connections. Finally weakened, he said, "I'll talk to her."

Relieved, but not reassured, May thanked him. For the time being he had done all he could.

He had known in his bones that one day he would see Inge again. Through the years he had imagined dozens of little scenes, and thought that he was prepared for at least one, which was not the case. He had visualized seeing her in a park where she was watching her children play—no, she would be watching someone else's children. In another scenario he had attended an art show of her works, where she was graciously acclaimed. Once they had met on a ski slope—she had fallen. The outcome of these little plays depended upon his mood at the time. Some had happy endings. In others he had walked away from her, uncaring.

He had not prepared for this, the most logical of them all.

* ** *

That May and Inge would meet again in Berchtesgaden was no idle coincidence. May was there because the Command hoped and believed the stolen art would be there. Inge was there waiting for Montag, because it was as close as she could get to Montag's ancestral home. Also, Berchtesgaden had an office of the Red Cross. Through the Red Cross the Germans were often able to locate missing family members and friends when local governments had completely broken down. Not to have run into each other in this little burg could hardly have happened.

CHAPTER FOUR

With Rasmussen's promise to see Inge, deciding he was ravenously hungry, May carried his memory of Inge to the club.

"Hey, May, come over here and settle something. Who won the World Series in 1932?" asked a voice from the present.

"The New York Yanks. Why?"

"See, I told you," Richards smirked, playfully poking at Walkowsky. Richards, a lanky dark-haired man of thirty, contrasted sharply with Walkowsky, a great lumbering Pole. Basic training and uniforms had considerably enhanced both; they did have good faces.

"I'm no authority on baseball, but I remembered that for all the wrong reasons. It changed my life, " replied May.

"How's that?" asked Walkowsky, always the one to bite.

"I had run away from my grandparents' farm. I'd walked about twenty miles and came to a general store. About six farmers were sitting out front listening to the Series. It would be the last game if the Yankees won. Well, I had to crap. Every decent pause I'd run to the outhouse. It was always occupied. By the time the game was over, I was almost doubled over in pain. There was a woodlot in sight, and I headed for it. I ripped down my pants and let go. Then I discovered I had shit all over my suspenders. I was so demoralized; I changed my life plan. I decided to make money so that this would never happen to me again. That meant walking back and continuing my education. I haven't struck it rich, but I haven't shit on myself since either."

They laughed.

"About that time Jimmy Foxx was really hitting them," said Walkowsky. "I was a coal miner. I worked my way out of the pits playing football for Penn State. Don't think I didn't have the shit kicked out of me a few times. Now here we are lording it over the cabbage heads. That's life. Win a few, lose a few."

"By the way," Richards warned. "We're going to be seeing a lot of loonies in this so-called 'designated rest and recreation center.' They're already coming in. These men are close to the breaking point, having seen too much front-line action. Don't make any quick, unsuspected moves around them. Last night one guy flipped out in the non-com mess, broke a glass and went for his buddy's ribs. He was hauled off crying and howling, "He wuz my best friend.""

The leaded windows of the Berchtesgadener Hof, made up of hundreds of round pieces of glass like the bottoms of coke bottles, were beginning to blur. May had not been keeping track of his drinks. "I've got to hit the sack. Goodnight all." He wasn't frightened over the loonies, but the talk of baseball had been a welcome distraction from a great feeling of uncertainty that had overwhelmed him from the moment he found Inge.

* ** *

The last person whom Inge expected to find in Berchtesgaden was Herr May—not that she hadn't thought of him often—with American soldiers everywhere. He looked older, more serious, and those remarkably vital, but now hardened eyes seemed to have gathered her in with more force than she had remembered him displaying. This was something she felt unequipped to deal with. The encounter resurrected the past with all its grief just when her life was finally coming into bloom. Kurt Montag had not been listed as *gefallen,* and she would soon be marrying him to live happily ever after.

On the other hand, the timing was fortuitous. The need for food and a roof loomed. When almost everyone was hungry or homeless, few could afford to be charitable to strangers. May's generosity might solve her immediate problems, but meeting him had brought back a time warp. Did he see that they were no longer the same people? Her heart became a tiny hammer.

She sat waiting to talk to the colonel. It seemed strange to see Americans in uniform, administering government in offices that only a few weeks ago had been populated by Nazi bureaucrats. Her existence now hung on a fine thread in the American hands. "The colonel will see you," announced a sergeant. "He's very busy," he warned.

Rasmussen looked up as she entered and nodded. "Please take a chair."

His eyes were upon her. They were like hazelnuts, just taken out of the mouth, wet and glistening. Totally disarmed, prepared opening lines were forgotten under their penetrating gaze. She felt her words would have to travel through a blinding storm.

"I'm good at lettering signs," she blurted. "My last job was in a department store. I could letter a sign in less then five minutes, usually saying what we were out of or that the price was going up... or something..."

Then she started to shake.

Rasmussen felt a rush of pity he could hardly contain. He sat back in his chair, watching her as if absorbed in a melodrama played out on a stage. Then he suddenly remembered his lines. "I'll give you a job. With it will come a room and one meal a day. There will be no fraternization with American soldiers, not even with your friend May, or I will certainly fire you."

She did not doubt him for a minute.

He forgot all about asking if she had been a Nazi.

For the first time in months she would be sure of eating and sleeping in a bed. Paper work followed. Later that day the billeting officer placed her in a German home, one judged substandard because it lacked a bathtub. In the billeting the daughter of the house lost her room to Inge and was relegated to a couch. Much as she would have loved to thank May, to do so would risk everything.

The Müllers considered themselves lucky. They could have lost the whole house. And working for the Americans, Inge might be able to bring home some unobtainable items, such as soap, toilet paper, light bulbs, disinfectants, a little sugar, or a leftover cup of coffee... if she liked them. Everything weighed on that.

Inge was well aware of their position. Their faces were transparent portraits of this particular time and station. Even before the war they were poor, but now they were not also homeless, and they considered themselves lucky *dafür*.

At the flea market, with May's money, she found a couple of secondhand dresses and a clumsy pair of wedge shoes. She also brought home some food. That night she hardly slept.

Work began. She saw May in corridors, and her eyes widened in fear that he would speak to her, threatening her existence; but he didn't, even though he seemed to hunger for greater contact, appearing more often than work could have demanded, scanning her face for words. The day she was hired, he went to the post exchange and bought whatever he saw that she could use: toothpaste, shoe polish, soap, aspirin, deodorant and a package of six men's handkerchiefs. The next day he carried the bag around until, on the street, he silently handed it to her. Recognizing the fright, like that of a trapped animal, he fled as if that would set her free. Clearly, the temper of her life was too harsh to further complicate.

Accepting the little package, she stood straight, looking grave in the afternoon light. The pink flowers rose and fell on her print blouse as she swallowed hard. Then without daring to look at her hoard, she hurried home.

May went back to his desk, angrily slamming drawers, and snatching a pen and his sunglasses. Putting his mind on automatic pilot, he grabbed his cap and, cursing Army regulations, headed for the bar.

*   **   *

May could be thankful for only one thing: Major Street was not on post. If Street knew that Inge was the Fraulein May had known in Berlin, he would fire her, even if he had to lie to do it. Street, anxious for results, had been pushing him without the concern that others had shown over the possible danger in the tunnels. He was also burdening him with reports when there was nothing to report.

A few days later in the club May sought out Kempe. "You're of German extraction, and tonight I'd like to talk to someone who is not still fighting the war."

Kempe laughed, "Is non-fraternization getting to you?"

May nodded.

"My grandparents were German. I grew up in Madison, then went to Purdue. I guess that's where I really grew up." Kempe sipped his rum.

Then May asked again, wanting to be sure his question had sunk in, "Then you're not still fighting?"

"You're almost intimidating, but the truth is, I'm fighting the peace. What are you doing?"

"At Street's insistence I've started work on Bormann's tunnel. It begins on a hillside beside a blockbuster crater about twenty feet deep. I've almost fallen in just getting to the shaft. There's a German 'burp-gun' by the entrance. One room is full of linen: tablecloths, napkins, sheets, pillowcases, feather comforters and men's nightgowns." May chuckled and continued, "Another room is full of Meissen. GI tourists have ripped a lot open. They really hit the wine. Further along the passage is another room loaded with furniture."

"I hear those tunnels are like catacombs."

"Some are, some aren't, but there are miles and miles of them. The whole city could have lived down there. There are apartments with playrooms for children, kitchens and servants' quarters. I've beamed lights down corridors that seem endless. I'm hindered by the fact that we haven't got a ventilating system going. Also some tunnels, like Göring's, may be ready to blow up. There has to be art down there by the crate. Göring would have had the best."

"How about water damage?"

"Possible. Do you know how to build a robot? That's what I need."

"Send in a couple of Nazis." Kempe swirled his drink.

"I would if I could. Haven't you heard? They've all disappeared."

They laughed.

"All joking aside, why not put out a directive to all commands, asking for as-built plans? There must be blueprints someplace, as well as people who know the tunnels." Kempe wanted to help.

"The blueprints were burned. What wasn't burned has been bombed to hell and back. Only the Devil and I could make use of those plans. But if you think a directive might help, cut the stencil. Really valuable stuff would have been well hidden. I'm sure that Göring thought one day that he'd inherit the earth. Then he'd get the stuff out. He would not have told anyone what he had."

Kempe faced May squarely. "Be careful."

"Are you married, Kempe?"

"My wife works in Washington."

"No wonder non-fraternization doesn't bother you."

"Hell, it's a godsend," he replied, chuckling.

Kempe had set May thinking.

The Müllers' half-timber house where Inge lived sagged under the weight of two hundred years of living. Tall men would have had to duck to pass through doors. Hooks lined one wall of the small entry where three worn but well-mended coats hung. The small living room was partitioned from the kitchen by a tiled furnace. The kitchen held a small sink, a few cupboards, and a heavy oak dining table under which the family had slept during air raids. Off the kitchen was a small toilet room. Upstairs there were two bedrooms each with a bed, dresser, night table (holding a candle), and an armoire for clothes. Wash bowls and pitchers stood on the dressers, there being no running water upstairs. The ceiling was not plastered, exposing the light wooden framework holding up the roof tiles. Diamond-like specks of sunlight shone through; still, the high-pitched roof did not leak. The partitioned cellar that once held coal, bins of potatoes, onions, barrels of apples, crocks of sauerkraut and lines of hanging sausage, now contained only drying laundry near two galvanized washtubs.

Frau Müller explained to Inge that they once had chairs in the living room, but they had sold them. "We didn't use them," she said proudly. Once plump, now like a little night moth, she flitted through long days with wary sureness, seldom taking time to sit on the lumpy cushions that softened the heavy kitchen chairs. She was always cleaning something. Religiously, once a week, using water and old newspapers, she washed the small many-paned windows.

"Without soap it's the only way I can keep on top of the dirt," she insisted. Her days were spent waiting in lines, hoping to buy food.

Inge put May's gift of toiletries near the kitchen sink where everyone could use them. When she saw that they went untouched, she protested. "If I hadn't wanted you to use them, I'd have kept them upstairs."

"When they're gone, do you think he'll give you more?"

"I'm sure he'll try to, but, of course, it's against regulations."

Frau Müller wilted visibly. The regulations were stymieing. "Someone may come in and see these things."

"Then put them out of sight. Don't worry about the MPs. They won't come here."

"But the neighbors?"

171

Ah, yes, thought Inge. They could be a problem. "Then you must hide the stuff." She left Frau Müller to the skillful plotting of her thoughts, wanting no more questions and no more fears.

Hans Müller stirred them. He was short and burly, not yet thin because he was always served first. "What does your soldier friend do?" he asked, dropping into a kitchen chair. Obviously, the gift had been well hashed over.

"He works in the tunnels looking for stolen art," she replied, accepting the interrogation as the man's due.

His eyes widened. "They're booby trapped. Does he know?"

"The colonel thought they might be, so he's been alerted. Do you know where these traps are?"

"*Ach,* perhaps, but only a few."

She stood leaning against the tile furnace, waiting for him to say more, full of questions while some great well of discomfort in her rose. Yet he sat there, drumming his fingers, waiting for food. "Would you be willing to talk to the Americans?" she asked.

"*Ach! Warum?* A few weeks ago these people were trying to kill me."

"Hansi, *menschlich sein.* The war is over. You gain nothing feeling that way," piped up Frau Müller, looking disapprovingly at her husband, then at Inge in a womanly exchange.

"Hush, woman! I feel the way I feel, and that's that!"

Now thoroughly frightened for May, Inge went to her room. She could report Müller's remarks to Rasmussen, but that did not seem the intelligent thing to do. Müller could deny everything. "What stupid ignorant clods," she muttered, utterly disgusted. There was nothing to do but write May.

"*Dear Friend,*

"*It is common knowledge that the tunnels are mined. Also you have never been properly thanked for my job, the roof over my head, my food, and my existence. There are not enough words.*

"*Love, Inge.*"

After a fitful night, she hurried to the Rathaus to catch May.

He breakfasted at the Berchtesgadener Hof, and from her upper window she could see him approach. Looking down, she could see a dense river of khaki caps, streaming along the sidewalk. Both May and Walkowsky, a good six inches taller than the rest, stood out among the bevy of Americans. A congestion of military vehicles, coughing autos and wobbling bicycles accompanied them. Every morning, as May reached the intersection and as he and Walkowsky stepped down to the cobblestones, he would look up at her. It was a fleeting look that she always caught, like a tossed ball. Then, whether he knew it or not, she could feel that he still loved her. The feeling brought more than a few misgivings and something like selfish comfort. On the other hand, her station had been intended merely to say, "Thank you," nothing more. Immediately she would step away from the window, turning to her drafting board, where she had to quiet an unsure hand before continuing to letter signs announcing the next USO show.

Every few days a new group of entertainers arrived, making a travel circuit through Europe to cheer the troops. Sometimes they included big names like Betty Grable or Bing Crosby, and the GIs could talk of nothing else. Other groups were not top-drawer, but they weren't bad, and they also went from club to club before moving on.

There were additional signs to be made in German concerning forbidden gatherings, the washing of hands, stealing, policy changes, and always denazification. The Americans were fanatical about that.

Some days it rained and the officers walked under umbrellas; then she could not see May's face until he peeked out from under. Today the sun shone brightly, taking with it the night's dew so that everything looked crisply in focus. Across the intersection May appeared. As if commanded, he looked up at her in the same intent way that she looked down. The others moved on, but he stayed still, his face raised, staring.

She leaned forward, her eyes wide with tension. He continued to stare, and their eyes met as if there were no distance between them. Then for the first time, she ducked behind the window jamb while waving to him, a quick summons. She felt a complex guilty concern and didn't dare breathe. Then confidently heartened by the small sign, he strode forward, smiling. She hurried to the head of the wide concrete stairs and watched him take them, two steps at a time. When he reached the top, she pressed her note into his hands, and turned, leaving him to read.

She knew then that there was still something electrifying between them. It seemed as if little flames were dancing around her heart. She looked down at her fingers, the ones that had held her note, now empty and trembling, still feeling his quick touch.

May read her note, having no real concern for himself. Her note hardly carried news, but it was important that she had written. He had given the problem considerable thought since talking to Kempe, and prompted by her warning, determined to act. He went directly to the colonel's office on the second floor. There he heard that the colonel had a meeting scheduled in five minutes. "Five minutes will do fine," he told the sergeant.

"Good morning, sir," said May, saluting. "You warned me of the possibility of the tunnels being booby-trapped, and I've reached a point where I think they may be. I believe Fritz Todt, now dead, would have been responsible for this work. Dr. Todt's position was taken over by Albert Speer, now awaiting trial at Spandau. Intelligence should be able to get Speer to name a person who could shed some light on this."

"An excellent suggestion. Get my sergeant to write up the order. I'll ask the general to sign it. That rank should get some action."

Sensing that his timing was on target, May pressed on. "One other request: Fraulein von Haas and I have scrupulously obeyed the non-fraternization order. Frankly, I need her talents badly—at least for a few hours now and then to draw up diagrams. Can she be made available to me for this work?"

Rasmussen cast him a squint-eyed look, then chuckled. The transparency of his officer's request was only too evident. "I knew this would come up. I'm just sorry I didn't bet on it."

May's heart fell. "You have a reputation for winning bets, sir."

"The race isn't always won by the fastest, or the battle by the strongest. But that's the way to bet."

May laughed. "I can't fault your judgment of human nature."

The colonel scowled and flipped a pencil. "Men are all human beings. They can't be any worse. As to your second request, it's reasonable. Be damned careful. I don't want any talk."

"Thank you, sir," said May, hastily retreating. The sergeant would contact Intelligence at Spandau. As one of the twenty-one top Nazis fighting for his life, Speer would probably cooperate.

May strode into Inge's workroom. He came no nearer than the doorway, and stood there, his eyes finding hers. "Fraulein von Haas, you will be assigned to me for a few hours of work several times a week. I need some diagrams drawn from rough sketches and measurements. The orders will come from the colonel."

He was saying something between the lines, and she was not sure that it was something she could handle. It would lead to closer contact. Frowning slightly, she put down her paintbrush.

Sensing misgivings, May again spoke. "You won't be working in the tunnels—at least until we are sure they are safe."

That they could not discuss things fully made the moment awkward. May turned and looked down the corridor in both directions. Seeing no one near enough to overhear, he added, "You must not think that I would ever damage your life." Then, before she could reply, he left.

He had raised a myriad of doubts. Working together there would be ample opportunity for private talks. After all his kindness, how could she tell him it was over? Now she loved Kurt Montag—whom she walked the streets looking for, who held her future. She knew May had made a promise he could not keep. She also knew that she could not make the same promise. Kurt Montag had not diminished in her thoughts not one bit. She kept telling herself that.

CHAPTER FIVE

To a great extent JCS 1067 reflected American feeling in 1945, stating that no steps toward economic rehabilitation or to strengthen the German economy beyond 1932 levels were to be taken. Of course 1932 levels were Depression levels. However, more mean-spirited details were spelled out, such as kindness to children was held as a misdemeanor; leftover food on plates was to be thrown away—not given to Germans. Even the gift of used coffee grounds was explicitly mentioned and forbidden. To May's dismay, General Eisenhower did not protest these directives. Embittered Jews, Lieutenant Cohen for one, did not either, giving rise to some heated mealtime discussions.

"Disease carrying germs can't tell the difference between an American and a German, and if the Germans get sick on a starvation diet, we will too, Cohen," said May. "Lord knows, I share your resentment over the treatment of the Jews, but our government's present policy is downright dangerous."

"I beg to differ," replied Cohen, sarcastically.

"You forget the Nazi pogroms never held a candle to the Russian ones, and they're now getting the German machinery. Also a lot of good Germans went into concentration camps because they opposed Hitler. Anybody who disagreed was silenced. That's the way they got away with what they did. It was a reign of terror—like in France after the Revolution. The Guillotine, of course, was more merciful."

"May, I'm sorry, but I'm ready to see these people pay for what they've done. You would too, if your family was gassed."

"I had friends destroyed. But if we stick to 1932 production levels as JCS 1067 directs, thousands will starve to death. Hardships of

1932 imposed by the Treaty of Versailles gave us Hitler. Now we are dismantling what little is left of German industry to ship it to Russia. It strikes me as incredible. We just don't learn!"

"May, you're digressing. We have treaties with Russia. Throughout the war they were our allies. The millions they lost, saved our necks."

"Like hell. We saved their necks when their backs were against the wall. They were our allies out of expediency—pure and simple. Russia will continue to see that we butter her bread, until she's strong enough to steal the cow she's milking: Germany." May looked at Cohen and leaned back. What could he say? His voice assumed a kinder tone. "Not only is our policy stupid, but we have no right to starve a lot of Germans to help the Russians. We'd be kinder to take them out and shoot them."

Cohen was unswayed. The suffering of his people had seared his heart. "It would be well deserved."

"Even before this last war, Germany could not produce enough food. It came from Eastern Europe. Now that food will go to Russia. I tell you, the Morganthau Plan—big, deep, dark secret as it is, and for damned good reason—will not be a credit to any American, Jew or Gentile."

"May, politics are not your forte. Stick to art."

"I will, and I'll see that it goes back to where it came from. Machinery is different. It's stamped out of scrap. Let the Germans pay for their crimes with work. If we don't, the American taxpayer is going to wind up paying for the whole stupid mess. The balance of power in Europe has been destroyed, and we'll have the Russians on our throats before we know what hit us."

"You're impossible, May. I suppose you'd arm the Germans again," Cohen argued, throwing May a look of disgust.

"When I consider Stalin, the idea has some merit."

Furious, Cohen moved away, and Richards moved over. "Mind if I take a warm seat?"

"It's more like a hot seat, but I'm glad to see you. You know, I'm sick of seeing suffering." May shook his head. "It's still no excuse to get into discussions like that with Cohen."

Richards cocked an eyebrow. "You sounded as if you were arguing, not discussing."

May shook his head sadly and fingered his glass. "The old Biblical tenet of mercy seems to have no place in this world. I try to keep my mouth shut unless I feel pretty strongly about what I have to say. The best way to win an argument is to be on the right side. But I've lost that 'my country right or wrong' attitude. Look what it did to the Germans."

"I agree, but I don't think you are ever going to teach Cohen anything on this subject."

"The sad thing is, he's not teaching me anything either," quipped May.

* ** *

Within three days May had his maven, *Oberfeldwebel,* or first sergeant Fiske, on the recommendation of Hitler's architect, Albert Speer. Speer was fighting for his life, doing everything possible to cooperate with the military government. Fiske had not designed the tunnel complex but he was fully acquainted with the 'As-built' layout. This was important since May knew the plans had probably been changed many times during the progress of the work, when underground streams and sand pockets were encountered during the tunneling.

Fiske would now be working for the Americans, like Inge, as a civilian employee. On learning that Fiske was a first sergeant, May expected a blustering, tough, no-nonsense individual, so the quiet, mild-mannered, middle-aged man who slipped timidly into his office, hugging an old hat, surprised him.

"Fiske reporting, sir." The German eyed the floor.

May smiled and turned to greet him. "Please take a seat, Herr Fiske. I realize this must be uncomfortable for you."

Obviously nervous, Fiske sat on the edge of his chair.

"We will be looking for art in the tunnels. Get rid of any animosity. The war is over, and although we were the victors, there will be many times when I will have to bow to your knowledge and judgment. It will be imperative that you speak out when necessary. I will regard you as trustworthy until you prove otherwise—then heaven help you."

"I'm sure that will never be the case, *Herr Leutnant.* I'm also relieved that you speak German. I worried about that problem."

May could see that Fiske was beginning to relax. "I've done a little exploratory work. If the art we're looking for is there, it might be booby-trapped. If it is, and if you don't know where and how to look for it, we may both lose our lives."

"I'm aware of some fortifications which may or may not be operable. It was believed that many civilians might need to use the tunnels as shelters, so the tunnels near the entrances were kept clear," Fiske explained.

"I didn't know your leaders were so merciful," murmured May, eyeing papers on his desk. Fiske said nothing.

"We'll be looking for stolen art to return to the Louvre, the Rijksmuseum and Stedelijk Museum in Amsterdam, the Narodni Galerie in Prague, Brussel's *Museee Royal d'Art et Histoire,* Ruben's House and churches in Antwerp, the National Museum in Luxembourg, and to many palace curators, *etc.* These and more have all filed claims. Even the Italians say art walked out of their country in the hands of the Nazis." May leaned forward looking into Fiske's eyes with an eyebrow askew. "The list goes on and on, Herr Fiske. However, every German museum was plundered, and much worse, many thousands of these works were purposely destroyed. But I expect much was hidden here, if only for protection."

Fiske did not seem embarrassed but immediately changed the subject. "Sir, is the ventilating system operating?"

"Poorly. I hope you can help there."

"I'm sure I can. Some of the vents are probably filled with rubble thrown about during the bombing. You have probably discovered there are two distinct systems of tunnels. Martin Bormann refused to be connected to Göring's complex."

"We'll see it all. Pick up your orders and come prepared for hard work. I'll have the mess sergeant pack us lunch everyday which will save a trip into town."

At the mention of food, the German brightened perceptively. In winter the food would do much to insure cooperation. "I'm grateful for the work, sir. I'll do my best."

"I would expect that. Be here at 7:30 if you'd like a cup of coffee and a *Brötchen.*"

"*Danke sehr, Herr Leutnant. Bis Morgen,*" Fiske replied, backing from the room.

"Auf Wiedersehen, Herr Fiske," May called out, feeling like the Pope.

Detained, Major Street overheard only the polite good-byes. He stepped into the office glowering. "I intended to get here for the interview with the German. You seem to have ended it on a friendly note. You could hardly have been exercising your authority in accord with our directives."

"Major Street, my life will be in that man's hands, and if you step into those tunnels, yours will be too."

Street was silenced only momentarily. "We've got to find that art, May. I intend to end my stint in the Army as a general."

"With the war over, promotions won't come along so fast."

"Results will do it—and international acclaim."

"If it's there, we'll find it, but I'm not going to get myself blown up to get a star on your shoulder."

Street's head came up sharply, then he took score. Without May, he'd have to work in the tunnels. For several years now he had noticed that he was uncomfortable in confined spaces. Perhaps it had begun with being locked up on the *Savoia*. He told himself that he was not claustrophobic, but that he must be careful about where he went. Again he was forced to acquiesce to May. "Utilize discretion then," he growled. "I don't want any complaints at staff meetings over fraternization by those under me."

Sensing a chink in Street's armor, May pounced. "Come down with me and take a look at what I'm up against. We needn't go into any areas that haven't been cleared."

Street didn't want to appear frightened but expressed himself as less than interested.

A beautiful ploy immediately took shape in May's brain. "Hundreds of GIs have already been down there. At some point you might have to go down alone. Suppose the General questions you?"

Pushed, Street relented.

Purposefully May selected Hitler's entrance because the five flights of stairs were frightening and sinister. No mine could have seemed so deep. The stairways grew darker and damper as they descended. Street, clinging to the railing as if it were a lifeline, grew more and more uneasy.

"It would be simple to get lost down here." May's flashlight caught Street's face for an instant. It had become a mask of terror. His dark pupils were so enlarged it seemed that no brown irises remained. Beads of sweat dotted his brow. "I can't believe this," Street muttered, extracting a handkerchief to wipe his face. Soon his breathing was coming in gasps, and in a merciful moment May almost regretted his strategy.

They left the stairs and were now in a wide corridor that descended into ultimate darkness. It was like slipping into a black sack of night. Footsteps echoed for blocks.

Street panicked but did his best to cover it. "Ahem, May, I just remembered I have a meeting scheduled. It's a shame to have gotten all the way down here, but now I must turn back. I knew there was a reason I shouldn't have come. Curiosity got the better of me. Now, *GET ME OUT OF HERE.*"

"Sorry, Major." May saw him back to the stairs.

Street left, climbing five flights in record time. May took his time returning, breathing the stale air left by more than one coward. As he walked to the Rathaus—quite a hike—he felt satisfied. Street had revealed a lot. Knowledge of his weakness would prove useful. It was always good to have an ace in the hole.

May had honestly grown tired of waiting around for a knowledgeable assistant. In straightening up the chaos following the surrender, most of his colleagues were overworked. All the functions of city government, which in the course of time had gone to the Nazis, now deposed, had to be kept functional or be resumed in places where they had been slowed to a halt. His own lack of activity, in the face of the pressures his associates were under, was embarrassing. At the same time he was tormented by the presence of Street. May had determined that Street was not nearly so knowledgeable as he pretended. By harassing May into endless meetings and reports that could produce nothing, Street managed to waste more of May's time than the longest day contained. With each day his animosity toward Street grew. He could not speak to Inge, the one person who could assuage his sense of irritation and isolation. The Germans, who could appreciate his distress over their lot, now looked at him as if he wore the Devil's horns. They dared not be openly rude, but his German was so expert that he never missed their innuendoes or the veiled insults that blanketed all their conquerors—

sympathetic or otherwise. More disturbing was the knowledge that, for the Germans, the worst was yet to come.

Americans, British, French, and Russians were settling in for years of occupation. An acute shortage of food was certain. Few Germans could have suspected what lay in the Washington directives, because their tone was so alien to all the pre-conceived notions they carried about the easy-going, free-spending Americans. It was the Russians they feared. Well, they had something to learn, thought May.

Throughout the war he had been grateful that he was not crawling in jungles in the Pacific or being shot at on the beaches of Normandy. Even when dull came to dullest, at least in Washington, there had always been a pretty face around. This was something different; somehow German surrender should have carried feelings of joyousness, and after that, normalcy. Instead he was left with deep feelings of frustration and remorse with no end in sight for the next five years. There was little to do but go to the officers' club and soak up booze. Germany in 1945 was no fun.

* ** *

Meanwhile word spread in the command that only a few miles away a cache of art had been found in a salt mine near Salzburg. A Third Army Monument's Officer, Captain Robert Posey, had received a tip from a dentist in Trier, directing him to a former SS Major, Herman Bunjes, as a source of information on stolen art. Bunjes had worked under Albert Rosenberg, the Nazi Party's philosopher who, coincidentally, had also been in charge of looting museums in France and the Low Countries for Hitler. Bunjes spilled the beans to Posey, who raced to the site.

Much to Street's envy, Posey found everything Bunjes said was true. Crates stamped 'A.H., Linz,' indicated that this cache had been intended for Hitler's proposed museum. The totals were astonishing: over six thousand oils, two hundred and thirty watercolors and drawings, almost a thousand etchings and engravings, as well as sculpture, pieces of furniture, tapestries, and rare books. Works by Michelangelo, Vermeer, Rembrandt, Hals, Breughel, Titian, Rubens, *etc.* had been sequestered 'for their protection' along with Belgium's *piece de resistance,* the eight panels of the *Adoration of the Lamb.*

The site was an ideal one for preservation, being both dry and devoid of temperature fluctuations, but not as easily protected as the Kehlstein in Germany.

While May rejoiced that at least some part of Europe's art treasures had not been destroyed, Street could only accelerate his hounding, if not with words but by glowering at May.

"For Christ's sake, be patient," May implored. "There's still a ton of unrecovered loot that's got to be someplace. We now know they were doing their best to preserve it. And let me remind you, the entrance to the salt mine was protected by six charges of dynamite."

* ** *

May's spirits rose as he recognized the sloppy handwriting of his old friend, Larry Price. He ripped open the thin airmail tissue to read:

"Dear Jimbo,

"Family news is such that old friends come to mind. It's marrying time for the Prices. Geraldine has me lassoed. Bachelor days—and I guess a lot of fun and games—will come to an end September 15, '45. I hope you can be best man. I should have written earlier but I've had my nose to the grindstone converting plants from defense to—happily—peacetime production. Right now Americans need everything.

"As if one wedding isn't enough, Betsy, despite her crush on you, is going to make her screwing legal. Her first fiancé was killed when his Flying Fortress hit a mountain. Mourning did not become Betsy. She's marrying a senator. Can't you see her out there politicking? Senator Barnes is 15 years her senior, but she has already taken about 10 years off him. Mother is in a dither with planning.

"Cable if you can make my wedding. If you can't, I'll get a stand-in. Any old senator will do.

"You'll be invited to Betsy's wedding, but I'll kill you if you show up and blow it! As to my wedding, the red carpet is out.

"Hail Columbia!

"Best, Larry."

The letter was from another world, or at least another planet, thought May. He saw no way to return just as his work was getting going. He cabled Larry congratulations and said his timing was awful and that he couldn't make Betsy's wedding either, because the general couldn't spare him for a single day. The specialist four who took May's cable looked askance at the message, knowing that the general had spent about four days on base during the last month, but he sent it anyway.

"It's a joke, of course," May said irritably.

The following day, having breakfasted and assembled flashlights, chalk, tape measures, paper and lunch, May and Fiske turned to the investigation of the tunnels. During the night Fiske had roughly diagramed locations of the major buildings on the Obersalzberg plateau (including Hitler's home, the Berghof, which had given the compound its name), showing roughly the way the tunnels entered the Kehlstein Mountain and converged.

Fiske explained: "All of the tunnels are entered by stairs. The tunnels cut deep into the mountain and then rise again with other stairs. I don't remember that any of these entrance tunnels had important storerooms. Only domestic hoarding took place there, although some had defense positions where gunners with machine guns could defend the entrances."

"I've spotted some of those."

"The real defense positions are further along. We'll find rooms of ammunition that, I venture, could have been used at the Front—any Front. The ammunition may still be there." Fiske had let this slip, his voice bitter in a moment of frankness. It was the first indication May had that Fiske might not be what he seemed. Then he dismissed the thought, not wanting to form a bad opinion of the man so early on.

Descending the tunnel off Hitler's pantry, May made a chalk mark and sent Fiske ahead with a lantern and measuring tape. Doors had been battered open by scavenging GIs, and goods had been scattered about. They found main generators for power and subsidiary generators for back-ups in rooms stocked with barrel after barrel of oil. There were water systems and pump rooms, which not only were intended to pump fresh water for drinking but also gray water from condensation and other waste. The utility areas had been roughly plastered and painted just as they would have been in homes or factories. The corridors extended for miles and miles.

Fiske knew where to find the panel boxes controlling the electrical supply, but because the generators were not operating, the lights would not either. A series of chimneys bored through the Kehlstein sucked out air, so that although the electrical ventilation systems weren't working, a natural one was, making drafts in the corridors. In some places they could hear the low whistle of the wind over the mountain above them, whipping the ventilating fans.

Some strategically scattered rooms had as many as twenty bunk beds and steel cabinets for clothing storage. "Here the guards were to be quartered," Fiske explained. "You will always find them near defense positions and supplies of weapons and ammunition." Nearby were shower and toilet rooms as well as kitchen and mess rooms.

"Serving here would have been like submarine duty," May noted.

"All of this cost millions of Reichmarks and was never used," said Fiske.

May ignored the lament.

The whole place was so eerie, so frightening in its complexity, and so dark that marauders, either Allied or German, had penetrated only a few square blocks from the two known entrances. With Fiske, who was thoroughly familiar with the tunnels, May felt infinitely more self-assured. He lost all sense of time, and it was 3:30 PM before he realized they had not stopped for lunch. Fiske's stomach was growling audibly.

"You'll have to remind me when it's time to eat. Your stomach is a better clock than mine," said May.

"That's all right, sir. If you don't mind, I'll take my meal home. I can eat it tonight."

"That's fine. I don't relish the thought of eating down here either. Let's check one more room and call it a day." The next door at the dead end of a hall happened to be red.

"Why do you suppose this door is red?" May asked, stepping back and raising the light to see Fiske's face, blank as an empty plate.

"It looks like a warning, but this would be a strange place to booby-trap. It's too far from everything."

May dropped his light to see the ground and spotted a brass ring in a drainage canal. It held one key, which he handed to Fiske. "Do you want to give it a try? It could be dangerous."

"I doubt it. Besides, the steel door would offer protection. The door opens in. Step back, sir."

Fiske cleaned the key on his trousers and inserted it in the lock, which turned hard. Slowly Fiske pushed in the door far enough to admit a flashlight beam. Moving the light along the walls, he said finally, "You won't like seeing this, sir."

"I'm afraid I have to," said May, stepping forward.

Three ghoulish mummified figures, mouths agape, were seated slumped together in a far corner of the small room. They wore the pajama-like uniforms of slave laborers. They had obviously been imprisoned and starved to death. In death their hands touched one another lightly.

"Shut the goddamned door," May barked in horror, "and lock it. I think we've seen enough for today."

For a few minutes they walked silently. May subdued his shock, gathering strength in his knees and breath in his lungs for the trek up and out of there. At the same time he felt amazed at his severe reaction and decided he would have made a lousy soldier. "How long would you guess they've been there?" he asked.

"Years, sir. I always thought this little corridor was empty. It was never lit."

"I'll go back and report. Tomorrow we'll work some other area while someone else gets them out. I feel green around the gills."

"It was unpleasant, wasn't it?" That was all Fiske could offer.

A brisk wind was blowing over the plateau, sending up white dust that stuck to May's damp khakis, which he was too distracted to notice. Street was not on post, so he reported to Rasmussen.

"May," said the colonel. "You look as if you've seen a ghost."

"Three of them. Fiske and I found three dead POWs, buried alive in a chamber."

The colonel blinked. "Well, now that you mention it, I'm not surprised. Incidentally I wasn't trying to be funny. You have white dust all over you."

May took out a handkerchief, wiped his face, and saw what the colonel meant.

"We'll get them out today. How do you like your assistant?"

"He's not what I expected as a German sergeant. He seems shy. I'm sure today's incident embarrassed him."

"He was embarrassed because we found the men—not that the

incident happened in the first place. It sounds as if you got in pretty deep—to find a dungeon."

May left the colonel's office with one small concern; Street would be pissed on missing the chance to report the grisly tidbit himself.

In need of a complete change of scene he went to the PX. For a long time he walked around, grateful for the distraction. He purchased two cans of nuts and a dozen candy bars—Baby Ruths, Mars Bars, and Mounds. Then he found a table of goods just arrived from France, the first shipment of luxury items available to send home as gifts. He bought two wedding presents, Lalique vases, to mail to the Prices, and a bottle of Chanel No. 5 for Inge. Then he went home to bathe for dinner.

May lived in a house in downtown Berchtesgaden. The Nazi owner had modernized two bathrooms that made it choice. It was shared with three other officers, one of whom ran the club and spent most of his time there. His two other housemates, Smith and Winchester, were pilots who also were away most of the time, ferrying top brass around Europe or delivering soldiers badly in need of rest and recreation.

The pilots came home exhausted. Once rested up, they were a little friendlier, but May, not wanting to disturb them, usually said little more than hello and good-bye. He commonly saw them through open bedroom doors, sprawled across narrow beds, half buried under feather *Oberbetten*.   With an end to Air Force duty in sight, both pilots spent most of their daytime waking hours writing wives or applying for jobs with Pan American, TWA, and other airlines. To them Berchtesgaden was a booby-hatch. Landing large troop transports on the small mountain-rimmed field, lent harrowing credence to this belief.

May showered and dressed. Picking up the small bag of purchases for Inge, he went downstairs. Just as he was ready to walk out, Winchester appeared in the kitchen doorway, holding a drink. An aged and honorable amber liquid swirled in his unsteady glass.

"How'ya doin'?" Winchester asked, smiling broadly, more friendly than May had ever seen him. He could hear Smith in the kitchen mumbling something about small ice cubes.

"As well as can be expected," May replied. "Right now I'm in need of food."

"Hold it a sec. We'll come with you," Winchester mumbled, downing his drink. Equally friendly, Smith appeared and greeted May. The pilots donned their caps in the entry, and May felt blown away by the sweet smell of bourbon on their breaths. Both were tipsy, although steady on their feet. Suddenly May remembered the package for Inge in his hand and decided he'd better part company with them.

"You two go on to the club. I'll meet you there in ten minutes. I want to deliver this package."

"We don't mind going with you," said Smith with a burp. The sweet air of Berchtesgaden will do us good. Huh? Win?"

"Sure," Winchester slurred.

"It's a few blocks out of your way. There's no point in my inconveniencing you."

"No trouble at all," said Winchester, pursing his lips in an effort to appear sober, yet now beginning to weave.

Accepting his companions with more reluctance than he wanted to show, May took off rapidly toward Müller's house with the pilots on his heels. As soon as there were a few yard's distance between them, Winchester called out, "State Department, take it easy. We're not running a race." May stopped. The cobblestones were damp and slippery, and the pilots were having trouble staying on their feet.

"I'll go ahead and save you some walking," said May.

"That's not necessary." Striving for momentum, Winchester waved his arms like two propellers determined to stick with May. With pale dismay, May trudged on. He would have ducked out of sight had there been any opportunity, but he was before them like a beacon. As they approached Müller's house, May broke into a sprint. Swiftly he ducked into the small yard and knocked. During the time it took Inge to get to the door, the pilots reached the gate. May thrust the package into her hands and wheeled around to face his companions. In the light of the doorway Inge lingered a second too long. Her prettiness and surprised smile penetrated Winchester's sodden brain, evoking a drunken stir. May raised both hands and shoved the pilots backwards.

"Who is she?" Winchester demanded, eyes alit.

"Fräulein Dinksboomps," May replied crossly. "Now let's get going. I'm hungry."

Winchester reared back. "Whoa...Fräulein Dinksboomps...YOO HOO, Fräulein Dinksboomps!"

"Come on. Let's get the hell outta here. Do you want to cause trouble?" May cautioned.

"Fräulein Dinksboomps… Hallo," continued the yodeler.

May spun around, furious at the commotion. Then Winchester, seeing the faint candlelight in the upstairs bedroom, playfully picked up a little pebble, no bigger than a marble, and although he should not have been able to hit the broadside of a coliseum, the small missile he threw pinged against one of Inge's small windows, breaking it.

May envisioned Inge's horror at the splintering glass. Even to him the shot was like a firecracker going off in his pants. The events of the day had him on short tether, but this was the last straw. His mind paralyzed, he lunged at Winchester with a crack to the jaw, flattening him.

"Christ Almighty!" May swore, looking down at Winchester, not believing what he had done. A flooding sense that this was all a bad dream, a play of nonsense, danced for a moment around his brain, then he looked again at the frightening reality on the ground. "Smith, take his feet," May ordered, reaching under Winchester's arms and heaving his torso upward. Docilely Smith obeyed. Together they staggered out the gate to the street, half dragging the limp pilot. With Winchester's legs in his hands, Smith wobbled like a wheelbarrow with a loose wheel. Then, looming out of the night, came a jeep with two MPs.

"What's going on here?" a trumpeting voice demanded.

"Nothing. Our friend hit a… house… a wall. He walked into it. Help us get him home." Sweat oozing from every pore, May cleaned up his story.

The doubting MPs peered sternly at a hapless Winchester. "I think he should go to the infirmary. His lip is bleeding." Just then Smith dumped his part of the load and belched. "You've been tying one on?" queried one MP, turning to May.

"I'm the soberest man alive," said May.

The two MP heaved Winchester into the jeep, while May helped Smith up. May stood during the ride to the infirmary, clinging to the jeep for dear life. Cold damp air pricked like needles into his face as fear took hold. He had slugged an officer of higher rank. Foreseeing doom, he felt thoroughly beaten. Not only could he be dishonorably discharged, he could be sent to prison.

CHAPTER SIX

1945, Berchtesgaden

May, Winchester and Smith survived the following day chiefly because Winchester and Smith had been too blind-drunk to remember diddley-squat, and other world-shaking events eclipsed their unfortunate evening. On August 6th the *Enola Gay*, a U.S. B-29, dropped an atom bomb on Hiroshima. Three days later another would follow, but the first was enough to convince the world that the United States had such a powerful weapon that for all practical purposes, World War II was over. American troops were ecstatic; the Germans were relieved. They had surrendered just in time.

May sent a glazier to the Müller house to repair the broken windowpane. When no MPs appeared at the door, Inge rightly assumed that somehow May had protected her, and in time she would get an apology. Meanwhile the candy and nuts were judiciously savored—they were almost too rich for her stomach—and satisfied her more than words, which could only be clumsy tools to convey things that worried them both.

The following day Inge was assigned to May, and for the first time in five years, they had a chance to talk leisurely. That bright and shiny morning he walked with her from the Rathaus to the Berghof ruins, a long but pleasant climb.

With the electrical generators working and the area safely cleared of explosives, May and Fiske discovered a small closet of what May considered disappointing minor art—not Old Masters. It was enough to convince Street that May's theory—that the cache could either be the first trace or the last remnant of a great hoard—was correct. May felt the former to be true, insisting, "Major, there's still too damn much missing!" With some reluctance Street permitted May to set up an office in the tunnels. The move gave May a measure of blessed independence. As long as he could feed Street information for his reports, he could keep the man at bay.

"There's so much to say, Inge, I don't know where to start," May said as they walked. "When my housemates attached themselves to me, I didn't realize how drunk they were. After that, I couldn't shake them. I tried, of course. I should have abandoned delivering the candy for the moment, but I felt you were hungry."

She listened with a reluctant smile. "I was frightened. I walked to Berchtesgaden with nothing, and now I don't want to lose my job. I feel as if some star led me here."

"When you selected this area, you must have had something in mind?"

Kurt Montag could not be mentioned. May would not understand. A remembrance of the hunger that was always there made her pause and influenced her reply. "I knew the Russians would take Berlin. I'd learned to expect the worst. It's easier to survive in rural areas." That was all true.

"And you were right. How long did you walk?"

She spoke without ever looking directly at him, lest they be observed. "For weeks. I had to stop along the way to work. Mostly I helped farmers. In all those little farm towns, pigs have to be slaughtered, cows have to be milked, and chickens need to be fed. Only the surrounding fields are fallow for lack of men. I slept in barns and was grateful. It was the smartest thing I could have done. The masses of refugees who came later had a much harder time. A woman walking alone was not a threat."

"My God, Inge...." May remembered his own ride to Berchtesgaden, seeing people trudging the highway. "I wish I could have spared you that. I tried..."

"Oh, don't think I didn't dream of how different life might have been."

"Where's Otto?"

"The Red Cross is searching for him. Somehow I feel he's all right."

She swallowed hard, putting down a rush of emotion. It was the first time in months that she had spoken of her brother to someone who had known him.

"Good. I've thought of him so many times." May kicked a stone. He had looked for magician/entertainers sandwiched between the female singers, playing the USO circuit, and kept thinking: could this be Otto? They all had stage names.

"That's kind of you. My parents were killed when a bomb hit our house, so since then I've felt responsible for Otto while being able to do nothing for him."

He gathered breath. "Inge, I'll do all I can—short of what would kick me out of the Army and the State Department—because then I couldn't help you at all." I wouldn't even be able to see you, he thought.

"Please, I know. My life hangs on a silly job painting signs."

"And instead of designing buildings, I'm measuring tunnels and calling on you to do a job I could have done in high school. But here we are, light years behind where we were five years ago."

"I didn't think of that."

"There are only so many hours in my day. I'll do what the State Department expects me to do: recognize art of intrinsic worth and get it back where it belongs. A lot, uncatalogued, came out of private homes in occupied countries. Many old pieces weren't signed, and aren't known to exist except by their owners—and the conquerors. We may find some of this. My government hopes I'll be able to sort it out."

They were now approaching the Berghof, where they could be observed, so Inge spoke rapidly. "I must tell you something else. I'm afraid that if I had my life to live over, I would have to live it as I did, as hard as it's been. I had my parents and Otto for two more years, but those years were important because of the time and fate, even if I paid a terrible price for them: losing you. As much as it hurt, it had to be that way."

He looked at her. "You're right. It hurt."

May felt himself picking up the pieces of his heart. He could not add, you never lost me, but he thought it.

She continued, "Each day meant only more rubble, and, of course, the question always loomed as to who did not survive the last raid."

They came to the entrance of the Berghof. There was a guard so they could no longer talk freely, but May wanted to approach the subject utmost in his mind. She had written mentioning a man who had attracted her. Had it been deeper than attraction? Wars always demanded a sort of desperate love, if only to insure survival of the race.

Now he knew how he felt about Inge, but it wasn't what he wanted at the moment. He never stopped loving her, and for a long period he almost convinced himself that he had. Seeing her again, he knew that he loved her; he felt as if he had been sleeping. Trapped in love with her, he could easily imagine the constant frustration he would feel, considering their awful circumstances. Besides, her recent past was still a secret…

Fiske was waiting for May at the tunnel entrance.

"Fräulein von Haas, let me introduce Herr Fiske, my assistant. He keeps me alive." May turned to Fiske, "Fräulein von Haas has been a friend for many years."

"*Freut mich sehr. Herr Leutnant* does his best to make a difficult job agreeable." Fiske smirked, obsequiously shaking Inge's hand.

May caught the attitude. Fiske had been artificially polite, too mannerly. Suddenly he realized that Fiske would rightly see Inge as a contender for the food supply and resented her. Well, he'd have to deal with that later…

Inge looked bewildered, not having expected another national in the tunnels. Now they were descending the stairs, ominous enough by themselves. May turned to her. "You can commence with some office work, down one more flight."

When they reached the workroom, May led her to a drafting board. "Break down the tunnels, corridor by corridor. Here's what I've done so far." He showed her the reports and diagrams.

For Inge, working in the tunnels was dreadful. She walked to the doorway, looking at the corridor and stairs in the dim light, planning an escape route were the power to fail—knowing that it always did—and doing her best to allay her fears.

May could not miss her anxiety. "Come on. I'll show you some more. You'll see the place isn't so frightening."

She followed him. The ground level first rose and then stretched for blocks, covering an area that May knew. "You see the numbering system that we've adopted. Knowing it, you can always find your way out."

"In the dark?"

"You'll always have a light."

They came to the red door. "Never open red doors."

"Don't worry about that."

Finally they returned to the office. May left for a few minutes to check a light with Fiske. In the course of the errand, he did his best to reassure Fiske that Fräulein von Haas would in no way effect his position—and its perquisites. He hoped he'd left Fiske satisfied. When he returned to the drafting room he found Inge drafting, her body rigid as a board. She jumped like a jack-in-the-box when he stepped into the doorway, then smiled in relief.

* ** *

Japan surrendered unconditionally and the club was packed with officers singing rousing songs. The MC had come straight from the Roney Plaza on Miami Beach. The drunken celebrants passed before May's eyes like so many hot air balloons. If only he could have celebrated with Inge. The club manager had promised a live band that would play as long as there was a living, breathing body to listen. After all, it wasn't often that the good old United States got into—or—out of war. And the war was over.

May felt extinct, out of everything.

Richards and Walkowsky joined him. "May, you don't look happy enough," said Richards.

"I can't seem to get drunk," May confessed. "This was one helluva day for Japan to surrender."

The musical group finished *I'll Be Seeing You* and moved into *As Time Goes By,* but, having been played too many times, cleared the room. May found himself immobile and incapable of communication, still reliving the last few days in slow motion. Finally he gathered a second wind and instead of going home, headed for the tunnels. It was now broad daylight, and the Germans were on the street walking to work. Where there was grass, large blackbirds hopped about with their pointed heads cocked toward the earth, listening for worms. On reaching the tunnels, the first thing he saw was a sign Inge had lettered:

DANGER RESTRICTED OFF LIMITS ONLY AUTHORIZED PERSONNEL. He wondered why he had not seen it before and how long it had been there. The night guards saluted and May returned their salutes. An empty whiskey bottle, which May ignored, indicated they had done a little celebrating on their own. He turned his back for a minute to sign in, and the bottle vanished. For a while he wandered numbly, then seeing a room furnished with bunks, he lay down. He was there sleeping when Inge found him hours later.

"Thank God," she breathed. It was enough to awaken him, and he sat up sharply. She stood in the doorway like the sun.

"What happened?" He jumped to his feet.

"Nothing except that you signed in, but we couldn't find you. Suppose one of those steel doors with no handle on the inside had closed on you? I've been sick with worry."

Her obvious concern made him feel lighthearted, happy and ready to celebrate. He looked down at his crumpled uniform, felt his stubby chin, and ran his tongue over his teeth to erase the awful flat taste his breath must have been telegraphing.

"Thanks," he said with a crooked smile. Looking such a mess, he dared not touch her. Then she was off.

An hour later he appeared at the tunnel office, bathed and refreshed, and as always, with food. The day was not conducive to work, and he hadn't the will to insist on it. Fiske had been uncrating art found in the closet, which obviously had come from Hitler's Festival of the Arts held annually in Munich. Two were by artists Inge knew.

"You remember the party at Gretchen Baumgarten's?" she asked. "Katz was there."

"I remember you, a Russian countess, an honest artist, who called himself Mr. Nobody, and a traumatic experience that lasted almost two weeks until I found you again. Since that party, my life has never been the same."

"Katz was Mr. Nobody."

"I'm afraid his aspirations were never high enough. His work will be confiscated and shipped to the States as Nazi Art—not to be seen again for a long time."

Inge's jaw dropped. "It's up to you to decide?"

"That's right. I'm evaluating him as he evaluated himself, but at the same time, now it's my professional reputation that's at stake. I honestly don't feel that by secreting his paintings, I'm withholding any deserved fame, power and glory. He's only a competent artist without real talent, who jumped on Hitler's bandwagon—by his own admission."

"If you thought that he had really great talent, what would you do?"

"The same thing, but with a lot more regret."

May felt that he had been given some sort of test, and he had no idea whether or not he passed it. If she were using his reaction to this incident as an indicator of how he felt about collaborationists, she had her answer.

Inge went to work, but because it required little concentration, she spoke as she drew. "Walking to Berchtesgaden wasn't too bad. I took back roads and crossed fields. I bathed every other day in public baths and washed my clothes in streams. My big worry was whether my shoes would hold up. By spring there was more to eat." She turned to May and added, "I ate tiny ears of corn."

"You told me once that only pigs ate corn." He well remembered the little rebuff.

"It wasn't very good," she replied. "In all fairness, I must make a confession. During the summer, when the farmers had harvested the white underground asparagus and let the plants grow—that was near Mannheim—I remembered you telling me that green asparagus was good. I feasted on them. Once I was strafed doing that, but that was by the British.

"Touché," May replied. "Some of my advice was good."

"Mostly I lived on mushrooms. To be safe I looked for the wormy ones and picked out the worms."

"All of this happened, Herr Fiske, because she refused to marry me," May responded with a joviality that carried a tinge of rancor. He later realized that this little piece of information could be used against him—or worse, against Inge. Revealing anything personal to Fiske had been a mistake.

"And how did you live during the war?" Inge asked.

"I rented an apartment near Washington, but rents were out of sight. Rent was one hundred dollars a month, while I made two. So I shared my place with a series of guys in order to eat. When my mother died, I sold her house and used the money as a down payment on a condo that I've rented out. I like the thought of owning a home someplace."

That evening when May returned home, he found airmen from the 101st packing up Winchester's belongings. "What goes on?" he asked.

"Sorry, sir, to give you the bad news, but Winchester was killed today in a crash near Berlin."

He felt stabbed. Clumsily he left Winchester's room. The fact that the war was over, made the needless dying incomprehensible. Smith took his friend's death with apparent composure. May awakened once in the night to hear him moaning but he felt powerless to comfort him in any way.

Together they walked to the Berchtesgadner Hof for breakfast. Smith would accompany the casket to Winchester's hometown, in itself, an onerous task. "We thought the premature dying was over. Well, it wasn't, " said Smith.

Although a ride was always available, May chose the long walk to the Obersalzberg. Had it not been for too much booze, living in the same house, he and Smith might have become good friends earlier. But, of course, there had always been Winchester with all his panache.

* ** *

"I think I've deactivated a crucial area," Fiske announced.

"Don't just think. Be sure."

"Small red wires would hardly be grounds. They don't operate lights or any other electrical systems that I know of. We'll need a locksmith. There are no keys."

"Can you recommend one?" May asked.

A long silence followed. "No, sir."

"What's the matter? Are you worried about implicating a fellow German?" There was no point in pussyfooting around. Their lives could be at stake, and May was in no mood for temerity. "Go to town and get one."

May hated to be dogmatic, but this was what Fiske responded to best. Within an hour he was back with a locksmith and a large supply of master keys. Clearly the man was awed by the place and by the defense positions, where burp guns were still stacked. May could see the color ebbing down through clear-lit levels of the locksmith's face, as they passed the widely spaced lighting fixtures, deeper and deeper into the mountain.

"Does this tunnel ever end?" the man asked.

May laughed. "We think it might in Italy or Spain. You're not thinking of bolting, are you?"

Finally they reached the area where Fiske had discovered the suspicious wires and a heavy steel door. Deftly and quickly the locksmith, unaware of the possibility of explosives, went to work. It only took a few minutes; May stepped forward and turned on a light. There, standing on end on a raised platform, was crate after crate of what were obviously paintings in a wide assortment of sizes. May grinned awkwardly. "They look pretty well protected. We're lucky." He wiped perspiration born of tension from his forehead, and turned to the locksmith. "You've done a good job. I'll call on you again. Fiske will see you to the exit. Thank you."

The locksmith did not look grateful.

May began examining crates, all bearing the addresses of museums stenciled on the wood. They had come from all over Europe. Holy Toledo, this is going to make a lot of museum directors happy—not to mention Street—thought May. The return of this stuff should foster some good will toward us, and at a time when we need it, considering those two explosions in Japan. He could do little but turn his back on the treasure and head for Street's office.

Bungle as his government might, there were some areas, fortunately, in which intelligence and sensitivity shone. The feeling was immensely satisfying. Instead of waiting for transportation, he chose to walk. Feeling the gladness of a patriotic little boy, naively believing in the right and might of his country, he found himself singing.

His news put Street in an equally good frame of mind, so May took a slight liberty. "If you can hold off interference so that I can get the stuff out in record time, you might soon have that silver oak leaf on your shoulder."

"It's overdue, May." Street began the serious tapping of a cigarette on its fine case, one May remembered from the *Savoia*. "Is the girl who is helping you any good?"

May felt a qualm of apprehension. He wanted no conversation with Street on this subject. "She and Fiske can do more to move our work along faster than ten others. Now I've got to get back."

"Just a minute, May. As a soldier, according to the terms of surrender, I'm entitled to one souvenir. If you come across something good," he hesitated, "that isn't, of course, claimed by a museum, I'll expect you to let me know about it."

For a moment May felt shocked speechless. "I hardly think that will be the case," he replied, stalking out the door.

He looked for Inge to give her the good news about the find. "What a wonderful thing for the whole art world," she said, "Wherever that is…"

"I think we'll find a world of art in the tunnels. By the way, I'll need you tomorrow." It was the understatement of the week.

He was becoming ravenously hungry for Inge. Until she had found him asleep in one of the bunks, he had been fairly sure that she did not share his feelings, despite the wall presented by non-fraternization. Because of her fears, she had been almost standoffish. But that incident had marked a subtle change, as if again, some chemistry between them was being re-stirred.

* ** *

The events of the last few days had fallen so pell-mell, May felt as though he had been whirled in a centrifuge. Smith could not yet have landed in the States, but it seemed as if Winchester's death belonged to a distant past. The reason for this, he decided, was the other world of the tunnels. Psychologically they were isolating—confining as a submarine.

Even Inge told him, "I'm frightened here. This is a sinister environment, conceived by satanic people. I have only to step outside and I get an instantaneous lift."

"Think of the guards. Only a colonel or a general could get in here," he replied. He subdued a small hurt that his presence was not enough to reassure her. "Forget the past and face the future."

She leaned back from the drafting table and looked at him. She didn't know what he was thinking, but she was thinking about Kurt Montag, while at the same time being unsure of what she felt for May. Love for him had faded so painfully slowly. Now he was back asserting himself, doing everything to retrieve what they once had. Again she was becoming aware of his body, and when they were not together, he was beginning to intrude on her mind. She was inexpressibly grateful to him, but unsure that it was love. Lately she had felt strangely free, untrammeled except for a sense of obligation toward two men—and one might no longer be alive. If May knew about Kurt, he would push her to make choices. She wanted only to make them wisely, as she sensed they would forge her fate for years to come—if not for the rest of her life. She had hurt May once. She did not want to hurt him again. She forced a smile.

"I promise to keep my imagination in check," she told him. "You know it has always been very active."

He brightened. She was beginning to regain her old beauty. The tan from living out of doors was fading, revealing a natural creamy skin. The gaunt look was gone, and she was slowly filling out. Her topaz eyes no longer pierced, but cast a warm light. He moved the lamp toward her face to see her better, and in so doing, upset a small dish of peanuts that scattered about, some on the floor. She scrambled quickly to retrieve them as if they were pearls. May felt a flush of pity.

"Don't worry Inge. You won't be hungry again."

"Did I look so… desperate?" she asked, as if he had been a mirror.

"You are always beautiful to me." Then he touched her shoulder, squeezing lightly. Throttled by desire for her, he murmured, "Will you come to my house this evening? No one else will be there."

Before she could make an excuse, Fiske's footsteps broke the stillness and he appeared in the doorway. "I hope I didn't startle you," he said, noting their strained expressions.

"The way footsteps echo in this place, you couldn't announce your presence more loudly if you came in blowing a horn," May replied.

They laughed, and the tense moment was broken. The situation undefined, Inge felt as if Fiske had suddenly reduced a fire on the stove just before the stew boiled over. Work began, but not before May placed a key and his address on her desk.

"I've requisitioned a small dolly," he told Fiske. "There's no reason to move pictures one at a time. We'll have to open every crate, carefully record the contents and condition, close the crates again, and sort them for shipment."

"You'll recognize every painting, sir?"

"Of course." His reply was more certain than he felt.

"Then you plan that we will do this work ourselves?"

"That's right. I'm not going to trust fifty thousand dollar paintings to a bunch of hammering GIs." He knew what Fiske was thinking—that such work was demeaning to an officer, but no matter.

As soon as possible May escaped. He dared not be alone with Inge to hear some excuse beyond regulations. He went by the commissary and stocked up on food and wine, at the same time, deciding that he should do that anyway. He was sick of the officers' mess. Also he might as well live with a greater sense of permanency. He would be here for years.

Smith would be gone for thirty days, and soon after that, probably for all time. New men would be moved in. As long as Inge's wellbeing was at stake, he had to protect her, which put a different light on his situation. GIs were hungry to know clean, hard-working German girls, and the girls were just plain hungry.

Characteristically he operated from a standpoint of preparedness, yet for this evening he felt woefully unprepared. He could not rehearse what he wanted to say because he wasn't sure that she would appear. He only knew that he wanted her, and the momentum of his emotions was impossible to arrest. Before he found her again, his self-image had been one of a sophisticated individual, one who could handle any situation like a gentleman. Suddenly, that posture was blown sky high, and he felt as unsure and tormented as a teenager.

His house was dark when he entered, grocery bags in his arms. Then he saw her sitting on the sofa, faintly illuminated by the tiny night-light that always burned by the stairs.

"Inge," his soft voice caught as he felt an immense sense of relief. "I'm so glad you came." She moved toward him to take some of the groceries, an unconscious gesture. There was something incongruous about a man handling food. Self-aware, he turned on a floor lamp.

"I shouldn't have come. We could both get into so much trouble." She also could have added, I'm hungry, but did not. Her eyes met his, and she followed him to the kitchen.

"The non-fraternization rule is breaking down *Blitzschnell.*"

"But not officially."

"I can stick you into one of Smith's uniforms. He's short." May added with a chuckle.

"And put a paper bag over my head?" They both laughed.

"My cooking ability leaves much to be desired, so I've planned a simple *Abendbrot*. Note the French cheeses and assorted crackers. The *Ami* bread is terrible. Are you hungry?"

"Perpetually…I'm famished, but it's all up here." She tapped her temple.

"Then I'll feed you. There must be some china here." He opened cupboards.

"You don't seem very familiar with your kitchen."

"I walked through it once. Smith and Winchester never did dishes. Early in the week they stored dirty dishes in the refrigerator, which is pretty small. When the cleaning woman got here she washed them. It was the system when I moved in, and it was more than I wanted to compete with. Men living without women can live like slobs."

"Where are Smith and Winchester now?"

"Winchester is dead, and Smith is accompanying the body."

"I'm sorry. I thought the war was over."

"So did I. It was an accident." May did not want to go into the depressing details, but he thought some sympathy would be nice. "Sometime I'll tell you about it, when it will be easier. There's so much to say. Your eyes keep interrupting me."

"You could always think of lovely things to say. I see you haven't changed."

"I've been tongue-tied by the Army."

With the table set and food on it, May opened the wine, making a little ceremony. He poured it with misjudged flourish so that a bit spilled. "I don't usually do that." His eyes were wide and candid. He sampled the wine and pronounced it good. "I drink to our past—yours and mine—and to our future. The wine is strong. Time is strong, too."

"I'm no longer afraid of time. It can only help," she replied in almost a whisper.

"You're boasting." He felt his confidence grow.

"No, not really. It's too complicated to explain right now. This tastes so good, and I'm hungry." She looked up at May, now self-assured, looking almost like the old May again. He got up and put on a stack of records. She continued speaking, "I've watched the way you handle Fiske. You seem to know when to be firm and yet you are never rude."

"Oh, I can be when I have to." He noticed that *Dancing in the Dark* was playing. "Will you dance with me?"

For an instant she hesitated, and then she stood up and went into his arms. He told her: "Once in England, I was terribly rude to a nice girl. I'd asked her out because she looked like you. She couldn't dance like you. She couldn't talk like you. Coming back to Germany, I was so lonely for you; I felt sick. I got terribly drunk. The next day I flew to Berlin." He knew he did not have to tell her how bad that was.

The record ended. "Now I'll let you eat, if you hurry." He seated her and resumed.

"The awful moment came with Dolly when the orchestra played *Poor Butterfly*. Do you remember dancing at the Adlon? When I saw the hotel, the memory of you in that white dress came back so vividly..."

"Oh, those dreams, they've haunted me."

The presence of her offered something like salvation. He was calm with controlled desire and anticipation. He had been careful not to press himself on her, but to woo her gently with words. Her young resilient body, arms as beautiful as those of Garbo, and her exquisite face shimmered before him. Another record dropped on the turntable, *It Had To Be You*. Again he pulled her to her feet and moved with her across the floor, until mercifully, the music reached a place where he could stand, holding her, swaying to the music. With infinite tenderness he kissed her neck, her cheek, her mouth. The lovely sweetness of her perfume mingled with her soft hair. One hand rose to cup her head and then moved to bring her body closer to his. Feeling her near him, he knew a delirious joy. The sweet mixture of passion and happiness almost swamped him. Again his lips found hers. He put a finger on her face, tracing the outline of her cheeks, feeling his hand tremble as he whispered her name.

He never knew how long they danced. Despite their growing need, even a move to the stairs seemed too divisive to bear. Somehow they made their way up the stairs, and tremulously he undressed her and handed her over to his bed while he undressed himself. Then he fell upon her and closed out the world, riding across skies almost agonizing in their sweetness.

"*Oh, Liebling,*" she confessed later, her voice caught with emotion, "I had thought that I remembered what love making with you was like.

But I hadn't, which was good—as I doubt if I could have lived." She began to weep uncontrollably.

Sometime during the night, May went downstairs to turn off the record player. They had not discussed the future. He felt to do so would have risked everything. He crept back to make love to her again in the first entire night they had ever spent together.

When he awakened in the morning, she was no longer in bed. Slipping into his robe, he went to the head of the stairs and bent over the banister to see into the dining room. She was at the dining table picking up scraps of food they had left, wrapping them in paper, and surreptitiously slipping them into her purse.

He stood shocked and unbelieving.

A few minutes later she came upstairs. "Would you mind if I take a shower now? I didn't want to waken you."

"No, please go ahead," he stammered, striving for composure.

"I should get back to the house before the Müllers get up. They could become upset and report me missing. They're such simple people, they could do something foolish."

"By all means. Hurry. I'll see you at work."

By the time she came out of the bath, fully dressed, he was calm and resigned. For a minute or two he took her in his arms, holding her and rocking her as he would a child. Then he kissed her, flush with desperation.

Five years of war had made more changes than were readily apparent. Not that he begrudged her a morsel; he despaired that she was reduced to stealing scraps. It dawned on him that she probably had to take something back to the Müller house to quiet them, and felt better. If they knew her absence would bring even small rewards, her nights with him would be encouraged.

Inge was a victim of her time, not quite innocent.

May found himself raging. How had it happened? How could the world leaders have allowed a maniac such as Hitler to wreck such havoc upon all of mankind before finally stopping him? Not only did millions die—the major crime—but how many had had their lives totally disrupted? Everybody he knew. Not one architectural student in his graduating class was practicing architecture. They had been doing submarine duty, or leveling airstrips in Latin America, or photographing things to bomb, if not actually bombing something. And potential talents, such as Inge, perhaps a budding Mary Cassatt, Doris Lee or Georgia O'Keeffe—Christ, there'd been so few women in art—had been reduced to painting signs and stealing table scraps. All of it made him sick. It also made him resolve that, if he ever got out of the goddamned Army, one way or another, he would work to see that such a thing never happened again.

Most Germans, utterly sick of the war, soon accepted defeat and were anxious to get on with rebuilding their lives, letting bygones be bygones. There were others who bore an ineradicable, venomous hatred for the conquering *Amis,* and among these dangerous few fanatics was Herr Fiske. He came to work for May simply because he and his wife were hungry, and the German authorities had ordered him back to the tunnels. There, alone with May, he would have ample opportunity to murder his commanding officer, but this would hardly serve his purposes. He hoped to bring down a horde of GIs and possibly a couple of generals in one last defiant gesture for the fatherland. He managed to disguise his hatred, and act almost friendly with May, while all the time he plotted one great tunnel blast. The sudden appearance of Inge on the scene complicated matters, because he would have less time to work alone. As he dismantled the wiring and explosives in one area, he hoped to reinstall them in another. This work would have to be hidden, and May, he knew, had quite an eye for detail.

CHAPTER SEVEN

The first important art May and Fiske found was considerable and predictable as they penetrated Hitler's tunnel. The inventory included a Boucher, two oils by Pieter Breughel the Elder, two Canalettos, two by Cranach, three van Dykes, a Goya, two Fragonards, three Franz Hals, one Leonardo da Vinci, four Rubens, a Rafael, four Tintorettos, a Vermeer, a Watteau, and naturally, two Wouwermans. Several bourgeois painters—Burkel, Lenbach and Makart—were also represented. May told Fiske, "They're here because Hitler thought they should be emulated to establish 'great contemporary painting.' But what we've found is real treasure."

Because Fiske was always withdrawn or even sullen, May was quick to give him credit for anything, hoping to change his attitude.

Unfortunately there was none of the modern art May was anxious for Inge to see. She had been too young to see the last 'degenerate' show in Munich in 1937, after which, modern art disappeared in Germany.

That afternoon when Inge came to work, May was attending a briefing, reporting the find. She looked for him and happened instead on Herr Fiske, inventorying a cache of clothing. Thinking himself safe, he had put on a Nazi uniform. When she interrupted him, he was strutting about the room, acting out a victorious posture of some sort. He was startled at first but then relieved that the intruder was only Inge. He laughed nervously.

Inge had never seen Fiske laugh. Then she saw the uniform and stiffened in shock. In a voice that was cold and flat, omitting the customary greeting, she announced: "I'm looking for *Herr Leutnant* May."

"I came across this and couldn't resist the temptation to once more wear our country's glorious uniform. I didn't hear your footsteps."

"You're lucky it was me. You could have lost your job."

Fiske drew himself up straight and tall, and she felt suddenly that she was looking at a frighteningly different man, one proud, arrogant and untrustworthy. "You wouldn't dare report me."

"I've never been *eine Landesverräterin*. Why would I do such a thing?"

"To displace me."

He did not have to add, 'for my share of the food.' She regarded him now with a cold stare and hissed. "I have more compassion for my countrymen than you realize, so I'm not going to report you, but you are a fool."

"The *Amis* are swine. Surely you feel it."

"I don't feel it. Fortunately you Nazis lost the war."

He snarled back, "So you've sold out for a mess of potage, and the *Ami* has become your lover. You whoring women are all alike—weak."

Inge's ire rose like a clap of thunder, giving her courage. "I should slap your filthy face. Keep your opinions to yourself. Herr May is doing his best to feed you, your wife, the three Müllers and me, or we would all be very hungry. Now get out of that disgraceful garment." She pivoted and wheeled from the room. By the time she reached the office, her adrenaline had ebbed and she was shaking.

Soon Fiske appeared, dressed in his tired civvies, shrunken in stature. He shuffled about the room while Inge walked to May's desk and picked up a sheaf of papers titled: *German Stolen Art*.

Berlin, Nationalgalerie—505 works; Kupferstichkabinett of the Nationalgalerie—647 works; Bielefeld, Städtische Kunsthalle—127 works; Bremen, Kunsthalle—165 works; Breslau, Schlesisches Museum—560 works; Chemnitz, Kunsthütte—275 works; Dresden, Kupferstichkabinett—365 works; Dresden, Staatliche Gemäldegalerie—150 works; Dresden, Stadtmuseum—381 works; Düsseldorf, Kunstsammlungen der Stadt—900 works.

Inge had gotten through the 'D's of the alphabetically listed cities in a line that totaled 15,997 works confiscated by the Nazis from German museums alone. She sat aghast, and then her mind reeled back to conversations with May when he tried to tell her about the treasure in art her government had denounced. How could all of those museum directors have been wrong?

Of course they hadn't been.

At the time May could not have had those statistics, yet how patient he had been with her.

This is incredible, thought Inge. The Nazis had plundered their own museums, a national heritage, with even greater zeal than they had shown in occupied countries. Visions of Kurt Montag, her family, friends killed in the war and cities in ruins flashed before her. And here was this old Nazi, this old fool defending them. Glaring at him with renewed disgust, she gathered saliva and spit at him. "Tell *Herr Leutnant* May that I'll see him later."

Fiske's jaw dropped with the insult he would not forget.

It was a serious lapse in judgment on Inge's part. She went to the Rathaus to paint signs. German film star Hildegard Neff would be singing for the troops.

* ** *

Street was positively ecstatic over the art that had been uncovered. For all the wrong reasons, thought May, now slumped in his chair, a prisoner of the assembled brass. Besides his work, the dull problems of administration were being hammered out. Finally he was freed and decided to walk home. A light drizzly rain had closed out the sky, leaving a wispy fog reminiscent of Berlin's bad weather. Before him on the street were two drunken GIs. Suddenly, from an alley four Germans appeared out of nowhere. This was enough to throw one of the Americans into an insane frenzy. He whipped out a pistol and began firing. Under the surprise attack the Germans crashed to the ground like felled trees. Parallel, May was going to be next.

The other GI, aghast at what his buddy was doing, stood for a moment as if in a catatonic trance. May felt a surge of terror. The man was off his rocker. May looked up, catching sight of an iron grating over a window, and a flash of Matcher's story aboard the *Nellie Bligh* ripped through his mind. May sprang at the duo, grabbed a pistol from the holster of the stupefied companion, and shot at the berserk warrior, hitting him in the forearm above the hand in which he held the gun.

The sound of the shots reverberated through the narrow streets bringing swarms of MPs, and, soon after, ambulances. The hubbub that followed would always remain a blur, including hours lost with the authorities. Two Germans were badly injured, but not mortally. The crazed GI would always have impaired use of his hand, and would be whipped back to the U.S. following court-martial. May was ordered not to discuss the incident.

What struck him, as he gave his story, and afterward, was that in a moment of crisis, he thought of Herr Matcher. He never discounted the profound impact that Germany had on him in '38 – '39, chiefly because of Inge, and his interest in fine art, in which she had become a catalyst. Now he saw the trenchant insights, the *savoir-faire* and refinement that Matcher exhibited—not to mention the scope of his intelligence—had become pilings on which he hoped to build his character. There was also the example of his sister, Frau Matcher, and her courage in facing death while disturbing no one around her. May had always considered the arrogant Herr von Haas on the deficit side of the ledger. Now he was willing to be more magnanimous. As Walt Whitman said: "Have we not learned great lessons from those who have pitted their strength against us and disputed the passage with us?"

There seemed to be no end to the disputed passages. They were part and parcel of the times.

Waiting to be interrogated, he sat thinking of the people who had been major influences in his life, for better or for worse. On a small piece of paper he listed seventeen names, including that of Adolf Hitler.

When he finally reached home, Inge was waiting for him. His pleasure soon dissolved in a sinking feeling.

"I did not come here tonight to eat or to make love to you, but to talk to you," she said.

He thought he had had enough trouble for the day. "Are you going to tell me that you're not coming here anymore?"

"No, but I want to clear the air."

During her wait she had seen that he had purchased packages of dried beans, chipped beef, powdered milk, and eggs, all still in the bag—not groceries he had bought for himself, but obviously for her, the Müllers, and perhaps even for Fiske.

Avoiding her eyes, he walked to the kitchen to open a bottle of wine.

Never had a drink seemed more necessary. Picking up two glasses, she followed him to the living room.

He threw his cap on a chair. "Come. Let's sit down."

Blessedly, his eyes left her. "I wrote you that I had met another man."

"I have the letter."

"You were gone. He may be dead. He was an Austrian tank commander sent to Russia, but he was also a charming Baron with an impoverished estate near Salzburg."

May took a deep breath. "So he was the reason you walked here?"

"And I learned I could not cross the border. On foot, I could never have gotten through 'No Man's Land.' I wrote him that I would marry him. I haven't heard from him since."

"Then I found you."

"You have also managed to rekindle much of what I felt for you years ago. I'm not using you for a meal ticket, although you are feeding me. *Liebling,* my parents liked Kurt. Remember, in my class, European marriages are arranged. I have never kissed that man! Now I feel like an opportunist, or a fickle child, moving whichever way the wind blows, except I know that is not the case."

"I suspected something like this. I've been frightened of losing you again, especially in light of my country's regulations."

She leaned to him and kissed him. Her eyes, swimming with tears, shone like amber pools. "You are the last man in the world I would want to torment. I can no longer bear the thought of not being honest with you, even though what I have said seems to pain you. I'm sorry, *Liebling,* but that's what happened."

He looked at her closely. "We've always been able to talk. That you came here caring for someone else complicates things, but even painful things you say, make me feel more alive than I ever felt without you."

Her head fell to his shoulder. "Don't be a jealous lover. A total commitment is impossible right now for reasons of your government alone."

"That's encouraging. Come, let's eat. Maybe the way to a woman's heart is through her stomach."

"This is just between us, please, but today I caught Fiske in a Nazi uniform. The transformation was astounding. I'm scared of him."

May did not react visibly. "Clothes make the man, they say. Was that all there was to it?" He turned his attention to the steak, now filling the room with a promising aroma.

"We had a fight. Then I looked down at your desk and saw the list of German art the Nazis stole. I was overcome by his stupidity on one hand, and your perspicacity on the other. I flipped. I spat at him."

What she said made May grimace, but before he could say anything, he looked up, shocked to see the club manager, Lieutenant Burns, the ever-absent fourth resident in the house, standing in the doorway. Inge froze.

"Inge, let me introduce Lieutenant Burns. Burns, meet Inge von Haas. I knew Inge before the war, and invited her to dinner. Will you join us?"

"I'm glad to know you, Inge, and I'm dying for a home-cooked meal. Do you have enough?"

For May the ground settled. "The porterhouse should feed four. Inge eats like three, but you and I can make out. Why don't you make yourself a drink and put on some music?"

"Say, May, I hear you shot a man today...." called Burns from the living room.

Again Inge froze, her eyes wide in astonishment. May had said nothing to her....

"Sorry, Burns, I can't discuss it," May quipped.

Burns returned. "Gotcha... I've hated the thought of coming back here since Winchester's death, but decided tonight I'd better face it. I must say, this is a pleasant surprise. You're so seldom at the club, I should have guessed there's a little life in the house." May laughed, only slightly embarrassed for Inge.

"Herr May has tried to keep me from starving."

"I understand," said Burns. "A lot of food walks out of the club, and not in some officer's stomach. I close my eyes to it. Mostly it's scraps and potato peelings, of all things! It's one thing to be businesslike, but I shudder at the thought of being downright cruel."

"It's un-American," said May, looking at Inge. "Many of us were brought up on farms where food was plentiful. Strangers were always walking up to our porch. My grandmother gave them a plate of food. While they ate, Grandpop pumped them for news. Sometimes they stayed a day or two to work. I was always sorry to see them go, because the chores would again fall to me, and the tramps made life interesting. They also made me hunger for travel."

May helped Inge carry food to the table. "Are you married?" he asked Burns.

By a cocked eyebrow Burns indicated he thought the question a bit ornery. "I was the last time I heard, but one never knows where one stands these days."

May couldn't have agreed more.

Soon after dinner Burns departed with a fresh supply of clothes.

May picked up the bag of soiled shirts that Burns had dumped on the sofa, and turned off the most irritating lights. "You've unsettled me."

"I told you I didn't want to do that," she whispered, as he flipped up her skirt to feel her, unfettered by clothes. Slowly he undressed her and himself, and put on a new stack of records. Drawing her to her feet, they danced. Her arms encircled his neck, and they moved with the music, joined by a chord, and perfect timing kept them in place. "I always wanted to dance this way with you. I knew we could."

"No other dancer in the world could do this. You lead perfectly," she said.

Finally when tension built to a distracting pitch, they went upstairs where he did his best to impregnate her.

Later she wanted to ask him about the shooting, but didn't dare. She went to sleep, somehow trusting him.

May slept only a few minutes. He found himself reviving the day's impressions, starting in the morning. Uncovering the art had given him the excitement of a parent watching a toddler's first steps, so the day had not been without its bright spot. But then he remembered Street's dishonest greed, his desire to 'liberate' something of value for himself, and hoped he could circumvent it. Street was knowledgeable enough not to be satisfied with one of Hitler's minor artists. His mind traveled to the incident of the berserk GI that, like fever or belly rash, was a symptom of a grave infection threatening their environment. For a moment it was simply too much to dwell upon—actually hopeless, considering the thousands of driven, homesick men stationed abroad. He was relieved that his aim was good enough not to kill. Then his thoughts drifted to a more personal matter. For Inge's benefit he had downplayed Fiske's little theater, but Fiske was unlikely to forget or forgive her reaction. Fiske was much more of an immediate threat to them both than he wanted to let on. Now he snapped to full wakefulness, his nerves jangling an alarm.

Not wanting to disturb Inge with his tossing, he went downstairs to mix himself a stiff Scotch. Standing, drink in hand, in the glare of the kitchen lights on white tile, he tried to figure out what Fiske could do to hurt them, beyond the obvious: tattling to Street or Rasmussen? Finally he decided he knew how to handle that. A small German roach appeared which he dispatched with a slipper to roach heaven, wherever that was.

As if in some bleary photograph, he thought of the Baron arriving to claim Inge—something he didn't know how to handle. The possibility was so unsettling; he made himself another drink and downed it quickly. The Baron, a captive tank commander, undoubtedly had been injured or he would have shown up. He would be no Rasmussen or Street to handle, but truly a loose cannon, a rogue elephant.

Turning off the lights, he trudged upstairs to the bedroom where Inge lay sleeping on her back as peacefully as before, her hair fanned across her pillow. For a minute he studied her intently, and fervently, as if praying for his own soul. Knowing that it had been a rough day he wanted to forget, he buried his head in his pillow and let the Scotch take over.

CHAPTER EIGHT

It grew colder, and the hunger of the Germans increased. The Morganthau Plan was still a well-kept secret, but its effects were very tangible. The Germans watched bonfires in which the precious commodities were wantonly burned, simply because the Nazis had hoarded them. This practice horrified May, but there was nothing he could do about it.

The winter of 1945 came early. May appropriated a down comforter from Hitler's hoard, and gave it to Inge with two cover sheets. "American soldiers are entitled to one souvenir each, so I'm stretching things—my neck—to give you these." It didn't seem like stealing since all the articles were to be burned anyway—as an object lesson for the Germans. They were allowed to get what warmth they could from the fires. May told Rasmussen, "These are the first fires I've ever seen that chill me to the bone." Being a wise commander, Rasmussen said nothing.

The Müller's house had three beds and three *Oberdecken*. The daughter slept on the sofa under the family's coats, so Inge's new comforter meant the girl could get her old covers back. May also had bought Inge a coat and a pair of boots. Larry Price got his bride to buy these articles for May in New York at a designer's outlet. The coat was camelhair, and May intended it as a Christmas present, not reckoning with the climate. When it got cold, he could not keep it hidden any longer.

Inge ran her hands over the soft silky wool. "It's the most beautiful coat I've ever seen," she murmured again and again. The only other women who were warm were farmers' wives who wore furs and diamonds that had been traded for food. With the coat came a letter from Larry.

"*Dear Jimbo,*

"*This should keep some nice lady warm. By the way, Betsy and her senator husband are touring Germany. Barnes is on some senate committee investigating military spending, etc. Betsy noticed Berchtesgaden on the agenda. If you've got any axe to grind, here's your chance. Betsy contributed heavily to his campaign, so he seems to listen to what she thinks. The old story, money talks. Your wedding present is our favorite gift. Geraldine will be thanking you in time—all she does these days is write little notes. Keep an eye on Betsy. Hail Columbia.*

"*Best, Larry.*"

May was appalled. Betsy! "Make use of her," Larry was saying. That was like saying, summon a hurricane to put out a candle. She was a smashing beauty, a nympho, a nut, a running case of trouble, if he had ever known one. He hoped they were on a whirlwind tour. In light of the deteriorating relationship between Inge and Fiske, he was alarmed at the thought of leaving Inge alone with him. Still, here was an opportunity to get in a good word with the powers that be, for the Germans and their desperate food situation. He'd beat Betsy's ear, while beating something else, if need be. But Lord, what a way to get an Act of Congress!

The timing was awful: Major Street's reports were due. Inge would need an explanation. He wiped a damp brow.

Later at dinner he could contain his problems no longer. "I won't be able to see you for a couple of days because a senator and his wife are here. Mrs. Barnes may want some escorting around while her husband is in conference with the brass. Lord, I hope the visit will be short."

"I understand." Inge visualized a plump, middle-aged dowager.

"It'll be a wonderful opportunity for me to get the story out over how bad things are for you Germans. I know a lot more about that than the general does—I'll tell the cockeyed world." He bent to kiss her forehead.

"Do you know these people personally?" She sensed that something about his kiss intended to pacify.

"Mrs. Barnes is the older sister of a friend of mine. Why?"

"You kissed me so funny, like you felt guilty about something."

"Don't read things into kisses. I kissed you impulsively because you looked so pretty."

"On the forehead?" She was smiling.

"If you'll just be quiet, I'll do a better job." He kissed her soundly. "Actually I'm nervous about this visit, because it is such a great opportunity, and I don't want to muff it. I care too much."

May said no more about the arriving statesiders. One thing was clear, he was not a good liar. Before the week was out, he was summoned to the colonel's office.

"How are things going, May?"

"Very well, sir. We're plugging along."

"I'm glad to hear that. I called you because Senator Barnes and his wife just arrived. The senator's wife has expressed a wish to have you escort her around. They would like you to join them for dinner tonight. I understand you're an old family friend."

"True," he replied, swallowing hard. "How long do they expect to be here?"

"Lord knows! These people think we have nothing to do but wine and dine them on taxpayers' money." Resignation flattened his tone. "However you may be able to do some real good." His eyes met May's.

"I'll give my all for my country, sir," he replied, smiling sarcastically. "Lord, colonel, unless Betsy Barnes has changed a lot—which I doubt— she takes some handling. She's a bombshell."

Rasmussen laughed. "I expected as much. She wants to play and relax."

May groaned and added, "Well, sir, here's our opportunity to get a message across."

"Right." Rasmussen nodded. His lieutenant had gotten the message.

Getting Inge straightened out was next.

"The Barnes' are here which will knock me out for a day or two. You and Fiske can get started on Göring's tunnel. Enter it where his bath was. Now I'm giving you strict orders in writing. You are not to probe any areas by yourself, and you are always to follow Fiske. Make him open every door. I know you're anxious to find modern stuff. Will you promise me to follow these instructions?"

"Yes, sir."

Still serious, May continued. "I may be able to get some important ideas over." He hoped he had not said that too often. "I'd rather spend the time with you. There's a lot going on that I haven't talked to you about. The Russians are being remarkably fast in returning art. They're doing this for a reason, and it's not generosity. I'm putting you in charge of Fiske." He sat down and put that point in writing in English and in German, which he signed. "Now be a good girl."

For some intuitive reason, Inge felt a tinge of jealousy.

Betsy Barnes had one reason for asking for him, and May knew it. She referred to her reason as 'a little nooky.' She was such a good-looking blond; he had always wondered why she had been so loose with her favors. Her hourglass figure was not built for Paris fashions, but she looked awfully good to men. When she bent over, and she bent over a lot, observers were certain that something embarrassing would pop out. Something did, but usually from her mouth. With Betsy, nothing was sacred, but a lot was funny. She could be coarse, but in such a jolly way, few objected. The senator adored her, and although the Press recognized her as a high-class tramp, not a word of this was breathed to constituents. Instead she was described as 'open, frank, fun-loving, and witty.'

Betsy had told the general, "While you're convincing my husband of what a good job you're doing, I want to be assigned to Lieutenant May. You take care of the senator in the daytime, and I'll take care of him at night." Then she winked. The general was flabbergasted. At the same time her smile dazzled him.

Barnes beamed proudly. The general followed orders. Major Street was furious over May's elevated status, temporary as it was. He voiced his objections to the colonel.

"Please, Street," the colonel said, "don't make me a present of your opinions—at least not quite so often."

* ** *

"I'm awfully glad to see you, Betsy," said May, speaking honestly. On seeing her, a sense of fun took over.

"Let's go to the bar for a Bloody Mary breakfast. Then we can talk."

May followed. They sat in the club bar, now an empty room. "Do you feel like being a Good Samaritan?" May asked.

"You always got from me what you wanted, Jimbo. I can't resist you. What's on your brilliant mind?"

"The same thing that's on yours, but we've got some talking to do first. You look positively great. Politics becomes you. I can hardly wait to vote for your husband."

"Darling, he's a rare bird, an honest politician."

"Betsy, an awful lot of people here need your help…"

"Tell me about it. I'm in the catbird seat."

"The message is a no vote-getter. We suffered three hundred thousand casualties during the war. There are a lot of families wanting to see blood. Add to them, the Jews who think of little but vengeance. Betsy, sometime soon we're going to have to bury the hatchet. Germany is our only real bulwark against Russia. We can't repeat Versailles. Right now the Germans are on a caloric allowance that is less than the people in concentration camps and slave laborers had. We can't sit here guarding forever; the Germans will either starve to death or go communist when we pull out. The Morganthau Plan stinks!"

"Baby cakes, that's a sacred cow."

"Betsy, don't think I'm not sympathetic to the Jews and what conquered people have suffered. I've been horrified by what the Nazis did—and I see more of that everyday. I also know how National Socialism happened. That's why I'm frightened."

"I'll give you a chance to spill it out to the senator tonight, but I also think you're throwing me a red herring. What's really eating you?"

May laughed. Betsy was smart. "Non-fraternization. Many of our forces haven't had a woman in years. The German women are clean and good-looking. By nature Americans are friendly and compassionate. They are given no contact with the people they're governing."

"And we're supposed to be teaching them democracy?"

"You get the picture beautifully."

"You know, Jimbo, you have an incredible talent for holding back on a girl. I've thought of that so often during the last few years. You never press; you simply heat the girl up. Do I have to hit you on the head to once again get your great dick?"

May blinked and smiled. "Okay, Betsy, let's have a little pillow talk." He reached for her hand. "Lieutenant Burns has given me a room here in the Hof for the duration of your visit. It will save me travel time. Why don't you look over my quarters? The décor is old Bavarian."

"I thought you'd never ask, darling, and how sweet of you to remember my interest in furniture." Betsy could be sarcastic.

Making love to Betsy stretched the concept of good, clean, bawdy fun. On entering the room, she stripped off her dress and pranced around in stockings, a black lace garter belt and bra, her nipples protruding from two round lace-trimmed holes. She pretended to examine the painted armoire and quaint decorated headboards while May undressed. The effect on him was terrific, taking him back years.

"I had totally forgotten what a garter belt can do," he confessed from a straight chair where he had just pulled off his socks and looked down at his erection. Betsy's eyes lit up. "Come here, woman." He begged, "Ease my pain."

"I thought you looked ready," she replied on her knees, taking him in her mouth for a few minutes, and then extracted a condom from her stocking and carefully inserted him for a little lap dance.

Larry was right. Betsy was still the extravagant, generous, madcap who had played cat and mouse with him and dozens of others for years. Once she had tormented him by stealing a car—or pretending to steal a car—to get to a dance. (The car, he later learned, belonged to her father). Another time she had disappeared at the beach, leaving him to think she had drowned. On the other hand, once when he wanted to see a movie playing in another city, she had commandeered her father's pilot and private plane to take them there. Her long crazy telegrams had bolstered his ego, coming as they always had, out of the blue. She had belonged to another world subsidized by her father; it was a very impressive world to a young college student, dwarfed by the pain of feeling poor. In self-defense he never gave her his heart for long. It seemed his only recourse.

While she enjoyed the veneer of game-playing, Betsy was basically immodest and free of inhibitions. She enjoyed dirty talk, which heightened May's arousal. "Take it easy, girl," he begged. "Let's draw this out a little longer…"

"Why do you always make me work so hard for it, then make me wait?" she asked. "This tight little pussy is always hungry."

"I like it that way."

"God, so do I. That must be the secret of your hold on me. I always have to be the aggressor," she said.

"I never knew I had a hold on you."

"I keep coming back."

That was true. "I haven't exactly fought you off." He wondered if that would always be so. Being with her was something like being with an ex-wife after an amicable divorce. At the moment he did not feel much guilt.

"You may someday."

Through some biological happenstance, which coincidentally added to her libido, Betsy enjoyed an elongated, doubled and extended clitoris, so that her vulva was strengthened and enlarged, giving her a lock on a man that was truly remarkable. So many tiny swollen blood vessels—as in a man's penis—were actually a deformity. Her consequent ability to afford a male exceptional pleasure had stimulated Betsy's libido so that from puberty on, she had spent an awful lot of time in the sack. She loved freedom, and her disagreements with men came about through their possessive attitudes, impinging on her independence. May had been the one exception; May also surmised that her husband understood his wife perfectly.

"I've always loved the way you make screwing fun," he told her at some point.

"I believe it should be our national sport. It's so much better than baseball or football, of all things."

"Get that into the next democratic platform. Organize a Fucking Olympics—that's even better," May murmured.

"It makes more sense than throwing javelins or the discuses, for heaven's sake. Some day I'll have a gold medal cast for you," she promised. "It's a shame your talents go unheralded."

"Don't jeopardize my amateur standing. With non-fraternization in effect, I have enough trouble keeping in practice."

"I'm not sure of that. You have not ejected prematurely," she mused.

"I've never minded playing with myself."

Later he would tell her, "I could have sworn you were going to get the captain of the fireboat to spray the *Savoia*. I was terrified."

"Oh, Jimbo, I was going to do just that, but I was distracted by the captain. I could see him swelling in his pants like a Pamplona toro. He was such a gorgeous bull. We circled Manhattan. I had a marvelous time."

Then she stopped talking, kissing him firmly while tightening muscles in the birth canal with a sort of churning motion that he was helpless to withstand. He roared like a lion in ecstasy.

Betsy hadn't changed. Nor would he have changed her, deciding her imperfections made her delightful. He also realized they'd been in bed for three hours. Not a record, but not bad.

* ** *

Except for an initial inspection, May had spent no time in Hitler's formal home, the Berghof, which Betsy wanted to visit. Wanting a better look himself, he drove her there. In the basement they discovered a narrow gray-walled shooting gallery, the sort of thing one would expect to find in a FBI school. They moved through rooms cluttered with overturned chairs, old magazines and newspapers, marveling at the wrack and ruin. They climbed the precarious stairs to Hitler's workroom that ran the width of the house. The walls had been thoroughly scorched and only a hideous *Kachelofen,* that once supplied heat, remained.

"I never thought I'd see this, " she exclaimed, "and what a great end for a bunch of cutthroats."

May nodded. Then a guard came up to May, saluted and announced the colonel had sent word that the elevator to the Eagle's Nest, Hitler's aerie perched on top of the Kehlstein, was now operable. "The senator was anxious for his wife to see it."

"You're lucky. I haven't seen it myself." May said. "It has to be one of the Seven Wonders of the World. It took three thousand workmen three years to build it. Hundreds died during construction."

They drove up the twisted mountain road toward the Eagle's Nest. A thousand feet below the summit, in a pocket cut out of the mountainside of the Kehlstein, May stopped the jeep before two magnificent bronze doors. They rode an elevator up.

"This must be one of the strangest places on earth," said Betsy. "It's overwhelming."

The furnishings reflected Hitler's celebrated bad taste. Betsy turned to a room that looked like a cheap bar and grill. "Yuck."

May opened a window and clouds swept through, carried by winds. Quickly he shut it. "I read this place was last used when Eva's sister married a general. Five hundred people came to get drunk. It must have been a madhouse, and wouldn't it have been funny if the elevator had gotten stuck?"

They laughed nervously.

The main conference room had a large oak table and blackout curtains. Betsy counted twenty-six chairs. Off this room was another great hexagonal room with forty-six chairs, one uglier than the next, all covered in pale blue, machine-made needlepoint. On the floor a large reproduction Chinese rug was centered under a huge white circular table. In one corner a red marble fireplace faced an incredibly ugly rust-colored sofa. The room was lit by garish gold-striped sconces, arranged fan-like to emulate flames. Betsy found bedrooms that would sleep eighteen. She turned to May. "So this is the way Superman lived. I'm aghast, Jimbo. The man was downright tacky."

"Obviously the budget ran short when it came to furnishings. I'd hoped to find some fine art, but art intended for this place must be stored in the tunnels below."

"Darling, it's fascinating. I wouldn't have missed this for the world. Just think, I'm the first American woman to see it."

Her remark was unsettling. May thought of Inge.

Outside the clouds cleared briefly, and they walked to a window. "That's Austria. Hitler could succeed with the Germans, as he never could have with his own people, the easy-going Austrians. He had to have the Germanic vitality and drive to manipulate, plus our mistakes at Versailles. Germans have the old work ethnic and an infinite capacity for self-sacrifice." He pointed to Berchtesgaden where the houses could have been stage settings for *Hansel und Gretel*. "Look at the clean, picturesque simple life the town suggests, and tell me how one equates it with the megalomaniac who built this and almost destroyed Europe."

Betsy, standing beside him, let her hand fall to his crotch where she could feel his sex while she gazed out the window. "I'll tell you what it all gets back to: quality of government. Now, in Hitler's bed, let's have a quick little fuck, and chart the course the American government should take so that we won't have to go to war again." With a delightful gleam in her eye, she opened his pants.

* ** *

May, Senator Barnes, Betsy, a general, Colonel Rasmussen, and a lieutenant colonel—the chief of the 101st Airborne Division administering the Berchtesgaden area—sat at a large round table in the officers' club. Slightly out of range, Street seethed.

"The tasks here are duplicated throughout Germany, Senator," said the general. "On Eisenhower's orders, we, the Military Government, are to provide for the needs of the American troops and to look after the thousands of United Nations' displaced persons, who were the victims of the Nazi slave labor system. Then we're supposed to start building a new democratic Germany."

Senator Barnes stared at him, nodding slowly, his fingers idly expanding and loosening a rubber band. "Well, that sounds mighty nice... What's being done on that last point, general—building a new democratic Germany?"

The general looked weary and grim. "That is going to take time."

Barnes turned to his wife with a meeting-of-minds exchange, possible only in a close relationship. He said, "We spent the morning with the Burgermeister, Dr. Rudolf Kries, an avowed anti-Nazi, who bowed so low I thought I heard his Bavarian lederhosen crackle. '*Jawohl, Herr Hauptmann,* I understand,' he kept repeating, waiting for commands— or at least a scolding. All I could think of was little boys in rompers. I couldn't detect a democratic bone in their...'" The senator let the rubber band fly.

"That's their attitude, sir," the general replied.

"It's not one I think we should foster. I've heard that this city is an exception in that water and electrical systems are operating. Houses are standing. However, transportation systems have broken down here as well as everywhere else, and that will only contribute to the food problem. Gentlemen, the food problem will be onerous, unless you get these people back to work." The senator sat back while the brass squirmed.

"We're ordering them to plant the equivalent of our own Victory Gardens."

Barnes scowled over the table. "What? The Military Government can stop ordering and start implementing, or the American taxpayer will have to feed these people or be accused of Nazi tactics. The Morganthau Plan is a disgrace."

Eyebrows rose around the table. The general coughed. May's heart gave a leap. Betsy had not had much time, but clearly his message had been carried home, and it had tallied with the senator's own impressions. He dared not throw even an acknowledging look Betsy's way, but Rasmussen's eyes twinkled. The general stiffened. "I don't like it either, but I'm stuck with it."

Barnes turned to May as he patted his face with a handkerchief. "I'd like to hear what you have to say, Lieutenant May. You speak fluent German, and you're an observer to the governing process. Speak frankly."

The senator was putting him on the hot seat, so May looked to Rasmussen who shot him a go-ahead nod. It was no time to be shy. Still, his heart was in his mouth, and Street sat with his ears cocked at a nearby table.

"Exactly as you have said, sir. It is easy to see that famine is inevitable." May then elaborated on much that he had told Betsy. "Walk around town and see how few food shops, bakeries, meat markets, and grocery stores are open. ONE business is alive and thriving—the brewery. Why? It pours out five hundred liters of beer daily to thirsty GIs. The attitude—let the Germans live off their fat—was all right for a while. Now the hoarded food is gone."

"I'm afraid you're right. I'm going to talk to Jimmy Burns and George Marshall about devising a realistic, far-sighted plan. It'll take months, even years. I suggest that you try to bend a little. Let me give you an example based on what I saw today. Nazi schoolbooks, flags, *etc.*, were being publicly burned. Book burning was a Nazi act, and THAT'S JUST WHAT WE'RE DOING. Lord knows, I'm in favor of the damned stuff being destroyed, every bit of it. However, I don't think we should make a public demonstration of it. That crap will end up being secreted and treasured, mark my words." Barnes shook his head over the problems—all of them.

May's eyes traveled to Street. His hostile stare foretold trouble later.

"If we're going to occupy this territory for the next five years with any degree of stability, we need an immediate building program of caserns and dependent housing, so that the Germans can get back into their own houses. This would afford work," interjected Rasmussen, looking pleased as if it were his birthday. "Also, schools, because of the war, have been closed for over a year. We should reopen them."

"Now!" said Barnes. His air and manner changed to an assured, relaxed tone. "Frankly, I like what I'm hearing. The great tool of democracy has always been enterprise and education. I'm delighted to have made this trip. My eyes have been opened; I'm sorry you are going to see more congressmen interfering with your day-to-day chores, because I can't turn things around alone, and I'm sure it needs to be done. We have an excellent President, whether you recognize it or not. Roosevelt let Stalin hoodwink him. Truman won't be bamboozled."

May got up and put a nickel in the jukebox. "Senator, I'd like the pleasure of dancing with your wife, if you don't mind."

"Be my guest. Tire her, please. I love having a young wife, but occasionally I could use a little relief."

"Now senator, you're the envy of every man here," said the general, brightening under the change of subject.

With Betsy to himself on the dance floor, May could speak freely. "You've been a princess, Mrs. Senator. I never could have reached your husband as you did in the short space before dinner."

"Perhaps I saw more than you thought, walking around this town. Not one person had clothes that fit. Hunger has a mean look…"

"As the shocking stories about the concentration camps sink in to the Germans, so does a great sense of guilt and shame. There's no way Germans can explain this to their children. That's why they have that attitude. They grovel."

"Don't expect quick changes, Jimbo. Washington doesn't work that way. But I promise, we'll get to work."

"I'm seeing a side of you I never saw before, Betsy. It's brighter and better than nice. Your brother and I have never done you justice. I apologize for us both."

"I grew up a lot when my fiancé died. I know I worried Larry. I can't speak for you."

"True art thou Cynara, in thy fashion," said May as he walked Betsy back to the table. The music had stopped and May did not want to draw attention by lingering.

"Yes, indeed, when you sign a marriage registry, life changes," Senator Barnes was saying, his eyes settling on Betsy as she sat down beside him.

The next day Barnes was ready to leave. May was not only exhausted, but also sore from satisfying Betsy's insatiable sexual appetite. He felt he had pulled every string, and turned over every stone, to get his message across without revealing anything personal. If Betsy learned of his attachment to Inge, his case for the Germans would be blown sky high.

"I'd love to stay, but he's anxious to get to Frankfurt/Main and Berlin. Where he goes, I go," Betsy purred, gazing fondly at her husband. Barnes gave her a slap on the behind, hurrying her into the car. From the backseat she waved to May.

"That was short and sweet, and I think productive, " sniffed Rasmussen. "May, you earned your pay."

* ** *

Back in the tunnels, May found Inge delighted over the first load from Göring's cache. Fiske was silent and glum.

"If you've been as successful as we've been, you're a lucky man," said Inge, her eyes dancing. Around her were dozens of uncrated pictures.

May stood quietly for a moment studying them. He did not want to talk about the Barnes' visit. "This painting is Thomas Couture's *Romans of the Decadence.* It was bound to appeal to Göring because of the nudes. In 1847, because the artist couched sex in togas and antiquity, he got away with it. Clearly, something sexual is going on."

"Tell me about your visitors," said Inge.

May felt a flush of guilt and ill temper. "I did my best for you. Leave it at that. I hope the powers that be in Washington will see that they won't gain a thing by starving the Germans."

"You sound angry."

"I don't mean to. I learned something interesting." He looked up at her. "In relationships there is a fuckor and a fuckee."

She turned abruptly. "I don't know what you mean." The ground was suddenly unsure, shifting. She knew what the words meant, but not the sense, not what was going on in his head. Was he talking about their relationship? And if so...

That evening after dinner he had no interest in making love to her. She was surprised, even a little hurt. Then she decided that he had been under a lot of strain.

* ** *

During the Barnes' visit, Fiske had raged silently. Inge, in her enthusiasm to find more of what May had been looking for, had hardly left him alone for a minute. With May's absence, he felt he had more important work to do. Only once during the entire time did she allow him to go from her sight to the *Stadt* for a brief meeting with Street, allegedly to tell him they had uncovered more important art. For Fiske it had been precious time wasted. More galling was the need to restrain himself around Inge, whom he had resolved to wipe out with the rest of the *Amis* in what would be the detonation of the year, making blasts at Hiroshima and Nagasaki look like explosions of popcorn.

Book V

CHAPTER ONE

1945, Berchtesgaden

Street, furious over having been given a backseat by Rasmussen during the Barnes' visit, nevertheless confined himself to testiness. "You've overplayed your hand, May," he sniffed. "The senator and his wife wasted too much of your time."

"You can say that again. Please remember that I did what I was ordered to do," May replied.

"Your critical work should never have been left to two nationals." Street tapped his cigarette on the overly familiar crocodile case, which by now was a tom-tom broadcasting the officer's frustration. "I see no reason why your opinions as an observer of the Military Government are relevant."

"I agree," replied May. "Betsy Barnes didn't come here for my opinions on the Military Government. She came here to get fucked—readily and steadily, too. Put that into your report if you want to. I assure you, Betsy wouldn't care." May shook his head as if dazzled by it all—which he wasn't.

Street, temporarily silenced, sat back and stroked his jaw.

* ** *

Pilot Smith had returned from burying Winchester and consoling the family. He heard May's complaints about the weather during a late Sunday breakfast.

"You've never lived in the mountains, have you?" Smith asked. "Late spring and fall in the mountains are hell, pure *Dreck*. What else have I missed?

"*Leutnant* General Berger," May answered, "second in command of the *Schutzstaffel,* whom we took prisoner some time ago, finally surrendered several million dollars in twenty-five currencies, including some nine million French francs and half a million Japanese yen. On top of that, on Himler's orders, he had buried mailbags of money under the floor of a barn. Since then I've come up with at least a hundred million dollars' worth of stolen art. We've had a senator and his wife here with some promise of improvement. And I've had a German girl here sleeping with me."

"What in the hell are you complaining about?"

"Now that you mention it, no snow!"

They both laughed.

"What's on at the movies?"

"*Gaslight.* I'd like to see it but I can't take Inge with me."

"It's good, but depressing. We have two choices left, May. Do we get drunk here or at the club?"

They spent the day talking. "I had a job to do. I did it well, saving my men, the plane, and my own skin, while stopping maniacs," Smith said. May also found a sympathetic friend.

"I first came to Germany with my head in the clouds. The *Gemütlichkeit* and a girl got to me. She's an artist, but she'd never seen any good modern art. When I got back to the States I gave art a lot of thought, and got into a new career."

"Do you think the Germans really had something?"

"I know they had. Modern art was cheap, and the only way to combat a rising inflation was to spend money fast. The art museum directors knew that and spent every mark they could, grabbing everything in sight."

"You've got to be kidding."

"No, but much was wantonly burned by the Nazis. The Army threw me into art in a big way. I love my country, but since that pre-war year in Germany, I've felt as if I've had one foot here and the other in the States. I've been straddling an ocean."

"Not a comfortable position. What happened to the girl?"

"Rasmussen gave her a job."

"For Christ's sakes, May!" joked Smith in playful exasperation.

Smith pushed away his coffee as if to push away something unpleasant. "I've watched the Germans cleaning up the Berghof. Hell, they're using paper and rags for gloves. I was interviewed in the States for a local human-interest story. I told the reporter how unbelievably bad conditions were here. You should have seen her freeze. 'It's just what they deserve, Captain. Let them suffer,' she said. I told her that this is a bit hard, in that most of us were brought up believing in the Golden Rule, Christianity, or something...." May sighed, "When the government won't let you give candy to children, something is drastically wrong."

Behind May, the Bavarian Alps glistened with a new cap of snow that would last throughout the winter, regardless of warmer weather in the low land. The house sat on steep ground so that the breakfast room, located in the back, afforded a spectacular view.

"May, when you look at these mountains turning purple as clouds shade them from the sun, you can't help but feel there's still some hope for mankind."

"Even the word hopeless, has hope in it," May remarked.

"And every time I have to put down one of those fat mamas on that little airport's runway, the earth feels mighty dear."

"By the way, speaking of touching bases, not long ago Burns started showing up for more than laundry. With Inge producing home-cooked meals, we've had some pleasant evenings."

"I hope I'll be included."

"No doubt."

As if destined, that night Burns brought over a roast and baking potatoes which Inge had never seen. "You, one of the great potato eaters of all time, have never baked a potato?" queried Burns.

"That's right," said Inge.

"May, you haven't taught this girl much," said Burns, turning to Inge. "You really are a cabbage head." They all laughed. It was the first time she'd been teased, and she took it well.

"Remember what Heine wrote: 'Luther convulsed Germany, but Sir Francis Drake calmed it down again. He gave the people the potato,'" said May.

The following morning May was called to Street's office. When he saw the severe expression on Street's face, he knew he was in for trouble.

"There's a report from a neighbor that Fraulein von Haas visits your home regularly. You know my orders on that score."

"Bullshit, Major. Occasionally she visits as a cook, which is hardly fraternization. Last night both Smith and Burns were there. They get tired of club food too."

"Von Haas has been doing a good job, but I'm forced to fire her."

May's stomach churned. "And, I suppose, haul me before the Adjutant General. Well, go ahead."

"I'm not going that far, not yet."

"Yes, you are. The loss of von Haas would slow up my work and your promotion considerably. She's trustworthy and intelligent. Fiske is not. The three of us have the most dangerous jobs in the command. I presume Fiske reported von Haas. He's a dyed-in-the-wool Nazi. She is not; Fiske resents the girl. When I'm not present, he must work under her. She's an artist and knows how art must be handled, how to stretch canvases, *etc*. Their roles cannot be reversed. Unfortunately you need them both, and without them, you lose me."

Street managed a wan smile, indicating that May had been right in thinking that Fiske had been the troublemaker. Fiske's report immediately became self-serving, since Street had no idea that Inge had been the top dog. In fact, he had assumed the opposite. But May had still another screw to turn. "Demolition, not art, is Fiske's field. If he doesn't do his work unerringly, he'll blow himself up, and he could take a few million dollars worth of art with him. Such a bungle could have very serious international repercussions…."

Street was forced to reconsider. "I'll admit you have a strong team. I won't rock the boat until I have to. However, I wouldn't want to defend you in front of Rasmussen."

"Major, don't worry about that. You won't have to. I'll defend myself."

"I would also like a home-cooked meal," Street admitted, hopefully speaking.

"Then you should really get yourself a cook, sir," said May departing. He left feeling that he had survived a close call.

There was no doubt about it, the animosity between Fiske and

Inge was growing; and it seemed to May that there was nothing that he could do about it. The best jobs in town were those working for the Americans, because with work came food. Among the Germans a lot of pettifoggery went on to discredit someone, to get a relative or friend into his or her place. He could not imagine Inge doing anything evil or malicious, but there was a lot he wouldn't put past Fiske. He could terrorize Inge by dousing lights or making strange noises. She might someway be hurt by this tomfoolery, and he didn't like it. Were she to go to Rasmussen asking for a different job, she'd get it in a flash. Luckily, she didn't know that. Until now, they'd been fortunate. Such great luck could not be expected to continue much longer.

* ** *

The Christmas season was upon them. May saw to it that the Fiskes and Müllers had coffee and cake for Advent. He bought heavy sweaters for the Fiskes and loden jackets for the Müllers. For Inge he had a leather portfolio made like the one he had given her in 1938. This time, instead of simply her initials, he had a jeweler work a butterfly in silver. Knowing this was an impractical gift, he included a beautiful purse made in France.

He bought a tree and announced, "We're going to have an international Christmas with lights, glass birds, and decorations from Nuremberg, and tinsel, and… whatever."

"Can we have real candles too?" she asked.

"Sure. I bought them." He thought she was struggling to say something and felt a sudden determination. "This is no time to be living in the past, not with your parents, me, or the Baron. All we have is right now. Let's make it good."

"I don't know why you included the Baron," she said. "My only memorable Christmas was with you."

More and more lately, May had thoughts of the Baron and frankly wished that he were dead. "You could find out quickly enough through Army channels," Smith had told him.

May admitted, "I'm too much of a coward. Remember, as an American, I'm disadvantaged as an oppressor."

Generally, that was true.

Inge was wrapping May's gifts for others when there was a knock at the door. Fearing MPs, coatless, she rushed out the back door. May answered the knock. It was Frau Müller, tense with excitement. May wondered: had the Baron arrived?

"*Herr Leutnant,* please excuse this intrusion, but I must find *die Inge.* The Red Cross sent a message. Her brother will be arriving any minute. She must go to the station."

Frau Müller's eyes mirrored apprehension since any change might greatly affect her. Otto's arrival could mean that Inge would be moved, and they would lose their benefactor. The boy would need a roof. May felt his pulse quiet momentarily.

"Is he all right?"

"I'm sure he is fine." She was smiling now.

"If Inge is not already at your house, I'll send her to the bureau. *Danke sehr,* Frau Müller."

Frau Müller disappeared into the night, and May hurried to the back of the house to call Inge. She stood shivering behind a bush.

"Come in. Put on your coat. That was Frau Müller. Otto will soon be at the Red Cross bureau."

Inge's face came alive with rare radiance. She grabbed at May's hand, her eyes glued to his face. "Oh, dear God, where shall I bring him?" Swamped with confusion, her voice trembled.

"Here, where else?"

"But how can you?"

"How can't I? He can't sleep outdoors. I'll think of something. Be off!"

Inge slipped into her coat and rapidly wrapped a scarf around her throat, her eyes never leaving May. Once again he was there, helping her as she laid her problems at his feet. "I can't dump everything on you. You've done too much for me already. Soon you won't be able to stand me. Remember: the fuckor and the fuckee?"

"I wasn't talking about you. That was something else."

"A fuckor or a fuckee?"

"That was a bad choice of words to represent using someone— someone whom in the past, I had not thought highly enough of. There's a lot of pleasure in being the fuckee."

"We'll talk about that later. Oh, my dear, *Er lebt.*..He lives!"

Inge rushed from the house, leaving May to sort out the tumultuous news.

Once again life was getting out of hand. Still, he had been drawn, as if by a maelstrom, into the turmoil of Inge's problems. When he looked into her eyes, and felt his own racing heart, he knew he had no choice. There are some things a kind, rational man must do without thinking. He wondered how long it would be before he would have to pay the piper? It was simply a matter of time....

The woman in charge of the Red Cross office had reopened that evening to receive and check in the arrivals being transported to Berchtesgaden by van. Otto was in the company of three natives of the Landkreis, who were finally well enough to be released from hospitals and shipped home. Families and close friends had packed the small office to receive their kith and kin.

It had been four years since Inge had seen Otto, due pretty much to his perversity. Too young for the army, he had been placed on a farm. He stayed there until he heard the rumble of what was known as 'Stalin's organs.' With the Russians approaching, Otto took off on foot, traveling toward Hanover. When Inge arrived in Berchtesgaden, she reported him missing, but because he was in the British Occupational Zone, it took the Red Cross considerable time to find him and get him under American jurisdiction. He was now seventeen, a tall, dark, still prankish boy, strangely recognizable.

While working on the farm he had killed a small field mouse and performed a fairly creditable job of taxidermy. Since then he had carried the stuffed animal in his pocket. The little gray creature enabled him to step up behind Inge, holding the mouse by the tail, and say, "Excuse me, lady, but you must have dropped this...."

Inge almost fainted before she broke into a laugh and took him in her arms. Bystanders in the little room were horrified, as was the Red Cross matron, who then processed Otto's papers with dispatch.

"Mousy moves things along," Otto confided.

A wave of relief swept through Inge who, for a moment, had considered the possibility that Otto was slightly deranged.

"You look good," Otto added, having noticed the Christmas coat and boots, but he found himself self-conscious, when it came to further complimenting his sister. "Where are we living?"

"We're going back tonight to Lieutenant May's house. Remember my first boy friend? Now he's an American Army officer. He's been good to me."

"I thought you were moving in court circles. What happened to your Baron Montag?"

"I don't know. May found me before I found Kurt. It's been very good. I got a job with the Americans."

Otto looked shocked. "They don't even speak to us!"

"That's right. Our presence puts Lieutenant May in danger of a sixty-five dollar fine. He has managed to avoid that, but you must be careful."

Otto shook his head in an exaggerated youthful way, digesting his sister's revelations and encampment with the enemy. He remembered that he had liked Herr May. His sister, beautiful and elegant, was cared for. Otto had been conditioned to shift rapidly into whatever condition presented itself with little emotional baggage. What he didn't realize was that much of the joy radiating from her came from finding him whole. For the moment, her concern—how to take care of him—was buried under unmitigated relief.

They walked in the darkness toward May's house, her arm through his, yet still leading, marveling at the way he had grown. Muscles bulged under his tight jacket. When she thought about it, her heart swelled with pride that, for this moment of entry into her life again, she would be able to bring him into something comfortable and infinitely more than others had. For the first time Otto would step into a home almost as fine as the house he remembered best. A Christmas tree with the odd colored lights May had insisted upon would be blazing in a corner, imparting a festive air. Herr May would welcome Otto, she was sure. It would be a wonderful Christmas.

Otto was her last living blood relative. Hounding the Red Cross in her quest to find Otto, she had learned that her Uncle Fritz had died of natural causes. He had owned a locomotive works. Like her father, he had been a quasi-Nazi. With his sons *gefallen,* his wife gone, and his property in ruins, she surmised that he had had little left to live for.

As they approached one of the few streets with streetlights operating, Inge took a long, harder look at Otto and felt a small panic. He looked like a man. Then she remembered that he had strained the patience of the von Haas household with his penchant for tricks and disregard of authority. Undoubtedly, he had been through a lot, for good or for evil. He could even be ready to break—for all she knew. He appeared to be dressed out of a ragbag. And needing a haircut, he looked like a chrysanthemum.

* ** *

Pacing the floor anxiously, May didn't know what in the devil he'd do with a seventeen-year-old. Burns had accepted Inge. He might be pushed too far when it came to secreting a teenager. And before too long, two more officers would be moved into the house, two totally unknown entities who could be two pricks like Street. The Housing Authority could push Inge into a room as a qualified specialist, but Otto would be about as necessary as a good case of mumps. He remembered the kid as bright, but hell, he could come in on crutches, thought May, making himself a stiff scotch. Then with a shudder he recalled himself at Otto's age. At least the refrigerator, all three cubic feet of it, was full.

May felt caught between Scylla and Charybdis. Doomsday was coming. It was only a matter of how soon. He gulped down the scotch and heard them at the door.

Otto filled the doorway. Inge peered from behind him, smiling, a reassuring sign.

"*Sapperlot!* Otto, I'm glad to see you." May wondered if he should act fatherly, but didn't quite know how. "You're a grown man." He took in the height, the thin parched face, and woolly hair—much as he had gulped down his last drink.

"He's up to his old tricks," said Inge. "Show Herr May *deine Feldmaus.*" She turned away, grateful for the distraction. Her brother's eyes in the bright lights of the Christmas tree were making little explosions in her heart.

"I'm braced with a drink, Inge. Make two for yourself and Otto while I take his coat."

May's first four sentences endeared him to Otto as nothing else could.

"You've made your sister's Christmas."

"Being here has made mine, sir."

They talked for over two hours, having moved to the kitchen, as Otto admitted to being hungry. Most of the conversation covered where he had been, how he had survived, and comparing notes with Inge. By the time May, having heard the highlights, excused himself and mentioned going to bed, the refrigerator appeared to have hosted a swarm of locusts. May touched Inge's shoulder. "Stay here and talk if you like. I'm bushed. Give Otto Winchester's room."

Once upstairs in bed, he felt a twinge of loneliness and would have appreciated Inge's presence, as if her body, freely offered, would have been a gesture of thanks. Then he realized that perhaps she was shy about toddling off to bed under the nose of her brother—with a man to whom she was not married; and he knew they needed to talk further without him. That settled, he fell asleep. Sometime later Inge crawled into his bed and into his arms. In the darkness, now warm and cozy, her lips left a trail of kisses as they sought his with ever increasing intensity. Her urgent trembling fingers massaging him completed his arousal, and in a fury of passion like some great storm, he was rewarded.

* ** *

The following morning May visited Colonel Rasmussen. There was no way that he could get away with harboring Otto under his roof for more than a day or two. With some trepidation he met the colonel's no-nonsense stare.

"Colonel, because there are only Smith and me in the house, the man who handles the coal furnace gives us short shrift. He's overworked because others are careless about leaving windows open—or so he says. I haven't availed myself of the services I'm entitled to. I want to hire a fire boy. He can sleep on a cellar cot near the furnace, and the German government can pay for it."

The colonel gave May a jaundiced look, but May had been right. He was within his rights under the terms of surrender. "Whom do you have in mind?"

"Inge's younger brother."

"That figures," growled the chief. "Okay, put him on the payroll." A glance to the papers on his desk indicated the meeting was over.

With Otto there for Christmas, May's shopping was not complete. The kid had come in with only the clothes on his back. May spent a long time in the PX, extending his role as Santa Claus. What fit him snugly would be right for Otto: a jacket, two shirts, two pairs of cord pants, some underwear, and a pair of gloves. Shoes would have to wait until after Christmas.

After dinner he eased into the subject. "Otto, you've moved into the American Zone where things might not operate like they seem." Then he went on to explain that he would have to work, and that he would only have the basement room. "There are other officers who live here, and you will have to accommodate their wishes. They come and go. I hope they'll like you; otherwise you'll have to make yourself scarce. Do you understand what I'm saying?"

"*Ich danke ihnen,* Herr May, and I won't mind eating in the kitchen if you think I should."

Obviously Inge had talked to him.

Otto strongly resembled his father. In that moment May wished that he smoked so that he could busy himself with something. Memories of Herr von Haas, the taskmaster, who could always play with inserting a cigarette in a holder and retain poise, not to mention a two-inch ash, undermined him. I don't want to be like him, thought May. "We'll simply have to play everything by ear, Otto."

May sighed as he sat regarding the young man, an enlargement of the boy whom he remembered so well—dashing over fields with exultant cries as his kite rose, or grinning silently as he waited for a trick to hatch. Thankfully, Inge had given him a haircut.

He's unspoiled, thought May in a wave of compassion usually reserved for Inge. At the same time he marveled over Otto's resiliency. With the lecture over, he retreated to the club.

There he was welcomed like the prodigal son returned. "Well, well, look who is here," greeted Walkowsky. "Long time no see."

"Come on. Don't you get sick of this place too?" queried May.

"Yeah, twice on Sunday. You haven't been seen since the dancing doll left."

"Obviously I have to work a good deal harder than you." May sipped his drink. "Where I work, you can hear the River Styx."

"There have been times when we've needed your sage judgment," said Richards.

"About what?" May replied, not taking him seriously.

"In Oberammergau we jailed John the Baptist for Nazi activities.

Also we discovered Pontius Pilate was more than a simple woodcarver—he was a *Volksturm* official."

The news fitted May's rebellious mood. He turned back to Richards, eyebrows knotted. "For heaven's sake, the Passion Play doesn't come up until 1950! Do we intend to keep these jokers in jail until then?"

"I should think not, but the people are concerned. Every ten years these roles are played by the same people. "

"This thing has been held every year ending in zero for over three hundred years. We can't begin to interfere with religious freedom." Then he remembered the American command was, indeed, capable of that. "I suppose now we have a new directive declaring the Passion Play, a Nazi ploy or a Fascist tool…"

"Somebody give this man another drink," yelled Walkowsky.

The liquor had its effect, and May remembered that quite a number of German *Feiertage* would be coming up: Corpus Christi, Fasching, October Fest, and even the Franconian Baroque Festival in Bayreuth. Were he to put on civvies, and not be too punctual about getting a haircut, the celebrations could be fun with Inge. He went home in a better frame of mind.

Inge had gone to the Müller house. May looked in on Otto, not yet asleep.

"I hope you're not upset about my being here, sir."

"No, Otto, not at all. Sleep well."

The following morning in the cellar where coal was stored, May examined a small adjoining room to the laundry room. It had a high window and an outside entrance. With a coat of paint, it would be adequate for Otto. He would requisition a bed, a chair, a desk, and chest of drawers.

Thinking of Inge, May said aloud, "I didn't know that she would take so much or that I would give it."

* ** *

Otto behaved himself perfectly when May was present, but having once been a venturesome teenager himself, May was inclined to give any youth a jaundiced eye. He remembered well a period of acting smart-alecky, feeling he knew more about everything than God himself, believing that he could do as he pleased and get away with it. The problem was that society and the consequences had changed. The U.S. Army was in control, not doting grandparents.

Not long after Otto's arrival, May happened to see Otto on the street with older companions who looked rougher and tougher than May would have liked. The group walked with a swagger, sporting a sense of lawlessness. May surmised that these older companions might have looked on Otto as a source of pilfered cigarettes, clothes, liquor, or whatever. Thugs would hardly let Otto hang out with them, unless he could be useful.

Soon May noticed that the liquor supply had gone down a lot faster than usual, but because there were other officers in the house, he felt both unsure and puzzled. For the time being, Otto was a misfit, and May knew that this was an uncomfortable position for any teenager. He could warn Otto that he might be set up by undesirables—to be someway used or framed—but he doubted that Otto would do anything more than politely listen. Besides, it was a ticklish subject to bring up with Inge.

CHAPTER TWO

1945, Berchtesgaden

Nursing a dream, May went to Bormann's tunnel and pulled out some beige silk, which, because it would be of no use to the Army, was scheduled to be burned. He wrapped the fabric in brown paper and walked out with it under his arm like a magazine, knowing that he was stealing, but only from a bonfire. When Inge finished work, he walked her across the Berghof grounds. Out of sight of the guards, he put the roll into her hands. "Go to a dressmaker and have an evening dress made for New Year's Eve." Before she could say anything, he left her. That he would steal for her, even from a bonfire, and that she would know, smarted.

* ** *

On Christmas Eve afternoon Inge delivered May's gifts to the Fiskes and Müllers. "You have no idea how I hated taking gifts to the Fiske's," Inge later told May. "You don't realize how dangerous that man is. The man is crazy."

"That's possibly true. You see things I miss, but I know you have a vivid imagination."

"He's a fanatic about everything—his shoe laces, his hair, his stubby little colored pencils…."

"What about his stubby little pencils?"

"They have a special order. If he takes one out, he sticks something in the slot. He almost slapped my hand for touching them. Around you, he plays a docile role. It's as if he's on stage, and it's a totally different story when you're not there."

"I need him, Inge."

"I think he would kill you if he could."

"He has had ample opportunity. All he would need to do is drag my body into some remote nook and cranny, and then blow it up. You'd be picking me off the walls."

Inge gasped. "Don't talk that way!"

"Well, I have to. Haven't you noticed that I always walk behind him?"

Inge's eyes fell to the floor. "Yes, and I thought that funny."

"I don't do it as a joke." He was getting irritated by the conversation that was leading nowhere. At this point he could do nothing about Fiske, and she knew it.

Inge had prepared a lovely dinner for Christmas Eve, using the house owner's best china and linens. The table was lit with candles and decorated with holly. She chose the traditional dinner of carp. For the gift giving that followed dinner, she had painted two watercolors and had them framed for May and Otto. They were taken from photographs May had made years before, when they enjoyed an outing on the Wannsee. Their love had been fresh and new, and both felt something incomparably unique and lovely was happening. For both it had colored life with a happiness they thought nothing could ever shake.

Both men were profoundly moved by their gifts. Otto, although not present on the outing, felt the scene reminiscent of an era blown to bits from which he had not one tangible token. For a moment they were silent.

"You don't like them?" she asked, apologetically. "I'm a little out of practice."

May reached for her hand. "How could you say such a thing?"

Inge felt better. "I found your old photographs. They included some shots of Otto, so I put him in a sailboat."

Otto rushed from the room, apparently overtaken with emotion, and Inge started after him.

"Inge, let him be," said May. "Just because you found him, doesn't mean you should start mothering."

The interference galled her. "But isn't that what I'm here for?"

"No, there are times when it is good to be alone."

Reluctantly, she accepted May's premise. Soon Otto was back with two small gifts. Wondering what in the world Otto would have found in so little time, they gingerly opened the lumpy packages. Inge looked down to see a platinum ring, set with two huge diamonds. There was a gold tiepin for May. Both were very fine and obviously valuable. Inge and May sat in shock. "Where did you get these?" Inge sputtered.

"I found them a long time ago."

"Where?"

"In Berlin."

"How did that happen?" Inge's tone rang with suspicion.

"I came out of an air raid shelter. I was the first out because I'd been the last in. A building had been hit, and there were bodies strewn about. I picked two rings off loose hands. The tiepin was on the street. I've kept them pinned inside my clothes. The little ring I had to sell to eat. The big one I saved for you. That's all there is to it."

Inge, aghast, swallowed defeat. "It's a magnificent ring."

Having opened her gift from May, she turned to him, aware of his faint smile. "I'm sure you know how I love this writing portfolio, so like another…"

*   **   *

May informed Inge and Otto that after the New Year came in, two more officers would be billeted in the house. They looked smitten. "Don't worry. We'll handle it." Still, he knew, it wouldn't be easy.

Inge's dressmaker would have the dress finished by New Year's Eve. "I want it to be like a dress I once had. The world has changed, and me with it, but many things remain the same," she told the dressmaker, who felt everything had changed. For the first time May would put on civvies, and he and Inge would appear in a public place, albeit a German locale—no longer the best. They had been taken over by the *Amis*.

Silvesterabend was not a repeat of the evening at the Adlon, yet it was gratifying. Inge's coat and purse hardly went with the dress, but the incongruity was matched a hundred times by others in the crowded room. The men's evening suits reeked of mothballs. Instead of being a poor student, May was now a big spender. They drank German sparkling wine and saw the old year out with horns and clatter. Otto made out well with the surplus women. With the Nazis gone, a whole new echelon of German society seemed to be coming out of cracks in the wall. Being exceptional dancers, Inge and May could not escape notice, and May's table was a great question mark: "Could he be an *Ami?*" Queries to waiters brought forth only, "I don't know, but the gentleman speaks flawless German."

The music was American to the note. The years of war, during which the ever-popular American and English music were banned on the *Volksradio*, left the Germans hungry for the sound. Groups that found work playing for the GIs were given sheet music, and heard records by Jimmy and Tommy Dorsey, Woody Herman, Glenn Miller, Stan Kenton, Gene Krupa, and Coleman Hawkins—which they were quick to imitate. In Washington May had learned to jitterbug, and with a little home instruction, Inge had picked up this jazz version of the two-step. The swing, balance and twirl—without the vigorous acrobatics—fascinated the Germans, and soon quite a few couples were trying the steps with them. Swing and sway tunes remained May's favorites, and one above all others, *Poor Butterfly.*

"We should find another song," he told Inge, "because the words never fit you. Its melancholy quality epitomized how bad leaving you was."

"It's always worse for the one left with the empty haunts," she replied, brushing his face with her lips. "If I didn't love you, I could never have accepted so much."

"I won't lie and say that finding you again has been easy, but for me there's only been you, despite the bag and baggage that have come with you. Under our circumstances I'm hopelessly frustrated. Now I'm concerned about Otto. He's a maverick. At heart, he's too bright, too inventive, and too rambunctious to thrive and develop in this hog-bound German/American society that has been forced on us."

His confession unsteadied her, and she wanted to blurt out that his fears over Otto were nothing compared to her fears over a confrontation with the Baron, who could also be just as dangerous as Fiske, and who might show up in a German locale. But Kurt Montag was a topic likely to spoil their magic moment. May's arms tightened around her. "Be patient with us," she said.

He stepped back to look at her and felt his love choking his throat.

He could see her breasts pulsating below exquisite satiny shoulders. Her long beautiful neck culminated in a face etched so strongly in his mind that it might have been branded there. Pre-war memories crowded him like a snare closing in around him. "Sometimes a man loves a woman more than it is sensible or wise, so that people say he's a fool. Perhaps I am. The good moments with you have been the greatest moments of my life. And that's the way it's always been."

Her eyes were shining, and above her, a slowly rotating mirrored ball beamed tiny prisms of light into her hair so that she seemed to shimmer. "After you left, if I'd been able to foresee what was going to happen, I probably would have killed myself. But by the time the future caught up with me, I could handle it. You know, because you do it all the time, there's a lot of satisfaction in putting someone else ahead of yourself." He did not know it, but these words would come back to haunt him.

The room seemed filled with light to the remotest corner. They both felt refreshed by the intimate confessions that there had been so little time to express. For the next few minutes they simply enjoyed the dance, reveling in the movement of two as one, with separations and returns, drawing back and stepping forward, relinquishing and reclaiming. The winning and losing seemed to be the tempo of life, and they had caught it. Then the band took a break. Otto had gone, leaving a note: "Am on to something promising. See you tomorrow. Thanks for a good time." Otto was no longer a child.

May seated Inge and continued with another point that was on his mind. "If the new housemates prove a problem, we'll move to the Eagle's Nest."

"Oh, no, not there!" she protested, pained at the thought, but reluctant to say more. Lord, a barn would be preferable.

Presently, they went out to face the New Year. Together in the star-spangled darkness they walked to his house, and for a while at least, forgot the past. After making love May fell into a deep sleep while Inge tossed. Within hours, the depressing thought of living in the Eagle's Nest, magnified into a distressing jail sentence.

* ** *

Inge did not think of the Baron Kurt Montag often, chiefly because of the distraction of Otto. Still, it was a holiday period, a time when

246

Montag was likely to appear. The stronger her attachment to May, the greater her feeling of foreboding, when she contemplated eventuality. Montag had written of hating May as the enemy. The reoccurring thought that he might hold back, observing her before making his presence known—for any number of reasons—was always frightening.

At the same time Inge was being exposed to a whole new world of art that was making a big impression. She carefully studied every crate that was opened as well as May's art books that were now available to her.

"I think Corinth really got to you," he said.

"Why do you say that?"

"Because looking at the watercolors you gave Otto and me, I can think of no one else."

May had sensed her troubled mood, and it had become apparent in her art. She felt unprepared to discuss Montag and covered up. "Yes, I had been looking at Corinth's *Walchensee – Blick und Wetterstein,* studying those blue tones. I didn't mean to copy his style, but you picked up on it. Nothing escapes you."

"Dear, that's what I'm trained to see. Many paintings are unsigned. I look for the feel of the artist. Picasso tried everything, but he still comes out Picasso."

"I saw an old bank calendar today with a beautiful reproduction," she said.

"Sketch something in that style and let me guess." He then busied himself with the lists that always needed updating; Street would be back soon expecting miracles. Inge grabbed a pad and sketched two embracing figures that she placed on his desk. "The clothes are gold, the background ocher with little squares."

"Gustav Klimt's *Der Kuss,*" he said, handing it back, looking bored.

"How do you know everything? How did you know to stop me from running after Otto, who has pulled rings off bodies? Or, that the only possession I ever loved was a writing portfolio from you? Your superiority is very hard on me!"

May laughed to make light of her outburst. Although he wanted to lead her to an empty chamber to make love to her, he could not. Fiske was approaching.

After May left, she turned to the sketch of the entwined lovers and added a locomotive. The flowers at the lovers' feet became clouds of steam. Around the couple she sketched other desperate people. Instead of a joyous reunion of a god and goddess, she now had a grotesque scene in a railroad station. The skillful transformation and distortion were remarkable. Then Fiske's obnoxious presence drove her home.

May did not doubt that Kurt Montag would show up one day. He knew Americans had no monopoly on berserk soldiers, and Montag could be one, but he considered Montag a threat to his happiness, not his life. His government had put him in the untenable position of competing with a castled nobleman, whom she had been conditioned from birth to appreciate. Plus, were he not a fine person, Inge would never have promised to marry him.

Betsy had once said, "Men never marry their great loves, but wind up marrying the women who want them. When you care too much, you don't know how to play the game." Unable to conceive of love as a game, May had been shocked. There had always been a lot of truth in what Betsy said. Inge left him once; she could leave him again.

* ** *

Captain Rex Wade took Winchester's old room. Wade's hair was red, his complexion flushed, peppered by freckles. Short and heavy set, he appeared to May as a composite of the Yokums: about as intellectual as L'il Abner, smart as Mammy, and lecherous as Pappy. If he didn't turn out to be a man with a mission, May felt he could handle him.

May explained, "A German girl fixes dinner for Burns and me. Her brother, only a kid, lives in the basement and keeps the fires burning."

"Is the girl good-looking?"

"Mightily so, and when non-fraternization is lifted I plan to marry her." May had decided to set the story straight from the beginning.

"Ho, ho! First dibs. Well, I'm glad you warned me."

"They were both pretty hungry when I took them in."

"Listen, the Germans all hoard food," said Wade.

"The hoarded food is gone. All they're hoarding now is despondence. Cellars, where they used to keep food, now have lots of people living in them."

"You get along with these people then?"

"I don't like to be around groveling, hungry, hostile people, especially in my own home. I'm dependent on them. A German saves me from being blown up about once a week."

"I get the message, but when they've done their best to kill you—you look at them differently."

"True, but Inge and Otto were kids when the war broke out."

"Do you have to look out for stealing?"

"Good Lord, no." Up until then, it was a true statement.

"I'm only asking. Are there house rules I need to know?"

"So far none have been necessary, other than consideration."

"That's something new in the Army."

May started to tell him to leave the Army at the door, but then softened his remark, "I hope you'll like living here. It's not home, but for now it is."

"Every monkey has his swing. I don't want to upset the applecart, but I also don't want to pay any sixty-five dollar fines."

"Nor do I." With that settled, May felt better. If nothing unpleasant happened for a while, May trusted Wade would be won over, if only by Inge's charm. Otto was warned to lay off the tricks and practical jokes.

May also wanted an ally in the house when it came to tackling a problem, one Inge had never given a thought to: Otto's education. It was May, not Inge, who had been shocked that Otto had not been in school for over two years, with a third one looming. In the rigid old system, Otto had become lost. He was seventeen with a German eighth-grade education.

Saying nothing to Inge, May had written Betsy Barnes explaining Otto's plight. Possibly among her prosperous friends, she might have one who would be willing to take Otto as a war orphan. In an American school, he might get back on track. There was no point in saying anything to Inge until an opportunity arose. He didn't want it to appear as if he wanted to get rid of Otto, which she might assume. It was a sticky wicket.

With Otto's education in another's hands, May tried to further Inge's artistic development. A Wassily Kandinsky turned up in Göring's cache. May let out a whistle. "See how he presents a turbulent earth? He painted wild terrain. He reflected the tense atmosphere in Germany and the apocalyptic mood Hitler exploited. Upheaval was his unique expression."

"Hitler would have hated this, but I can't take my eyes away. The brilliant colors make me think of clashing sounds," said Inge.

May beamed. "You don't know how happy I am that you're finally seeing these things."

"What a voice!"

His lips closed on hers, and his hand pulled hers down to the throbbing bulge in his khakis. Fiske was on an errand in town, leaving them free to make love.

Separating and tidying up themselves, he told her, "I never knew Kandinsky was that exciting."

She quieted a still racing heart.

"We don't know how many of his paintings were destroyed—in the hundreds," he murmured.

"I was looking forward to more."

He slapped her fanny.

She regarded him seriously. "You make a great teacher. I don't feel as though I'm looking at art, but at a gathering of personalities, all coming alive, all saying something in their own way with so much more variety than I'm used to. I'd like to know these people better, to learn their languages, because they all speak differently."

"Most people have no idea what the Weimar Republic could have given the world."

"You must admit, it takes study."

"Everything does."

"Then I shouldn't feel stupid not having heard the silent voices?"

"Not at all. You'll soon know more than I do because you have the natural insight of an artist. I'll be reduced to keeping you happy in bed."

"Don't underestimate the free flow of emotion," she replied, running her hands through her hair and laughing.

Moved by her words, he stepped behind her and with both hands, stiffened her shoulders. Everything went well when they were alone. It was only when they emerged to the outer world that estrangement threatened him. Her people were struggling to stay alive. She was as much as part of this as he was of the military. They were 'the Krauts.'

Crude remarks about their hairy legs and armpits, dropped loudly by GIs—when there were no razors to come by—were only minor irritations. Despite warnings of court-martial—and the death penalty—GIs frequently raped German women. Defense lawyers, juries of men, portrayed women as whores, and the soldiers always got off. As non-fraternization droned on, more and more of these incidents occurred.

The first night Wade was in the house, Inge fed Otto early, which suited him fine. Downstairs in his room he was tinkering with an old radio that was close to operating.

"I think I should eat alone in the kitchen," Inge said.

"You will not."

"For a little while...at first, it might be wise, certainly safer."

"You're going to be safe. No more of this talk."

Inge took her place in the dining room, but she said almost nothing as if her silence complied with the directives. May talked non-stop. He told Wade about the tunnels and the POWs that were found. "A day never passes that both Inge and I don't discover another crime of Hitler's regime."

Wade looked at May and then Inge. "I'm surprised that you talk so openly about the Germans. It must be an uncomfortable subject for Inge."

May gave her no chance to speak. "If you had your family and home destroyed, and if you had walked here from Berlin, you wouldn't be embarrassed by anti-Nazi sentiment. You'd agree wholeheartedly. Without killing her, their policies destroyed everything she had—except for one brother."

"Her beauty is still intact," said Wade, smiling.

"Thank you," she replied, almost in a whisper.

"As are her mind and talent," May added.

"I know nothing about your art, but your cooking is great." Wade was a flirt.

Before dinner was over, May saw that Inge had taken the right tack in handling Wade. He would be unlikely to hurt her now, whereas had she been pushy or possessive about the house, he would have been irked. In the soft light of the room, she looked particularly lovely, and May felt his heart crowded by pride in her. Inge cleared the table and started doing the dishes. May came to help.

"I'm going back to Müller's tonight. Let's break Wade in slowly," she whispered. "Listen to me this time."

"If you insist, but have Otto walk with you." This instruction was ignored.

They finished the dishes and she kissed him quickly. "Good night, sir," she said to Wade, slipping into her coat, leaving May to spend the evening talking to the captain.

"She's a lovely girl. I understand how you feel."

May smiled. "You can't really, but I must say, you're catching on remarkably fast."

* ** *

The walk to the Müller house was through twisting, cobblestone streets to a poor section of town. Inge had walked it many times, but not since Otto's arrival. Times had been changing rapidly however. Cold weather kept people off the streets, and the shortage of fuel forced Germans to bed early, so there were fewer lights from houses, fewer still from *Kneipen*. Even though it was not late, the town seemed closed up tight.

As Inge approached an intersection illuminated by one small light bulb, she heard a group of GIs talking loudly as they came to the corner. She stepped into the light first and began crossing the street in full view. She was not immediately frightened, but then she realized they had picked up their pace. As their footsteps grew closer, she started to run.

"Let's get the Kraut," one called out. As if seeing a checkered flag or hearing a shot, they broke into a run after her.

The men were naturally faster, but they had been drinking, and the cobblestones were slippery. Inge had spent a lifetime holding her footing on precarious ground, and the daily climb to the Berghof had proved a worthwhile exercise. Mobilized by fear, like a fox pursued by a pack of hounds, she gained ground for awhile. The blocks were short and once she slipped into an alleyway as they ran past. Panting, she regained her breath. Knowing they would be back, combing the alley, she started out again, running in the opposite direction. Hearing her footsteps, they started back after her. Fortified by the few minutes rest, she was able to gain some distance. But, spurred by the thrill of the hunt, they remained on her heels.

At this point Inge had no idea where she was, or where she could find a police station, or even a hospital to get help. Under American orders many of the street names had been changed. Adolf Hitler *Strasse* had become Maximilian *Strasse,* and Horst Wesselberg was now Moosweg. These were main streets, but many smaller commemorative names had been painted out, leaving Inge and the pack behind her totally lost. Once again she was able to slip into a doorway while the men ran past. The group soon discovered their mistake and wheeled back. The pause spared her a collapse in complete exhaustion, but starting out this time, she lost momentum and losing her stride, became careless. She fell. Within seconds they were around her, also heaving and panting.

"Don't you dare touch me," she gasped. "I'm under Colonel Rasmussen." As always, her English was perfect, and she had hit upon the right words, 'Colonel Rasmussen.'

"Christ, she must be a nurse. Let's get the hell out of here," someone said. Visions of repercussions for having attacked an American had their effect, and the men barreled off.

Slowly Inge picked herself up. Bruised and aching, she began staggering around, looking for a familiar landmark. She began to sob. In a daze she saw a jeep with two MPs, and waved them down.

"Help me, please. I've been chased by your soldiers," she blurted, before giving way to near hysterics. Blood streamed from her head.

"Did you notice any name plates," asked the driver.

"I had no chance."

"Then there's not much we can do other than report the incident. They didn't rape or beat you?"

"No, but they would have, if I hadn't said that I work for Colonel Rasmussen. They were five, a pack of wolves. I ran for miles."

Contritely, they drove her around, looking for the men, but apparently they had split up. Inge was driven home.

The following morning Inge was too ill to show up at work. When she was half an hour late, May began to fuel his panic. Something had happened. By the time a driver arrived to take him to the Müller house, he could hardly restrain his anxiety. Frau Müller answered his knock, and her pained expression confirmed his fears.

"She's upstairs," she murmured as May rushed past her. His presence awakened Inge. Only her bruised face was visible. Through tears, finally the story came out.

"You're sure no bones are broken?"

"I don't think I could've walked."

"I'll be back with some medicine," he promised.

At the infirmary May found a doctor he knew slightly. On hearing the story, against regulations, he gave May a painkiller and some sleeping pills. "She's lucky," said the doctor. "A mob of men can be brutes."

He watched Inge take the dosage, and went to see Rasmussen.

The colonel listened to the story, shaking his head in chagrin. "It's one of the things that comes with an army, May. This sort of thing is happening more and more. We're never going to eradicate it completely, but we can certainly make more noise."

"If we don't want the Germans patrolling the streets with hidden clubs to protect their women, we'd better protect them, sir."

Rasmussen concurred. "Lawlessness is growing. It's not just the U.S. Army. The German crime rate is on the rise."

May thought of Otto's friends, then felt guilty over the thought.

The following day, appearing better, Inge told May, "It has occurred to me, having such a strong will, I could have died from exhaustion. It's better to be raped than dead."

"Still, you shouldn't have to endure it. Psychopaths will always prey on society. The brutes attacking you were not mentally ill—just men out of control. It's a wonder you don't hate all Americans."

His expression struck Inge as pathetic. "You redeem them all, *Liebling*. When you get upset with the Army, remember that.

* ** *

Later that evening May and Inge heard voices in Otto's room and rightly assumed he had guests, let in through the cellar door. "I've seen some of his friends on the street," said May, "and, frankly, they don't look so hot to me. I haven't wanted to say anything."

"Then why are you now?"

"Because I wanted to discuss it with you first."

"All Germans look pretty awful. What is it you say? Don't judge a book by its cover."

"I'm not referring to the way they're dressed. It's an attitude and not a nice one."

"If this is something you feel sure about, I'll say something to him. But can you understand my reticence? I've had to put so many restrictions on him. He's so out of place."

"Yes, but I think it would be prudent. They're older, and a sort of mean looking bunch. They can only be interested in using Otto. I don't quite know how. I do know that when I think about them, I don't feel good. It's just one more thing we don't need to worry about."

"I'll say something."

"Try not to use me as a big stick."

She looked chagrined. "You're giving me ammunition but no gun. Still, I'll try."

May doubted that she would.

CHAPTER THREE

Within a few days, out of sympathy for Inge as well as May's persuasive arguments, Captain Rex Wade warmed to Inge and Otto. "It's so good to talk to people who aren't in the goddamned Army." Wade was speaking after a particularly frustrating day. The Army's a fucking machine."

"A machine fucking illegally, too," corrected May.

Wade, in maintenance, was having problems with his men. The older ones, sick of Europe, were becoming careless with safety standards. "I have to hammer away at stuff that ought to be self-evident. And for every well-trained man who goes home, I get some eighteen-year-old from the States who doesn't give a rat's ass about what he's doing, and he's bound to be homesick tomorrow. The kids don't realize that there are about two decent flying days a year on this continent. Pilots need everything they can get out of a machine."

* ** *

May was awakened by a call from Street, and he knew immediately that Street wanted a favor—his tone was too cordial. "My furnace has conked out. This house is like a refrigerator, and my houseman can't get it going. I wondered if you'd lend me Otto for the day. I'll pay him gladly."

"Oh, sure," May replied. "I'll send him over. Probably it simply needs a good cleaning."

In the course of the war, a good many mechanical chores usually done by men went begging. May was right. A lack of cleaning was the problem, and Otto worked there all day, opening valves and shoveling out clinkers. On that same day May and Wade were robbed. May did not discover the theft until evening when the family converged at around 6 PM. Otto was covered with soot like a chimney sweep. May called the MPs and the local police, because two of the heavy wool blankets taken from the house belonged to the German owners. The thief, or thieves, found everyone's money, all the gold and sterling silver the men possessed, as well as two Leicas, and some film recently purchased at the PX.

Entrance and an exit had been gained through Otto's cellar door, and May immediately suspected his unsavory friends. Much to May's relief, Otto had worked all day at Street's, which put him in the clear. Wade's Leica was brand new, but May's had been bought years before when he first went to Germany, and he felt he had lost an old friend. Inge sensed this.

The theft came on the heels of Inge's episode with the GIs, and despite the fact that she lost nothing, together the two incidents combined to destroy her self-confidence. "I feel stymied," she told May while at work. "It extends to my art. I'd like to find direction, my own style."

"You want to do in a few months what other artists took years to achieve," May countered.

"The theft upset me, but talking to you always makes me feel better. I've always had an inner tension…"

"Under such a calm exterior. Now I've a briefing, and I want to pick up my mail. Stay here until I get back. I don't want you walking across that rocky, debris-strewn plain alone."

Nor did she want to, but she felt even more constrained, almost physically handicapped. Certainly she loved May, but sometimes inadvertently, he made her feel so… flawed.

* ** *

An expected letter from Betsy arrived. May soon sat down while reading it.

"Dearest Jimbo,

"Your letter re Otto is before me. I have just talked to several high school principals and spent last evening talking with my husband. Now, brace yourself for a surprise. We would like to take Otto ourselves! Apparently, I

*won't be having any children of my own, so I might just as well start with
a teenager. It might be one worthwhile thing I can do with my life.*

*"The schools here are familiar with students from God- knows- where,
and push them along. Having a senator for a hubby will cut the red tape.
Perhaps your assistant can give Otto some English tutoring before he comes.
It would help.*

*"General Marshall is deeply involved with a plan for the European
recovery, so take heart. I warned you about time, didn't I?*

*"Being with you was great. What a lover! Well we've always had a ball
in the sack.*

*"I'm so excited about this I can hardly write. Shall I come over? Write.
Write. Write.*

"Soonest—you Darling!

"Love, Betsy

"P.S. Send snapshots. "

Holy Toledo, thought May, never having dreamed he was stirring
up a caldron so fast. He couldn't let Inge see the letter, and surely she
would want to. There was nothing to do but destroy it immediately. A
quick search produced a match, and soon he was breathing normally.
He'd have to tell Inge that the information came with a 'top secret'
cable. But he decided, sure as a gun's steel, there'd be more letters from
Betsy, dozens of them, all personal, all exuberant, all incriminating!
Furthermore, in Washington, Otto would surely spill the beans about
Inge.

May went back to the tunnels with the dilemma weighing like a
sack of cement.

His silence did not go unnoticed. "Obviously, I upset you today."
Inge was straightening up her drafting board.

"No, you didn't. I have something else on my mind"

She pressed. "You don't want to talk about it?"

"I'd rather wait until dinner. Right now I'm tired. Street was a pain
in the ass." For once he hadn't been; he actually had expressed concern
for Fräulein von Haas.

"Shall I brace myself?"

"Well, it certainly isn't urgent. How long before Corpus Christi?"

"I'll check it out tomorrow," she replied, relieved.

Wade was there for dinner and so was Burns, which knocked out the 'top secret' excuse. He could swallow his tongue for a few days, but Inge was highly susceptible to his moods and too often misunderstood them. Trying to help Otto, he felt caught in a vise.

Inge had prepared a beautiful platter of *hors d'oeuvre,* and soon they were all enjoying drinks before dinner. "It's been too long since I've been here," said Burns, helping himself to a thin roll of ham and asparagus. "What have you been up to besides protesting hoodlums, May?"

May propped his feet on the ubiquitous Moroccan hassock, trying to relax. "We were lucky today. Fiske unpacked a Pissarro."

"I thought they were called *pissoires,*" replied Burns.

May turned to Inge. "See how uncouth and uneducated Americans are?" Even Otto understood enough English to laugh.

"I was awfully glad to find one. There aren't many, and history never gave him his due."

"How come? He has a big name?" continued Burns.

"He taught Gauguin, Monet, Cézanne, and especially Renoir, but during the Franco-Prussian War, German soldiers in his house used stacks of his paintings for floor matting and butchers' aprons. Twenty years of his labor were lost."

May could hardly concentrate on his little monologue, feeling the weight of Betsy's communication. Finally, he decided to bite the bullet. Trying to assume an air of nonchalance, and avoiding Inge's eyes, he turned to Otto. For clarity he spoke in German.

"I received a letter today that concerns you. In the fall, how would you like to go to school in the States? Of course your sister would have to approve. Friends of mine have offered you a home."

Otto's eyes bulged. "You've got to be joking, sir?"

May felt Inge's stare. "No, not at all." Then he translated for Wade and Burns. "Senator Barnes and his wife have no children, and apparently there's a big movement in the States to help war orphans. Otto would qualify. The schools are gearing up to help by placing them by age, rather than completed grades. When the Barnes' were here they were shocked that German schools have been closed for over two years." Only then did he dare look up at Inge.

"So that was what was on your mind," she said, doing her best to hide her distress.

"That was one of the things. The other is 'top secret.' Otto would not leave before fall. Also there would have to be a lot of preparation. Otto, you would have to work seriously on your English. Inge would have to help you."

"Wow, a senator! " Wade turned to Inge. "It would be a great opportunity."

"I'd call that luck," added Burns. Then he turned to Inge. "Now, if you'd just forget May, and give me a chance to get rid of my wife, we could join him."

"That sounds like a great idea," Inge countered, making all laugh except May.

"What would this cost you, my dear?" Inge asked May.

"It sounds like it would cost me you. But if you mean in money, probably nothing. Betsy gave me no details, only the line that it might be the most worthwhile thing she could ever do. She's worth millions."

"It's a good attitude," said Wade. "No one ever offered me that."

The silence was stunning.

"It's a big decision that could be a turning point in your life," said May, looking at Otto.

"It's something I never would have dreamed of," said Otto.

"There's a price, of course. It means a separation of you and your sister, which will be hard, especially for Inge."

May knew Inge's mind was traveling back to when she wanted to go to America with him. Now her father's shoes were on her feet and they pinched. "This is not something we have to decide tonight. Lots of things can happen between now and Fall." She threw Otto a loving glance that bounced off a face beaming with joy. He was already far away.

"My master plan calls for taking Inge to the States," May added. "For the moment, I have a contract with Uncle Sam."

"What city will I be living in, sir?" asked Otto.

"Alexandria, just outside Washington, D.C."

Inge excused herself and went to the kitchen. With a lift of eyebrows promising trouble, May followed.

"I wish you had spoken to me about this first. Why did you keep me in the dark?"

"I didn't keep you in the dark. And 'why'? It's his life. You can't live it. You have only your own."

"I'd like to see the letter." She spoke more quietly, closing a drawer. Her nostrils quivered.

"You can't do that. There were confidential things in it regarding government policy. The letter contained classified material. It has already been shredded and burned."

"There are other secrets which you keep from me?" Now her voice trembled.

"Of course. The military government is none of your business. Let me add, there are other areas in your life in which I never probe. Please, accord me the same courtesy. I tell you everything that is important to me personally. That should be enough." He carried a bowl of vegetables to the dining room table, gratefully fleeing her gaze.

During dinner Wade and Burns talked about their own problems, while May jumped back and forth between English and German, answering Otto's questions. Otto was a veritable question box, wanting to know all about American life and schools. "I want you to know I appreciate this, sir," Otto said, finally excusing himself.

"That's nice of you to say that, Otto, and, whatever you do, please don't lose those beautiful manners."

His departure was a *fait accompli*. Later May had tried to cheer Inge who had remained silent during Otto's exuberant chatter. "Darling, I know how you feel, and I hate to ask you to make sacrifices—you, of all people. Dispense with the thought that I might want to get Otto off my hands." He reached for her, held her a moment, caressed her hair, and then released her to continue undressing. "I don't pretend to have all the answers, but I'd like to give Otto some options. I'd like to open the world to you both." He flipped his buttons into a dish on the dresser, making a small clatter. His shoe hit the floor with a resounding thud.

"Otto makes me feel more secure with you…" said May.

"You're impossible to combat." Finally, a smiled curled his lips. She ran her fingers through her hair, pulling it back from her forehead. "Yes, I'm pained. I'm also grateful. It's just awfully sudden." Slowly she began undressing, neatly leaving her clothes where she could jump into them on a moment's notice should the MPs knock on the door. They no longer talked about—or no longer even noticed—this little routine except on nights when one or the other was upset. May cringed. Her mind racing, Inge was beyond noticing something so habitual and small.

"This comes on the tail of a bad experience, so the timing is awful." May's other shoe fell. He rolled his socks and aimed them at a dirty clothesbasket, which he missed. He stood up and continued undressing. Finally, the smelly socks landed where they belonged.

For a moment Inge studied him, then she put on a pair of his pajamas, and sat down on the bed as if she wanted something warm around her. "Always before, you referred to the senator's wife as Mrs. Barnes. Tonight you called her Betsy."

"Darling, I was talking to Americans. She'll tell Otto to call her Betsy." God, thought May, she never misses a trick.

"Oh."

At the bathroom's small lavatory, they brushed their teeth. Foam spared further embarrassment. Finally he could say, "Get out of those pajamas and get in my arms."

Later feeling better, she whispered. "Nothing is ever easy, is it, *Leibling?*"

"Lord, no," he replied, grateful for the darkness.

Not long after, there was a much bigger robbery at the PX. Once again the inspectors came knocking, believing that Otto was involved. "Honest, Herr May," Otto swore, "I never would have done such a thing! Believe me!"

He looked innocent. "I believe you, but I also believe you've been careless about your friends."

"If that's the case, I'm sorry..."

"So am I, but that doesn't do much good at this time," May growled.

A few days later it was film from the U.S.A.—stolen from May's house—that trapped a ring of thieves when one tried to get it developed at an atelier. The other thugs were named, but one culprit laid the theft of the cameras at Otto's feet.

"I worked all day at Major Street's house," Otto remembered in his suffering. "You offered my services."

When May asked Street to confirm Otto's alibi, Street refused. "I'm sorry, May, but I can't remember which day Otto worked for me, and frankly, I don't want to be involved."

"Major, this is important," May insisted, almost pleading. "An innocent kid may go to jail—and lose a trip to the States for schooling." Street seemed to take considerable pleasure in putting May through a wringer and stood firm. "Listen, May, you've chosen to bed with the Krauts; now lie in it."

"He's so naïf, how could anyone think Otto could be guilty?" Inge asked, embarrassed, sick at heart.

"Regretfully, dear, a good many kids make mistakes growing up. We want Otto to learn a lesson without being burned at the stake. But, a lot is at risk, such as his trip to America. As a jailbird, he'd never get into the country."

At last Otto remembered that Major Street had paid him with a check on a stateside bank that Otto had not yet cashed. The check, well marked with coal dust, was dated the day of the robbery. Otto was exonerated. Street was somewhat subdued, "You have to admit, May, Otto looked guilty as hell."

"Please, Major, let this topic die. And the next time your buns get cold, get someone else to fix your damned furnace." May's tone was so vicious, Street paled.

May knew there was one answer to the problem of Otto. He told Inge, "I'm sorry, my dear, but I have to get him to the States before he gets in more trouble."

Inge knew May was right and came close to putting him under house arrest.

* ** *

The coming of spring was hard on Inge. Otto, wildly enthusiastic about the trip to America, wanted every spare minute of her time for help with his English. She made him read aloud to her, and because this was painful for others to listen to, many of her evenings were spent in his basement room. The United States was likely to come out, 'U-ni-ted Sta-tes,' causing Inge to cry, "Whaaaat was that again?"

For the 'th' sound Inge made up tongue twisters such as: Thirty-three thirsty theologians thanked the thoughtful thespians for Thursday's thoroughly thrilling theater.

"What does that mean?" asked Otto.

"The pastors had fun. Now say it again."

"The pastors had fun." "Otto!"

On the whole he tried so hard, she swallowed his impudence with good humor, and occasionally caught herself looking forward to his departure.

* ** *

June of 1946 finally brought an end to the non-fraternization rule, but with comical overtones. Inge could appear with May in public. However, to do this she needed a social card, proving that she was not a prostitute or a criminal. She could dance with him at the officers' club, but he could not buy her food or drinks there. Now he could go with her to German locales without pretending to be German. And sometimes to eat out with her, he used her ration cards, which heretofore had gone to the Müllers or the Fiskes. It was no longer obligatory to black out their house at night in case of an air raid, but instead, it was now necessary to shut out the glances of a prying neighbor.

A trickle of American women appeared, joining their husbands overseas. But they tended to treat Inge coldly, as if for the past year their husbands had been playing around with such gorgeous creatures, while they sat home alone and worried. At the same time Inge looked at them aghast at the way they appeared on the street in robes or housedresses with their hair in curlers—something no German woman would ever do.

"Before Otto leaves in the fall, I hope we can be married," said May. "I shudder at the red tape the Army regulations will demand, but it will make a difference."

"Imagine. I can be served at a table with you."

"I never exposed you to that!" he retorted.

"Because you're a gentleman. I'm perfectly aware of the regulations."

Knowing that these regulations pained him more than her, he said nothing. They were walking, crossing the rocky plain toward the tunnels. The Eagle's Nest perched above them like a beacon and was beautiful only in the distance, an enigma in stone and glass destined to fascinate the world. It seemed to May a polar opposite to the confining tunnels. There would not be much work there, but May had kept the place in mind as a possible retreat, the purpose for which it was built.

"There's only a little more work here in Berchtesgaden—with some of that in the Eagle's Nest. Then I'll have to go to Spandau where more art is hidden. There we may find stolen Rembrandts that have not shown up yet. They may not be true Rembrandts; many so-called Rembrandts bear his signature, but they may have been only partially painted by him or just supervised by him. Some fine artists—Gerard Dou, Govert Flinck and Ferdinand Bol—mimicked Rembrandt's style."

"Can you tell the difference?"

"Perhaps. That's why Street wants me there now. Won't you be glad for the change?"

"In a way. Berchtesgaden is entire. Berlin is nothing but rubble."

"So then we finish up and go someplace else."

It seemed so simple.

* ** *

Neither May or Inge noticed Fiske's delight that they would be working in the Eagle's Nest, allowing him time to set a new explosive trap. "There's very little art there," said May, "so we won't be there long." Then he turned to Fiske, catching his changed expression. "You almost look disappointed."

May continued. "In modern times there have been great engineering feats—the Panama and Suez Canals, Hoover Dam—but they were not built for one man's fancy."

"How about the pyramids?" asked Inge.

"They probably had a practical use, such as surveying or astronomical tools. The Eagle's Nest was simply a retreat—and not one intended to honor or glorify even a wife, like the Taj Mahal at Agra."

"I hope I'll have a chance to see the place," said Fiske.

"You will." May promised.

"I'm sure Hitler thought other more public monuments would spring up all over Germany in his memory," said Inge, slipping into her coat. She and May were off.

Finally they stood at an open window gazing at the view that stretched for miles, a *mise-en-scene* that presented a storybook fairyland of beauty and contentment, totally alien to the misery that came with a closer look.

May's impression of the Eagle's Nest was that it was wildly private, built to satisfy a maniac. "Someplace in this mountain must be a secret stair or ladder," he told Inge as they entered the great bronze doors. "I can't believe that Hitler would stop at one entrance and one exit." The security system seemed such that only the wind and field mice could penetrate. May soon found a half-empty cardboard box of powder labeled, 'An absolute guarantee against *Feldmause.*'

Inge fairly tiptoed from room to room, noting the poor taste and outlay of money. Then she found something else. Off the main bedroom in a bath, a used condom floated in the toilet. For a long minute she stood staring at it.

She was well aware of the security placed on the building, it being the only surviving building belonging to Hitler. The elevator had not worked until recently, and marauding soldiers had not plundered it. May had admitted to bringing the senator's wife here. After Betsy left, May had not been interested in making love. And, he had withheld *her* letter.

The discovery came as a crushing blow, sickening in its impact. She pushed the flush button, watching the damning evidence resist removal, due to the captured air as the water swirled. Finally, utterly distraught, she covered the offending article with wads of toilet paper and flushed again. This time the Trojan was carried under with all that remained of Inge's peace of mind.

CHAPTER FOUR

Taking Nietzsche's words literally, 'Superman lives on the mountaintop,' the master of Europe went into the clouds, May decided, looking at the jagged peaks surrounding the Eagle's Nest. He cracked a window. A cold, white alpine wind whistled, moaned, and choked as it fought for entrance and succumbed to the erratic plan of the house. He closed the window immediately, and hearing Inge's footsteps said, "I doubt if Hitler ever spent a night here. This place is much too close to the elements."

He turned, and seeing the distressed expression on her face, knew she was dreadfully upset. Her skin, now blanched white, rimmed eyes like yellow fires. She glared a moment before she found her voice and managed to choke out, "So you were Mrs. Barnes' lover!"

His stomach plummeted, but May's defense was an offense, as a look of shocked irritation flushed across his face. He wheeled to face her squarely. "What in the world gave you that idea?"

"A floating condom in the toilet," she replied haughtily, pointing a trembling finger toward the bath.

"Did it have my name on it or could you tell by the size?" His reply carried all the cool annoyance he could muster.

"You told me she was here with you."

"She was, and any number of brass as well. It's none of my business what they may have done, and I certainly would not have mentioned it to you. I don't even like this subject now." Somehow he found the strength to glower at her.

"I'm sure that's all true," she replied evenly as May strengthened his case and hers faltered. "Remember you were too tired to sleep with me after she left…"

"She left me exhausted. You never know what she'll do next. She wields a lot of power, and I'd been given an assignment by the general. For Christ's sake, Inge, she's a bride!"

He had tried to sound disgusted, and his intimidating tone was meant to throw her into the wrong without his resorting to outright lies. That was the line—somewhat wobbly—that he would hold. Much as he hated deceit, he had had important goals to achieve and had taken a devious way of achieving them. By playing with Betsy, he had gained her support. Betsy had never taken rejection lightly. He knew that from years of experience; he was not about to test her and risk everything again.

The first shock waves subsided, yet she had caught the suffering in his eyes, born of his guilt, and fought for equilibrium. Her tall figure slumped, while a nervous hand swept through her hair, as if pushing away the pain.

"A few officers, married men, have access to this place. Don't think or talk about what you saw." The confidential tone was meant to mollify her, yet they both knew some great damage had been done. He pivoted away from her, giving her his back, and looked out the window. "How can you doubt my love for you?"

He knew the question was unfair, but she had cornered him, and he was desperate not to hurt her.

Now, more aware of his pain than her own, she reached for him, swallowing hard.

"I don't, *Liebling*. Let's get out of this place. It must be haunted. I couldn't spend five minutes here without you. There are even strange noises." She pulled at him to see his face, and he managed to look at her squarely, her words having given him more normal poise. "There must be hundreds of ghosts hanging around. Think of all the slave laborers who died in building this dump and in those tunnels below. What a shame your airmen didn't manage to drop a single bomb on this. What a crying shame!"

Together they walked to the elevator, too tense to say more.

During the slow decent, without looking directly at one another, both could observe each other's face reflected in the shiny pink copper walls. For a fleeting moment, each one caught the other's unguarded expression, before the secret of the mirroring was apparent.

May's soul was filled with despair, which Inge could not miss. In defense, he had added one wrong to another. Ashamed, he would have loved to explain it all, and yet he knew he never could, and never would. He would have to bear the burden of his sins without her absolution. Nervously he churned the keys in his pockets.

Inge had been hurt, but while he was there beside her, she could be generous to him, suppressing a loss of pride and innocence. She had trapped him, and then survived the terrible moment that came, and now she must forget. "Scold me when I'm jealous," she whispered.

The elevator stopped without May having a chance to reply. Stepping into the dim entry, he suddenly drew her into his arms, holding her tightly for a long moment. Before he kissed her, one hand cupped her head tenderly. The act brought tears to her eyes. Does the suffering never end? She asked herself. Then he reached for the switch that illuminated the great bronze chandeliers, and light burst around them.

* ** *

The following day, carrying some fresh food, they returned to the Eagle's Nest. Both determined to ignore their wounds. They went to work immediately and discovered numerous paintings.

"Here's a portrait I knew we'd find somewhere," May exclaimed.

It was by Fritz Erler, and had been reproduced hundreds of times during the Third Reich. Against a background depicting the ancient Egyptian hawk god, Horus, and other deities, Hitler's full, uniformed figure stood before a powerful youth. Scattered building blocks suggested Hitler's obsessive self-image as an architect.

"Such a painting as propaganda shows how the legend of Hitler's strength and invincibility could have grown in Germany," said May.

"Can you imagine, I once wondered if I could ever paint that well?" she replied, laughing at herself.

"I'm sure everything we find here will be artistic mediocrity, though technically proficient, of course. The Americans won't be turning this picture loose, so take one last look at the *Portrait of the Führer*."

"My father was greatly impressed by Erler's *Sea* in the main hall of the Reich's Central Bank. He wanted a mosaic for his bank and approached Erler. Erler said, 'Give the commission to your daughter. She's a better artist than I am.' Nothing was done because Father found the idea ridiculous."

They inventoried gigantic nudes painted by Ivo Saliger. Another *Leda, Blessings of the Earth, Workers,* and *Mars and Venus* came out of closets. "Not even the titles are distinguished," Inge sighed, waving at the stack of canvases. "What cheap tricks! And I was taken in by all of this."

"You were young. Now you've matured. It's like sex. Once you've had it, kissing isn't enough."

By evening the weather was worse. "We should stay here tonight," May commented, looking out the window. "The jeep is wide open, and we'll freeze before we get to town."

Light flurries of a spring snow whipped around the few bushes clinging to the rocks outside the building. Below, the snow would melt into a cold pelting rain. The furnace took away the worst of the chill, but suddenly it seemed woefully inadequate. The heavy blue velvet drapes took unexplainable moments to start swaying as they closed them, and when touched, grew dead still. Inge shivered.

May made a fire, not a roaring one, but a steady warming, dancing fire, nourished by some granular chemicals that had been stored nearby. A sprinkling of the pre-war product imbued the yellow flames with streaks of blue, green and purple. A good supply of dry wood had been cut and cleaned, waiting for just such an occasion, which the Führer was never destined to enjoy. May pulled the cushions from the rust-colored sofa to the floor, making a deep pallet facing the fireplace. There, yoga-fashion, they dined on bread and cheese, washed down by a great burgundy, a Romanee-Conti, which someone had the taste to select for Hitler.

Inge talked about the war. "There was always a little wood for fires from bombed out houses. Naturally everyone was after it, scrounging like cockroaches." Now she could laugh about it.

"I'm intrigued by what it took to survive," May replied. "Survival is always grasping at straws. Little things become so important."

Both thought of the perilous moments of the day before. The near loss of each other drew them together now with an awareness of having survived something dangerous but not lethal. They had made love the night before, but their feelings had been too raw and turbulent for satisfying release. Now, in their closeness, something infinitely more tender and binding washed over them. They undressed before the fire, glorying in each other's nakedness as god met goddess in two shimmering beautiful bodies.

"For years the memory of our lovemaking sustained me. When the world is in ashes at your feet, if you think of those moments, you'll find a will to survive," she told him. Then she found his lips and met his passion with her own.

Later they dressed as Inge wanted to leave. May was disappointed, but the weather had calmed. Besides he would not have refused her a star, much less a whim.

In Hitler's bedroom he discovered a beautiful mink lap robe and a square silk scarf, possibly intended for Eva Braun. With no pangs of conscience he took them. Both had Hermes labels. Downstairs he wrapped the scarf around Inge's head. Once in the jeep he tucked the warm fur around her. "I doubt if this beauty was ever paid for," he said, aware that he was stealing. It occurred to him that he was getting very used to stealing.

"You mean with money?"

"I mean at the time. It will be paid for eventually."

What the Nazis had done to the world would take a toll on the Germans for a long, long time. The loss was irreparable.

The Eagle's Nest produced no fine art. The one shocking discovery was a condom. Now that speaks for all of this, thought May.

*   ** *

The next day found them back at the Eagle's Nest. By mid-afternoon May and Inge had run out of the food that they brought with them. "Don't panic," said May, ever mindful of her stomach. "I know there'll be something to eat here."

The building had two kitchens and one enormous pantry. Every cupboard and every drawer had a lock and key, even the refrigerators. May put each key in its lock, and they began a search. Inge tackled the main kitchen, and May took the smaller diet kitchen and pantry.

"I've found some sardines," he heard her say, "and enough olives for the world's biggest cocktail party. There are dozens of restaurant-sized cans here. Even tins of crackers and cookies from England."

Distracted by curiosity, he did not abandon his search, but continued checking cupboards. In one cabinet he found an unopened manufacturer's box. Using a key to slit the carton, he opened it and pawed through the excelsior packing. Soon he reached an object in red velvet. With the suddenness of a burst of sunlight he found himself gazing at an intricately engraved gold goblet, emblazoned with the initials 'AH.' He gasped, then carefully repacked it. The box held six. Behind that box was another and another, all the same size. Carefully, he replaced the packages. They would be so easy to steal.

Another sealed carton held sterling silver service plates, equally well packed. Other boxes held serving dishes, silver table ornaments and flatware, all as if waiting for some victory celebration. May knew that none of these things would have been seen by the household help, nor were there records of their purchase. Awaiting the *Götterdammerung,* at every turn the Nazis had destroyed their records. May's gaze returned to the boxes containing the gold goblets. Then Inge appeared, making him feel slightly guilty.

"Sardines await you, sir," she said, smiling.

Dutifully he followed her, drinking in the fresh air.

"There's a little Fort Knox in the pantry," he told her, putting a sardine on a cracker.

"Armaments?" she asked, not understanding.

"Gold. The United States keeps its gold in Fort Knox."

"Oh." She was too occupied with food to comment further.

Later May came to grips with the fact that he had considered a gigantic theft. Never in his life had he seriously thought of such a crime; he was shocked at himself.

Once as a child, he had stolen a yo-yo, allegedly as a gift for his mother. Knowing that he didn't have a quarter to buy it, she had questioned him relentlessly, showing little or no appreciation for the gift. Lying, he had been forced to point out where he had found the money. Stubbornly he stuck to his tale. The subject was dropped, but nobody had been fooled. His mother returned to the city and took the yo-yo with her, something he had not counted on. He never saw the coveted toy again. Agony over the incident convinced him that crime did not pay. After that, what he could not pay for, he did not get. In time he grew interested in things of the mind. The desire for wealth, that initially led him into a higher education, diminished to nothing by the end of the war. The rich, cushioned in life by their checkbooks, died just like the poor.

"You're awfully quiet," she murmured, bending to kiss his cheek.

He smiled wanly. The goblets were not *objets d'art:* only precious, well-crafted metal. They could have been stored anywhere and blown to bits. The contents of the Eagle's Nest were considered Hitler's private possessions, paid for by him. State gifts were displayed and later wrecked in the Berghof. He remembered Street's covetousness and felt revulsion wash over his own conscience.

"This place is chilly. Let's go home early tonight," he said abruptly.

"That would suit me just fine."

"Then put on your coat. We started early, we can quit early."

What a strange thing for me to think of stealing, thought May. I'm not desirous of possessions, and certainly Inge isn't. Subconsciously I must feel that the Third Reich deprived her of so much, she has some indemnity coming. He shivered inwardly, remembering the *Oberbetten,* the Hermes lap robe, and the scarf that his sticky fingers had latched on to—always for Inge. He hoped he was not becoming a thief out of love.

Suddenly, May heard a low muffled boom.

"What do you suppose that was?" he asked, frowning.

"It couldn't be target practice at this hour."

May stood, waiting for a repeat. When none occurred, he immediately thought of Fiske. He grabbed Inge's hand, and they bounded from the room toward the elevator.

The ride down was slow, designed to be comfortable. May winced, but tried to be patient, thinking aloud, reviewing the options. He muttered, "Fiske may have become careless. There are also buried gas tanks that may have exploded—certainly if someone threw a cigarette in the wrong spot. Or possibly an old bomb has been detonated. Hidden ammunition could have blown. If it is Fiske, he's had it..."

They whipped down the mountainside to the entrance of the tunnels where a crowd was already gathering. A guard held everyone back waiting for an authority, and certainly May was one.

"There's been an explosion in the tunnels, sir," the guard announced, grimly.

"Has anyone gone in?"

"No, sir. The lights are all out."

"Have you got a flashlight?"

"Yes, sir."

"Then give it to me. Hurry. Fiske was in there."

May addressed another GI. "You come with me." He rightly thought that if Fiske were injured, he would need help carrying him out.

Together they disappeared while Inge waited outside. She thought of Hans Müller, her old landlord, whose hands were now bloodied by Fiske's death—not by those of an *Ami*. A great inner rage swelled, venomously directed toward Müller, who might have prevented this. She bore Fiske no love, but Fiske had protected May, and for that—for a few minutes—she felt she could forgive his stupid political leanings. She would soon change her mind.

Within a few minutes May appeared, ashen. "He never knew what hit him. Thank heaven for that." He remembered how foolishly they had thought a steel door might protect them.

"And the other guards?"

"Almost deafened."

"And the art?" she asked.

May was slow to reply. "It's okay."

"You look very strange. What did you discover?"

"That the area that blew had already been cleared. Do you understand what that means? Fiske was running a new line. I'm sure he wanted to kill me." He paused. "I must report this, and then I'll have to talk to Frau Fiske. I don't know when I'll be back."

She understood. She sat down on the guard's chair, fearing that her knees were going to give way.

They had been working on a powder keg with a maniac. She remembered what May had said once, "It was ammunition the Nazis were protecting, not their art." Well, the Nazis had been stupid people.

* ** *

The next afternoon they sat opposite each other in the breakfast room. Considerately, other members of the household left them alone. The setting sun was huge and red, its base sliced by mountain peaks. Alpine green gave way to pink then mauve. Rocks shimmered against the sky while the light drained. May had spent the day dealing with the aftermath. Inge had been thinking about many things.

"Inge, we must put what happened yesterday behind us. By luck we survived a very close call."

"*Liebling,* you're right." She paused for a while. "Someday I would like to do something exceptionally generous or kind for the Jewish people." She spoke out of the blue.

The full story of Hitler's handling of the Jews had not broken publicly in Germany. From time to time May had heard shocking reports, but never discussed them with her. The reports were highly secret and incomplete. He felt that one day the whole story would come out, but she didn't need to hear it from him. Still, her statement was startling.

"My sweet, I doubt that you could do much alone, and I don't think your admirable aspirations would find much support among your countrymen. Your people are going to want to forget Hitler and the plight of the Jews like a bad dream."

"Still, perhaps someday I can do something."

"Become a successful artist and set up a foundation that would offer scholarships or orphan relief. Until that time, you'd better think of your own hide. Such projects take a lot of organization, popular support, and money. In your case, all of these ingredients happen to be lacking. Besides Fräulein Dinksboomps, the Germans are going to have to pay and pay plenty for years to come. You just don't know...."

"I'd like to do anything that might redeem us a little..."

She was almost making him angry. Such childish naïveté was exasperating and frightening in light of the financial bind he had been under since he found her. She didn't let go of her ideas easily.

"When you have earned the wherewithal to be charitable, that will be the time for it. Please don't be charitable with my commission in the United States Army, because your bit of *noblesse oblige* could be just that."

"Those were just idle thoughts."

"You've never had an idle thought in your life," he muttered.

Although his words were complimentary, she knew he was displeased. He had crumpled his napkin. She gathered courage. "All right, they were not completely idle thoughts. For years I've had a guilty conscience. It's been an awful burden. Sadie, a Jewish friend, came to me begging me to hide her father and uncle in our attic. The Gestapo was looking for them. I refused. The men disappeared, but Sadie got out to England. My father profited by the sale of their stock in our bank. It's a sordid story, isn't it?" With a grimace she looked at him, scanning his face for some morsel of comfort. "I feel a little better having told you."

His heart ached for her. "Inge, I think you've probably looked for redemption under every stone and around every corner since. National Socialism wasn't your fault. Suppose you had secreted the men, and suppose some servant or neighbor discovered them. You might have doomed yourself and your parents to the very same fate."

"I know that, but it doesn't help much. Where was my loyalty and an obligation to a true friend?"

May withheld a sigh. "I'm glad you finally told me about this. It makes you easier to understand. Please forget it. Lord, don't feel you should suffer to atone. We can't do anything about the past, but learn from it."

"Sadie begged me. That made it so bad."

He despaired, finding it hard to budge her. "The only thing we have any control over is right now—not yesterday which was bad enough—not even tomorrow. You must learn to forget."

Her eyes scanned the floor, avoiding his. "I guess you're right."

* ** *

The focus of activity in the house centered on Otto. When his departure date was moved up, Betsy wrote a note that May could let Inge read: *Having a senator in the family is like using a magic wand with bureaucrats. In Washington Otto would make much faster progress with his English, and have time for tennis, riding, swimming lessons—you know what I mean—those social skills that boost one's ego and make life so much more FUN.*

While she would not admit it, Inge knew Betsy was right. Perfunctorily, she had been given those skills that Otto had missed. She also saw that holding on to the scheduled departure date would have been cruel and possibly futile. Otto reacted to her reluctance with such hostility that she backed down in shock. He was of another ilk, and only May could control him.

May had not been permitted to see much of their conflict, but the spoor of it filtered through the air. "You could end up with a rebellious teenager on your hands," he warned. "In front of Otto, I'll be supportive of you. But privately I want to tell you, it's a mistake. What you really want is the pleasure of his company and that could become dubious."

Her shoulders slumped. Knowing she was beaten, she acquiesced.

"There are times, dear heart, when you must let go of people in order to hold them," May told her, not knowing that one day soon he would want to eat those words.

Another problem came to light, throwing May into despair: the government frowned heavily on the marriage of American soldiers to German girls. Abolishment of the non-fraternization ruling had been a superficial gesture, a sop for horny men, designed to cut down on charges of rape. The aftermath of this policy—thousands of fatherless German/American children—was one nobody had the foresight to consider.

By law, paperwork and screening delayed all marriages for nine months. Then marriages would be permitted four months prior to the soldier's return to the States with no-reassignment to Germany possible. This applied to everyone attached to the Armed Forces abroad.

Were May to resign his commission, Inge could not enter the U.S. as a 'War Bride,' but would have to wait until the quota system permitted her entry. Now that work in Berchtesgaden was complete, May was needed in Spandau. Because they would have to travel through other occupational zones, May's hope of taking her to Spandau entailed as much red tape as entering the United States. As an army officer, he had a coveted position in Europe that included a paycheck. Back in the States, building materials were not yet available, so the prospect of finding architectural work at home was still premature. May's professional life had become a can of worms.

Street was totally unsympathetic, finally enjoying a revenge that he had long and impatiently waited for. Smirking, Street sat back in his chair, ugly self-confidence communicating itself as he tapped his foot. "The fact is, a policy exists, and if one exception is made for you, others will expect it. You're an old friend," he spoke sardonically, emphasizing the word friend. "I'd leave myself open to censure in requesting an exception. Put your application in writing and sit back and wait like everybody else."

The removal of the non-fraternization ruling had brought May's relationship with Inge to light, and fired Street's envy. May saw clearly that no favors would come from Street. Always, when he left Street's office, he left Street smiling like a Cheshire cat.

For as long as possible he kept the depressing news from Inge, but finally the situation had to be explained. He thought she took it well, better than he had expected. *"Liebling,* we must learn to expect nothing. Then we won't be disappointed."

"It's so unfair to you. I'm trying to do everything I can," he told her. This included talking to Rasmussen who was sympathetic, but willing to offer only advice.

"Once you reach my age, you stop sticking your neck out. If your relationship can't weather this, you shouldn't get married. Policies are changing every day now. Take it easy. File your papers, and wait it out."

May knew the colonel was right. Their hardship was intangible. Inge was not pressing for marriage. Only he felt insecure, unable to offer his ladylove her rightful place in his society. The fact that Otto would embark on a great opportunity through the courtesy of his actions—and that this opportunity deprived Inge—only made him more sensitive. Otto was still considered a child, but she was an adult and an undesirable alien.

Inge sat in the kitchen where she had been snipping the ends from green beans, talking to May about Otto's departure—his shots, papers, toiletries, his clothes. Her gaze did not meet his, but traveled nervously from the beans to the corners of the room so that her words permeated the shadows. She appeared to have surrendered everything.

"Take heart, Fräulein Dinkboomps. Within a few days you'll get into a new routine, and his going won't hurt anymore. In fact, you'll get a lot of pleasure out of his progress."

"I'm just envious. You're the one who has had the responsibility."

He did not refute that. He didn't want to talk anymore about Otto, but he would have liked to buy her a hat. He had heard that buying a hat always made a woman feel better.

Otto's excitement was contagious, and the final farewells came off better than May expected. Knowing that after May had seen him off, May would come home wanting a drink. Otto had cleverly used a small salvaged spring and some folded paper to construct a Jack-in-the-box in the cap of the Scotch bottle. May almost jumped out of his skin when he opened it. A chain of paper flowers popped into the air like a rocket for the May Queen. He almost dropped the bottle.

"Damn it! I should've expected this," May roared, turning red. Inge collapsed in laughter.

For a minute he resented her glee. "The whole goddamned house may be booby-trapped," he muttered, a little embarrassed.

Tears of laughter filled her eyes. "I would never have believed that I would cry for joy over his departure."

Nor would May.

* ** *

He did not buy her a hat—at least he felt he *could* not buy her a hat—but he did have a fine gift for her. Thinking something would be called for on Otto's departure, in the PX he spotted the first shipment of real pearls from Japan. At the same time he learned that his condominium in Washington had been rented to new tenants at a much higher rent. Feeling flush, he purchased a beautiful string of pearls.

As soon as he downed a bit of his drink, he remembered his purchase and extracted the round flat velvet box from a drawer and handed it to her. "Don't weigh these against food or you won't enjoy them."

"Oh, my God," she cried, her eyes wide in astonishment. "They are so beautiful. How could you afford them?"

"Our finances are looking up, and your day is coming. I've neglected your wardrobe, but we'll be able to correct that eventually. The PX has more things for women everyday."

"I trudge around with my Reichmarks, but there's nothing to buy." She dangled the long necklace in her hand so that it swung and glowed like a warm, creamy pendulum; it had picked up the light of her smile and refocused on him. "They're like the pearls my grandmother had which, I remember, had to be sold at some point to save the bank."

"At least they weren't blown to smithereens. Also the price of pearls has dropped since the Japanese began their oyster farms."

She kissed him soundly, and he suggested, while feeling her behind, that she take off her clothes and model her pearls. She gladly complied and gave him his prize, doing it just the way he liked.

Finding those pearls and being able to buy them for her had made him incomparably happy. For a few hours, making love, he was able to forget all of life's other irritations, and better still, make her forget them. As Betsy said, he was awfully good in bed.

Book VI

CHAPTER ONE

Earlier May had anticipated Inge's feeling of loss over her brother's departure, and from the States, had ordered a wide selection of oil paints, brushes, and assorted-size canvases. He had kept the large bulky packages hidden at the club, otherwise she would have found the mountain they made—at home or in the tunnels.

Just as he had hoped, they enabled her to throw herself into creative work. He soon saw that, although she had had no opportunity to paint in oil during the last five years, with a little fresh practice in mixing paints, it wasn't before long she had made a quantum leap in her development as an artist. Her work bore no reference to the ideas she espoused in Berlin in 1938. Her eyes had been opened.

"You've got to admit, my dear, that getting you some first-rate supplies was one of my smarter moves," said May, nodding and admiring a landscape she was working on.

"Of course, *Liebling,* having the tools makes such a difference."

"They make it easier, but the real difference is here," he said, tapping her temple.

"There's always a certain mental brutality when I try to wrest something from nature and prove my own intuition, my own way of seeing something, " she told him, tension making her almond-eyed.

"Some people call that work," he commented wryly.

"Yes. Paintings are layers and layers of thought. The concentration leaves me exhausted. When I get my concept to come out right, it's such a wonderful feeling. Sometimes I work so hard, and then I come back later and see that it's not right. I haven't captured something here." Then she pointed to her head. "I haven't delighted myself or even engaged the viewer. It may be proficient, but it's boring." She sighed. "Then I go back to try to figure out what happened. At what level did I go wrong? It's like I've given birth to a defective child—no, no, of course, not that bad, because I can do it over. But, the great expectations, the magnificent promise that I felt when I first took up the brush didn't come out. I flubbed! Somewhere I lost the vision."

"Fräulein Dinksboomps, none of that is ever wasted. You're digging in your head to find something, something you know is there, somewhere…"

"And when you find it, it jumps out at you."

They were taking a long evening walk, and when she was speaking, she was waving her arms, sweeping the dark sky, full of stars.

The mention of a child jarred May. For months he's been trying to get her pregnant, but he let that go and went on. "You had to endure a lot to learn what you are now expressing or trying to express in painting. You've gone beyond pretty visions and nice pictures into bold gripping statements. That's a big step. You can be very proud."

"Not really, because you've put something of yourself out in the open, up for judgment by others. You've exposed yourself to condemnation or ridicule. If those you care about do not accept your work, it can be crushing. It makes you scared."

"I'm not much good to you if I can't criticize in trying to help," said May. "If I weren't frank, you wouldn't trust me, at least not for long."

"You're different."

"Not really. There are always those who will take pot shots at you. Ignore them and plug on with your vision. Accept the fact that progress will be sporadic, one painting will be brilliant followed by some less so. In time they'll all be brilliant. Even unimportant artists create a masterpiece now and then. Great artists produce nothing but masterpieces."

"I think you're wrong," said Inge, now daring to disagree. "I think even the masters had ideas that didn't gel when they tried to put them on canvas. They simply became smart about painting over their mistakes before the world had a chance to see them."

May's eyebrows rose in the darkness. He knew differently, but he didn't want an argument. Lately it seemed that she knew her own mind, and there was no longer anything that he could tell her about painting she didn't already know. He sensed she thought that she'd gone beyond him, and he felt displaced.

The attitude of independence that he had fostered, feeling that it was something that she needed, now was backfiring. Grateful for the night that hid his discomfort, he let her talk on, her voice ringing with conviction.

"Painting is taking over my life in a way I never dreamed possible. It's all I think about. I'm transported into a different world. There are demons, but I can overcome them. I'm not swamped by army regulations that I cannot overcome—no matter what I do or don't do. Sloppy American army wives who snub me are unimportant. The precious American movies, which for so long you couldn't take me to, are a waste of valuable time. With one hand tied behind me, I can cook a better meal than you can get at your American army officers' club."

May's anxiety grew. Deeply throttled resentments, which she now claimed unimportant, undermined him when she aired them. In this state, he could refute nothing. Finally, resignedly he said, "That army fed you."

"You fed me. I also earned my food."

Knowing her, he knew the remark was intended to be kind, but in his unsteady position, he imagined that it indicated a lessening of feeling for him. He went to bed feeling gloomy, leaving Inge to her world of art in which, for the time being, the sun rose and set.

The little exchange did not reflect a lessening of her love for him, but it was an expression of individualism that she was beginning to show more freely. She had been reviewing the past, and revising her notions of many things, including how the world turned, or at least her world. May was at the mercy of an army of occupation that could sweep him away from her in the time it took to type a new assignment. She had to be prepared for this eventuality, and her art might be her salvation—the only thing that could save her from loneliness. It meant that she had been going through an introspective period in which she thought of herself, and worried about her existence more than usual. In itself, this self-absorption was not a dangerous mood, but it desensitized her to May's need, and the timing was unfortunate.

He felt bereft and was unable to express it. Something had gone seriously wrong.

Then May discovered Inge's purse left open, its contents spilled. Seeing a little leather case he had never seen before, he opened it to gaze on the utterly drop-dead handsome face of Kurt Montag. It didn't occur to him that keeping the picture of a former fiancé in its worn leather folder was not important to her, except that it was the only remaining possession from the past, and as such, it represented something entirely different. It was simply something she was reluctant to throw away.

Fearing that Inge still loved the man, it took May several moments to pull himself together, and put the folder back. A depression hit him that Inge was aware of, but other discomfiting changes—beyond being unable to marry her—could also account for this. That afternoon he and Wade had been notified that they would have to move to bachelor quarters.

In the end the easing of restrictions had not helped at all. An increase in dependents from the States was awaited, and May's house was better suited than most for married officers with children. Desperate, May went to Rasmussen.

"I'm sorry, May, but that's the way the ball bounces. I can't interfere with housing. You're asking me to play musical chairs, or should I say, musical beds. Just relax."

It wasn't the sort of thing that he could relax about. His life was on a roller coaster, going from bad to worse, and he didn't know how to stop it. There was one possibility. "Can you move me to the Eagle's Nest? It's too isolated for dependents, cut off from the PX, commissary, and everything else."

"Good point, May," conceded the colonel. "There's a lot of space, but it sure is inaccessible. It would take a long distance runner to keep the place clean."

May hadn't thought about this, but then decided that two rooms could be maintained as an apartment. "Until permission comes through for Inge and me to be married, it would solve my problems."

"All right, May. Are you still finding much valuable art?"

"Good old, bad new: Hitler's taste, sir. He leaned toward the explicit. His pictures instantly tell their story despite generous assistance from their titles."

Rasmussen laughed. "Be off with you. I'll give you your castle in the sky or love nest, whatever."

When May told Inge where they would be living, she was dismayed. "*Liebling,* I really don't want to stay there."

"Darling, I have to. It's the one place where I can still live with you, which colors everything. Wade has to move to the BOQ." He was hurt and showed it.

"I want to live with you too, but...*bitte, bitte.* The place needs a staff."

May looked grief stricken. "We'll have to imagine that we have a dozen servants. I promise it won't be for long. You'll have good light. You won't have that at Müller's."

She looked at him. "*Mein Gott.*" How stupid can I get? she thought. The man was hurting. Her voice dropped. "Of course I'll go with you to the Eagle's Nest."

Much as she hated the place, they would be together. It was safe from intruders. She couldn't think of another advantage.

May thought she wanted the light.

* ** *

Moving their relatively few possessions was easy. May ordered a mammoth bouquet of flowers in scale with the round table in the main salon for Inge's arrival. It was an expensive gesture, but he felt guilty, and knew she was doing her best to accommodate him. Late in the evening he helped her set the table for a supper. He unlocked the cabinet with Hitler's flatware. Sterling silver settings for twenty-four were the most complete either had ever seen. There were fish knifes and forks, oyster forks, asparagus and escargot clamps, bread and butter knives, soup spoons, bouillon spoons, cereal spoons, and nut picks, not to mention serving pieces. "We might as well use the silver service plates, the Meissen, and the silver candelabra, too," he said.

"Probably never before was a large can of Texas chili served in such style," she replied, wanting to be nice.

"I'm not so sure. There's a lot of oil money in Texas." He started to make a fire.

"Don't make a fire. It would compete with the flowers."

"You mean we'll be cold for a week?"

She laughed.

He did not unlock the cabinet where the gold goblets rested, nor did he mention them, but he thought of them. He opened a 1929 chateau Bordeaux, and the beautiful garnet liquid was like velvet in their mouths. "Don't spoil this with the chili. We can drink it later with cheese," he advised.

"I'm afraid I'm getting a taste for things I can't afford."

"Me too," she admitted.

When dinner and the wine were finished, he picked up the empty bottle, cradling it in his hand. He wished only he might have bottled the essence of life's lovelier moments and preserved them, as the wine had been preserved to grow and bloom after having aged for seventeen years. Suddenly the glorious flush abated. The candles, all still burning, gave a diminished light, and he saw that Inge looked forlorn. "The room has gotten dark," he said flatly. "Perhaps it's the generator."

"The flames are all there. Maybe they don't light our faces as well. The light source is lower," she murmured. "Are you uncomfortable?"

He replied, "Not exactly. My mood has changed. I feel insecure with you, perhaps because I know you don't like this place, and I can't do a goddamned thing about it!"

"It's a dreadful place, an ugly hotel closed for the season. I hate it." Her eyes scanned the room.

"Do you love me, Inge?" he asked, finding her eyes.

"How could you doubt that? I'm here." She had pulled the same question on him, when his back was to the wall, and he had lied over fucking Betsy.

"Perhaps I should ask, 'Do you still love Kurt Montag?'" He had to know.

Her eyes were clear, and she could not lie. "Why? Would you throw me out?"

"You're returning questions with other questions, not answers."

A little streak of perversity and self-preservation bolstered her defense. She loved May exclusively, but she didn't want to tell him so. In a womanly way, she felt insignificant and angry. Not necessarily angry for herself, but for all women who seemingly had no power over their lives, and loved too much.

"I wish I knew how I felt about Kurt Montag," she said, frankly.

"Perhaps I won't know until I see him—if I ever do and if he is still alive. It was not a 'real' love, because we had no time together. It was a fantasy, and that's why it has been hard to get rid of. I only wish that I'd never met him, because I feel guilty over ever having cared for him, when I should have saved all my love for you, trusting that the forces of good would overcome those of evil. But I did care for him." Tears that did not fall made her eyes wider, shimmering with moisture. "I think the feeling, the caring, stemmed from the period."

May stood up, grabbed her by the wrist and drew her into their bedroom where he bolted the door as if to hold her there forever. Then he threw her down on the bed, ripped off her underwear, opened his, and made love to her in a wild impassioned, lustful pounding manner that he had not demonstrated since they were in Norbert Buth's apartment in Berlin. When he finally let go of the great stream of sperm that had been building up for some days, he also let out a horrible howl like that of the banshee, rocking both their souls.

Later, still dressed, coming close to hysteria, standing before him as his wasted sperm dripped down her legs, she found the words to tell him: "*Liebling,* this place was the home of the man who ruined my beautiful country, murdered millions, destroyed much of Europe, blew up my parents in our home, and almost wrecked my life. Can't you understand that this place sets my teeth on edge? I'm so deranged here, I doubt if I can work."

He buried his head in Hitler's pillow.

CHAPTER TWO

Everything happened so quickly in the end.

May bought two small trunks, thinking their presence would cheer Inge. They did. The two footlockers were evidence that he did not intend to subject her to the Eagle's Nest any longer than was absolutely necessary.

Despite her fears about being able to work there, the light was good, and work would have been impossible at the Müller's. The job in the tunnels had dried up for Inge. However, in order to maintain her employee status, she continued to work part-time on other jobs within the command. Even though one or two officers had mentioned wanting to buy one of her paintings, she didn't feel ready to let anything go.

Sunday came, a raving beauty of a day. The glorious afternoon brought German families streaming from their homes into the parks and woods, either in small celebrations of nature or out of sheer gratitude for the change in the weather. Because the weather was so often bad on good days, the clean air, the beauty of the countryside, and simple breathing space beckoned with an irresistible lure. Even May was not immune. "Let's go outside with the rest," he suggested, looking down to the street, seeing people strolling below. "God is having a great giveaway, and it won't last long."

"Take your binoculars," she suggested. "We may see some birds."

Emotionally, he felt stabilized. Inge's spirits had lifted, buoying his own. He had pressed for other living accommodations, demonstrating again, the lengths that he would go to for her. She felt something precious in their love, which she could convey, but not easily verbalize.

Their regained rapport freed May's tongue to talk about art where he felt surefooted.

On days like this, when the sun shone, there were people and landscapes crying to be painted at every turn—green mountain flanks rose, and frothy white streams rushed down shattered granite staircases. Inge and May could see these pictures in their minds' eyes with the vibrancy of a master's brush and hashed them over, as they might picture postcards in a drugstore.

They passed a picturesque mill with a small bridge over the River Ache—quaint, devoid of advertisements, almost too pretty to be real.

"This scene reminds me strongly of an early Piet Mondrian painting, *Landscape with Mill*, though the windmill is missing. I spent a long time studying Mondrian because so many of his paintings were missing. He went through quite a number of developmental stages I had to track. Look carefully." May continued, pointing out repeated motifs. Inge followed his comments, using her fingers to frame a scene, moving them right to left to find a balanced composition. May pointed to the bridge. "The timbers of the bridge make those dark shadows in the water, just as they do in the painting."

"Yes, I see," she replied, squinting at the view.

"Mondrian moved to abstract painting and became obsessed with rhythm. Then he painted *Composition in White, Black and Red* that uses only seven lines and one small block. It's a condensation of the earlier landscape, with a perfect balance of tension."

May went on talking about how he had to trace different artists' development in periods of thirty and forty years. "My time in Washington was a lot pleasanter than fighting in Europe or Japan would have been— I'll tell the cockeyed world."

He was so absorbed in reflection that he did not notice Inge's fixed stare and sudden silence.

"It's a lot of fun when you figure out—and put together—two separate artists' views of the same scene." He gave an amused chortle.

"*Liebling,* please let me see those binoculars," she said, helping him take them from his neck and then peering through them herself. "Let's go back," she said abruptly, breathlessly.

"Sure, if you want to…" He turned to face her. For some reason she appeared to be very uncomfortable. He put out an arm, which she readily accepted. "Are you tired?"

"Yes," she snapped.

Inge had seen a man she was certain was Kurt Montag, only he was missing an arm, part of his shoulder, some of his face, perhaps more… It was a shattering revelation, and one that she was incapable of facing with May present. She clung to him, as if he were a savior. She was reasonably sure Montag had not seen her since he had not moved or even stiffened, and it was imperative to get away before he did. She had to have time to think. Summoning every ounce of self-control, she turned with May blocking a view of her, and walked with measured paces in the direction from which they had come. After a minute or two her silence concerned May. "Are you really all right?" he asked.

"Yes." Her tone was nicer.

For some time they had been hoping that she was pregnant only to be disappointed each month. May naturally hoped that her strange behavior had something to do with her menstrual cycle. Her apparent discomfort might have meant a cramp or two—not what he wanted, but not serious.

There was no way at the moment for her to escape from May without distressing him greatly, and she didn't want to distress him, even for a moment. They were having such a wonderful day. Oh, dear God, what shall I do? She prayed silently, numb with shock.

Now she knew Kurt was in Berchtesgaden, undoubtedly staying in a pension, going out on sporadic forays, looking for her. She was secluded from nationals on U.S. Army property. She would have to find him, which would be easy because he, an Austrian, would be registered with the police. They would have to resolve something once and for all. The missing arm and slumped shoulder explained his earlier inability to write. Perhaps he had found someone else. Men often fell in love with their nurses. That would solve everything. In the *Kreutzer Sonata* Tolstoy had written: To say that you can love one person all your life is like saying that one candle will continue burning for as long as you live. May deserved her total devotion. She loved him above everything in the world.

When they got to town, May stopped a taxi. "No more walking. I don't think you're well."

She did not protest. "I love you, *Liebling,*" she said, meeting his eyes. "You are such a good, dear man."

The words were strangely discomforting, as if she feared she were dying. "What in the world brought that on?" he inquired, shaking his head, not expecting an answer.

They returned to the Eagle's Nest, and she threw herself on the bed, Hitler's bed. That fact made no difference now.

"I wish you would tell me what the trouble is." He sat down beside her, feeling her forehead, concern clouding his face and hammering at his heart.

"I'll be all right, *Liebling.* Just leave me alone for a little while."

"Did I do anything, say anything to hurt you?"

"No. Heavens no."

The emphasis was not reassuring. Taking her at her word, he left her, blaming the Eagle's Nest.

She knew he would be in the kitchen fixing food she could not eat.

Soon he was back at the bedroom door. "Would you like a little soup? I'll be glad to bring it to you."

"Danke, nein."

Her voice carried a tinge of irritation, and he backed away, feeling as helpless as a rebuffed child. She had never behaved this way. He told himself that she'd feel better if she went to sleep, but this solution was unsatisfactory. Certainly she was not pregnant. It was no passing mood. Clearly, she was greatly troubled, in great mental pain, and he felt powerless to help until she was ready to confide in him. Was she struggling with some great principle? He wondered. No way. He felt some of the most foolish things in the world had been done because of somebody's misguided principles.

Baffled, eating alone, he reviewed the afternoon, step by step. Everything had been hunky-dory until they reached the bridge. He had been talking about Mondrian, looking at reflected timbers in the water, and she had listened closely, clearly interested. He had recalled the early painting and compared it with their view. Why had she suddenly become silent and wanted the binoculars? Why had she appeared afraid? Perhaps it was too much of a likeness—the similarity of two different realities. No, she wasn't *that* philosophical. He reviewed the scene. There was one minor difference. A man had been leaning over the bridge, a small figure in the distance, oddly sagging, bending morosely toward the water, conceivably considering suicide? Was Inge, with her wild imagination, foreseeing that? There had been no figure in the Dutch painting, so May had ignored him. Clearly, the sight of this person stunned her, and she wanted a closer look. Only one man would have elicited such a powerful response: Kurt Montag! She had recognized him and fled, fearing recognition. That was the only possible explanation. May felt a sudden sickening that came with a sense of impending loss. He wanted to rush to her, to hold her tightly and prevent any thought of separation, but he resisted the urge. She had shut him out. He would not beg. His interpretation of her behavior meant only one thing: she still loved the man.

He had lost her once before, and he had survived. He presumed he would again, but Lord, how painful it would be.

Once during the night, awakened by Inge's impassioned kisses, he made love to her. He had not expected her frenetic outburst, stemming from distress, guilt, and true love, yet he matched it with his own.

She had been weeping, her skin was salty, her body tense. The tears made him feel all the more certain that their conjunction was a good-bye. In this most critical time, when verbal communication was so crucial, both conveyed only silent despair.

It was near dawn when he awakened and found her gone from their bed. Panicked, he sprang up and darted from the room, thinking she had already left. He discovered her sitting in a chair in the great ugly salon, staring into the distance. He was over his panic now, but consumed by the unfairness of life. Behind them, forty-five ugly chairs formed an empty theater. The fat lady hadn't yet sung.

"You saw Kurt Montag, didn't you?" he asked, standing near her, aching at the thought.

"Yes." Her voice was soft and pained. "I think so. He's lost an arm and a lot of his shoulder. He looks perfectly awful, terrible."

It was worse than he had expected. "You're going to see him today?" His arms hung limply at his sides.

"I don't want to." She looked up at him. "I guess I must. I'm afraid he's been waiting here for me. Lord knows how long." Agony and self-hatred were written on her face. It's awful for us both, but there it is. I'm trapped."

She felt ready to start hiking back to Berlin, or at least running for the hills, except she knew there would be no escape. Kurt would have to see that they were now two very different people. As gently as possible she would have to tell him that her American lover had returned and that she was going to marry May, and hoped that he would set her free.

May closed his eyes. "There's nothing that I can say. I've already said it all so many times." He left the room to make coffee or to get dressed or to be busy doing something.

She followed, wanting to explain that she had no idea that her innocent correspondence could boomerang in such a fashion—but what was the use. Instead she said, "I don't know what he'll say or expect. He may be nasty and angry, and that would make it easier. Seeing him destroyed has upset me terribly. You have no idea how I'm hurting over this."

"Yes, I do." He turned to face her. "Do you think as a German that you have a monopoly on pain and suffering? I'm hurting the same way you are. You'd better not go to work. See him this morning. Get it over with. Please, don't keep an axe hanging over my head."

However the meeting turned out, it was bound to be bad.

* ** *

The German police had the address where the Baron was living. He was in a pension, an over-crowded, run-down establishment left for German use. Inge had no difficulty finding it. She sat down in a dilapidated chair in the foyer to wait, knowing that in the next hour, he and all the other boarders, would have to appear for breakfast. No one would forego a meal. Soon she was joined by three other guests, waiting for the French doors in the dining room to open. Then there he was, stepping out of the elevator. Trying to look only at his eyes, managing a smile, she rose to greet him.

"I knew you would come," he cried, an arm outstretched, half of his face smiling, the other half cracked in distortion and partially hidden by a veil attached to his cap. "But you see, I'm not all here."

Inge's heart sank, standing close, feeling half an embrace. One side of his face was dreadfully scarred. "What does it matter? Kurt, you're alive!"

He walked her back to the line of chairs, and sat down slowly beside her, offering her his good profile. "We have so much to talk about."

Her mouth felt dry, and she groped for words, finding only the most prosaic. "Are you in pain?"

"I was until I saw you… Honestly, I just get bad headaches."

The brave sentiment was like a knife in her back.

Other hotel guests entered the foyer and greeted him. Smiles broke out when they saw she was there. To avoid interruption, he stood up and led her to a small writing room where they had more privacy. "Don't come to me out of a sense of pity. I could not stand that. I've learned to live with what's left of me. Until I reached that point, I couldn't look for you. I needed operations, therapy, and time. Can you understand and forgive me? I knew this… this…," he pointed toward the missing arm, "disfiguration would make no difference to you, but it made a great deal of difference to me."

"I'm not here out of pity."

The missing arm and disfigured side of his face did make a difference, but one she guessed anyone could get used to in time. The problem was simply that she loved May, not this dear, sweet, ravaged man, now monstrously disfigured.

Kurt gave her no chance to speak further. "So many operations were necessary to restore even this much of me. You've no idea the mess I was in. Through it all there was always your face before me, giving me something to live for. The few hours that we were together in Berlin became an epiphanic turning point for the rest of my life. Isn't that remarkable?"

Then I've already served you, thought Inge. Shouldn't that be enough?

At this point he was careful to turn so that she could not see his disfigurement. Only his love poured out of him. She listened, choked by a great swell of pity, horrified by her position. Other guests, having filled the foyer, suddenly swarmed into the small writing room waiting for the dining room doors to open. A beaten young couple that could have posed for Degas's painting, *The Absinthe Drinkers,* stared sadly at Inge and Kurt over a small table. That this was their first meeting after the war was all too clear. They were observing her, seeing all—how she had taken his appearance, the love pouring from his eyes, and her misery, shaming her passivity before a man who had sacrificed so much for *Das Vaterland*. The snare of her people grew tighter.

"You never know when you're living, which hours will be the important ones," she stammered. "It's only later, perhaps at the end of one's life…"

"You're right about that. I could never have foreseen at the time how I would fight like a madman because of your face—how it would give me strength and endurance. The thought that the Russians would march toward you always obsessed me. I fought for you."

Inge's heart sank. "You hardly knew me, Kurt. I doubt that I'm worthy of such love. You fought for an ideal—all women, perhaps." She was getting nowhere.

"Oh, you can learn a lot about someone through letters—enough to focus on one face that stood for all women. No, dear, you never wore a mask. Your kindness, love of beauty, diligence, and tender heart could be read in every line. How else could I have fought for that maniac Hitler as I did, except to protect you? And through my love for you, I found the strength for the ultimate act." Then his voice broke.

"What?" Her lips trembling, her eyes wide, she opened the trap.

"In the end a Russian with a flame-thrower got the nozzle into our tank, dooming us to the most painful death possible. I had to shoot my men, my friends. My dear, they were like brothers." His hand rose to shield his eyes. "I'd have killed myself, but I couldn't reload."

Inge listened, moved. A great sense of pity and compassion took over and an awful sense of duty weakened her resolve. She would have to let Kurt down slowly. It was impossible to tell him about May right now.

"Kurt, I need a little time. You've been through an ordeal. You need time, too."

Seemingly, he didn't hear her, still lost in some tank battle on the Steppes of Russia. "*Jawohl, meine* Inge, I've killed for you, and I would again. I'd hunt down any man who would take you from me, if it took me until the end of my life." He shrugged, but the fire in his eyes alarmed her. "I'd have nothing to lose. *Gar nichts.*"

Now, out of fear for May's life, she was overwhelmed. She would have to make herself love this man again. Looking into his eyes, seeing the adoration, she felt the trap close.

"Please Kurt, don't talk that way. The world has seen enough killing. You have to forget. She looked up to see that they were the center of attention in the room. People listening were whispering to each other.

"Liebling, your family... how are they?" she asked.

"They're planning a warm reception for you."

He smiled, and Inge could think of one thing. She had to get this man out of Germany, and the sooner the better. Then she could tell him about May. For the next hour she sat numbly, holding his hand, acquiescing to his marriage plans. She prayed for strength, having no idea where it could come from. May had been her strength.

There were no regulations against Germans marrying Austrians, and the Germans would see that the usual red tape was circumvented for a war hero and nobleman in pain. She knew her duty, her *Pflicht.* She had done it before. It was all so *déjà vu.* May already knew that she might leave him; she had seen it in his eyes. By evening Kurt would have them on the night train, but he could not accompany her to get her things on the U.S. Army facility. " I must resign my job," she told him.

Very soon May would have to leave for Spandau for an undetermined length of time. She could not accompany him. The pieces in the puzzle that were her life were all falling together by themselves, and she hated the picture they were making. She would have to become an actress. I'm strong. I can do it. I must, she told herself.

"You look very serious for a bride," he told her, radiating love. His dreams were coming true.

"All brides are frightened. I'm shy, you know..."

Kurt seemed satisfied. Colonel Rasmussen was not, when she visited him. She told him that the Baron, once her fiancé, had been badly injured. She didn't tell him the whole story—that May would be in great danger if the Baron were to learn about him—but Rasmussen knew his officer would be hurt by the loss of this German girl.

He studied her. "Fräulein von Haas, how well do you know this Austrian?"

"Really only through letters, sir. But they revealed a lot. This is something I must do. Please don't make me talk about it. I am distraught."

If she told Rasmussen that Kurt could be ready to kill May, he would be thrown in jail, but he would soon be out, ready to stalk again. A lawyer would call her opinions hearsay.

Rasmussen remembered the first time he saw her, and the way the skinny girl had trembled. May had taken good care of her, filled her out. Damn stubborn Germans, he thought. Certainly the Baron sounded like a super-sensitive, suffering invalid. How long did she think she could keep up a charade with him? Well, it wasn't his business. The girl was obviously demoralized. He could see that he could not change her mind. Too bad army regulations had been so hard on his capable officer, which was where his interest lay. "Call me if I can help you in any way," he said finally, but his tone was cool. Theatrical sacrifices were no favor to a real man.

She went back to the Eagle's Nest to wait for May. A few hours later, unable to work, he came home. Seeing the desolation on her face, he knew her decision.

"I refused you once. Today I love you a hundred times more than I did then, but again, I know what I must do. That it hurts you breaks my heart. I can't help it…" She sobbed. She could not talk about her fear for his life. He would not have listened, much less understood.

May said nothing, his disappointment binding his lips like a muzzle.

Fighting for composure, she gathered her possessions in a paper bag. May folded the Hermes lap robe and handed it to her. "My wedding present," he said. "I don't want you ever to be cold."

Inge shuddered.

As they descended the shiny copper-clad elevator toward the grand marble foyer where the jeep waited, neither looked to the walls, fearing to see the other's face reflected. May remembered that she had caught him in an unfaithful act, and she had given him a way out. Now he was giving her a way out—with no idea of the sacrifice that it was.

He looked at the dashboard of the jeep, and for a moment he thought of letting the motor run, of simply sitting there with her, while carbon monoxide fumes put them both into a long sleep. Then he banished the thought and hit the button controlling the great bronze doors of the foyer. In town at the PX he stopped and bought her a suitcase. He knew she would not be ashamed of the paper bag, but he was. When he got back to the vehicle, he almost expected to see her gone. She was still there, immobile as a wax figure. She had long given up ever telling Kurt about May.

"You'd better repack," he said.

Standing by the jeep, she threw her few things into the suitcase. He stood watching mutely, now certain that some wild force was playing havoc with his life. A capricious wind whipped around them, scurrying dust that was a blessed distraction. Something awful was happening, and yet they were moving as if it were nothing.

* ** *

He was sent to Berlin. At least Berlin offered some signs of rebuilding, new faces, and the absence of Street's. May often wondered whether or not Street got his one souvenir—and how fine an *objet d'art* it was.

Berlin also offered several good beers that helped him through nights. In a few lonely months he finished up the work in Spandau. All joy was missing from the task, despite the fact that considerable art had been stored there. As promised, Rasmussen saw to his promotion, so he was now a captain. He ordered a car from the States. His new red Ford was one of the first off the peacetime assembly line. As soon as it came, he requested leave. Like everything else, the car was unsatisfying.

CHAPTER THREE

1947, Mondsee

Kurt Montag's arrival in Mondsee quite naturally overshadowed Inge's. His mother and sister were thankful simply that he had survived, and it took several days before Inge came seriously under their scrutiny. Much to Kurt's chagrin, he found that he and Inge could not be married immediately. His mother saw to that. The astute *Baronin* was not about to give up her title until she was sure about her son's choice of a bride. She had received Inge graciously, but for Kurt's sake, she wanted to be sure that the girl could handle her role. Because of the extent of Kurt's injuries, she was more than wary, but plans for an elaborate wedding would give her time for a closer, harder look.

This was not easy because almost immediately Inge turned into a recluse. She soon saw that not showing up for meals so disrupted the peace in the family that she made it a point of being there in body, if not in spirit. Still she had very little to say. Soon after she arrived the *Baronin* gave her a tour of the castle. Inge noted that many of the paintings were in bad shape, and she asked for permission to restore them, one by one, which was gratefully granted.

This work, which was tedious and time-consuming, was also blessedly diverting. Further, it gave her an escape from conversation and scrutiny. Years of smoke, grime, and fly specks first had to be removed from the art by soap and water. Then the old, yellowed lacquer could be removed. Finally, with the original colors bursting through, Inge could again seal the cleaned canvas, retouch the frame, and return the hallowed ancestor or landscape to its wall. Because the work chewed up time, it afforded a tad of satisfaction. In the meantime, to keep her son busy, the *Baronin* suggested that machinery from an abandoned quarry be utilized to build a ski lift. Kurt was overjoyed. It was the second step in his dream.

Inge happily soon saw that the Baroness was clearly in control. She could only apologize for being unable to handle any of the wedding plans herself, having no family, no money, further unsaid—no interest. The fact that her country had just lost a war was again a blessing. "I'm sure that whatever you plan will be lovely," she murmured. She could not even give the Baroness a list of people to invite. "There is no one, Madam. What you see is what you get—just me." Even mentioning American Army officers, the only people she knew, would have been a mistake.

The *Baronin* drew a deep breath. The girl would take some getting used to. "The wedding must be a big affair. The whole village will celebrate. After all, Kurt inherited the barony," she needlessly pointed out. "Also we must treat him like a normal human being—as if he still were the handsome young man with a beautiful soul that he once was. And of course, Inge, you must be received in the Catholic faith."

"Whatever you say, Madam."

This development suited Inge well. It gave her an opportunity to walk to the village everyday whether she showed up for the religious instruction or not. At home she could not help but feel herself under a microscope. Further, she had no will to attempt her own painting. Her concentration was not there. One canvas, which she had started, a picture of a black and white cow sat idly on its easel. She didn't think much of it, and knew May wouldn't have either. For some odd reason the subject seemed appropriate. But her cow gave her an excuse to lock herself in her room. The art in the *Schloss* was not bad, but could not hold a candle to what she had seen in the tunnels.

The *Baronin*, an attractive woman for her age, at first made a conscious effort to be charming, but she soon decided that Inge was utterly spineless. "She mindlessly agrees to anything and everything," she told Kurt, unabashed. It was up to Kurt to explain to his mother that Inge's former friends and all her possessions had been lost, but he could vouch for her completely acceptable background. At any rate, the few possessions she had, her pearls, a massive diamond ring and Hermes mink lap robe, spoke of taste, as well as lost wealth. The lap robe proved a godsend. Often when Inge felt depressed, like a sick animal needing to lick her wounds, she could go to her room, curl up under a warm fur, feel close to May, and find strength to go down to dinner or whatever.

The Baroness, studying the tall beautiful girl with the sad face, nursed strange misgivings. Here was not a happy bride. But also, here was no title-seeker or money-hungry belle either. She baffled her future mother-in-law on one hand, but then on the other, the *Baronin* enjoyed the free hand she seemed to have in planning the nuptials. "The girl is an enigma," she whispered to her daughter Olympia. "Try to sound her out. I can't." Olympia, still inwardly shaken by Kurt's condition, only shrugged.

Inge gratefully accepted Kurt's preoccupation with the ski lift. Kurt, busy and optimistic over the future, moved in a dream world, bowing to the dictates of both his mother and Inge. He and Inge had had so little time together, been alone so seldom, he was reluctant to press her into bed, and she would not let him in her room. Something at cross-purposes with a new faith, as Inge, dreading a sexual encounter, quickly explained. Such was the rational thinking of an irrational man whose years in Russia had driven him too far.

There were moments when working on the dredging machinery with simple day laborers, cursing and frustrated over the loss of his arm, he would branch into blind uncontrollable rages. This terrifying behavior went unobserved by the family. Nevertheless, Olympia and Kurt's mother, through devoted servants whom they knew loved Kurt, heard alarming stories of insane tantrums and cruel beatings, totally out of character with the man they knew. As a matter of course, they kept these tales from Inge.

The Baroness tried to excuse Kurt. "The Nazis did it to him," she told Olympia. "Inge will help him. There's nothing like the love of a good and beautiful woman to tame a man. Haven't you noticed that she brings out the best in him?"

"Yes, *Mutti*, when she's with him, but that's only at meals. She's never alone with him." Troubled thoughts were written on her face. "I spent the war working in the quarries, and I know the men, *Mutti*. They're trustworthy, good, simple, hard-working people. Handled rightly, they give their all. They cringe in fear of Kurt," she confided.

The Baroness recoiled. "You've seen this?"

"No. He behaves himself around me and certainly around Inge, but I'm telling you what I've heard. The villagers, seeing his disfiguration, are ready to make allowances. Stories come out slowly. The work is dangerous. These people have never built a ski lift. Kurt demands too much of unskilled labor."

"The new work will soon be finished, then the men can go back to what they know. In time Kurt will adjust."

A few days later the Baroness called Olympia to her suite, which she wanted to refurbish for the newlyweds, and wanted suggestions. Olympia limped in, listened to her mother, but engulfed in sadness changed the subject. "Things have been getting worse, not better."

"What?"

"*Mutti,* there's a volcano in Kurt that will soon erupt."

The weight in the Baroness's heart grew heavier. Olympia had been housebound too long for a girl with a handicap—and yet? She must have some reason for her statement, the mother decided. She loved her brother too dearly for idle criticism. "A wedding is always a stressful time."

"I don't think you should give up the master suite either. I'm sure that would make Inge very uncomfortable. She's not particularly comfortable as it is. Does she see anyone besides the village priest?" Olympia asked. "She gets no mail. She writes no letters. She doesn't telephone or get any calls. She seems to enjoy the library, but that is escapism...."

The Baroness ignored the question and her daughter's remarks, as if sweeping dirt under a rug would make it go away. She too had noticed Inge's absorption with the new religion—as if she were searching for solace or grasping for some fountain of strength, which, of course, Inge was. Kurt did not revolt her. It was simply that she hungered for May, and needed every ounce of strength she could muster, to act like a blushing bride while living without him. She hoped renewing her faith would help, but decided it was easier to believe in Santa Claus or the Tooth Fairy.

"She doesn't seem to care about the bridesmaids' dresses," said Olympia, "which she's left for me to design, while she's the artist. That's strange."

"Don't go imagining things. Because she can't pay for anything, she would be reluctant to suggest spending our money." The Baroness could laughingly gripe about a shortage of money and having to make do, but even Inge had noted there was no shortage of help.

"I don't think she's a happy bride, and I don't think Kurt sees it. She's been here weeks, and we don't know her any better than we did the day she arrived."

"She's quiet."

"Too quiet, for my taste, *Mutti,* dear. Something's not right. I hate to think it could be his disfigurement."

It was late fall before the wedding day arrived. The entire village came alive for this occasion. The mountains were decked in fresh glittering snow. Inge, resplendent in her mother-in-law's wedding dress, lengthened by an underskirt with a deep band of shirred lace, held her emotions under control, as they had been for weeks. A pearl tiara held a long veil in place, and matched the string of pearls from May.

Olympia, grave and darkly beautiful, and three of her friends preceded the bride down the aisle of the cathedral as *The Bridal Procession and Chorus* from Lohengrin swelled and rose like a flight of birds. An old family friend of the Baroness escorted Inge at a metered pace. Kurt, calm from a resource of happiness, waited. Inge made her replies. Then suddenly the ceremony was over. Kurt led her to a white stagecoach drawn by six white horses. In her mind she had just taken part in a mock pageantry. Smiling wanly, she waved to well-wishers. She had behaved herself through the traumatic event in splendid fashion; she didn't quite know how. May was someplace in a sleeping memory, and this was her new life. Due to the food shortage, guests threw artificial rice.

How symbolic, she thought, not daring to look at the man now in the rapturous delight of a child, riding beside her.

"I hope I can make you very happy," she told him as they bumped along, feeling that some kind, sweet, tender statement was called for.

"You've done that by being my bride, and by being true to me for such a long time," he whispered. "Don't be afraid. I know you're a virgin. I'll be very gentle."

Oh, dear God, thought Inge. Will this charade never end? Give me strength…

A lavish reception followed, provisions having been acquired gradually on the black market during the summer. Her mother-in-law found *ways*. People in the country had their own resistance to occupation. Despite Olympia's disapproval, the master suite had been readied for the bridal pair; travel for a honeymoon was prohibited. A seamstress had fashioned a beautiful nightgown for Inge out of scraps of silk and lace assembled by Kurt's mother. Any other bride would have greatly resented her mother-in-law's dominance, but Inge could not have been more grateful. They liked each other in a strange way. During the reception she watched the *Baronin,* and knew exactly what it was about her that had caught her—the sensation of power, clothed in unbeatable Austrian charm. Today it seemed beautiful.

The Baroness had observed her son very carefully on his wedding day. Despite careful refitting of his cutaway by his tailor, Kurt was dissatisfied. His proper pre-war wedding attire had been refurbished. The striped trousers, stiff white shirt and turned collar, gray and black striped four-in-hand tie, a gray glove, black kid shoes, and gray silk top hat—with a gray silk veil on his right side pleased him. But the coat, slightly let out, was binding and uncomfortable. It threw him into an uncontrolled rage that settled on his valet. The Baroness, hearing the commotion, interrupted Kurt beating the old man with a cane. Kurt's frenzy at the sight of his mother subsided, but the valet was seriously injured, and the Baroness was thoroughly shaken. Sick with apprehension that she hid even from Olympia, she steadied her nerves by telling herself that, with the outburst over, Kurt would be subdued. To her great relief, in the cathedral he was.

It was during the wedding reception with the public rooms of the castle filled with guests—fires roaring in the two massive fireplaces—that Kurt seemed overly tense, even strange to his mother. The fires, made with great logs as customary on such occasions, had been necessary, but a mistake she realized. Fortunately the reception line in the entry distanced the wedding party from the fires. Yet Kurt's tension was such that twice he snapped the stems of fine champagne glasses. The problem of being unable to offer his right hand to old friends repeatedly frustrated him. When his eyes rested on Inge, he grew calm; his high artificial laugh dissipated. By the time the last guest departed, the Baroness was strained to the point of exhaustion. Despite her misgivings, she had been the epitome of charm, dazzling all her guests with her smile.

"Be sure to lock up well," she ordered the houseman. "Silver wedding gifts on display in the library might lure thieves." The gifts were magnificent, coming from titles all over Europe. Inge could hardly believe the windfall. Father would have appreciated this, she thought several times. His dream had come true. Too bad it wasn't hers.

Inge bent to kiss her mother-in-law. "Thank you for a perfectly beautiful wedding. I'm sure no one here will ever forget it. I never will." She turned to Kurt, smiling. "I never would have believed that such a magnificent wedding would be mine." The Baroness was touched. Kurt was ready to die of happiness. Olympia kissed Inge and then her brother. "Dear brother, you were great. I know it was a strain." It had been—for all concerned.

Everything is going to be fine, thought the Baroness.

* ** *

It was early in the afternoon, after the last busload of guests had left for Salzburg, before Inge could slip back to her old room to get out of her wedding finery. It was there, assisted by an unbuttoning upstairs-maid, that she learned of Kurt caning the valet. She was even more alarmed to learn that such outbursts occurred often in the recent past, and carefully had been kept from her.

"Why wasn't I told?" She was incredulous.

"I think the *Baronin* feared you would call off the wedding. She felt you would be very good for him. Please, don't tell anyone that I told you or I might lose my job. I thought I should warn you never to cross this man. He has a terrible temper. I wouldn't want him to turn it on you." The maid had whispered, wanting to endear herself to Inge.

Inge was shocked but also grateful for an ally. "Thank you," she replied, determined to make the wedding night turn out well. She slipped into a becoming afternoon dress, and set out in search of her husband. She found him in the library.

Still dressed in his wedding attire, Kurt smiled broadly on seeing his bride. Then his expression changed as he noted she was no longer in her wedding dress. "Apparently you don't want to appear as a bride for very long," he said.

"It was not the most comfortable dress. Did you expect me to wear it all day?" Her tone was not particularly warm, but it wasn't cold, just full of surprise. "Your mother had a very small waist. Besides, the dress should be saved for our daughter."

"My coat is not comfortable, but I'm still wearing it."

"I heard that. I just learned of your outburst this morning, and that your valet was seriously injured. Kurt, I'm shocked. This is serious. Perhaps you need psychiatric help."

"I don't need help. A wedding is a stressful event. I was very disturbed by the fires."

"Do you get angry often?" She did not know her husband.

"Inge, are we going to quarrel on this… our wedding day?"

"I hope not."

"Then don't tell me what I need. I need an arm, a shoulder, a face," he cried, now glaring at her.

"I can't handle your bad humor. You must stop attacking. Verbally you're attacking me now," she replied shaken, but mustering a soft tone, hoping to quiet him.

After a silence he said, "You don't love me."

The pathetically childish ploy only angered Inge who, turning her back to him, stooped to play another equally unkind game. "That's not true, but perhaps I also love another." The quarrel snowballed.

Kurt pounced, his rage growing. "You have seen your American? The one you told me about in Berlin, and later wrote me about?"

"Herr May was in Berchtesgaden. He gave me a job." Why am I telling him this? she asked herself, except that I am at the end of my tether. Finding no answer, only aware of guilt, she hoped to retreat.

"I knew it. I could feel it. You have never been happy here. You have not grieved for me. You have grieved for him. You have lied to me, betrayed me!"

"Never."

"I'll kill that man. I swear." His eyes were murderous.

"Perhaps you already have," Inge muttered, now without fear, as she had no idea where May was; very probably he was no longer in Berchtesgaden, but safe behind the walls of some other casern. She was still angry, so angry she had forgotten the maid's warning. "At least you don't have to look at yourself." She stopped there, not adding but thinking, I do.

Mercifully, summoning the strength to restrain himself, Kurt stalked from the room, heading on foot to the quarry that had become his haven.

Inge fled to her old room where she threw herself down on the bed. She had made a terrible mistake, and didn't quite know how to remedy it. Someway she would have to fight to save her marriage. Kurt, in time, could be won over. She hoped.

The butter-yellow quarry office sat in a treeless valley a kilometer behind and out of sight of the *Schloss*. The small solitary building sat amidst an accumulation of rubble left from years of stone cutting. The yard around the shop was littered with old, dilapidated and abandoned cutting machinery, a broken-down tireless truck, and worn out motors, all rusting beside scrap metal too troublesome to haul away. Much of the morning's light snow had melted with the afternoon sun, but enough remained to mingle with the coarse quarry dust and shimmer, belying the mess lying beneath the surface.

Kurt entered the building, left the door ajar, and threw himself down on a Thonet chair. The high, many-paned windows filtered an eerie greenish light that danced about the oppressive dust, coarse to the touch.

Kurt was heartbroken. Inge could not have hurt him more had she plunged a knife into his heart.

Her revelation had first stunned him, and in his mental illness he was ready to believe the worst. After a few minutes his pain turned to anger, first toward Inge and then toward her friend, Herr May. Undoubtedly, they had been lovers. He had been totally deceived. That business of her being a virgin was a crock. He had done so much killing that one more would not matter. How can I get to May? he wondered. How can I rid the world of this pox, this man who has truly ruined my life, who tried to rob me of the little bit of happiness that was left to me?

From the back of a shallow drawer under an old table he extracted a Luger.

He should not have wondered. The mountain would come to Muhammad.

CHAPTER FOUR

1947, Berlin

While in Spandau, May received a disturbing letter from Otto. It came just as he was sitting down for a coffee that, in his frustration, he immediately spilled. Betsy had been very pleased with Otto's progress and wrote: "*If you don't hear from him you know he is busy, busy, busy—and happy.*" Knowing what a chore letter writing was to a teenager, May had not expected to hear from Otto often. When the first letter came after Inge left, May thought: he needs money. This was not the case; still he would send some.

> "*Dear Herr May,*
> "*I have been awfully upset to learn that Inge is in Austria, planning to marry the Baron von Montag. Knowing how much she loves you, she is making a terrible mistake. How can you let such a crazy thing happen? Can't you stop her? Bark an order, Herr May. She's German. She'll obey. That guy cornered her, pressured her, and wheedled her into self-sacrifice, knowing her character. She doesn't love him. She says, quote, I will learn to. I have to. Unquote. Inge is difficult to understand because she is so good and is always willing to be the sacrificial lamb.*"

May's hand, grasping the letter, fell to his lap, while the old familiar pain that he lived with once again swelled from deep in his chest, rising to his throat. Tears dampened his eyes. Somewhat calmed, he returned to the letter.

> "*Frankly, I think the guy is dangerous—a loonie—and he may have*

frightened Inge. Needless to say, I'm unhappy with what I hear from her, and only hope you will take some action.

"Betsy is tops. I often wonder why you did not marry her, as once she admitted that in college she was crazy about you. I guess much of life is timing, isn't it. The timing sure was right for me when we met.

"There is no way that I can thank you with words. I only hope that you will forgive Inge. Better than that, stop her.

"I miss you.

"Love, Otto."

Good try, Otto, thought May, dourly. When you leave duty in the U.S. Army without leave, it is known as AWOL, for which there are jail sentences. Otto didn't seem to realize that he always knew Inge loved him. The problem was that she apparently loved Kurt Montag or Montague more.

May read and reread the letter, then wrote Otto a brief note, thanking him, and—just to be safe—enclosing more money. He wrote: *"When it comes to timing, I've not been very lucky, Otto, despite a concerted effort on my part to make my own luck. You will soon learn that you can't or shouldn't marry all the great women you will meet and love. Whatever, I'll always be your friend."*

Eventually, when the work in Spandau was finished, May was ordered back to Berchtesgaden to wait for the wheels of time, oiled by the U.S. Army that would issue him further orders. Sometimes he permitted himself to gaze hungrily toward Austria, wondering when he would muster the strength to cross the border. He dare not move closer to Inge, knowing he would be making a perilous journey.

Sometimes he entertained curious thoughts about her, as to whether she was happy or not, but because such musings depressed him, fueling his loneliness, he tried not to think of her—much less to inquire. With all the joy of his life gone, May gritted his teeth and settled down in the BOQ. Street still lusted for one souvenir painting, but May clearly considered this unethical to the point of criminality. Street certainly would not have wanted it spread around the command that he had taken, as his souvenir, a piece of art the Nazis had purloined from an occupied country. The one souvenir that soldiers were permitted, had to come from the Germans themselves, not their victims. Street backed down and became a little easier for May to tolerate.

"Wrap-up operations are always a bore," Street said. May couldn't agree with him more, wondering what experience Street was drawing on.

Street and May were in the Rathaus in the Fine Arts and Monuments office when a call came in from Rasmussen. "A general just rang. It seems a priest in the village of Mondsee discovered a cache of hidden art that may be stolen and called us. I think we have to look into it."

The story of the recovered stolen art had broken in European newspapers along with the news that the U.S. Army was returning all of it to the rightful owners.

"You know what's going to happen, don't you, May?" moaned Street, looking at a map. "This is only the beginning. Every little boondocks will be finding...well luckily, Mondsee is only about forty klicks as the crow flies."

May frowned. "We're not crows." A full day's outing with Street was nothing to look forward to. "It's a pretty mountainous region." The fact that he would be getting perilously close to Inge, he could not even think about. So near and yet so far. Pain still crowded his heart.

"You heard the general's order. Let's go!"

"If we're going to visit a parish priest, and we want anything from him, we should come bearing booze," said May, remembering European protocol from years ago. "Say a bottle of schnapps or something 100 proof."

"Good thinking May. We'll pick up a bottle at the club." May would pick it up, and May would pay for it. No matter. It was cheap enough.

The drive to Mondsee in a jeep was endured passively by May simply because of the superb scenery. He listened patiently to a new recital of Street's ambitions, and was actually glad that Street could distract him, if only with irritation.

This day Mondsee had put on her best dress. There were garlands everywhere and free drinks at every *Kneipe*. On the street Austrian women showed off their embroidered velvet dirndls, and the men donned their squeaky lederhosen. The reason came to light when they stopped to ask directions to the church.

"Have a drink on the house, actually the old Baroness," crowed the patron. "Her son married this morning." He pushed a beer toward May who, paling slightly, graciously refused, saying that he had a meeting with a priest and shouldn't have beer on his breath.

So today the possibility of a life with Inge is finally, definitely, permanently over, he thought, and, of all the crazy things, I'm here in Mondsee to celebrate the closure. It was enough to gag a goat, and made him want to cry. Hope, regardless of how vague, always had a way of sneaking into May's psyche. It undermined reasoning, and yet, if not lifting his spirits, at least it had preserved him.

He and Street located the church. They found the priest and were led to an apse, where at least a hundred candles were burning.

"A gift of the *Baronin* for this day," the kindly old priest acknowledged, beaming and waving toward the candles. "Cleaning up, we found these paintings that apparently had been hidden in the church with no record. I read about the stolen art, and simply want to be sure they don't belong to somebody else."

The dusty art was unframed, and it took May only two minutes in the brilliant, dancing candlelight to ascertain that the stations of the cross—the usual fourteen images—had been painted by an amateur and were worthless as art.

"I'm glad you brought them to light," said May, trying to be both tactful and kind, stepping over to a tall wrought iron candelabrum for further inspection. He stalled, looking to Street for confirmation.

Street concurred by nodding and murmuring under his breath, "Crap."

Then May continued, "I know where the artist copped this from. It's from a mosaic in the House of Faun in Pompeii, representing the battle of Alexander the Great and Darius III that took place in 333 BC. In the horse-drawn battle scene, Alexander pursues a fearfully pleading Darius, swords, spears and mayhem surrounding them. Obviously these paintings were donated by somebody seeking redemption, but whoever was in charge here at the time, recognized that they weren't worthy of this beautiful building, and hid them as best he could—possibly at least fifty years ago."

At that moment Baron Kurt Montag burst into the room.

While stewing in the quarry office over his confrontation with

Inge, Kurt had decided that being a rational man, he should speak with the priest who had handled her conversion into the Catholic faith and who had given her the necessary instruction. The first thing he saw on stepping into the room was the light of a hundred candles. One hundred little fires carried him back to the war in Russia as if he had stepped back in time, thrusting him into months of pain. Then he saw the two U.S. Army uniforms, and the insignia that had become so familiar to him while in Berchtesgaden. Reading May's name pinned on his uniform, Kurt Montag went totally berserk.

Much of what followed on this most awful day of his life, May would not remember. He did remember Montag crying out, "May, you've come here on my wedding day to steal Inge, whom you've debauched, and I'm going to kill you." With that he pulled out his Luger from his vest holster. Facing the three men head on, as if in a showdown, the one-armed Baron stepped forward, totally in command of the situation. He held the pistol and aimed directly at May.

Immediately the brave priest stepped forward, hands extended, imploring, "My friend, Kurt, please let reason prevail. Stop this insanity before someone is hurt. I beg of you. Don't spoil your own wedding day."

Without hesitation, the Baron turned and fired point blank. The bullet slammed into the holy man's chest, imploding his heart, knocking him backward off his feet so that he crumpled with a thud to the stone floor. Both May and Street, horrified, knew the man had died instantly and that they, too, were in mortal danger.

Montag first turned to Street who stood motionless, mouth agape, the bagged bottle of brandy still in his hand. "You will die because you have chosen the company of your friend May on this day. What rotten timing you *Amis* have."

When Montag turned to May, Street decided to take some evasive action—at least to save himself. There was no point in placidly supporting death in May's honor. Seeing his chance, he swung the full bottle of brandy at the Baron's head, using all the force he could muster. Montag ducked and fired. The bottle missed Montag's head, but instead hit the prosthesis with a loud crack that surprised everyone. The bottle disintegrated into glass shards, scattering about, while the brandy doused Montag's formal morning suit. The shot went wild, missing May and Street, but freezing Street in his shoes. May dived at Montag, felling him like a tree. One of the men on the floor accidentally tipped over the candelabrum. May would always remember the way the flames jumped in mid-air toward Montag and his brandy-soaked clothing. By now Street had gained his senses and intervened to step on Montag, allowing May to get up. May grabbed a painting, intending to use it to put out the fire blazing on Montag. But Montag, who still had the Luger in his hand, lying flat, fired into his own mouth, killing himself. Immediately the gunshots brought out the villagers, police, and the authorities.

May would always believe that Montag, finally looking through a window of sanity heretofore closed, in the last minute of his life, suddenly saw the world and realized what he had done. The flames of Russia, having followed him for the last several years, finally caught up with him, like Darius pursued by Alexander. Noble cause was not a warm gun in his hand. Possibly it had come to him as he saw the priest fall. May would never know for certain. Perhaps Inge's face has been the last thought of Montag's life; May knew she would be his.

There would be authorities to deal with: the U.S. Army, the provincial Austrian government, the national Austrian government, and the Papacy. For the moment, however, May needed to speak to only one person, Inge.

From police headquarters he asked for a phone to call the castle. Street remained stunned in the next office, dutifully following all the requests and assignments the various authorities presented. May stood, telephone in hand, looking out a window toward the church, wondering how he would break the news of the Baron's death to *Freifrau* von Montag, the only woman he would ever truly love. He felt at a complete loss for words, but somehow he hoped that she would find a way to understand him. He asked the guards to leave the room and honor his privacy for the call. They kindly obliged.

Through an operator the phone rang several times—a long buzzing ring. Finally he heard the click of a receiver being handled and felt his stomach plummet.

May spoke in German with his slight American accent in as calm a voice as he could muster. "Baronin Inge von Montag, *bitte sehr.*"

"The Baroness is not available," came the voice back with a reaction typically curt, considering the importance of the day.

That he should have expected. He drew a deep breath, "This is the American Occupational Government," he barked, avoiding his name. "I wish to speak with the Baroness Inge Juliana von Montag, *sofort.*"

"*Moment, bitte.*"

There was a long pause while May listened to his own breathing, aware of every ounce of his one hundred and ninety-five pounds of acute discomfort standing in his shoes. Then she was there, and he felt the muscles of his chest constrict, crowding his heart.

"Von Montag, *hier.*"

"Inge," he whispered. The name came out like a devotion. "I must talk to you. Please forgive me—but I'm afraid you never will."

"Herr May, is that really you? What are you talking about?" Her voice sounded uncertain, but then gained force. "No, my friend, you must forgive me. But I have to ask you again, what are you talking about? You sound so strange."

"I have shocking news that I can't deliver to the *Schloss*, yet I won't let you hear it from anyone else." He paused for a moment. "Inge, how does a man tell the woman he loves on her wedding day that her husband is dead, and that he had a part in this tragedy—a terrible part?"

"Where are you? You're talking crazily."

"I'm in Mondsee. Trust me. I came here on official business that had nothing to do with you. The Baron attacked me and my commanding officer at the church. He killed the priest. He tried to kill us. Then he killed himself."

The words spilled out like sap from a bitter vetch that he feared would gag her. A long pause ensued.

"Oh, my God, are you hurt?"

He had not expected that. What a fool question, he thought, still feeling sick at heart and confused. "I'm okay, but your husband is dead."

Finally what he said registered, and she looked for words to respond. "We had a confrontation after the wedding. I saw today that my husband was stark raving mad, and I didn't know how to handle it. I was terrified. It is one thing to marry a man you don't love, and another to learn that he is dangerously insane. *Liebling,* now excuse me please. I must deal with Kurt's mother and sister, but you must come to the castle with the authorities. Please! Come here. I can't deal with this without you."

Before Inge called Olympia, she was weeping profusely, not necessarily for Kurt, but for all of them, and for all the pain and suffering jointly they had endured. Would it never end?

Within the hour May, Street and two policemen arrived at the castle. Inge walked into May's arms for an entirely decorous embrace. She even embraced Street. Already quite a few people, all strangers to May, had assembled. The older Baroness had been heavily sedated and put to bed. Olympia held court, asking questions, while Inge drew May aside for a few private words. "I'll be all right, but *Liebling,* you must understand that I have to publicly grieve. I must carry on with this charade a little longer. Please forgive me. You are—have been—the only man I love. I can't remember not loving you. I can't even talk sensibly at this point. I'm so ashamed. I'm so ashamed that I'm relieved of a terrible burden that, once more, you took on for me. Oh, dear, God, is this to be the pattern of our lives?" Her hands pressed a grief stricken face.

"I can only hope for that." May turned to view the assembly, and saw that nobody was noticing them. He grabbed Inge's hand. "Where is your room?"

"Follow me." Apart and silently, they slipped out of the room and upstairs, where she bolted the door and fell into his arms. Not even bothering to undress, Inge's marriage was consummated. In less than five minutes, fortified by each other, separately and unmissed they rejoined the group.

Olympia and her mother took Kurt's death reasonably well. Quite naturally the older Baroness wondered if the marriage had been consummated and dared to ask Inge. Inge was shocked by the inquiry and replied, "I am not a virgin."

Two weeks later Inge's morning sickness began. Most of the next two months she would spend in bed.

With the possibility of an heir, the Baroness was delighted. "Apparently they couldn't wait," she told Olympia. The older woman knew that, despite vigilance, lovers usually find ways to get together alone.

All the European tabloids jumped on the tragic story, running handsome photographs of Kurt before the war, the wedding carriage, the snow-lined *Schloss*— with the great black banner signifying a death in the family hanging over the main entrance—and finally, three beautiful women in black at the grave site. Inge's pearls shone from under a fine lace veil, matching the whites of tear-filled eyes. For a while she was a victim of her celebrity, but she could talk daily with May, who waited while she dealt with her widowhood properly. For three months, they could only meet secretly, as it was important not to embarrass Kurt's family.

It was with May's approval that she put Olympia's name on the *Schloss* title as a joint owner. Olympia would see that the ski lift was finished and would eventually develop and run the property. The attorneys were speechless by her generous offer, but there were considerable other properties in the barony. She was suddenly a wealthy woman, just as if she had found a treasure chest under a palm tree on some tropical beach—some great source of unearned wealth.

* ** *

After the horrible conflagration at the church in Mondsee, Street treated May differently, and May was relieved to find their relationship infinitely less antagonizing. They would never become buddies, but they had shared an unforgettable experience that engendered mutual respect for the way both had behaved under fire. The brush with death had made Street a more humble man. May would never again go out of his way to avoid Street. Like the adversaries depicted in the mosaic on the House of Faun, the two warriors, Darius and Alexander or Street and May, realized the futility of their actions. Besides, May was secretly ecstatic over Inge's pregnancy.

The whole story was, of course, grist for Rasmussen's mill. Certainly with the war over, he would have suffered greatly over the needless loss of his two Fine Arts and Monuments Officers, but they had survived, and he was reassured that his prognostication on Inge's marriage had been right on target—just sorry he had not bet on it.

* ** *

In time, Inge could step into May's car at the gates of the castle, and the trying story of that year would unfold only as a memory—and a bad one at that. No matter, they were together again.

They would pass the magnificent views of the Salzkammergut region, the lakes enclosing steep mountains that rose majestically straight out of their depths, catching only fleeting glimpses. The breath-taking panorama lay in each other's eyes—the absolving, comforting, warm feeling in each other's touch.

EPILOGUE

In 1947 General George Marshall, then Secretary of State, proposed the Marshall Plan. After three years of deplorable conditions in all of Europe following the German surrender, the United States Congress became alarmed. In a great turnabout, Congress enacted the European Recovery Act, authorizing and funding the new plan

The interim, between 1945 and 1947, revealed the shortsightedness of keeping free Europe in shambles, while Russia became more and more difficult as an ally. Possibly because of the quality of the German government, the strength of Konrad Adenauer as a leader, and the energy of the people, the world experienced what became known as the *Wirtschaftswunder*. Five years after the end of the war, U.S. Army caserns were completed to house the occupational forces, and German housing, or what remained of it, was returned to the Germans.

May never learned that in a moment of rage at the Eagle's Nest, Inge had stolen the golden goblets as well as Hitler's sheets. She packed these things in the two trunks that May had bought, feeling sure that she would be the one to unpack them. The contents were never added to the inventory. Inge, having done the work herself, was sure May was never aware. He was distracted with other problems—in particular, his inability to marry her. Trustingly, he took her word that the work in the Eagle's Nest was complete. If he had ever been questioned about the goblets, his only thought would have been one of relief that he had resisted the heist—expressed with a pang of guilt that he had even thought of it.

While May was in Spandau, some GI found the trunks. Being the soul of honesty, he checked records, but not thoroughly enough. He found a home address for May in New York belonging to May's spinster

319

second cousin. The trunks were shipped to her. May actually forgot that he had ever bought the trunks, this stressful period becoming blocked out of his mind after Inge's departure for Austria and his for Spandau.

Certainly, Inge, also stressed almost to the breaking point, totally forgot packing the goblets, sheets and memorabilia in the trunks, and later surely would have denied ever having done so. Possibly at some point of delirium, she felt the goblets could be sold for the benefit of the Jewish people, as had been her dream.

One embarrassing incident did occur, years later, that May would never mention, but one that moved him profoundly. He was checking into the Vier Jahreszeiten, an elegant hotel on Maximilian Strasse in Munich, because Inge was having an opening of her art show at the Museum of Modern Art. "Here is your key, Ambassador May," said the clerk. A portly bald man next to the ambassador overheard the name, and took a long hard look at May's face. Then he got down on his knees and kissed May's shoes. A Jew, he had escaped from Germany on May's passport in 1938. "My name is Herschel Cohen," he explained, "and you saved my life with the use of your passport."

"*Bitte, bitte,*" said May, completely taken aback. "I'm sorry, I never knew your name, which might have been a good thing at the time, but I believe you were never thanked for a beautiful silk tie, which I still have." May then turned to Inge and a young girl. "Let me introduce my lady, the *Baronin* Inge Juliana von Montag of Mondsee and our daughter, Gertrude Victoria von Montag."

Thirty years passed before the goblets turned up in New York City. Due to Bob Hermes's good sense, the goblets were judiciously disposed of, and the Hermesdorf Trading Company avoided bankruptcy. Neither Bob Hermes nor his partner, Mike Dorf, would ever hear of the Salzburger bull-washers or the Viennese foam-gatherers, but they managed to down considerable suds in celebrating the unrecorded theft.

As it happened, the noted philanthropist, Aaron Hirschfeld, in time found the gold goblets strangely unsettling, and put them on the market. The *New York Post* reported the $300,000 sale to the wealthy socialite, Betsy Price Barnes, Washington's 'Hostess with the Mostess' and widow of the late Senator R.R. Barnes (D – N.Y.). Hirschfeld donated the proceeds of the sale to the National Jewish Relief Fund, and was believed to have enjoyed a healthy tax write off.

THE END

ABOUT THE AUTHOR

Martha Melahn is a world traveler, fluent in four languages. Having traveled and spent over two decades abroad, Melahn now resides in South Florida. She began her professional writing career in the early 1960's as a reporter in Germany for United Press (precursor to U.P.I.) and the American newspaper, *The Overseas Weekly.*

Currently, she writes for local newspapers as a contributor to *The Miami Herald, Miami Magazine,* and *The Coconut Grover* (where she penned "The Gardening Corner" and a cooking column).

Stealing Eyes is Melahn's extensively researched fictional novel. It follows *Wave of Destiny, Encounter with Destiny* and *Legendary Dining.* Melahn writes within romantic themes, based on historical events. She is the daughter of Dr. John Clayton Gifford, famed botanist, noted writer and Florida pioneer, for whom the Gifford Arboretum at the University of Miami is named. Melahn was formerly married to architect Alfred Browning Parker, and European expatriate entrepreneur, Harold Melahn. She is the mother of six children.